Anton Kerner von Marilaun, Francis Wall Oliver, Mary Frances
Macdonald, Marian Balfour Busk

## The Natural History of Plants

Their forms, growth, reproduction, and distribution - Vol. 1

Anton Kerner von Marilaun, Francis Wall Oliver, Mary Frances Macdonald, Marian Balfour Busk

**The Natural History of Plants**
*Their forms, growth, reproduction, and distribution - Vol. 1*

ISBN/EAN: 9783337775513

Printed in Europe, USA, Canada, Australia, Japan

Cover: Foto ©Andreas Hilbeck / pixelio.de

More available books at **www.hansebooks.com**

THE

# NATURAL HISTORY of PLANTS

## THEIR FORMS, GROWTH,
## REPRODUCTION, AND DISTRIBUTION.

* * * * * * * * * *

FROM THE GERMAN OF

### ANTON KERNER von MARILAUN,

PROFESSOR OF BOTANY IN THE UNIVERSITY OF VIENNA,

### BY F. W. OLIVER, M.A., D.Sc.,

QUAIN PROFESSOR OF BOTANY IN UNIVERSITY COLLEGE, LONDON.

WITH THE ASSISTANCE OF

MARIAN BUSK, B.Sc., AND MARY EWART, B.Sc.

* * * * * * * * * *

**With over 1000 Original Woodcut Illustrations**

and

**Sixteen Plates in Colours.**

* * * * *
* * *

KERNER'S NATURAL HISTORY OF PLANTS, now for the first time presented to English readers, is one of the greatest works in Botany ever issued from the press. Its province is the whole realm of Plant Life, and its purpose, as conceived by the author, Professor Anton Kerner von Marilaun, of Vienna University, is to provide "a book not only for specialists and scholars, but also for the many".

To the preparation of the work Professor Kerner has devoted a quarter of a century of earnest labour, bringing to bear upon it the highest professional knowledge, experience, and skill. It is thus in nowise a sweeping together of current views, but has the rounded completeness of an original work of art; it might indeed be fitly named The Epic of Plant Life.

With the grasp and mastery of a thorough botanist and skilled expositor, Professor Kerner shows us the plant in its varied natural surroundings, and tells in plain terms, shorn of needless technicalities, the story of its life—how its food supply is obtained under all sorts of conditions and built up into its own substance; how it grows, adapts itself to its environment, reproduces itself, and dies. He explains and describes the various mechanisms for furthering nutrition, growth, and reproduction, and the manner in which each discharges its particular function.

That plants, like animals, are possessed of instinct and endowed with sensation; that in fact no marked boundary-line exists between the world of plants and the world of animals, are curious truths, of which the fewest of us were aware, but which are here made plain. The reader will indeed find matter of novel and entrancing interest on every page. He will read of rootless plants free to move from place to place, of plants whose roots hang suspended in mid-air, of strange carnivorous plants that capture their prey in traps and pitfalls of cunning device, of parasitic plants that live and are nourished, some on fellow-plants, others on animals. He will find described, not merely our own familiar vegetation, but the whole world's flora, in its relation to the Science of Biology.

While, therefore, all lovers of nature will find THE NATURAL HISTORY OF PLANTS an inexhaustible treasure-house, to the specialist and serious student of Botany the variety and freshness of its facts and the beauty and fidelity of its illustrations render it a necessary possession. Very many of the facts recorded are the result of the author's long-continued observation, and are here made accessible for the first time.

The English translation has been carried out by Professor F. W. Oliver, University College, London, assisted by Marian Busk, B.Sc., and Mary F. Ewart, B.Sc. It possesses the great merit of maintaining at once the simplicity and readableness, and the scientific accuracy and precision of the original.

The pictorial illustrations, executed under the author's own supervision, form a very notable feature. They consist of about 1000 engravings on wood, and 16 plates in colours. The woodcuts have, with a few exceptions, been specially drawn and engraved for the work, and are remarkable for beauty, as well as for truth to nature. The coloured plates, also original, while imparting brightness to the pages, are not merely decorative, but are of much scientific value as exhibiting the plants in their natural surroundings. Indeed, they form in themselves a contribution to Botany of no mean order.

While the book has been written in the main in untechnical language, it has nevertheless been thought well to append a glossary to it, in which such technical terms as could not be dispensed with will be explained.

*The Work will be printed with the utmost care on fine quality paper, and issued in sixteen monthly parts, imperial 8vo, price 2s. 6d. each, nett; also in six half-volumes, handsomely bound in cloth, price 9s. each, nett.*

*This edition will be sold exclusively by Subscription, through authorized Agents, and no order will be accepted unless for the complete work.*

BLACKIE & SON, LIMITED; LONDON, GLASGOW, AND DUBLIN.

A. Kerner von Marilaun

# THE
# NATURAL HISTORY OF PLANTS

## THEIR FORMS, GROWTH,
## REPRODUCTION, AND DISTRIBUTION

FROM THE GERMAN OF

### ANTON KERNER von MARILAUN
PROFESSOR OF BOTANY IN THE UNIVERSITY OF VIENNA

BY

### F. W. OLIVER, M.A., D.Sc.
QUAIN PROFESSOR OF BOTANY IN UNIVERSITY COLLEGE, LONDON

WITH THE ASSISTANCE OF

### MARIAN BUSK, B.Sc. AND MARY F. EWART, B.Sc.

WITH ABOUT 2000 ORIGINAL WOODCUT ILLUSTRATIONS AND SIXTEEN PLATES IN COLOURS

## DIVISIONAL VOLUME I.

LONDON: BLACKIE & SON, LIMITED
GLASGOW, EDINBURGH, AND DUBLIN
1896

# CONTENTS OF DIVISIONAL VOLUME I.

## LIST OF ILLUSTRATIONS.

## INTRODUCTION.

## THE LIVING PRINCIPLE IN PLANTS.

## ABSORPTION OF NUTRIMENT.

# THE
# NATURAL HISTORY OF PLANTS.

## INTRODUCTION.

### THE STUDY OF PLANTS IN ANCIENT AND IN MODERN TIMES.

Plants considered from the point of view of utility.—Description and classification of plants.—
Doctrine of metamorphosis and speculations of nature-philosophy.—Scientific method based on
the history of development.—Objects of botanical research at the present day.

### PLANTS CONSIDERED FROM THE POINT OF VIEW OF UTILITY.

SOME years ago I rambled over the mountain district of North Italy in the
lovely month of May. In a small sequestered valley, the slopes of which were
densely clad with mighty oaks and tall shrubs, I found the flora developed in all
its beauty. There, in full bloom, was the laburnum and manna-ash, besides
broom and sweet-brier, and countless smaller shrubs and grasses. From every
bush came the song of the nightingale; and the whole glorious perfection of a
southern spring morning filled me with delight. Speaking, as we rested, to my
guide, an Italian peasant, I expressed the pleasure I experienced in this wealth
of laburnum blossoms and chorus of nightingales. Imagine the rude shock
to my feelings on his replying briefly that the reason why the laburnum was so
luxuriant was that its foliage was poisonous, and goats did not eat it; and that
though no doubt there were plenty of nightingales, there were scarcely any hares
left. For him, and I daresay for thousands of others, this valley clothed with
flowers was nothing more than a pasture-ground, and nightingales were merely
things to be shot.

This little occurrence, however, seems to me characteristic of the way in which
the great majority of people look upon the world of plants and animals. To their
minds animals are game, trees are timber and fire-wood, herbs are vegetables (in
the limited sense), or perhaps medicine or provender for domestic animals, whilst
flowers are pretty for decoration. Turn in what direction I would, in every
country where I have travelled for botanical purposes, the questions asked by the
inhabitants were always the same. Everywhere I had to explain whether the
plants I sought and gathered were poisonous or not: whether they were efficacious
as cures for this or that illness; and by what signs the medicinal or otherwise

useful plants were to be recognized and distinguished from the rest. And the attitude of the great mass of country folk in times past was the same as at the present day. All along anxiety for a livelihood, the need of the individual to satisfy his own hunger, the interests of the family, the provision of food for domestic animals, have been the factors that have first led men to classify plants into the nutritious and the poisonous, into those that are pleasant to the taste and those that are unpleasant, and have induced them to make attempts at cultivation, and to observe the various phenomena of plant-life.

No less powerful as an incentive to the study of herbs, roots, and seeds, and to the minute comparison of similar forms and the determination of their differences, was the hope and belief that the higher powers had endowed particular plants with healing properties. In ancient Greece there was a special guild, the "Rhizotomoi," whose members collected and prepared such roots and herbs as were considered to be curative, and either sold them themselves or caused them to be sold by apothecaries. Through the labours of these Rhizotomoi, added to those of Greek, Roman, and Arabic physicians, and of gardeners, vine-growers, and farmers, a mass of information concerning the plant-world was acquired, which for a long period stood as botanical science. As late as the sixteenth century plants were looked upon from a purely utilitarian point of view, not only by the masses but also by very many professed scholars; and in most of the books of that time we find the medicinal properties, and the general utility of the plants selected for description and discrimination, occupying a conspicuous position and treated in an exhaustive manner. Just as men lived in the firm belief that human destinies depended upon the stars, so they clung to the notion that everything upon the earth was created for the sake of mankind; and, in particular, that in every plant there were forces lying dormant which, if liberated, would conduce either to the welfare or to the injury of man. Points which might serve as bases for the discovery of these secrets of nature were eagerly sought for. People imagined they discerned magic in many plants, and even believed that they were able to trace in the resemblance of certain leaves, flowers, and fruits to parts of the human body, an indication, emanating from supernatural powers, of the manner in which the organ in question was intended to affect the human constitution. The similarity in shape between a particular foliage-leaf and the liver did duty for a sign that the leaf was capable of successful application in cases of hepatic disease, and the fact of a blossom being heart-shaped must mean that it would cure cardiac complaints. Thus arose the so-called doctrine of Signatures, which, brought to its highest development by the Swiss alchemist Bombastus Paracelsus (1493–1541), played a great part in the sixteenth and seventeenth centuries, and still survives at the present day in the mania for nostrums. The inclination of the masses is now, as it was centuries ago, in favour of supernatural and mysterious rather than simple and natural interpretations; and a Bombastus Paracelsus would still find no lack of credulous followers. In truth, the great bulk of mankind regard Botany as subservient to medicine and agriculture, they look at it from the purely utilitarian point of view in a manner not essentially different from that of two hundred—or even two thousand—years ago, and it may well be a long time before they rise above this idea.

In addition to the botanical knowledge thus initiated by the necessities of life, a second avenue leading to the same goal was early established by man's sense of beauty. The first effect of this was limited to the employment of wild flowers and foliage for purposes of ornament and decoration. Later on, it led to the cultivation of the more showy plants in gardens, and ultimately to the arts of gardening and horticulture, which at different periods and in different countries have passed through such various phases, corresponding to the standards of the beautiful which have prevailed.

## THE DESCRIPTION AND CLASSIFICATION OF PLANTS.

A third path leading to botanical knowledge springs from the impulse which actuates those who are endowed with a keen perception of form to investigate structural differences down to their most minute characteristics. Workers in this field arrange and classify all distinct forms according to their external resemblances, give them names appropriate to their position and importance, catalogue them, and keep up the register when once it has been started. Many people possess, in addition, the remarkable taste for collecting, which causes them to find pleasure in merely accumulating and possessing enormous numbers of specimens of the particular objects on which their fancy is fixed.

This tendency of the human mind has played a very important part in the history of botany. The first traces of it can be ascribed with certainty to a period long before the commencement of our era; for such descriptions and other notes as are contained in the *Natural History of Plants*, written by Theophrastus about the year 300 B.C., are founded, for the most part, on the observations and experiments of "Rhizotomoi," physicians and agriculturists, and it is obvious from the text of the book that in some cases those authorities did seek out plants, and learn to distinguish them for their own sakes, and not solely for their economic or medicinal value

At the time of the Roman Empire and in the Middle Ages, it is true, no one troubled himself about plants other than those known to be in some way useful. But there was a revival of the practice of hunting for plants for the purpose of describing and enumerating all distinguishable forms, at that great epoch when the nations of the West began to study the treasures of Greek thought, endeavouring to adopt the point of view of antiquity, and to harmonize their own circumstances with it. It was at this same period that art too shook itself free from the traditions of the Middle Ages, and became actuated by a new ideal based on the study of the antique; but science, particularly natural science, has as good a claim as art to regard that memorable time as its period of renaissance. Although the ancient Greek writings on natural history, to which people turned with such youthful enthusiasm in the fifteenth century, could not satisfy their thirst for knowledge, yet there is no doubt that, as in art, the effect was to stimulate and reform; and that this study led up to the source, so long forgotten, whence the ancients had themselves drawn their knowledge, that is, to the direct investigation of nature, which has invariably given to every branch of human knowledge new and pregnant life.

As regards botanical knowledge in particular, the study of old Greek writings on the part of western nations in both Northern and Southern Europe had the immediate effect of instituting an eager search for all the different kinds of indigenous plants; and, besides arousing a passion for investigation, it evoked untiring industry in this pursuit, the results of which preserved in a number of bulky herbals still excite our wonder and respect. If these folios, dating for the most part from the first half of the sixteenth century, are perused in the hope of their revealing some guiding principle as a basis for the arrangement of the subject, the reader will no doubt be obliged to lay them aside unsatisfied. The plants were described and discussed just as the authors happened to come across them; and it is only here and there that we find a feeble attempt to range together and make groups of nearly-allied species. Only cursory attention was paid to the facts of geographical distribution. Plants native to the soil, herbs which flowered in gardens and had been reared from seed purchased from itinerant vendors of antidotes, and plants whose fruits were brought to Europe as curiosities from the New World recently discovered—all these were jumbled together in a confused medley. The whole endeavour of the time was directed to the enumeration and description of all such things as possess the power of producing green foliage and maturing fruit under the sun's quickening rays.

Owing to the fact that researches were then limited to the native soil of the student, most of the botanical authors of that day had but dark inklings of the extent to which the floras of various latitudes and areas differ. They assumed that plants of the Mediterranean shores, which had been described centuries before by Theophrastus or Dioscorides or Pliny, were necessarily the same as those of their own more inclement countries. The German "Fathers of Botany" (Brunfels, born about 1495, died 1534; Bock, 1498–1554; Fuchs, 1501–1566, are the best known) applied the old Greek and Latin names without scruple to the species growing in their own localities. They were so firmly convinced of the identity of the German, Greek, and Italian floras that even the numerous inconsistencies occurring in the descriptions did not disconcert them, or prevent them from discussing at great length whether a particular name was intended by Theophrastus and Dioscorides to indicate this or that plant. It was by slow degrees that botanists first began to abandon these fruitless debates concerning the Greek and Latin names of plants, with which it had been the custom to fill so many pages of the herbals. Step by step they became conscious that although the yellow pages of the ancient books deserved all gratitude for the stimulating influence they had exercised, yet the green book of nature should be set above them. This led to their devoting themselves entirely to direct researches in the subject of their native floras. The herbal of Hieronymus Bock, which appeared in 1546, and in which "the herbs growing in German countries are described from long and sure experience," contains a passage treating of the controversy of the day as to whether the Latin name *Erica* was applicable to the German Heath or not; and in the midst of the discussion the author expresses the opinion that "the plants we know best were the least known to the Latins;" and at last he exclaims: "Be our heath the same as Erica or not, it is in any case a pretty and sturdy little shrub, beset with numerous brown rounded branches, which are clothed all over with small green leaves; and its appearance is like that of the sweet-smelling Lavender Cotton." And again in a number of other places, after making lengthy philological statements relating to the old names, he ends by losing patience and declaring that the proper thing would be to lay aside all disputes concerning this nomenclature.

At length a Belgian, Charles de l'Écluse (1526–1609), whose name was latinized into Clusius, emancipated himself entirely from the hair-splitting verbal controversies of the day. He was also the first to abandon the utilitarian standpoint; and in his extensive work, which appeared at the end of the sixteenth century, he was guided solely by the desire to become acquainted with every flowering thing. He therefore endeavoured to distinguish, describe, and where possible to draw the various forms of plants, to cultivate them, and to preserve them in a dried condition. It was just at that time that collections of dried plants began to be made. Such a collection was at first called a "hortus siccus," and later on a "herbarium." All museums of natural history were forthwith furnished with them. Moreover, Clusius, actuated by the wish to see with his own eyes what the vegetation on the other side of the mountains looked like, was the first man to travel for the purpose of botanizing. In order to extend his knowledge of plants he roamed over Europe from the sierras of Spain to the borders of Hungary, and from the sea-coast to the highlands of the Tyrol. Journeys of this kind in pursuit of botanical knowledge were by degrees extended to wider and wider limits, and thus an abundance of material was brought together from all latitudes and from every quarter of the globe.

An immense number of isolated observations were accumulated in this way, till, at length, in the first decades of the eighteenth century, the desirability of sifting and arranging this chaotic mass became urgent. When, therefore, the Swedish naturalist Linnæus (1707–1778), by the exercise of unparalleled industry, mastered in a fabulously short space of time the detailed results of centuries of labour, and afforded a general survey of all this scattered material, he obtained universal recognition. Linnæus introduced short names for the various species in place of the cumbrous older designations, and showed how to distinguish the species by means of concise descriptions. For this purpose he marked out the different parts of a plant as root, stem, leaf, bract, calyx, corolla, stamens, pistil, fruit, and seeds. Again, he distinguished particular forms of those organs, as, for instance, scapes, haulms, and peduncles as forms of stems, and in addition also the parts of each organ, such as filaments, anthers, and pollen in the stamens, and ovary, style, and stigma in the pistil; and to each one of these objects he assigned a technical name (*terminus*). With the help of the botanical terminology thus formulated it became possible not only to abridge the specific descriptions, but also to recognize species from such descriptions, and to determine what name had been given them by botanists, and to what group they belonged.

Linnæus selected as a basis of classification in the "System" established by him the characteristics of the various parts of the flower. In this system the number, relative length, cohesion, and disposition of the stamens formed the ground of division into "Classes." Within each Class, "Orders" were then differentiated according to the nature of the pistil, especially the number of styles; and each Order was again subdivided into more narrowly defined groups, which received the name of "Genera." To the 23 classes of Flowering Plants (Phanerogamia) Linnæus added as a 24th Class Flowerless Plants (Cryptogamia), which were divided into several groups (Ferns, Mosses, Algæ, and Fungi) in respect of their general appearance and mode of occurrence.

This system took immediate possession of the civilized world. Englishmen, Germans, and Italians now worked in unison as faithful disciples of Linnæus. Even laymen studied the Linnæan botany with enthusiasm; and it was recommended, especially to ladies, as a harmless pastime, not overtaxing to the mind. In France Rousseau delivered lectures on botany to a circle of educated ladies; whilst even Goethe experienced a strong attraction to the "loveliest of the sciences," as botany was called in that day. Linnæus had introduced for the first time the name "flora" to signify a catalogue of the plants of a more or less circumscribed district. He had himself written a flora of Lapland and Sweden, and by doing so had stimulated others to undertake the compilation of similar catalogues; so that by the end of the 18th century floras of England, Piedmont, Carniola, Austria, &c., had been produced. By this means a certain perfection was attained in that field of botany which has only in view the examination of the fully-developed external forms of plants, together with the distinguishing, describing, naming, and grouping them, and the enumeration of species indigenous to particular regions. Later on, unfortunately, botanists lost themselves in a maze of dull systematizing. They either contented themselves with collecting, preparing, and arranging herbaria, or else devoted their energies to endless debates over such questions, for instance, as whether a plant, that some author had distinguished from others and described, deserved to rank as a species, or should be reckoned as a variety dependent on its habitat or on local conditions of temperature, light, and moisture. They took delight in now including a group of forms as varieties of a single species, now dividing some species as described by a particular author into several other species. For this purpose they did not rely upon the only sure method, the determination by cultural experiment of the fact of the constancy or variability of the form in question; nor did they, in general, adhere to any consistent principle to guide them in this amusement.

Aberrations of this kind constituted, however, no serious barrier to progress. On the contrary, the passion for collecting continued to extend its range. The vegetation of the remotest corners of the earth was ransacked by travelling botanists without any material advantage being gained, though they not infrequently ran considerable risk to their health, and sometimes sacrificed their lives. As one generation succeeded another thousands of students of the "scientia amabilis" made their appearance in every country. Swept along by the prevailing current of thought they devoted themselves to the examination of native and foreign floras, or to a detailed study of the most insignificant sections of the vegetable kingdom. Those who are not under the spell of this passion cannot conceive the joy experienced by the discoverer of a hitherto unknown moss. To such it is inexplicable how anyone can devote the labour of half a lifetime to a classification of Algæ or Lichens, or to a monograph of the bramble-tribe or orchids. The progress achieved eventually in this department of botany is best appreciated when the wide difference in the numbers of species described in botanical works of different periods is considered. Theophrastus in his *Natural History of Plants* (about 300 B.C.) mentions about 500 species, and Pliny (78 A.D.) rather more than 1000; whereas, by the time of Linnæus, about 10,000 were known; and now the number must be all but 200,000. It should be remarked, however, that half the plants described since Linnæus lived fall into the category of Cryptogams, or non-flowering plants, the examination of which was first rendered possible by the wide-spread use of the microscope in recent times.

The microscope led also to discoveries concerning the internal architecture of plants. A faint attempt in this direction, made 200 years ago, had died away without leaving any trace behind; but at the commencement of this century the "*inward construction* of plants" was studied all the more eagerly by means of the microscope. In buildings belonging to different styles of architecture it is not only the forms of the wings, stories, rooms, and gables that differ, but also and in no less degree those of the columns, pilasters, and decorations. The same is the case with plants. They possess chambers at different levels, vaults, and passages. They have pipes running through them, and beams and buttresses, some massive and some slender, to support them. The pieces of which they are built vary in size, and their walls are sculptured in all kinds of ways. It was the business of the vegetable anatomist to dissect plants, to look into all these structures under the microscope, to describe the various component parts as well as the ground-plan and elevation of the plant-edifice as a whole; and to name the different forms of structure after the manner of Linnæus when he invented terms for the different forms of stems and leaves, and for the several parts of the flower and fruit.

## DOCTRINE OF METAMORPHOSIS AND SPECULATIONS OF NATURE-PHILOSOPHY.

Side by side with this immense volume of research, which was directed to the separation, description, and synoptical arrangement of mature forms only, there arose about the year 1600 another school which considered vegetable forms from the point of view of their life-history, and endeavoured to trace them back to their origin. Tracing the development, from one stage to another, of all the different species, of the multitudinous forms of leaves and flowers, and of the various kinds of cells and tissues, the student of this school has to detect identity in multiplicity, to show that the connection between forms which have arisen from one another is in accordance with fixed laws, and to express those laws in definite formulæ.

The attention of botanists was in the first place directed to the wonderful series of changes in the form of the leaf which occur in all phanerogamic (i.e. flowering) plants as the delicate seedling gradually turns into a flowering shoot. At the circumference of the stem which constitutes the axis of the plant, foliar structures are produced at successive intervals. All these structures are essentially the same; but they exhibit a continuous modification of their shape, arrangement, size, and colour, according to their relative altitudes upon the stem. To discover the causes of this structural variation was an attractive problem, and very diverse theories were suggested for its solution. The earliest explanation, which was given by the Italian botanist Cesalpino in 1583, is founded rather on superficial analogies and remote resemblances existing between tissues than on careful observation. According to this theory the stem is composed of a central medulla highly endowed with vitality, and surrounded by concentric layers of tissue, those namely of the wood, the bast, and the cortex. Each of the foliar structures put forth from the axis is supposed to originate in one of the above-named tissues, the idea being that the green foliage-leaf and calyx grew out from the cortical layer, the corolla from the bast, the stamens from the wood, and the carpels from the medulla. It was believed, also, that the outer envelope of a fruit arose from the rind of the fruit-stalk, the seed-coats from the wood, and the central part of the seed from the medulla.

Early in the eighteenth century there came to be connected with this theory the doctrine of so-called "prolepsis," which was founded on more accurate comparative observations. It was thought that the medulla of the stem breaks through the rind at particular spots to form at each a bud, which subsequently grows out into a side branch. Owing to this lateral pressure of the medulla the ascending nutrient sap becomes arrested beneath the rudimentary bud, and, in consequence, the cortex develops under the bud into a foliage-leaf. In the bud the different parts of the future annual shoot are already shadowed forth in stages one above the other; and each is produced always by the one beneath it. As soon as vegetative activity is resumed after the expiration of the winter rest, the bud sprouts. If only that part of it develops which constitutes the first year's rudiment, a shoot furnished with foliage-leaves is produced. But the embryonic structures belonging to succeeding years, which are concealed in the bud, may also be stimulated to development; and when this happens, these premature products do not appear as foliage-leaves, but in more or less altered forms as bracts, sepals, petals, stamens, and carpels. If no such anticipatory activity has been excited, the rudiment which in the previous case would have developed into a bract does not appear till the following year, and then as a foliage-leaf; whilst that which would have formed a calyx in the first year lies dormant till the third year, when it too emerges simply as a leaf. This transformation of the leaves, or metamorphosis as Linnæus called it, is, therefore, the result of anticipation; and it was assumed by the Linnæan school that the cause of this metamorphosis or hastened development was a local decrease in the quantity of nutriment. The idea was, that in consequence of the limited supply of sap the incipient leaves were not able to attain to the size of foliage-leaves, but remained

Fig. 1.—Seedlings with Cotyledons and Foliage-leaves.
¹ *Cytisus Laburnum.* ² *Koelreuteria paniculata.* ³ *Acer platanoides.*

rudimentary, as is the case with many bracts; and further, that the axis was no longer capable of elongating, so that the leaves proceeding from it remained close together, became coherent, and thus formed the calyx. The supporters of this explanation relied particularly on the experience of gardeners, that a plant in good soil with a liberal supply of nutriment is apt to produce leafy shoots rather than flowers; whereas, if the same plant is transferred to a poorer soil, where its food is limited, it develops flowers in abundance.

But yet a third attempt was made to explain this process of transformation, by the theory that parts which are identical so far as their origin is concerned, subsequently receive the stamp of distinct foliar organs. The diversity in the development of parts, originally alike, was supposed to depend on a filtration of the nutrient

sap, the idea being that identical primordial leaves issuing from the axis of a particular plant were fashioned with more and more delicacy as the sap became clarified
and refined in its passage through the vessels.    This explanation of metamorphosis
was first given by Goethe (1790) in a treatise which was much discussed, and which
exercised a most important influence in initiating researches of a similar nature.
Goethe's interpretation of metamorphosis may be briefly reproduced as follows.    A
plant is built up gradually from a fundamental organ—the leaf—which issues from
the node of a stem.    First of all, the organs which are called seed-leaves or cotyledons
(fig. 1) develop on the young plant as it germinates from the seed; they proceed
from the lowest node of the stem, and are frequently subterranean.    They are of
comparatively small size, are simple and unsegmented, have no trace of indentation,
and appear for the most part as thick, whitish lobes, which are, according to Goethe's
expression, closely and uniformly packed with a raw material, and are only coarsely
organized.    Goethe explains these leaves as being of the lowest grade in the evolu-
tionary scale.    After them and above them the foliage leaves develop at the succeeding nodes of the stem; they are more expanded both in length and breadth;
their margins are often notched, and their surfaces divided into lobes, or even composed of secondary leaflets; and they are coloured green.    "They have attained to
a higher degree of development and refinement, for which they are indebted to the
light and air."    Still further up, there next appears the third stage in foliar evolu-
tion.    The structure called by Linnæus the calyx is again to be traced back to the
leaf.    It is a collection of individual organs of the same fundamental type, but
modified in a characteristic manner.    The close-set leaves, which proceed from
nodes of the stem at what is, in a certain sense, the third story of the plant-edifice
as a whole, and which constitute the calyx, are contracted, and have but little variety
as compared with the outspread foliage-leaves.

On the fourth rung of the ladder by which the leaf ascends in its effort to perfect
itself, appears the structure named in the Linnæan terminology the corolla.    It
consists, like the calyx, only of several leaves grouped round a centre.    If a contraction has taken place in the case of the calyx, we have now once more an expansion.    The leaves which compose the corolla are usually larger than those of the
calyx.    They are, besides, more delicate and tender, and are brightly coloured; and
Goethe, whose mode of expression is here preserved as far as possible, supposes them
to be filled also with purer and more subtle juices.    He conceives that these juices
are in some manner filtered in the lower leaves and in the vessels of the lower
region of the stem, and so reach the upper stories in a more perfect condition.    A
more refined sap must then, he says, give rise to a softer and more delicate tissue
(fig. 2).    Above the corolla and at the fifth stage of development there follows the
group of stamens, structures which, though not answering to the ordinary conception
of leaves, are yet to be regarded again simply as such.    In the circle of the corolla
the leaves were expanded, and conspicuous owing to their colour; on the other
hand, in the stamens they are contracted to an extreme degree, being almost filamentous in part.    These leaves appear to have reached a high degree of perfection,

and in the parts of the stamens termed anthers "pollen-grains" are developed "in which an extremely pure sap is stored." Adjoining these pollen-producing leaves,

Fig. 2.—Metamorphoses of Leaves as exhibited by the Poppy.

1 Germinating plant with cotyledons. 2 and 3 The same plant further developed and with foliage-leaves; in 3 the cotyledons and lowest foliage-leaves are already withered. 4 The same plant with a flower-bud showing the closed sepals. 5 The bud open and with petals, stamens, and carpels (pistil) developed.

where contraction has reached its extreme limit, is the sixth and last story, which is composed of leaves, once more less closely-set, and exhibiting a final expansion on the part of the plant. These are the carpels, which surround the highest part of the stem and inclose the seeds, the latter being developed from the tip of the stem. Thus the plant accomplishes its life-history in six stages. It is built up of leaves, the "intrinsic identity" of which cannot be doubted, although they assume extremely various shapes corresponding to the six strides towards perfection. In this process of transformation or metamorphosis of the leaf there are three alter-

nate contractions and expansions, whilst each stage is more perfect than the one next below it.

Whilst seeking to explain metamorphosis in this manner, and endeavouring, with greater perspicacity than all his predecessors and contemporaries, "to reduce to one simple universal principle all the multifarious phenomena of the glorious garden of the world," Goethe conceived the notion of a typical plant, an ideal, the realization of which is achieved in nature by means of a manifold variation of individual parts. This abstract notion of a plant's development with its six stages corresponding to "three wave-crests" or expansions (Leaf, Petal, Carpel) and "three wave-troughs" or contractions (Cotyledon, Sepal, Stamen) is expressed graphically in figure 3. It still holds its ground at the present day under the name of Goethe's "Urpflanze," and the credit of its invention is entirely his. But it is not quite right to claim for Goethe, in addition, the title of founder of the doctrine of vegetable metamorphosis; for in reality he only offered another interpretation and mode of representation of a phenomenon already included by Linnæus under the term metamorphosis. Linnæus had instituted a

Fig. 3.—Goethe's "Urpflanze."

comparison between the metamorphosis of plants and that of insects; in particular, he likened the calyx to the ruptured integument of a chrysalis and the internal parts of a flower to the perfect insect (Imago). He also made many different attempts to establish analogies between the development of plants and that of animals; and in so doing he opened up a wide field for the speculations of the "nature philosophers" in the earlier part of the nineteenth century.

An extensive study of this subject now commenced; and writers on nature-philosophy worked indefatigably at the amplification and modification of this theme, first broached by Linnæus.

"A plant is a magnetic needle attracted towards the light from the earth into the air. It is a galvanic bubble, and, as such, is earth, water, and air. The plant-bubble possesses two opposite extremities, a single terrestrial end and a dual aërial end; and so plants must be looked upon as being organisms which manifest a continual struggle to become earth on the one hand and air on the other, unmixed metal at one end, and dual air at the other. A plant is a radius, which becomes single towards the centre, whilst it divides or unfolds towards the periphery; it is not therefore an entire circle or sphere, but only a segment of one of those figures. The individual animal, on the contrary, constitutes of itself a sphere, and is therefore equivalent to all plants put together. Animals are entire worlds, satellites or moons, which circle independently round the earth; whereas plants are only equal to a heavenly body in their totality. An animal is an infinitude of plants. A blossom which, when severed from the stem, preserves by its own movement the galvanic process or life, is an animal. An animal is a flower-bubble set free from the earth and living alone in air and water by virtue of its own motion."

Page after page of the writings on *Nature-philosophy* of Oken (1810) and other contemporary naturalists is filled with interminable statements of the same kind. At the present day it seems scarcely credible that such propositions were then received with admiration as profound and ingenious utterances, and that they were even adopted as mottoes for botanical and geological treatises. For example, it is worthy of record that as late as the year 1843 the Austrian botanist Unger made use of the last of the flowers of rhetoric above quoted from Oken's *Nature-philosophy* as a motto for one of his first works on the history of development, the title of which is *Plants at the Moment of their becoming Animals.*

The general divisions or systems of the vegetable kingdom which were evolved by adherents of the school of Nature-philosophy were, as may be imagined, just as absurd as the speculations on which they were based. In his *Philosophical Systems of Plants* Oken develops in the first place the idea that the vegetable kingdom is a single plant taken to pieces. Inasmuch as the ideal highest plant is composed of five organs, there must likewise be five classes: root-plants, stem-plants, leaf-plants, flower-plants, and fruit-plants. The world is fashioned out of the elements: earth, water, air, and fire. Hereupon is founded a classification of root-plants into earth-plants or lichens, water-plants or fungi, air-plants or mosses, and light-plants or ferns. Proceeding from the assumption that all the groups are parallel and that the principle of classification for each group is always given by the one preceding it, we have next, to take one instance, the second class—that of stem-plants—divided (in accordance with the subdivision of earth into earths, salts, bronzes, and ores) into earth-plants or grasses, salt-plants or lilies, bronze-plants or spices, and ore-plants or palms.

## SCIENTIFIC METHOD BASED ON THE HISTORY OF DEVELOPMENT.

Though as we see the doctrine of metamorphosis, with its conception of a typical plant, degenerated thus into the most barren of fancies, still from it originated the line of research based on the history of development which has since borne fruit in every department of botany. Observers arrived at the conviction that every living plant undergoes a continuous transformation which follows a definite course, and that accordingly every species is constructed on a plan fixed within general limits and exhibiting variation in externals only. These, it is true, are often more conspicuous at first sight than the direction and disposition of the parts which are really fundamental, and secure the stability of the entire structure. But in order to ascertain the plan of construction it was found necessary to go back to the very first visible appearance of each organ; to determine how the original rudiments of the embryo and the beginnings of roots, stems, leaves, and parts of the flower are formed, and to see what rudiments succeed in opening out, branching and dividing, and what remain behind to perish and be displaced by organs growing vigorously in close proximity to them.

These researches into the course of development of the separate parts of flowering plants, and to a still greater extent the observations of the development of cryptogams or spore-plants (rendered possible by improvements in the construction of microscopes), led naturally to a study of the history of the elementary structures of which all plants are composed. Previously three kinds of elementary organs had been supposed to exist, utricles, vessels, and fibres. The observations of Brown and Mohl (1830–1840) resulted, however, in the identification of the cell as the common starting-point of all these elementary organs. This led to the further discoveries that protoplasm is the formative and living part of a cell, and that each cell is differentiated into a protoplasmic cell-body and a cell-membrane. It followed that the envelope of the protoplasmic body, the cell-membrane, which had hitherto been considered the primary formation, was in reality a *product* of the protoplasm enveloped by it, and this discovery resulted in a complete revolution in the conception of cells generally. Further investigation led to the conclusion that the various modes of growth and multiplication depend on definite laws. That even in the mode of juxtaposition of daughter-cells arising in reproduction, a certain plan of construction may be distinguished in each species which must stand ultimately in some causal relation to the structural system of the whole plant. The progress achieved along these lines in the course of a few decades has been extraordinarily great, no doubt due to the peculiar fascination which the study of the life-histories and transformations of living organisms and the observation of mysterious processes invisible to the naked eye have had for the mind of the inquirer.

In that group of plants which includes the forms classed together by the earlier botanists under the name of Cryptogamia an altogether new world was revealed. An undreamed-of variety was discovered to exist in the processes of propagation and rejuvenescence of these forms of plants by means of single cells or spores. Objects which, having regard to their external form, had been assigned to widely different groups, were found to be connected with one another as stages in the development of one and the same species; and one result of these discoveries was the establishment in this division of the vegetable kingdom of an entirely new system of classification based on life-histories. The systematic arrangement of Flowering-plants or Phanerogams also underwent essential alteration. The Linnæan system, founded on the numerical relations between the different parts of the flower, had indeed already been displaced by another method of classification, that of the French observers Jussieu (1789) and De Candolle (1813), who framed systems said to be natural when contrasted with the artificial system of Linnæus. At bottom, however, these classifications only differed from the Linnæan in the fact that they multiplied and widened the grounds of division. The main division of Phanerogamia into those which put forth one cotyledon (or seed-leaf) on germinating (Monocotyledones) and those whose seedlings bear two cotyledons (Dicotyledones) is the only one that could serve as a starting-point for a system based on the history of development; but when we come to the grouping of Dicotyledones into those destitute of corolla (Apetalæ), those with the corolla composed of coherent petals (Monopetalæ), and those with the corolla composed of distinct petals (Dialypetalæ), we have already to admit something forced, and a reliance on characteristics merely external.

The system which is the outcome of the study of development starts with the idea that similarity between adult forms is not always decisive evidence of their belonging to the same group, and that the relationships of different plants is much more surely indicated by the fact of their exhibiting the same laws of growth and the same phenomena of reproduction. Plants exhibiting widely different external forms in the mature state are nevertheless to be looked upon as closely allied if they are constructed according to the same plan, and *vice versâ*. There can be no question that a system based on these principles means a material advance. At the same time it cannot be overlooked that great difficulties are involved in hitting upon the right selection from among the number of phenomena observed in the course of a plant's development, and in determining which of these phenomena are to be referred to a mode of construction common to a number of plants, and therefore treated as fundamental properties, and which should be esteemed merely as outcomes of the conditions of life affecting the existence of the plant in question.

### OBJECTS OF BOTANICAL RESEARCH AT THE PRESENT DAY.

DESCRIPTIVE BOTANY only concerns itself with the configuration of a plant. COMPARATIVE MORPHOLOGY endeavours to trace back to a single prototype the extremely various forms exhibited by mature plants. The history of development deals with the growth and differentiation of such forms. But all these paths of research shirk the problem of the biological significance of the different forms. The line of investigation starting from the conception of a plant's life as a series of physical and chemical processes, and which attempts to elucidate the configuration of a plant in the light of its environment, could not be developed with the slightest prospect of success until physics, chemistry, and other allied sciences had reached a high degree of perfection, and till botanists had become convinced that the phenomena of life are only to be fathomed by means of experiment.

The earliest attempts to define the biological significance of the several parts of a plant do, it is true, take one back as far as Aristotle and his school; but the ideas of vegetable life entertained at that time are scarcely more than fantastic dreams; and the recognition now accorded to them springs rather from a reverence for antiquity than from any intrinsic merit which they possessed. The first experimental investigations into the vital phenomena of plants were published by Stephen Hales in 1718; but it was not till a hundred years later that this kind of research really came into vogue. It brought with it the conception of a cell as a miniature chemical laboratory, and looked for mechanical interpretations of the phenomena of nutrition, sap-circulation, growth, movement—in short, all vital processes—and for some connection between these processes and the external form. Whereas, in the case of descriptive and speculative botany, and in the study of development, the entire plant was first taken into consideration, next its several parts, and lastly the cells and protoplasm; in the new department of inquiry, on the contrary, the complete histories of the ultimate organs were studied first of all, then the significance of the different forms of the several members, and lastly the phenomena occasioned by the aggregate life of all the various kinds of animals and plants.

Modern science, governed as it is by the desire to lay bare the causes of all phenomena, is no longer satisfied with knowledge concerning the existence of cells, the arrangement of the different forms of cell, the development of their contents, and the changes undergone by cell-membranes. At the present day we inquire what are the functions of the various bodies which are formed within the protoplasm? Why is the cell-membrane thickened at a particular spot in a particular manner? What is the meaning of all the tubes and passages which exhibit such great diversity of size and shape? What part is played by the peculiar mouths of these channels, and why do they vary so greatly in shape and distribution in plants which are subject to different external conditions? We are no longer content to determine in what manner the rudimentary organ of a plant is produced, or how it expands in one case and frequently divides, or else is arrested in its growth and shrivels up; but we inquire the reason why one rudiment grows and develops whilst another is obliterated. For us no fact is without significance. Our curiosity extends to the shape, size, and direction of the roots; to the configuration, venation, and insertion of the leaves; to the structure and colour of the flowers; and to the form of the fruit and seeds; and we assume that even each thorn, prickle, or hair has a definite function to fulfil. But efforts are also made to explain the mutual relations of the different organs of a plant, and the relations between different species of plants which grow together. Lastly, this department of research (the rapid growth of which is due to Darwin) includes amongst its objects a solution of the problem of the ultimate grounds of morphological variety, the causes of which can only be sought for in a qualitative variation of protoplasm. Specific relationship is explained by attributing it to similarity in the constitution of the protoplasm of allied species, and the affinities exhibited by living and extinct plants are used as means of unfolding the hereditary connection between the thousands of different sorts of forms, and of tracing the history of plants and vegetable life all over the earth.

The various lines of botanical research described in the foregoing pages, with their particular problems and objects, have but slight connection one with another. They run side by side along separate paths, and it is only occasionally that a junction is apparent which establishes a communication between one path and another. The subject-matter, however, is always the same. Whether we have to do with the perfected form or with its growth, whether we try to interpret the processes of life or to trace the genealogy of the vegetable kingdom, we always start from the forms of plants; and the ultimate result is never anything more than a description of the varying impressions which we receive at different times from the objects observed, and which we endeavour to bring into mutual connection. All the different departments of botany are accordingly more or less limited to description; and even when we endeavour to resolve vital phenomena into mechanical processes we can only describe, and not really explain, what happens. The processes which we call life are movements. But the causes of those movements, so-called forces, are purely subjective ideas, and do not involve the conception of any actual fact, so that our passion for causality is only ostensibly gratified by the help of mechanics. Du Bois Reymond is not far wrong when he follows out this train of thought to the conclusion (however paradoxical it may sound) that there is no essential difference between describing the trajectory (or particular kind of curve) in which a projectile moves on the one hand, and describing a beetle or the leaf of a tree on the other.

But even though the ultimate sources of vital phenomena remain unrevealed, the desire to represent all processes as effects, and to demonstrate the causes of such effects—a desire which is at the very root of modern research—finds at least partial gratification in tracing a phenomenon back to its proximate cause. In the mere act of linking ascertained facts together, and in the creation of ideas involving interdependence among the phenomena observed, there lies an irresistible charm which is a continual stimulus to fresh investigations. Even though we be sure that we shall never be able to fathom the truth completely, we shall still go on seeking to approach it. The more imaginative an investigator the more keenly is he goaded to discovery by this craving for an explanation of things and for a solution of the mute riddle which is presented to us by the forms of plants. It is impossible to overrate the value and efficiency of the transcendent gift of imagination when applied to questions of Natural History. Thus when we inquire whether certain characters noted in a plant are hereditary, constant, and inalienable, or are only occasioned by local influences of climate or soil, and hence deduce whether the plant in question is to be looked upon as a species or a variety; when we conclude from the fact of a resemblance between the histories of the development of various species that they are related, and place them together in groups and series; when we unravel the genealogies of different plants by comparing forms still living with others that are extinct; when we try to represent clearly the molecular structure of the cell-membrane by arguing from the phenomena manifested by that membrane; when we investigate the meaning of the peculiar thickenings and sculpturings of the walls of cells, or when we discover the strange forms of flowers and fruits to be mechanical contrivances adapted to the forms of certain animals, and judge the extent to which these contrivances are advantageous, or the reverse, to the plants—in all these and similar investigations imagination plays a predominant part. Experiment itself is really a result of the exercise of that faculty. Every experiment is a question addressed to nature. But each interrogation must be preceded by a conjecture as to the probable state of the case; and the object of the experiment is to decide which of the preliminary hypotheses is the right one, or at least which of them approaches nearest to the true solution. The fact that when the imagination has been allowed to soar unrestrained, or without the steadying ballast of actual observations, it has frequently led its followers into error, does not detract at all from its extreme value as an aid to research, notwithstanding the fact that it is responsible for the wonderful fantasies of nature-philosophy of which a few specimens have been given. Nor should we esteem it the less because enlargements of the field of observation and improvements in the instruments employed have again and again led to the substitution of new ideas for those which careful observers and experimentalists had arrived at by collating the facts ascertained through their labours.

For the same reasons it is unfair to regard with contempt the ideas of plant-life formed by our predecessors. It should never be forgotten how much smaller was the number of observations upon which botanists had to rely in former times, and how much less perfect were their instruments of research. Every one of our theories has its history. In the first place a few puzzling facts are observed, and gradually others come to be associated with them. A general survey of the phenomena in question suggests the existence of a definite uniformity underlying them; and attempts are made to grasp the nature of such uniformity and to define it in words. Whilst the question thus raised is in suspense, botanists strive with more or less success to answer it, until a master mind appears. He collates the observed facts, gathers from them the law of their harmony, generalizes it, and announces the solution of the enigma. But observations continue to multiply; scientific instruments become more delicate, and some of the newly-observed facts will not adapt themselves to the scheme of the earlier generalization. At first they are held to be exceptions to the rule. By degrees, however, these exceptions accumulate; the law has lost its universality and must undergo expansion, or else it has become quite obsolete and must be replaced by another. So it has been in all past times, and so will it be in the future. Only a narrow mind is capable of claiming infallibility and permanence for the ideas which the present age lays down as laws of nature.

These remarks on the limitations of our knowledge of nature, the importance of imagination as an aid in research, and the variability of our theories are made with a view to moderate, on the one hand, the exuberant hopes raised by the belief that the great questions connected with the phenomenon of life will be solved, and to correct, on the other, the habit of not appreciating impartially the various methods which have been and are still employed by different botanists. In our own time, adhering as we do to the principle of the division of labour, it has become almost universal for each investigator to advance only along a single, very narrow path. But owing to the fact that one-sidedness too often leads to self-conceit, the lines of study followed by others are not infrequently despised, just as overweening confidence in the infallibility of the discoveries of the present day leads to depreciation of the labours of former times.

For the building-up of the science of the Biology of Plants everything relating to the subject has its value, and is capable of being turned to account. Whether the materials are rough or elaborated, massive, fragmentary, or merely connective, howsoever and whensoever they have been acquired, they all are useful. The study of dried plants made by a student in a provincial museum, the discoveries of an amateur regarding the flora of a sequestered valley, the contributions of horticulturalists on subjects of experiment, the facts gleaned by farmers and foresters in fields and woods, the disclosures which have been wrested from living plants in university laboratories, and the observations conducted in the greatest and best of all laboratories—that of Nature herself—all these results should be turned to account. Let us take for the motto of the following pages the text:

"Prove all things; hold fast that which is good."

# THE LIVING PRINCIPLE IN PLANTS.

## 1. PROTOPLASTS CONSIDERED AS THE SEAT OF LIFE.

### Discovery of the Cell.—Discovery of Protoplasm.

### DISCOVERY OF THE CELL.

What is life? This ever-interesting question has seemed to approach nearer solution on the occasion of every great scientific discovery. But never did the hope of being able to penetrate the great secret of life appear better founded than at the time when, among other memorable developments of science, it was discovered that objects could be rendered visible on an enlarged scale by the use of glass lenses, and the microscope was invented. These magnifying glasses were expected to yield, not only an insight into the minute structure of living beings which is invisible to the naked eye, but also revelations concerning the processes which constitute life in plants and animals. The first discoveries made with the microscope, between 1665 and 1700, produced a profound impression on the observers. The Dutch philosopher Swammerdam became almost insane at the marvels revealed by his lenses, and at last destroyed his notes, having come to the conclusion that it was sacrilege to unveil, and thereby profane, what was designed by the Creator to remain hidden from human ken. The observations of Leeuwenhoek (1632 1723) with magnifying glasses formed by melting fine glass threads in a lamp, were for a long time held to be delusions; and it was not till the English observer Robert Hooke had confirmed the fact of the existence of the minute organisms seen by Leeuwenhoek in infusions of pepper, and had exhibited them under his microscope in 1667 at a meeting of the Royal Society in London, that doubts as to their actual existence disappeared. Indeed a special document was then drawn up and signed by all those who were satisfied, on the evidence of their own eyesight, of the accuracy of the observation; and this clearly shows how greatly people were impressed with the importance of these discoveries. Of the different forms of the tiny organisms, amounting to nearly four hundred, which were at that time distinguished, and all included under the name Infusoria, because first seen in infusions of peppercorns, some only are at the present day reckoned as animals. In many cases it has been ascertained that they are the spores of plants, whilst others again belong to the boundary-land where the animal and vegetable kingdoms are merged.

The presence or absence of movement used to be considered as the most decisive mark of the difference between animals and plants, and, accordingly, all the minute

beings which were seen bustling about in watery media were described and labelled
as animals. No movement was found in the higher plants which were studied with
the microscope about the same time by Dutch, Italian, and English observers; but,
on the other hand, these investigations led to a recognition of the quite special
peculiarities of such structures as leaves and stem, wood and pith. These parts of
plants appeared under the microscope like honey-combs, which are built up of a

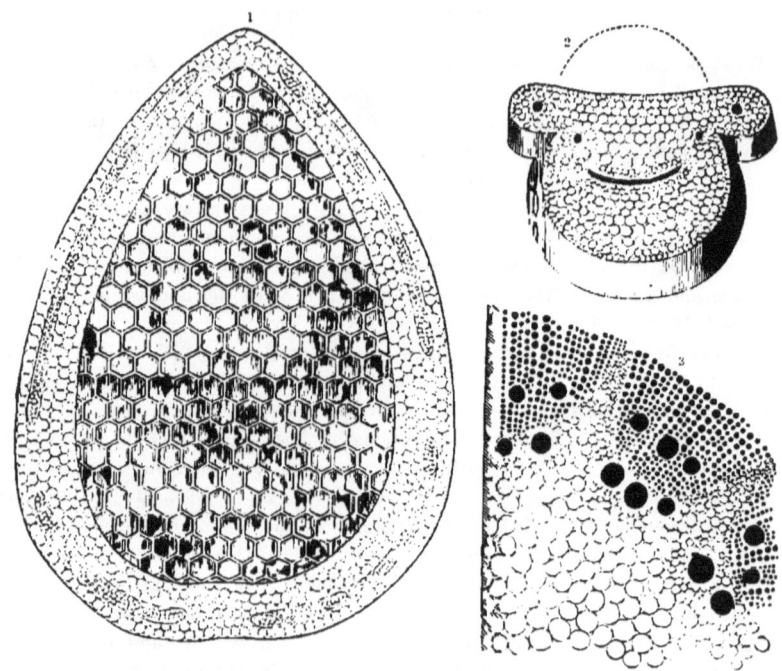

Fig. 4.— Vegetable Cells (from Grew's *Anatomy of Plants*).
¹ Longitudinal section through a young apricot seed.   ² Transverse section of the petiole of the Wild Clary.
³ Transverse section of a pine branch.

great number of cells, some empty and some full of honey. From this similarity
the term "cell" arose, which later was to play so important a part in botany. In
the drawings of parts of plants as seen under the microscope the resemblance to a
honey-comb is very apparent; indeed, it is sometimes rather more striking than
when seen in reality, as, for instance, is the case in the above reproduction of three
engravings from Nehemiah Grew's fine work published in London, 1672. It was
also noticed that, besides the structures which resembled honey-comb, there were
little tubes and fibres which were distributed and aggregated in very various ways,
and were bound up together into strands and membranes, and into pith and wood;
further, all these things were seen to increase in size and number in the growing

parts of plants. How growth and multiplication took place, and where exactly the seat of a plant's life lay, remained, of course, obscure. It was, however, natural to assume that the walls of these small cells constituted the essential part and living substance of plants, that they drew materials from the fluids which rose by suction in the tubes, and so increased in size and were renewed.

It was as yet hardly suspected that the slimy substance which filled the cells of a plant, like honey in a honey-comb, was the basis of life. The observation made again and again at the beginning of the nineteenth century, that the cell-contents of certain algæ are extruded in the form of globules of jelly, and that each globule moves independently and swims about in the water for a time, but then comes to rest and becomes the starting-point of a new alga, might undoubtedly have led to this conclusion. The accounts of these occurrences were, however, considered incredible by the majority of contemporary observers; and it was not till recently, when Unger established the phenomenon as an indubitable fact, that a proper estimation of its value was accorded. In the year 1826 this botanist investigated under the microscope a water-weed found at Ottakrinn, near Vienna, which had been described by systematic writers as an alga, and named *Vaucheria clavata*. To the naked eye it appears like a dense plexus of dark-green irregularly branched and matted filaments. These filaments, when magnified, are seen to be tubular cells which wither and die away at the base whilst growing at the apex, and developing sac-like branches laterally. (Pl. 1.) The free ends of these tubes are blunt and rounded. The substance they contain is slimy, and, though itself colourless, is studded throughout with green granules; whilst near the blunt end of each filament these green particles are so closely packed that the entire contents of that part appear of a dark-green colour.

Now, there comes a time in the life of every one of these filaments when its extremity swells and becomes more or less club-shaped. The moment this occurs, the dark-green contents withdraw somewhat from the extremity, leaving it hyaline and transparent. Almost simultaneously the contents of the swollen part of the tube nearest the apex become transparent, whilst further down the colour becomes very dark. (Pl. 1., fig. *a*.) Twelve hours after the commencement of this change, that portion of the tube's contents which occupies the club-shaped end separates itself entirely from the rest. A little later, the cell-wall at the apex of the tube suddenly splits, the edges of the slit fold back, and the inclosed mass travels through the aperture (fig. *c*). This jelly-like ball, having a greater diameter than the hole, is at first strangulated as it struggles forward, so that it assumes the shape of an hour-glass and looks for an instant as if it would remain stuck fast. There now arises, however, in the entire mass of green jelly an abrupt movement of rotation combined with forward straining, and in another instant it has escaped through the narrow aperture and is swimming freely about in the surrounding water (fig. *d*). The entire phenomenon of the escape of these bodies takes place between 8 and 9 A.M., and, in any one case, in less than two minutes. When free, each individual assumes the shape of a perfectly regular ellipsoid (fig. *d*), having one pole of a lighter green than the other; it moves always in the direction of the former, so that the lighter end may be properly designated the anterior. At first the ball rises to the surface of the water towards the light, but soon after it again sinks deep down, often turning suddenly half-way round and pursues for a time a horizontal course. In all these movements it avoids coming into collision with the stationary objects which lie in its path, and also carefully eludes all the creatures swimming about in the same water with it. The motion is effected by short processes like lashes or "cilia," which protrude all round from the enveloping pellicle of the jelly-like body and are in active vibration. With the help of these cilia, which occasion by their action little eddies in the water, the whole ball of green jelly moves in any given direction with considerable rapidity. But at the same time as it pushes forward, the ellipsoid turns on its longer axis, so that the resultant motion is obviously that of a screw. It is worthy of note that this rotation is invariably from east to west, that is, in the direction opposed to that of the earth. The rate of progress is always about the same: a layer of water of not quite two centimetres (1·76 cm.) is traversed in one minute. Now and then, it is true, the swimming ellipsoid allows itself a short rest; but it begins again almost immediately, rising and sinking, and resumes its movements of rotation and vibration. Two hours after its escape the movements become perceptibly feebler, and the pauses, during which there is only rotation and no forward motion of the body, become both longer and more frequent.

At length the swimmer attains permanent rest. He lands on some place or other, preferably on the shady side of any object that may be floating or stationary in the water. The axial rotation ceases, the cilia stop their lashing motion and are withdrawn into the substance of the body, and the whole organism, hitherto ellipsoidal and lighter at its anterior end, becomes spherical and of a uniform dark-green colour. So long as it is in motion the gelatinous body has no definite wall. Its outermost layer is, no doubt, denser than the rest; but no distinct boundary is to be recognized, and we cannot properly speak of a special enveloping coat. No sooner, however, is the ball stranded, no sooner has its movement ceased and its shape become spherical, than a substance is secreted at its periphery; and this substance, even at the moment of secretion, takes the form of a firm, colourless, and transparent membrane. Twenty-six hours afterwards, very short branched tubes begin to push out from the interior, and these become organs of attachment. In the opposite direction the cell stretches into a long tube which divides into branches and floats on the water. After fourteen days the free ends of this tube and of its branches swell once more and become club-shaped; a portion of their slimy contents is, as before, separated from the rest and liberated as a motile body, and the whole performance described above is repeated.

## DISCOVERY OF PROTOPLASM.

The study of Vaucheria led, then, to the discovery that there are plants which, in the course of their development, pass through a motile stage, propelling themselves about the water as tiny balls of jelly with ciliary processes, and giving exactly the same impression as infusoria. Hand in hand with this discovery went the further observation that a portion of the plastic cell-contents in all plants lies, like a lining, in contact with the inner face of the cell-walls, so that we find that these latter, at a certain stage of maturity, are made up of two layers lying close

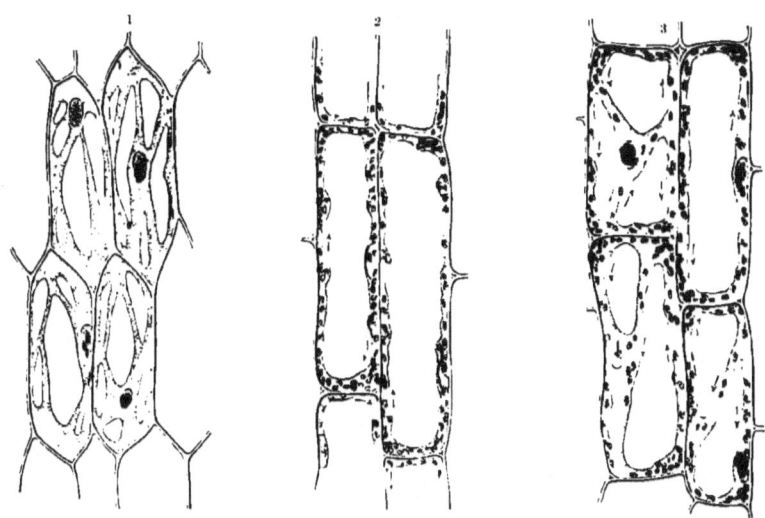

Fig. 5.  Protoplasm inclosed in Cells.
1 Protoplasm in cells of *Orobanche*.  2 Streaming protoplasm in cells of *Vallisneria*.  3 Streaming protoplasm in cells of *Elodea*.

together, the outer one firm and the inner soft. The name of " primordial utricle" was given to this inner layer. On further investigation it turned out that this primordial utricle belongs to a body of gelatinous, slimy consistency which lives in the cell-cavity like a mussel or a snail in its shell. At first it is shapeless and fills the whole cavity with what appears to be a homogeneous mass; but later on it is differentiated into a number of easily-recognizable parts — *i.e.* into the above-mentioned lining towards the inner surface of the cell-membrane, and into folds, strands, threads, and plates stretching across the interior of the cell. (See fig. 5.) Mohl of Tübingen, the discoverer of these facts, applied in 1846 the name of *protoplasm* to the substance of which the cell-contents are composed.

It is possible for protoplasm, under certain conditions, to exist for a time without any special protective envelope; but, as a general rule, it secretes at once a firm, continuous coat, and, so to speak, builds itself a little chamber wherein to live. We may therefore distinguish naked protoplasm from that kind which inhabits the interior of a cell of its own creation, and compare the former to a shell-less snail, and the latter to a snail that constructs the house in which its life is spent. Still better may we compare the firm and solid cell-membrane with which the protoplasm clothes itself to a protective coat, a garment fitted to the body; and, following out this analogy, the protoplasm must be designated the living entity in the cell, and the secreted envelope must be considered as merely the skin of the cell. Consequently, although this cell-wall was the part which was first revealed by magnifying glasses, and was called a cell on account of its form, this is not the essential formative element, which has the power of nourishing and reproducing itself. It is the body within the cell, the slimy, colourless protoplasm in full activity within the surrounding membrane made by itself, which must be taken to be the essential part of the cell and the basis of life.

The term cell had become so naturalized in the science that protoplasm which had escaped from a cell-cavity was also called a cell, and the unfortunate name of "naked cell" was brought into use to designate it. More recently many of these older designations have been abandoned as unsuitable. We now include under the term "protoplasts" all these individual organisms, consisting of protoplasm, which occupy little chambers made by themselves, living either alone like hermits or side by side in sociable alliance in more or less extensive structures, able under certain circumstances to leave their domiciles, laying aside their envelopes and swimming about as naked globules.

Only when the protoplasts live in innumerable little cavities congregated close together in colonies, and when these cavities are bounded by even walls and are for the most part uniformly developed in all directions, does the part of a plant composed of them look under the microscope like a honey-comb, and each cavity like a cell. But even in these cases of external similarity there is the essential difference that in a honey-comb each of the walls separating individual cells is common to both the adjacent spaces, and, accordingly, the cells of the comb are like excavations in a continuous matrix; whereas, in sections of cellular plants, every cell possesses its own particular and independent wall, so that in them every partition-wall between neighbouring cavities is composed, properly speaking, of two layers (fig. 6). These two layers are scarcely distinguishable in the case of delicate cell-membranes newly secreted by the protoplasts. Later on, however, they are always to be made out clearly (fig. 6$^2$). Frequently the layers separate one from another at certain spots, and thus channels are formed between the cells (fig. 6$^1$); these are called "intercellular spaces." One often sees cells, too, whose entire surfaces are, as it were, glued together with a kind of cement, and then this substance which is stored between the two layers is called "intercellular substance" (fig. 6$^3$).

By loosening the intercellular substance, where present, by mechanical or chemical means, we can easily separate adjacent cells from one another; the two layers of the partitioning cell-walls come asunder, and then each separate cell exhibits a complete envelope. The individual cell-cavities are often elongated and shaped like either rigid or flexible tubes; or the wall of such a cavity may become very thick and encroach to such an extent on the cavity that the latter is scarcely recognizable. Cells of this kind look like fibres and threads, groups of them look like bundles and strands, and do not resemble even remotely the cells of a honey-comb. The term "cellular" is hence no longer suitable in the case of these structures.

The expression "cellular tissue" is calculated also to occasion a wrong idea of the grouping and connection of the single cell-cavities. By a tissue one would surely understand a collection of thread-like elements so arranged that some of the threads run parallel to one another in one direction, whilst similar threads crossing

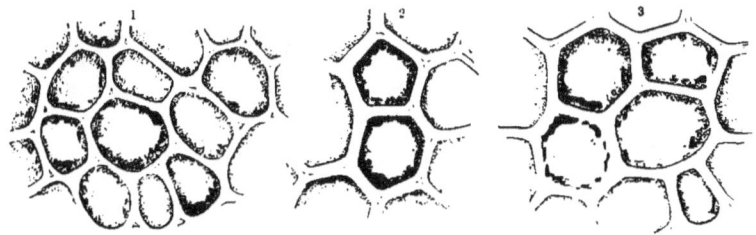

Fig. 6.—Cell-chambers Showing Intercellular Spaces (1 and 2) and "Intercellular Substance" (3) in the Partition-walls of the Chambers.

the first at right angles are interwoven with them. In such a tissue, as of woven silk or the web of a spider, the threads are held together by intertwining; but this is by no means the case with the collections of cells which have been called cell-tissues. Even where the parts of a so-called tissue of cells are tubular, thread-like, or fibrous, they lie side by side and are joined as it were by a cement, but are never crossed or twisted together like the threads in a woven fabric.

Again, cells have been compared to the bricks of a building, but this analogy is not exact. The process of formation of a cubical crystal from a solution of common salt may perhaps be compared to the piling up of bricks; but when a leaf grows the process is not for one layer of cells to be superimposed from the outside upon another previously deposited. The development of new cells proceeds in the inside of existing cells and ensues from the activity of the protoplasts inclosed within the cell-walls; and these protoplasts not only provide the building materials, but are themselves the builders. It is in this very fact indeed that we grasp the sole distinction between organic and inorganic structures, and on this account especially the above analogy is inadmissible and should be avoided.

Cells and cell-aggregates may be conceived most clearly by considering their analogy to the shells of living creatures, as we have already done more than once in the foregoing pages. Protoplasts are either solitary, inhabiting isolated cell-cavities; or else they live in associated groups, the cells being crowded close together in great numbers and firmly attached to one another—each cavity being inhabited by one such protoplast. When the latter is the case, division of labour usually takes place in a plant, so that, as in every other community, some of the members undertake one function, some another. The older cells in these plants often lose their living protoplasts, and then, for the most part, serve as an uninhabited foundation to the entire edifice, which may thus be penetrated by air and water channels. The protoplasts have meanwhile erected new stories for themselves and their posterity on the old deserted foundations, and are pursuing their indefatigable labours in the little chambers of these upper stories. This work of the living protoplasts consists in absorbing nutriment, increasing their own substance, maturing offspring, searching for the places which offer most favourable conditions with a view to an eventual transmigration and to colonization by their families; and lastly, securing the region where all these tasks are performed against injurious external influences. The sequence of these labours is always governed by conditions of time and place. Many of them are only to be observed with difficulty in their actual performance and are first recognized in their perfected products, while others are attended by very striking phenomena and are easily followed in their progress.

---

## 2. MOVEMENTS OF PROTOPLASTS.

Swimming and creeping protoplasts.—Movements of protoplasm in cell-cavities.—Movements
of Volvocineæ, Diatomaceæ, Oscillariæ, and Bacteria.

### SWIMMING AND CREEPING PROTOPLASTS.

Among the most striking phenomena observed in connection with living protoplasts are, without question, the temporary locomotion of the protoplast as a whole and the displacement and investment of its several particles. The freest motion is of course exhibited by protoplasts which are not inclosed in cell-cavities, but have forsaken their dwelling and are wandering about in liquid media. Their number, as well as the variety of their forms, is extremely great. These naked protoplasts are evolved by several thousands of kinds of cryptogamic plants, at the moment of sexual or asexual reproduction in these plants. The escape from the enveloping cell-wall alone takes place in countless different ways, though the process, as a whole, is conducted in the manner already described in the case of *Vaucheria clavata*. Sometimes a single comparatively large protoplast glides out of the opened cell by itself: at other times, before the cell opens the protoplasmic body divides into several parts—often into a great number—and then a whole swarm of protoplasts struggle out.

These swarming protoplasts differ considerably in form. Usually their outline is almost ellipsoidal or oval: but pear-shaped, top-shaped, and spindle-shaped forms also occur. Often the body of the protoplast is spirally twisted like a corkscrew, and has in addition one end spatulate or clavate. Thread-like processes, definite in number and dimensions and arranged variously, according to the kind of protoplast, project from the surface of its body. In some instances the whole surface is thickly covered with short cilia, as in *Vaucheria* (fig. 7 [1]); in others the cilia form a close ring behind the conical or beak-like end of the pear-shaped body, as in *Œdogonium* (fig. 7 [2]); and in others again, one or two pairs of long and infinitesimally thin threads, like the antennæ of a butterfly, proceed from some spot, generally the narrow end (fig. 7 [3] and 7 [4]). Many forms are provided with a single long lash or flagellum at one extremity (fig. 7 [5]), and yet others are spirally wound and are beset with cilia, thus presenting a bristly or hirsute appearance (fig. 7 [11]).

These ciliary processes have a combined lashing and rotatory motion, and by their means the protoplasts swim about in water. In many cases, however, swim-

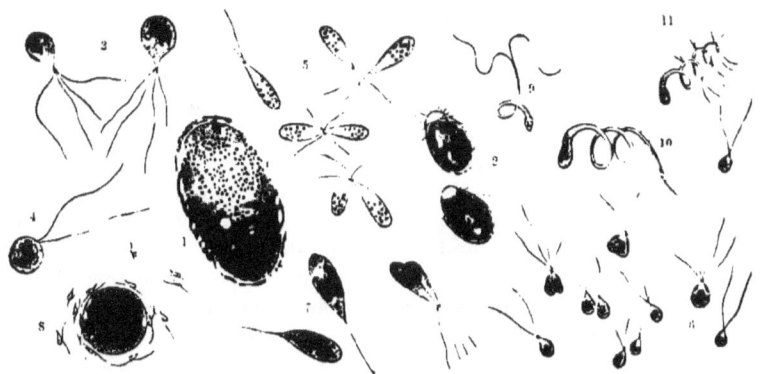

Fig. 7. Swimming Protoplasm.

[1] *Vaucheria*; [2] *Œdogonium*; [3] *Draparnaldia*; [4] *Coleochœte*; [5] and [7] *Botrydium*; [6] *Clothrix*; [8] *Fucus*; [9] *Funaria*; [10] *Sphagnum*; [11] *Adiantum*.

ming is hardly an appropriate expression; certainly not if one associates the term with the idea of fishes swimming with fins. In point of fact there is, associated with progression in a particular direction, a continuous rotation of the protoplast round its longer axis, and on this account its motion may be compared to that of a rifle-bullet, since in both cases the movement of translation takes place in the direction of the axis round which the whole body spins. The movement in question is not unlike the boring of one body inside another; according to this, the soft protoplasts bore through the yielding water, and by this action make onward progress.

The microscope magnifies not only the moving body, but also the path traversed; and when one contemplates a protoplast in motion, magnified, say, three hundred times, its speed appears to be three hundred times as fast as it really is. As a matter of fact, the motion of protoplasts is rather slow. The swarm-spores of *Vaucheria*, described above, which traverse a distance of 17 millimeters in a minute are amongst the fastest. The majority accomplish an advance of not more than 5 m.m., and many only 1 m.m. per minute.

As was mentioned in the description of Vaucheria the locomotion of ciliated protoplasts lasts for a comparatively brief period. It gives the impression of being a journey with a purpose: a search, as it were, for favourable spots for settlement and further development; or else a hunt after other protoplasts moving about in the same liquid. Green protoplasts always begin by seeking the light, but after a time they swim back into the shadier depths. Many of these, especially the larger ones, avoid coming into collision, and are careful to give each other a wide berth. If numbers are crowded together in a confined space, and two collide or their cilia come into contact, the motion ceases for an instant, but in a few seconds they free themselves and retire in opposite directions.

Contrasting with these unsociable protoplasts are others, which have a tendency to seek each other out and to unite; and protoplasm acts in many cases on protoplasm of identical or similar quality, perceptibly attracting it and determining the direction of its motion. It is very curious to watch the tiny pear-shaped whirling protoplasts of *Draparnaldia*, *Ulothrix*, *Botrydium*, and many others, as they steer towards one another and, upon their ciliated ends coming into contact, turn over and lay themselves side by side (fig. 7 $^5$); or, to see one pursued and seized by another, the foreparts of their bodies brought into lateral contact, and, finally, the two, after swimming about paired for a few minutes, fusing together into a single oval or spherical protoplast (fig. 7 $^6$). Even the minute fusiform protoplasts which are moved by cilia proceeding from the sides of their bodies (fig. 7 $^8$), as well as the spirally-coiled forms (figs. 7 $^{9, 10, 11}$) endeavour to unite with some other protoplast. They always move towards larger protoplasmic bodies at rest, cling to them closely, and at last coalesce with them into single masses (fig. 7 $^8$).

As a rule no striking change is to be perceived in the inside of motile protoplasmic bodies during the rotatory and progressive motion caused by their cilia; and the granules and chlorophyll-corpuscles dotted about in the body of the protoplast seem to remain, throughout the period of locomotion, almost unchanged as regards both position and shape. It is only in the vicinity of certain little spaces, called "vacuoles," in the substance of the protoplasm, that changes in many instances are observed, which indicate that, during the motion of the whole apparently rigid mass, slight displacements may also occur in the interior, somewhat in the same way as, when a man walks, the heart inside his body is not still (relatively to the body), but continues to pulsate and cause the blood to circulate. The changes observed in vacuoles have, moreover, been described as pulsations, because they are accomplished rhythmically and manifest themselves as alternate expansions and contractions of the vacant space.

In each of the motile protoplasts of *Ulothrix* (fig. 8) there is found, near the conical end, which is furnished with four cilia, a vacuole which contracts in from 12 to 15 seconds, and dilates again in the succeeding 12 or 15 seconds. In the swarm-spores of *Chlamydomonas* and those of *Draparnaldia* two such vacuoles may be observed close together, whose rhythmic action is alternate, so that the systole (contraction) of the one always takes place synchronously with the diastole (expansion) of the other. The contraction often continues until the cavity entirely disappears. It must depend, as also does the expansion, on a displacement of that part of the protoplasm which immediately surrounds the vacuole. But such a motion as this in the protoplasmic substance, even if only visible in a small part of the whole body, can scarcely be without its effect on other more distant parts; and it may, therefore, be concluded that the interior of a protoplast, endowed with ciliary motion, rotatory and progressive, does not remain quite at rest relatively, as seems on cursory inspection to be the case.

Protoplasts whose motion is effected by means of cilia have no more need of their vibratile organs when once they have reached their destination. The cilia,

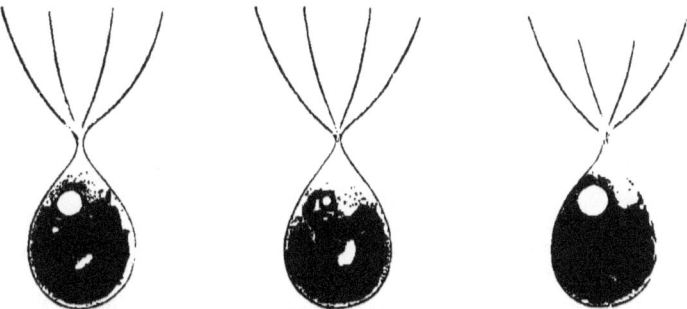

Fig. 8.—Pulsating Vacuoles in the Protoplasm of the large Swarm-spores of *Ulothrix*.

whether numerous or solitary, whether short or long, first of all become stationary and then suddenly disappear. Either they are drawn in or else they deliquesce into the surrounding liquid. Whether the motile protoplasts have come to rest because they have reached a suitable place for further development, as happens in *Vaucheria*, or because they have united, like with like, into a single mass, the form taken by the resulting non-motile body is always spherical. The final act is the development around itself of an investing cell-membrane, so that its soft and slimy substance may be protected by a firm covering from external influences.

Essentially different from the motion just described is that of certain protoplasts which are unprovided with cilia, but perpetually change their outlines, thrusting out considerable portions of their gelatinous bodies in one direction or another, and at the same time drawing in other parts. At one moment they appear irregularly angular, shortly afterwards stellate; then, again, they elongate, become fusiform, and gradually almost round (fig. 9). The protruded parts are sometimes delicate, tapering off into mere threads; sometimes they are comparatively thick, and have almost the appearance of arms and feet in relation to the principal mass. The motion is not in this case like boring, but is best described as creeping. As one or a pair of foot-like appendages is thrown out

in one direction, others on the opposite side are retracted, and the protoplast as
a whole glides over the intervening space like a snail without its shell. The
analogy is all the more exact since the protoplast, as it glides onward, leaves a
slimy trail in its wake, so that the latter is marked by a streak resembling the
track of a snail. When two or more of these creeping protoplasts, or plasmodia,
meet, they merge into one another, flowing together somewhat in the same way
as two oil-drops on water coalesce into one—leaving no distinguishable boundaries
between the united bodies. Thus, slimy lumps of protoplasm, which may attain
to the dimensions of a closed or open hand, result from the coalescence of great
numbers of minute protoplasts. And it is a very remarkable fact that these
plasmodia can themselves change their form, putting out lobes and threads, and

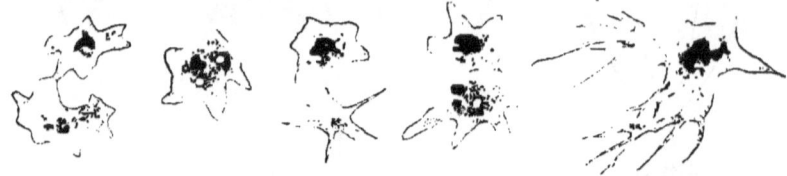

Fig. 9.—Creeping Protoplasm.

creeping about in the same way as the single protoplasts from whose fusion
they have arisen.

Creeping masses of jelly sometimes move in the direction of incident light; at
other times they avoid light and hide in obscure places, wriggling through the
interstices of heaps of bark or into the hollows of rotten trunks; or they may
creep up the stems of plants, or glide over the brown earth in a viscous condition.
On these occasions they resolve themselves not infrequently into bands, cords, and
threads, which surround fixed objects, divide, and combine again, forming a net-work
of meshes, or else perhaps frothy lumps like cuckoo-spit. If foreign bodies of small
size are enmeshed by the viscous threads of the reticulum, they may be drawn
along by the protoplasm as it creeps; and if they contain nutritive material, they
may be eaten up and absorbed. Plasmodia are, for the most part, colourless, but
some are brightly tinted; in particular may be mentioned the best-known of all
plasmoid fungi, the so-called "Flowers of Tan" (*Fuligo varians*), which are yellow,
and *Lycogala Epidendron*, which comes out on old stumps of pines, and is vermilion
in colour.

## MOVEMENTS OF PROTOPLASM IN CELL-CAVITIES.

In the case of a protoplast which is not naked, but clothed with an attached
cell-membrane, the movements are limited to the space included by the membrane,
that is to say to the cell-cavity. Until the protoplasmic cell-body is differentiated
into distinct individual portions no very lively motion can in general take place
in the coated protoplast; though it is not to be assumed that it abides completely

at rest at any time, except perhaps during periods of drought in summer and of frost in winter, and in seeds during their time of quiescence. This applies particularly to immature cells. In them the protoplast forms a solid body whose substance entirely fills the cell-cavity. The young cell, however, grows up quickly, its cavity is enlarged, and the space, hitherto filled by the protoplast, becomes two or three times as large as before. But the increase of volume on the part of the protoplast itself does not keep pace with the enlargement of its habitation. It is true that it continues to cling closely to the inner face of the cell-wall, thus forming the primordial utricle; but the more central part of its body relaxes, and in it are formed vacant spaces, the vacuoles above mentioned, wherein collects a watery fluid known as the "cell-sap." The portions of protoplasm which lie between the vacuoles resolve themselves gradually into thin partitions bounding them; and lastly, these partitions split up into bands, bridles, and threads, which stretch across the cell-cavity from one side of the primordial utricle to the other, and are woven together here and there where they intersect. With these protoplasmic strands we have already become acquainted.

But the protoplasm in the interior of a growing cell, whilst relaxing and breaking up, also becomes motile if the liquid attains a certain temperature, and then the appearance presented is like that of a lump of wax melting under the action of heat. These movements may be observed very clearly under the microscope in the case of large cells with thin and very transparent cell-membranes, especially when the colourless, translucent, and gelatinous substance of the protoplasm—not always sharply defined in contour—happens to be studded with minute dark granules, the so-called "microsomata." These granules are driven backwards and forwards with the stream, like particles of mud in turbid water, and their motion reveals that of the protoplasm wherein they are embedded. Seeing particles gliding in all directions through the cell-cavity, arranged irregularly in chains, rows, and clusters in the protoplasmic strands, we are justified in concluding that this motion takes place in the substance of the strands itself. The movement, moreover, is not confined to isolated strands, but occurs in all. Granular currents flow hither and thither, now uniting, now again dividing. They often run in opposite directions even when only a trifling distance apart; sometimes two chains are drifted in this way when actually close together in the same band of protoplasm. The streams pour along the primordial utricle and whilst there divide into a number of arms, meeting and stemming one another and forming little eddies; then they are gathered together again and turn into another strand of the more central protoplasm. The individual granules in the currents are seen to move with unequal rapidity according to their sizes; the smaller particles progress faster than the larger, and the larger are often overtaken by the less, and when this happens the result often is that the entire stream stops. If so, however, the crowded particles are suddenly rolled forward again at a swifter pace, like bits of stone in the bed of a river as it passes from a level valley into a gorge. The course of the streaming protoplasm remains throughout sharply marked off from the watery sap in the vacuoles, and none of the granules ever pass over into the cell-sap from the protoplasm.

Larger bodies, such as the round grains of green colouring-matter or chlorophyll, are in many instances not carried forward, but remain stationary, the protoplasmic stream gliding over them without altering them in any way. Further, the outermost layer of the protoplast, contiguous with the cell-membrane, is not in visible motion in most vegetable cells. On the other hand, occasionally the entire protoplast undoubtedly acquires a movement of rotation, and then the larger bodies imbedded in its substance, i.e. chlorophyll corpuscles, are driven along like driftwood in a mountain torrent (fig. $5^2$ and $5^3$). On these occasions a wonderful circulation and undulation of the entire mass takes place: chlorophyll grains are whirled along one after the other at varying speeds as if trying to overtake one another; and yet another structure, the cell-nucleus presently to be discussed, is dragged along, being unable to withstand the pressure, and, following the various displacements of the net-work of protoplasmic strands in which it is involved, is at one moment pulled alongside of the cell-wall, at another again is taken in tow by a rope of central protoplasm and hauled transversely across the interior of the cell (fig. $5^3$).

When the rate of the current itself is estimated by the pace at which the granules are driven along, results which vary considerably are obtained, depending chiefly on a qualitative difference in the protoplasm, but secondarily also on temperature and other external conditions. A rise in temperature up to a certain point as a general rule accelerates the rate of the stream. Particles of protoplasm in particularly rapid motion pass over 10 m.m. in a minute; others in the same time traverse from 1 to 2 m.m.; and some, in still less haste, advance only about a hundredth part of a millimeter. Larger bodies, especially the bigger chlorophyll grains, move slowest of all. So it is often hours before chlorophyll grains lying near one side of a cell are pushed through the protoplasm over to the other side, a distance only equal to a small fraction of a millimeter.

The minute granules, as well as the larger grains of chlorophyll and the cell-nucleus, are entirely surrounded by protoplasm; and the protoplasm, whether in the form of bands or threads, whether a peripheral lining or an indefinite mass, must be conceived as always composed of two layers, the outer "ectoplasm" being tougher and denser than the inner "endoplasm," which is softer and somewhat fluid. The former is homogeneous and non-granular, so that it is the more transparent and has the effect of a skin clothing the inner, softer layer, which is granular and turbid. It would be incorrect, however, to think of this as a very strongly-marked contrast, sufficient to mark off one layer clearly from the other. In reality there are no such sharp boundaries, and the tougher ectoplasm passes gradually into the softer and more mobile endoplasm. Of course the granules and corpuscles which one sees drifting in streaming protoplasm are situated within the more yielding endoplasm. It is true, minute particles often appear to glide from one side to the other upon a delicate protoplasmic strand as if it were a tight-rope; but on closer study it is apparent that the granules which seem to be travelling on the proto-plasmic thread are covered by a delicate and transparent protoplasmic pellicle. Thus, these granules imbedded in the substance of protoplasts have no independent motion, but are pushed along by the spreading protoplasm.

Each stream of protoplasm is shut off from its environment and limited by a layer tougher than the rest. But this does not prevent the currents, with their crowds of drifting granules, from changing their direction. In fact we have only to follow for a short time the course of one such granular stream to remark a continuous series of changes: a current from being in a straight line bends suddenly to one side, it broadens and contracts again, now it runs close alongside another channel, now breaks away once more, divides into two little arms, and loses itself finally in the primordial utricle. On the other hand, fresh folds start from the primordial utricle, stretch and grow until they have pushed across the cell-cavity to the other side in the form of bands, or the protoplasm may be drawn out into threads, which elongate until they encounter other similar strings and form a junction with them. The same processes then that are observed in free creeping protoplasts take place to some extent here. Imagine a protoplast captured whilst on its travels—creeping along the level ground—and imprisoned in a completely closed vessel; it would spread itself out over the inner surface of the vessel, would branch and creep about and have just the same appearance as the protoplasts, just described, which inhabit cell-cavities from their earliest youth. This is but the converse of the power possessed by a protoplast set free from its cell, which enables it to move, stretch out, and draw in its various parts, and so to effect locomotion.

Another motion, differing from the creeping, gliding, and streaming action of protoplasts, manifests itself in the so-called swarming of granules contained in the protoplasm. It may be best observed in the cells of the genera *Penium* and *Closterium*, both of which are shown in Plate I., figs. *i*, *k*, though the same phenomenon is to be seen in many allied forms, living in lakes and ponds either singly or congregated in colonies, and remarkable for their bright green colour. The above-mentioned genus *Closterium* includes delicate unicellular forms having a curved or scimitar shape unusual in plants, whence one of its species, in which the semi-lunar form is most striking, has been named *Closterium lunula*. The cell-membrane in all these little water-plants is clear and quite transparent. The greater part of the cell-contents consists of a dark-green chlorophyll body longitudinally grooved; but the protoplasm which is visible in the two sharply tapering ends of the cell-cavity is colourless, and embedded within it is a swarm of microsomata. These granules or microsomata appear to be in a most curious state of motion so long as the protoplast lives. They are to be seen plainly within the limits of the tiny cavity, jumping up and down, whirling, dancing, and rushing about without really changing their position. One is reminded of the apparently purposeless journeyings to and fro within reach of their homes of ants or bees, and the movement has been called not inaptly "swarming." It is difficult to imagine the kind of motion possessed by the protoplasm in which these swarming microsomata are embedded; but however closely it is confined, there must be continual rapid displacements in its substance, which is very fluid, and it may be assumed that here again it is not so much the tiny grains that bestir themselves as the protoplasm which holds them. Probably the protoplasmic matter spreads and stretches out and rotates, and individual granules are carried about by it. This, of course, does not exclude the possibility of the granules possessing a vibratory motion of their own within the mass of protoplasm.

Similar, but not identical, is the swarming movement of protoplasm observed in cells of the Water-net (*Hydrodictyon utriculatum*), and in several other plants allied to it. *Hydrodictyon* looks like a net in the form of a sac, and composed of green threads. The meshes of this net, which are generally hexagonal, consist, however, not of filaments but of slender cylindrical cells joined together by threes at their extremities, somewhat in the same way as are the leaden frames of the little hexagonal panes of glass in gothic windows. The protoplasmic body of one of these cells in due time breaks up into a great multitude (7000–20,000) of tiny clots, which begin to move and swarm within the cell-cavity in what appears to be a disordered medley. In half an hour, however, the excited mass is again restored to rest: the minute particles take form and arrange themselves in definite order, each having two others at either extremity, making an angle of 120° with it; and, lastly, all unite to form a single tiny net having exactly the same shape as the one whose component cell constituted the arena of this process of construction. The miniature water-net so formed then slips out of the cell, the latter opening for the purpose, and in from three to four weeks it grows to the same size as the parent plant.

In the above we have an instance of a protoplast producing a whole colony of cells, which are obliged to leave their home for want of space. In cases previously considered we have found the protoplast stretching and elongating in all directions, drawing itself out into bridles and spreading as a delicate lining to walls, and so endeavouring generally to expand and present the greatest surface possible. Again, we have seen it wandering freely, creeping, swimming, and rotating, and by this method also covering as much space as it can. But, conversely, there is a time when a protoplast tends to the other extreme; the expanded mass of its body gathers itself together again, contracts more and more, and at length becomes a resting sphere, that is to say, it assumes the configuration which exposes the least surface to the environment.

This process exhibits itself with particular clearness within the cell-cavities of the green algæ known by the name of *Spirogyra*, a species of which is represented, magnified three hundred times, in Plate I., fig. 1. In this alga the protoplasm in each mature cell-cavity forms, as a general rule, a very delicate parietal lining wherein green chlorophyll bodies are embedded, arranged in a spiral band. All of a sudden, however, this lining strips itself off the inner

# SWARMSPORES AND ZYGOSPORES.

## FORMS OF CHLOROPHYLL-BODIES.

a – d  Development of swarmspores in the tubular cells of *Vaucheria clavata*.

e  h  Swarmspores and resting-cells of "red-snow" (*Sphaerella nivalis*), mixed with pollen grains of Pines.

i – k  Forms of Chlorophyll in cells of Desmidieæ (i. *Closterium Leibleinii*, k. *Penium interruptum*).

l  Formation of zygospores and spiral arrangement of Chlorophyll-bodies in cells of *Spirogyra arcta*.

m  Star-shaped Chlorophyll-bodies in cells of *Zygnema pectinatum*.

n  o  *Gloeocapsa sanguinea*.

p  Protonema of *Schistostega osmundacea*.

q  Transverse section of the foliage-leaf of Summer Savory (*Satureja hortensis*).

r  Transverse section of the leaf of the Passion-flower.

s  Relative positions of laticiferous tubes and palisade-cells in the leaf of a Spurge (*Euphorbia Myrsinites*).

All the figures greatly magnified.

PLATE I.

SWARM-SPORES AND ZYGOSPORES. FORMS OF
CHLOROPHYLL-BODIES.

Printed from the originals by the BIBLIOGRAPHISCHES INSTITUT, Leipzig.

face of the cell-wall and shrinks together so as in a short time to present the appearance of a sphere occupying the middle of the cell-cavity. Again, just as this contraction is an instance of a special form of protoplasmic motion, so also the further change which the contracted protoplast in a cell of *Spirogyra* undergoes is reducible to displacements in its substance, and must be mentioned as a special kind of protoplasmic movement. For the conglomerated protoplast remains but a short time in the middle of the cell-cavity. It leans almost immediately to one side, thrusting itself into a protuberance of the cell-membrane, which is concurrently developed, and which, when further developed, forms a passage leading over into another cell-cavity. Its body becomes longer and narrower, and at last slips through the passage into the next cavity, where a second protoplast awaits it; and the two then unite, fusing together into one mass. It is not premature to remark that all these displacements and investments of the protoplasmic substance in cells of *Spirogyra*, including the phenomena of contraction, as well as those of pushing forward, escape, and coalescence, are not produced as the results of a shock, impulse, or stimulus from without, but are to be looked upon as movements proper to the protoplasm, and resulting from causes inherent in the protoplasm.

## MOVEMENTS OF VOLVOCINEÆ, DIATOMACEÆ, OSCILLARIÆ AND BACTERIA.

Very remarkable is the movement of those wonderful organisms which are comprised under the name of Volvocineæ. One species, *Volvox globator*, was known to so ancient an observer as Leeuwenhoek; but he, and after him Linnæus, took it to be an animal on account of its extraordinary power of locomotion, and it was named the "globe-animalcule." A Volvox-sphere consists of a large number of green protoplasts living together as a family and arranged with great regularity within their common envelope. They appear to be disposed radially, and to be linked together and held firm by a net-work of tough threads, their poles being directed towards the centre and the periphery of the sphere respectively. From the peripheral extremity, which in each protoplast is marked out by a bright red spot, proceed a pair of cilia, and these protrude through the soft gelatinous envelope of the whole sphere, and move rhythmically in the surrounding water. A Volvox-globe rolls along in the water propelled by regular strokes, like a boat manned by a number of oarsmen, as soon as the protoplasts, which form the crew of this strange vessel, begin to manipulate their propellers. The effect is exceedingly graceful, and has justly filled observers of all periods with astonishment; indeed no one seeing for the first time a Volvox-sphere rolling along can fail to be impressed and delighted.

Another plant allied to the foregoing, the so-called "red-snow," has always excited wonder in no less degree from the remarkable phenomena of motion which it exhibits, but also because of its characteristic occurrence in situations where one might suppose all vital functions would be extinguished. It was in the year 1760 that De Saussure first noticed that the snowfields on the mountains of Savoy were tinged with red, and described the phenomenon as "red-snow." Once on the look-out for it, people found this red-snow on the Alps of Switzerland, Tyrol, and the district of Salzburg, on the Pyrenees, the Carpathians, and the northern parts of the Ural Mountains, in arctic Scandinavia, and on the Sierra Nevada in California. But red-snow has been seen on the most magnificent scale in Greenland. When Captain John Ross in 1818 sailed round Cape York on his voyage of discovery to Arctic America, he noticed that all the snow patches lying in the gorges and gullies of the cliffs on the coast were coloured bright crimson; and the appearance was so startling that Ross named that rocky sea-shore the "Crimson Cliffs." On the occasion of later expeditions to the arctic regions, red-snow was observed off the north coast of Spitzbergen, and in Russian Lapland and Eastern Siberia, but never in such surprising luxuriance as on the Crimson Cliffs of Greenland.

If a snow-field coloured by red-snow is examined near at hand it is found that only the most superficial layer, about 50 millimeters in depth, is tinged. It is also present in the greatest quantities in places where the snow has been temporarily melted by the heat of summer, particularly therefore in depressions, whether big or little, and towards the edges of the snow-field, where the so-called snow-dust or Cryoconite extends regularly in the form of dark, graphitic smeary streaks. Examined under the microscope, the matter which causes the redness of the snow appears as a number of spherical cells having a rather substantial colourless cell-membrane and protoplasmic contents permeated by chlorophyll. The green colour of the chlorophyll is, however, so disguised by a blood-red pigment that it is only possible to detect it when the latter has been extracted, or in cases where it is limited to a few definite spots in the cell. These spherical cells do not move, and so long as the snow is frozen they show no sign of life. But as soon as the heat of the summer months melts the snow, these cells acquire vitality, visibly increasing in size and preparing for division and multiplication the moment they have attained a certain volume. The growth, so far as it depends on nutrition, takes place at the expense of carbon dioxide absorbed by the melted snow from the atmosphere and of the inorganic and organic constituent parts of the dust. We shall frequently have occasion to return to this dust, but at present it is only necessary to observe, for the comprehension of the drawing of red-snow as seen under the microscope (Pl. I., figs. e–h), that in the Alps, amongst the organic materials which constitute the dust, pollen-grains of conifers occur with great frequency, especially those of the fir, arolla, and mountain pine. These pollen-grains have been swept up into the high Alps by storms, and are already partially decayed. In all the material that I investigated I found the red-snow cells mixed with pollen-grains of the above-mentioned conifers. The pollen-grains are oval in cross-section, of a dirty yellow colour, and swollen laterally into two hemispherical wings, as is shown in Pl. I., figs. e–h.

As has been stated, the red cells are nourished by the constituent elements of the dust, which are dissolved in the melted snow. They grow and at last divide so as to form daughter-cells, usually four in number but often six or eight and less frequently two only (Pl. I., fig. $f$, $g$). As soon as the division is accomplished, the daughter-cells, so produced, free themselves, assume an oval shape, and display at their narrower extremity two rotating cilia by means of which they move about in snow-water with considerable vivacity. The interstices of the still unmelted, but now granular, snow, are filled with water from the melted parts, and through these the red cells swim away and are thus diffused over the snow-field. At the moment of escape and first assumption of movement the cell-body appears to be uninclosed. But it soon clothes itself with an extremely delicate, though clearly discernible skin, which, curiously enough, does not lie close to the protoplasm, which is withdrawn slightly and inclosed as in a distended sac (see Pl. I., fig. $e$). Only in front, where the two cilia carry on their whirling motion, does the skin lie close to the body of the cell; and it must be presumed that the cilia, which are simply extensions of the protoplasmic substance, are projected through the envelope. The swarm-spores afford an example of an unusual type of protoplasts, namely of those that move about singly in the water by means of cilia and at the same time carry their self-made cell-membranes with them.

How long the motile stage lasts under natural conditions has not been determined for certain. On the mountains of central and southern Europe, where hot days are followed, even in the height of summer, by bitterly cold nights, causing the melted snow which has not run off to freeze again in the depressions of the snow, the movement no doubt is often interrupted. On the other hand, in high latitudes, where the summer sun does not set for weeks together, such interruption would be exceptional. In any case, however, the locomotion of the red cells with their hyaline cell-membranes is not limited to so short a period as is that of naked ciliated protoplasts. Moreover they have the power of nutrition and growth like the red resting-cells from which they originate, and they have been observed, in a culture, to increase in size fourfold within two days. When at last they come to rest they draw in their cilia, assume a spherical shape, thicken their cell-membrane, which now once more lies close to the protoplasmic body, and divide anew into two, four, or eight cells (Pl. I., fig. $f$, $g$). The fusion of the protoplasts of the red cells in pairs, and their sexual propagation, which has been observed in addition to the above-described asexual multiplication, will be the subject of discussion later on. At present we need only add with reference to this remarkable plant that it was named *Sphærella nivalis* by the botanist Sommerfelt, and that not only in mode of life, but also in form and colour, it most closely resembles a kind of blood-red alga, which makes its appearance in Central Europe in little hollows temporarily filled with rain-water in flat rocks and slabs of stone, and also inside receptacles exposed to the open. This alga has received the name of *Sphærella pluvialis*, and also that of *Hæmatococcus pluvialis*.

Lastly, we have to consider the mysterious movements exhibited by many Diatomaceæ, and by the filamentous species of *Zonotrichia*, *Oscillaria*, and

*Beggiatoa.* As regards the Diatoms, some of them are firmly attached to a support, and are not generally capable of locomotion; but others are almost incessantly in motion, and these little unicellular organisms steer themselves about with great precision near the bottom of the pools of water in which they live. Their cell-membrane is transformed into a siliceous coat, and this coat, which is hyaline and transparent, but very hard, consists of two halves shutting together like the valves of a mussel. The entire cell thus coated has the form of a gondola or little boat, with a keel either straight or curved (*Pleurosigma*, *Pinnularia*, *Navicula*), and is provided with various bands, ribs, and sculpturings on its siliceous walls. Driven by inherent forces, these little protected cruisers pursue their way at the bottom of the water or over objects which happen to be in the water. They either glide evenly over the substratum, or else proceed by fits and starts at rather long intervals, and apparently with difficulty. For some time they may hold a straight course, but not infrequently they deviate sideways without apparent cause, and after deviating return again. They double round projecting objects or push them out of the way with one of their hard points, which are often thickened into nodules, and cause the obstructing objects to slip by alongside the keel of the little vessel. Yet no paddles or cilia are to be seen projecting from it, as in the case already described of Volvocineæ; nor does the siliceous coat exhibit any sort of motile processes whereto the movements might be attributed. But the strong analogy between the structure of these Diatomaceæ and that of mussels seems to justify the assumption that the two siliceous valves, which are fast shut during the period of rest of the Diatoms in question, move a little apart, so that the protoplast living within can push out one edge of its body and creep along over the substratum by means of it.

The movements of the filaments of *Beggiatoa*, *Oscillaria*, and *Zonotrichia* are explained in a similar manner. These filaments are made up of a number of short cylindrical or discoid cells, and are attached by one end, but with the other execute most striking movements. They stretch themselves and then contract again, coil up and straighten out like snakes, and, most characteristic of all, make periodic oscillations in the water. The belief is that the mechanism of this motion is similar to that of the preceding, that infinitesimally fine filaments of protoplasm inserted spirally penetrate the cell-walls, and that these act like the propeller of a ship.

On looking back over the multifarious examples of movement that have been described, the conviction that the capacity for motion is inherent in all living protoplasts is difficult to resist. In many cases, of course, the displacement and replacement of the substance no doubt takes place so slowly that it is scarcely possible to express its amount numerically. Movement may even entirely cease for a time; but, as necessity arises, and under favourable external circumstances, the protoplasmic mass always becomes mobile again—the direction of its motion being determined by inherent forces. There is still much to learn, no doubt, concerning the objects and significance of the different movements of protoplasm;

but in this connection we are justified in assuming that all these movements
have to do with the maintenance and multiplication of the protoplasts. For
instance, amongst the objects of the various movements are the search for food, the
elimination of useless material, the production of offspring, the discovery of the
rays of sunlight necessary to the existence of chlorophyll-bodies and of suitable
spots to colonize. This conception has been brought out frequently in the course
of the foregoing description, and will again engage our attention in succeeding
pages.

---

## 3. SECRETIONS AND CONSTRUCTIVE ACTIVITY OF PROTOPLASTS.

Cell-sap.—Cell-nucleus.—Chlorophyll-bodies.—Starch.—Crystals.—Construction of the Cell-wall and
Establishment of Communication between Neighbouring Cell-cavities.

### CELL-SAP.—CELL-NUCLEUS.—CHLOROPHYLL-BODIES.—STARCH.—CRYSTALS.

In addition to the powers which the living protoplast possesses of shifting
its parts, of expanding and contracting, of dividing and of fusing like with like,
it has also the properties of adapting different parts of its body to particular
functions, of building up various chemical compounds, and of separating them out
when necessary. As the protoplast stretches and expands, spaces and depressions
arise within it, and these form ultimately, when the protoplast is limited
to a peripheral layer lining the walls of the cavity, a single central vacuole.
In the spaces there is secreted, in the first instance, the cell-sap, a watery fluid
containing a variety of substances either suspended or in solution, of which the
chief are sugar, acids, and colouring matters. Moreover, in the interior of the
protoplasm itself, structures with quite different forms occur, and are easily recognizable by their contours; these are the cell-nucleus, chlorophyll-bodies, and starch-
grains.

The principal feature of the cell-nucleus is that, although the substance of
which it is composed is only slightly different from the general protoplasm of
the cell, yet it is always clearly marked off from the protoplasm. In the un-
developed protoplast the nucleus is usually situated in the middle, but in mature
protoplasts it is either pressed against one wall of the cell or suspended in a sort
of pocket of protoplasmic filaments in the interior (fig. 5¹ and 5³). It may
be pushed along by the streaming protoplasm and dragged into the middle of
the cell, and in that case its shape is sometimes altered and it becomes for a time
somewhat elongated and flattened. The nuclear substance, which, as has been
already mentioned, differs but little from ordinary protoplasm, is colourless, and
studded with microsomata, and is liable to internal displacements similar to those
of the entire cell-body. When a protoplast divides, the nucleus plays a very

important part in the process, and it will be necessary later on to discuss its significance in this connection.

The chlorophyll-bodies, mentioned already more than once incidentally, are green corpuscles, roundish, ellipsoidal, or lenticular in shape, and grouped in a great variety of ways (Pl. I., figs. i, k, l, m, p). They are produced generally in great numbers by the protoplast in special sac-like excavations in its body, but nowhere except where they are necessary, that is, in those cells wherein the transmutation of inorganic food-stuffs into organic matter takes place. This transformation, so important to the existence of the organic world, will be considered in detail later on. Chlorophyll-corpuscles are not, as regards their material basis, essentially different from the substance of the protoplasm in which they are formed, and in which they remain embedded for life, but their green colour distinguishes them very clearly from their environment. This greenness is due to a colouring matter stored in the protoplasmic substance of the corpuscle; and our ideas of plant-life are so intimately associated with this remarkable pigment, that a plant that is not green seems to us to be almost an anomaly.

Besides the nucleus and the chlorophyll-bodies or corpuscles, protoplasts produce starch-grains, aleurone-grains, crystals of oxalate of lime, and drops of oil, all of which will be dealt with presently in their proper place. They are evolved in accordance with the requirements of the moment and with the position held in the edifice of the plant by the cells concerned. Moreover, the walls of the cells themselves are the work of the protoplasts, and it is not a mere phrase, but a literal fact, that the protoplasts build their abodes themselves, divide and adapt the interiors according to their requirements, store up necessary supplies within them, and, most important of all, provide the wherewithal needful for nutrition, for maintenance, and for reproduction.

## CONSTRUCTION OF THE CELL-WALL AND ESTABLISHMENT OF CONNECTIONS BETWEEN NEIGHBOURING CELL-CAVITIES.

Of all these performances, the construction of the cell-wall shows the greatest variety from the nature of the case. For the envelope with which each individual protoplast surrounds itself serves at once as a protection for the delicate protoplasm, and as a firm support for structural additions; and, at the same time, it must not impede the reciprocal action between the protoplasts and the external world, or the intercourse between those living in adjoining cavities. These cell-walls are accordingly very wonderful structures, and we shall often have occasion to discuss them, especially with reference to the significance of variations in their structure in particular cases. At present it is sufficient to remark that the original envelope which is secreted from the body of a protoplast and which appears at first as a delicate skin, is made of a substance composed of carbon, hydrogen, and oxygen, belonging to the class of carbohydrates.

The name of cell-membrane, usually applied to the original envelope formed by the cell-body, is one quite suitable for the purpose. But this earliest covering undergoes many modifications. The protoplast is able to store up in it suberin, lignin, silica, and water in greater or smaller quantities, and by this means it either makes the envelope more flexible than it was in the first instance, or else hard and stiff, converting it into a shell-like case. Even the shape is seldom preserved as it was originally. The solitary protoplast surrounded by its cell-membrane is generally in the form of a roundish ball, and its envelope, which is closely adherent, exhibits a corresponding configuration. Young cells, aggregated together, have outlines too which remind one of crystalline forms, such as dodecahedra, cubes, and short six-sided prisms. But when a protoplast has produced its first delicate covering it does not come to rest, but goes on working at the membrane, distending and thickening it, transforming a cavity which was originally spherical or cubical into one of cylindrical, fibrous, or tabular shape, and strengthening its walls with pilasters, borders, ridges, hooks, bands, and panels of various kinds. Where a number of protoplasts work gregariously at one many-chambered edifice, cells of most diverse forms are produced in close proximity to one another. These varieties are, however, never without method and design, but are invariably such as to adequately equip each cell for the position it holds and for the particular task allotted to it in the general domestic economy.

The volume attained by cell-cavities in consequence of the expansion of their walls varies within very wide limits. The smallest cells have a diameter of only one micro-millimeter, i.e. the thousandth part of a millimeter; others, as for example yeast-cells, measure perhaps two or three hundredths of a millimeter; and yet others have outlines perceptible to the naked eye and have a volume amounting to one cubic millimeter. Tubular and fibrous cells often stretch longitudinally to such an extraordinary extent that some with a diameter of scarcely the hundredth part of a millimeter reach a length of one, two, or even as many as five centimeters. An instance may be seen in the filaments of *Vaucheria clavata* (Pl. I., figs. *a–d*), and again in the fibrous cells from which our linen and cotton fabrics are manufactured.

The enlargement of a cell-cavity, or, in other words, the growth in area of its walls, ensues in consequence of the intercalation of fresh particles between those which, by their mutual coherence, form the delicate skin of the protoplast —the earliest stage of the cell-wall. When these intercalated particles are situated in the same plane as are those already deposited, the cell-wall resulting from this method of construction will increase in area without adding to its thickness. But when once the cells are full-sized, the constructive activity of the protoplasts has to be directed in many cases to the strengthening and thickening of their walls, so that later on they may be able to perform special duties. From the appearance of this thickening one would judge that a number of layers were deposited on the thin original wall according to requirement, and in many instances no doubt the process corresponds to this appearance; but, as a rule, the thickness of the wall is increased by intercalation, on the part of the protoplasts, of additional material between the original particles, a process which has been termed "intussusception."

The appearance of stratification in thickened cell-walls is naturally most striking where substances of different kinds have been deposited alternately in the different parts of the wall, and when successive layers take up unequal quantities of water. The thickening may at length result in such an extreme restriction of the cell-cavity that its diameter is less than that of the inclosing wall. Sometimes nothing remains of the cavity but a narrow passage, and then the cells are like solid fibres. Formerly they would not have been classed with cells at all, but would have been distinguished under the name of fibres, from the forms resembling honey-comb cells. The protoplasts in these contracted cells languish and often die, especially when the walls of the self-made prison are greatly thickened and do not allow of intercourse with the world outside. But generally a protoplast takes care, in constructing its dwelling, not to close itself in entirely, nor to cut itself off permanently from the outer world. It either makes from the very beginning little windows in the walls of its house, leaving them quite open or closed only by thin, easily-permeable, membranes; or else, after constructing a completely closed envelope, it redissolves a piece of it, thus making an aperture through which in due time it is able to effect its escape. The scope of this work does not admit of an exhaustive treatment of the formative power possessed by protoplasts needful for these results; it will be sufficient to give a general description of some of the more important processes which have for their object the establishment of a connection between adjacent cell-cavities and of communication with the external world.

The new particles of material, or cellulose, which are to strengthen the delicate original cell-membrane, are in many instances not deposited or intercalated evenly over the entire surface of the protoplast. Little isolated spots are left unaltered, and these may be compared in a way to the small glazed windows in a living-room, or cabin port-holes closed by thin panes of glass. The part of the thickened wall which immediately surrounds the little window, and which so to speak constitutes its frame, has, besides, often a very characteristic structure, being elevated so as to form first a ring-like border, and eventually a hood, arching over the window and perforated in the middle (see fig. 10[1]). A comparison of this structure, arched over the thin spots in a cell-wall, to the iris spread in front of the crystalline lens in an eye would be still more appropriate. A similar annular border projects likewise from the window-frame on the other side, facing a neighbouring cell-cavity, so that the window appears symmetrically vaulted on both sides by mouldings with round central apertures (fig. 10[2]). Supposing someone wanted to pass from one cell-cavity to the other he would have in the first place to go through the hole in the moulding on his side. He would then find himself in a roomy space, which we will call the vestibule, and would next have to break through the little window, which is somewhat thickened in the middle, but elsewhere is as soft and thin as possible. On the further side again would be a vestibule, and it would not be until he had emerged from this through the aperture in the second moulding that he would reach the interior of the adjoining cell. Seen from in front, the outline of one of these windows, or rather the outline of the common floor of the vestibules, appears as a circle, whilst the aperture or opening in the moulding—which is exactly in the centre of this circle—is seen as a bright dot or pit encompassed by the circle which defines the limits of the vestibule. Hence these curiously protected window structures are named bordered pits. They are shown in fig. 10[1] and 10[2], and are to be seen in great perfection in the wood-cells of pines and firs.

Whenever bordered pits are formed, the thickening of the cell-membrane is comparatively slight; the frame of the window in the cell-wall is never more than

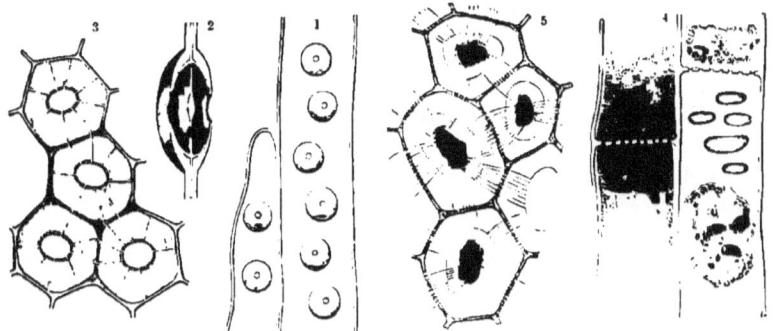

Fig. 10  Connecting Passages between adjacent Cell-cavities.

[1], Bordered pits.  [2], Section of a bordered pit.  [3], Mode of connection of adjacent cells in the bundle-sheath of *Scolopendrium*.  [4], Sieve-tubes.  [5], Group of cells from seed of *Nux-vomica*, the protoplasts of adjoining cell-cavities connected by fine protoplasmic filaments.

five times as thick as the window-pane itself. In other cases, however, the cell-wall becomes twenty or thirty times as thick as it was at first, and the interior of the cell is thereby seriously diminished in size. But even if, little by little, the cell-wall augments in thickness a hundredfold, any spot where thickening has not taken place from the first, and where, accordingly, a little depression occurs, is not subsequently covered with cellulose, but is carefully kept open by the protoplast as it builds. A greatly thickened wall of this kind resembles a fortification provided here and there with deep, narrow loopholes. Where two cells thus provided adjoin one another, the windows in the one occur, normally, exactly opposite those of its neighbour, and the result is the formation of canals, very long relatively, which penetrate through the two adjacent cell-walls and connect the neighbouring cell-cavities together (fig. 10[3]). A canal of this kind is still closed, it is true, in the middle by the original cell-membrane as though by a lock-gate: but this slight obstruction may be removed later by solution, and the contiguous cells have then perfectly open connection through the canal.

Very frequently provision is made in the very first rudiments of a cell-mem-

brane, destined to constitute a partition-wall, for open communications such as the
above. For segments of the wall of various sizes are made from the beginning with
sieve-like perforations, as is shown in fig. 10 $^4$, which represents diagrammatically
portions of tubular cells called "sieve-tubes." The pores are crowded close together
on the perforated areas of the walls of the sieve-tubes, and their dimensions are
relatively broad and short. Thus, when two neighbouring protoplasts reach out to
one another through these pores, that is to say, when there is continuity of the
protoplasm of the two cell-cavities, the connecting filaments, which pass through the
pores and which fill them completely, are short and thick and have the appearance
of pegs or stoppers.

But in many cases the pores through which adjoining cell-cavities communicate
are drawn out to a great length, forming infinitesimally slender passages. They are
situated close together in great numbers and penetrate transversely through the
thick cell-walls (fig. 10 $^5$). Neighbouring protoplasts may be brought equally well
into mutual connection by means of these canals, or perhaps it would be better to
say that their connection may be equally well maintained. For it is very probably
the case that in the first rudimentary partition-wall, which is produced between the
products of division of a protoplast, minute spots remain open and are occupied by
connecting threads common to both halves of the protoplasm as they draw apart.
Then in proportion as the partition-wall between the two protoplasts, produced by
the division, becomes thicker, the openings take the form of fine canals, and the connecting filaments are modified into long and exceedingly fine threads which fill the
canals. These protoplasmic threads pierce through the thickened cell-wall in the
same way as a dozen telegraph-wires might be drawn through a partition from one
room into another. Often a number of protoplasts living side by side and one
above the other are linked together by filaments of this kind, which radiate in all
directions.

This species of connection, of which an intelligible idea is given by fig. 10 $^5$,
escaped the notice of observers in former times owing to the extraordinary minuteness of the canals, and delicacy of the protoplasmic filaments. Another method of
communication between protoplasts in adjoining cells has, on the other hand, been
long known and often described, its phenomena being very striking and visible when
only slightly magnified. The connection referred to is that which is afforded by
the formation of so-called "vessels." By vessels the older botanists understood
tubes or utricles, arising from the dissolution of the partition-walls between a series
of cells. Either the partition-walls in a rectilineal row of cells vanish, in which
case long straight tubes are produced; or portions of the walls of cells arranged at
different angles to one another are dissolved, and then tubes are formed having an
irregular course, and sometimes branching or even uniting, so as to make a net-work.
In instances of the first kind the lateral walls of the series of cells which are to lose
their transverse partitions are previously thickened and made stiff by the protoplasts, which also provide them with various mouldings and panellings, and above all
with bordered pits. This task accomplished, the protoplasts forsake the tubes, whose

function thenceforth it is to serve as passages for air and water; thus the continued presence of the protoplasts is no longer advantageous. On the other hand, in the second class of vessels the lateral walls of the cells, which have coalesced to form them, exhibit no thickening, but are soft and delicate, and resemble flexible tubing. These tubes, moreover, are not deserted by their protoplasts; but, after the coalescence of a number of cells into a single duct has taken place, the protoplasts in the cells are themselves merged together, and the entire tube is then occupied by an uninterrupted mass of protoplasm, which generally persists as a lining to the wall.

As the initiation and construction of cell-walls are the work of the living protoplast, so also is their removal. The home it has made for itself the protoplast can also demolish—either partially or completely. But this demolition is preluded by the importation of particles of water into the portions of the wall which are to be destroyed. The introduction of water brings the wall into a gelatinous condition; the cohesion of its constituent particles is loosened, little by little, and at length completely abolished.

---

# 4. COMMUNICATION OF PROTOPLASTS WITH ONE ANOTHER AND WITH THE OUTER WORLD.

The transmission of stimuli and the specific constitution of protoplasm.—
Vital Force, Instinct and Sensation.

## THE TRANSMISSION OF STIMULI AND THE SPECIFIC CONSTITUTION OF PROTOPLASM.

As has been already intimated, the breaking down of individual cell-walls and the formation of the various pits, sieve-pores and fine canals in thickened membranes, in the manner described in preceding pages, are processes of great importance to the life of protoplasts. In the first place, many of the resulting structures are the means of preserving the possibility of intercourse with the outside world. In a space inclosed by evenly thickened walls, the absorption of air, water, and other raw materials from the environment would be very difficult if not impossible; the protoplast inside would soon lack the provisions needful for further development, and would at last die of starvation, drought, and suffocation. But the little windows, whether open or closed by thin permeable membranes, enable it to supply itself with all necessaries of life. Another advantage is derived, in the case of many of these structures, inasmuch as the protoplasts on occasion escape through the open doors and settle down in some other part of the cell-colony, where they are able again to make themselves useful. Lastly, one of the most important benefits of all is due to the fact that mutual intercourse between protoplasts, living together as a commonwealth, is rendered possible by the canals which join them together. And such an intercourse must of necessity be presumed to exist. When one considers the unanimous co-operation of protoplasts living together as a colony, and observes how neighbouring individuals, though produced from one and the same mother-cell, yet exercise different functions according to their position; and, further, how universally there is the division of labour most conducive to the well-being of the whole community, it is not easy to deny to a society, which works so harmoniously, the possession of unity of organization. The individual members of the colony must have community of feeling and a mutual understanding, and stimuli must be propagated from one part to another. No more obvious explanation offers than that the protoplasmic filaments, which run like telegraph-wires through the narrow pores and canals in the cell-walls (see fig. 10[5]), serve to propagate and transmit stimuli from one protoplast to another. These threads of protoplasm may indeed be likened to nerves which convey impulses determining definite actions from cell to cell.

Imagination takes us further still, and raises the cell-nucleus to the position of the dominant organ of the cell-body  For the nucleus not only determines the activity of the individual protoplast within its own cavity, but continues in sympathetic communion with its neighbour by means of all the threads and ligaments which converge upon it. This last idea in particular derives support from indications that the filaments uniting neighbouring protoplasts have their origin in specific transformations in the substance of the nucleus itself. When a protoplast living in a cell-cavity is about to divide into two, the process resulting in division is as follows:—The nucleus places itself in the middle of its cell, and at first characteristic lines and streaks appear in its substance, making it look like a ball made up of threads and little rods pressed together. These threads gradually arrange themselves in positions corresponding to the meridian lines upon a globe; but, at the place where on a globe the equator would lie, there then occurs suddenly a cleavage of the nucleus—a partition-wall of cellulose is interposed in the gap, and from a single cell we now have produced a pair of cells. In this way, from the nucleus, and from the protoplast of which the nucleus is the centre, two protoplasts have been produced, each having a nucleus of its own, and they thenceforth live side by side, each in its own chamber. It has been proved that in this process of division the substance of the nucleus is not completely sundered by the partition as it grows, but that, as we have already mentioned, minute pores are kept open in the cellulose wall, and that the pair of protoplasts continue joined together by threads running through these pores.

When we realize that every plant was once only a single minute lump of protoplasm, inasmuch as the biggest tree, like the smallest moss, has its origin in the protoplasm of an egg-cell or a spore; and when we consider how, by growth and repeated bipartition, thousands of cells are evolved, step by step, from a single one, whilst their protoplastic bodies still remain united by fine filaments, we arrive of necessity at the conclusion that the whole mass of protoplasm, living in all the myriads of cells whose aggregation constitutes a tree, really is, and continues to be, a single individual, whose parts are only separated by perforated sieve-like partitions. Every member of this community occupies a particular compartment or cavity, and is governed by a central organ, the cell-nucleus; but being linked to its fellows by connecting threads of protoplasm, a mutual understanding is thus established among them.

The physical basis of such an understanding may in this manner be represented with tolerable certainty. But it is extremely difficult to throw light upon the process of this mutual intelligence, the actual method whereby the cell-nuclei not only govern within their own narrow spheres, but also co-operate harmoniously for the good of the whole. And yet the problem involved in this unanimity of action, with a view to a systematic development of the plant in its entirety, is of such extreme importance that we cannot evade it even if, in the endeavour to solve it, we have to move altogether in the region of hypothesis.

In every attempt at explanation of the kind we must, at all events, bear in mind that the agreement in question, as well as the processes which take place in pursuance of this agreement, such as the nutrition, growth, and the organization of the entire plant, are reducible to the subtlest atomic agencies in the living protoplasm. They may be resolved into the motion of minute particles, into attractions and repulsions, oscillations and vibrations of atoms, and into re-arrangements of the atomic groups called molecules. Again, these movements are the result of the action of forces, especially of gravity, light, and heat. As regards gravity and light, experiment shows, however, that, when acting on living protoplasm, they give rise to varying effects even under the same conditions; and this fact, which will be discussed frequently later on, indicates that these forces are at any rate only to be conceived as stimulative and not coercive, and that they have no power to determine the kind of form. It is characteristic of the processes set up by gravity and light, especially when they take place in the continuous protoplasm of a great cell-community, that the coarser movements visible to the naked eye are often manifested in members comparatively remote from the part immediately affected by the stimulus. We cannot well represent this to ourselves except by supposing that the stimulus, which is the cause of the movement, is propagated through the threads of protoplasm from atom to atom, and from nucleus to nucleus. But the great puzzle lies, as already remarked, in the circumstance that the atomic and molecular disturbances occasioned by such stimuli and transmitted through the connecting filaments are not only different in the protoplasm of different kinds of plants, but even in the same plant they are of such a nature, according to the temporary requirement, that each one of the aggregated protoplasts in a community of cells undertakes the particular avocation which is most useful to the whole, the effect of this joint labour conveying the impression of the presence of a single governing power of definite design and of methodical action.

That a stimulus causes different occurrences in different species of plants, and, more especially, that cell-communities arising from different egg-cells develop into different forms, though under identical conditions and subjected to the same stimuli, are phenomena which have parallels in the inanimate world. A different sound is produced by striking the key of a piano which is connected to an A-string from that resulting from the transmission of a similar impulse to an F-string; and the difference depends on a difference of structure and an inequality of tension in the strings. Again, solutions of the sulphate and of the hyposulphite of sodium in similar glass vessels are indistinguishable at sight, both being colourless and transparent. These solutions will preserve their liquid condition when cooled down gradually to below freezing-point if they are kept absolutely still; but the moment the vessels are touched and a vibration thereby transmitted to the contents, they freeze. Crystals are formed in the apparently identical liquids, but crystals of different kinds, Glauber's salts in the one case, hyposulphite of sodium in the other. The variety of form depends simply on the sort of atoms, and on their number and mode of grouping.

In a similar manner must be explained the variety of forms in many plant-species developed under the same conditions and affected by the same stimuli. Dozens of kinds of unicellular Desmids and Diatoms are often developed at the same time in a single drop of water in close proximity to one another. Although the protoplasm in the spores of these different species is absolutely identical to our vision, aided by the best microscopes, yet the mature cells exhibit a multiplicity of form which is quite astonishing to the observer on first inspection. One cell is semi-lunar, another cylindrical, a third stellate, a fourth lozenge-shaped, and a fifth acicular. In one specimen the cell-membrane is smooth, in another it is beaded; some are provided with siliceous coats, whilst others have flexible envelopes.

The same thing holds good with respect to the vegetable structures, which are composed of myriads of cells, and develop into huge shrubs or tall trees. The protoplasm in the egg-cell of an oleander is produced close to that of a poplar on the same river-bank, and under exactly the same external conditions. The cells divide, and partition-walls are introduced in the proper direction in either case, according to a plan of structure which is adhered to with marvellous precision by the protoplasts engaged in the work of construction. In each species, stem, branches, foliage, and blossoms have invariably a particular form and arrangement, have the same colour and smell, and contain the same substances. How utterly different are the mature leaf, the opened flower, and ripe fruit of the oleander from the corresponding parts of a poplar. Yet both were nourished by the same earth, were surrounded by the same atmosphere, and encountered the same rays of sunshine. We cannot otherwise explain it than by the supposition that, in a case like this, the difference of form in the perfected state is based upon a difference in the self-developing protoplasm, and that the atoms and molecules of this protoplasm, which appears to us to be uniform, vary in kind, number, and grouping in the two species of plants. Consequently, we must assume that every vegetable organism, every species of plant that appears invariably in the same external form when mature, and develops according to an invariable plan, has a protoplasm of its own of a certain specific constitution. And, further, we must assume that this specific protoplasmic constitution is transmitted from one generation to another, so that the protoplasm of the oleander, for example, had exactly the same constitution thousands of years ago as it has to-day. Lastly, we must assume that each special kind of protoplasm has the power to reproduce its like, ever anew, from the raw materials occurring in its environment.

## VITAL FORCE, INSTINCT, AND SENSATION.

The phenomena observed in living protoplasm, as it grows and takes definite form, cannot in their entirety be explained by the assumption of a specific constitution of protoplasm for every distinct kind of plant; though this hypothesis will again prove very useful when we inquire into the origin of new species. What it does not account for is the appropriate manner in which various functions are distributed amongst the protoplasts of a cell-community; nor does it explain the purposeful sequence of different operations in the same protoplasm without any change in the external stimuli, the thorough use made of external advantages, the resistance to injurious influences, the avoidance or encompassing of insuperable obstacles, the punctuality with which all the functions are performed, the periodicity which occurs with the greatest regularity under constant conditions of the environment, nor, above all, the fact that the power of discharging all the operations requisite for growth, nutrition, renovation, and multiplication is liable to be lost. We call the loss of this power the death of the protoplasm. It ensues upon assaults from without if they succeed in destroying the molecular structure so entirely as to render reconstruction impossible; but, furthermore, death may take place without external cause.

If cells of the blood-red alga, previously mentioned as allied to the red-snow, are collected from hollows in stones, casually full of rain-water, and are kept dry for weeks and then again moistened, the water is found to have a very powerful effect. The protoplasm becomes mobile, and swarm-spores are formed which put forth vibratile cilia, propel themselves about for a short time in the water, and then settle down in some favoured spot, draw in their cilia, come to rest and divide, producing offspring which again are motile. This alga may be kept dry for months, nay even over a year, and still its cells exhibit the movements above described when put into water. But if a mass of it is preserved under these same conditions for many years and then moistened, the little cells will, it is true, take up additional water, but motile cells are no longer formed. The cells do not move, nor grow, nor divide, but gradually become discoloured; are first disintegrated and then dissolved. We say then that in them life could no longer be recalled, and we describe them as dead.

The same thing is observed in great cell-communities. The seeds of many species of plants preserve the capacity for germination for an incredibly long period, especially when kept in a dry place. If after ten years such seeds are transferred into moist earth, the protoplasm in the majority of cases begins to bestir itself and to move, and the embryo grows out into a seedling. After twenty years, perhaps, only about five per cent of the seeds preserved would germinate. The rest are not stimulated by damp earth to further development; their protoplasm no longer possesses the power of augmenting its volume by absorption of matter from the environment, or of developing a definite form, but is disintegrated by the influx of air and water and breaks up into simpler compounds. After thirty years hardly one of the seeds would sprout. Yet all these seeds were kept throughout the time at one place and under precisely the same external conditions; nor can the slightest change in their appearance be detected. Gardeners express the fact by saying that the capacity for germination becomes extinct in from twenty to thirty years. But what kind of a force is this which may perish without a physical change of the substance concerned affording the basis of the extinction? In former times a special force was assumed, the force of life. More recently, when many phenomena of plant life had been successfully reduced to simple chemical and mechanical processes, this vital force was derided and effaced from the list of natural agencies. But by what name shall we now designate that force in nature which is liable to perish whilst the protoplasm suffers no physical alteration and in the absence of any extrinsic cause; and which yet, so long as it is not extinct, causes the protoplasm to move, to inclose itself, to assimilate certain kinds of fresh matter coming within the sphere of its activity and to reject others, and which, when in full action, makes the protoplasm adapt its movements under external stimulation to existing conditions in the manner which is most expedient?

This force in nature is not electricity nor magnetism; it is not identical with any other natural force, for it manifests a series of characteristic effects which differ from those of all other forms of energy. Therefore, I do not hesitate again to designate as vital force this natural agency, not to be identified with any other, whose immediate instrument is the protoplasm, and whose peculiar effects we call life. The atoms and molecules of protoplasm only fulfil the functions which constitute life so long as they are swayed by this vital force. If its dominion ceases, they yield to the operations of other forces. The recognition of a special natural force of this kind is not inconsistent with the fact that living bodies may at the same time be subject to other natural forces. Many phenomena of plant life may, as has been already frequently remarked, be conceived as simple chemical and mechanical processes, without the introduction of a special vital force; but the effects of these other forces are observed in lifeless bodies as well, and indeed act upon them in a precisely similar manner, and this cannot be said of the force of life.

Were we to designate as instinctive those actions of the vital force which are manifested by movements purposely adapted in some manner advantageous to the whole organism, nothing could be urged against it. For what is instinct but an unconscious and purposeful action on the part of a living organism? Plants, then, possess instinct. We have instances of its operation in every swarm-spore in search of the best place to settle in, and in every pollen-tube as it grows down through the entrance to an ovary and applies itself to one definite spot of an ovule, never failing in its object. The water-crowfoot, in deep water, fashions its leaves with finely divided tips, large air-passages, and no stomata; whilst, growing above the surface of the water, its leaves have broad lobes, contracted intercellular spaces and numerous stomata. *Linaria Cymbalaria* (see fig. 11) raises its flower-stalks from the stone wall over which it creeps towards the light, but as soon as fertilization has taken place, these same stalks, in that very place and amidst unchanged external conditions, curve in the opposite direction, so as

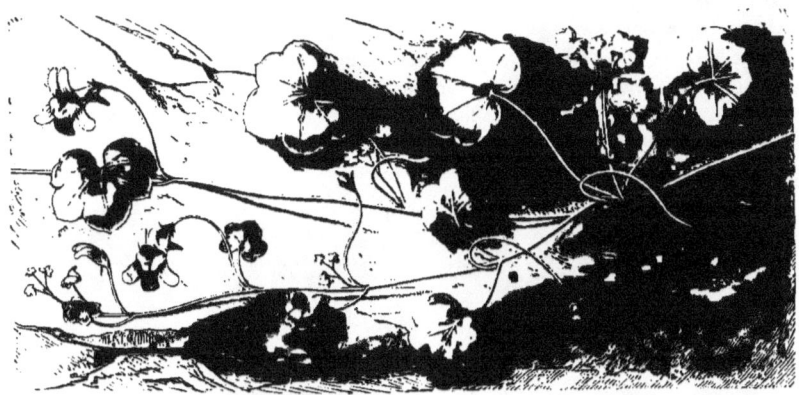

Fig. 11.—*Linaria Cymbalaria* dropping its Seeds into Clefts in the Rocks.

to deposit their seeds in a dark crevice. The flower-stalk of *Vallisneria* twists itself tightly into a screw and draws the flowers, which previously it had borne upon the surface of the water, down to the bottom when their stigmas have been covered with pollen-dust at the surface. These are all cases of unconscious action for a definite object, that is to say, they are the result of instinct.

If, however, we attribute instinct to living plants, it is but a step further to consider them as endowed with sensation also. Feeling in animals is the concomitant of a condition of disturbance in nerves and brain caused by a stimulus, which acts on the organs of sense, and is conveyed by nerves to the central organ. The transmission of the stimulus and the excited state of the brain and nerves are only molecular movements of the nervous substance, or, let us say, of the protoplasm, for nerve-fibres and nerve-cells are simply protoplasm developed in a particular manner. But the state induced by the stimulation of protoplasm, which is what we call sensation, cannot be essentially different in vegetable protoplasm from what it is in animal protoplasm, since the protoplasm itself, the physical basis of life in both plant and animal, is not different. In isolated plant-cells, indeed, it may amount to such a concentration of the condition of stimulation as to be called sensation, for the cell-nucleus is to all appearance a central organ in relation to the protoplast that lives in a solitary cell. It is not of course to be supposed that within a whole plant-structure, that is in the community of live protoplasts which constitutes an individual plant, such a concentration of stimulation could occur as is the case with individual animals which have nerve-fibres all converging into the brain; but between the sensation of animals without nerves and that of plants no essential difference can exist.

Hence we infer that there is no barrier between plants and animals. The attempt to establish a boundary-line where the realm of plants ceases and the animal world begins is a vain one. If we naturalists, all the same, agree to separate plants and animals, we do so only because experience shows that a division of labour conduces to a speedier attainment of our object. On the intermediate ground where animals and plants meet, zoologists and botanists encounter one another, not, however, as hostile rivals with a view to exclusive possession of the field, but as colleagues with a common interest in the administration and cultivation of this jointly tenanted region.

# ABSORPTION OF NUTRIMENT.

## 1. INTRODUCTION.

### CLASSIFICATION OF PLANTS WITH REFERENCE TO NUTRITION.

The object of a plant's vital energy, next in importance to the resistance of such influences as are likely to bring about the death of the protoplasm, is growth, *i.e.* the addition of substance to its body, or, in other words, the absorption of nutriment. A living plant, whether consisting of a single cell or of a vast community of cells, takes up food from its environment in quantities varying according to the needs of the moment. But its method of action—how it sets about acquiring possession of this raw material, how it manages to incorporate the substances absorbed from without, how it contrives to retain only such part as is useful to it, and to reject and get rid of, like ballast, what does not subserve its own growth—is infinitely varied. This variety in the processes of food-absorption corresponds, on the one hand, to differences in the habitat of plants, and, on the other, to the requirements of particular species, which requirements in their turn depend upon a specific constitution of the protoplasm in each species concerned. The difference must be very great between this process as manifested in plants which are immersed in water during their whole lives and the same as it occurs in plants which live in desert sands and are not supplied with water for months together. And again, absorption in those fungi which grow luxuriantly on damp timber in the deep obscurity of a mine must take place very differently from the corresponding process in the delicate alpine plants which on our mountain slopes are exposed periodically to the most intense sunlight, and then, for weeks at a time, are wreathed in sombre mists. So, also, the reciprocal action between plants and their environment must have a character of its own in the case of parasitic growths which absorb their food from other living organisms, and in those remarkable plants, too, which catch and devour small insects, and in such minute organisms as yeast, the vinegar ferment, and others, which play so important a part in our daily life, and lastly, in the gigantic trees which form our forests.

To acquire a general notion of these forms, with reference to their varieties as regards nutrition, it is best to classify them in the first place in groups according to their habitat, viz.: into water-plants or hydrophytes, stone-plants or lithophytes, land-plants, and epiphytes. But here again it is necessary to remark that no sharp line of demarcation exists between these groups; all are connected by numerous intermediate links, and there are forms which belong to one group at one stage of development and to another at another stage.

The distinctive property of aquatic plants is that they derive their nourishment either entirely or principally from the surrounding water. Some preserve their freedom, floating or swimming about in the liquid medium; but the majority are fixed somewhere under the water by special organs of attachment. Many plants that are rooted in the mud at the bottom of pools are able to derive their food from the water when it is high, and when it is low, from the atmosphere as well: such amphibious organisms form a transitional group between water-plants and land-plants. The number of lithophytes is comparatively very small. They include those lichens and mosses which cling in immediate contact to the surface of stones and derive their food in a fluid state direct from the atmosphere. All lithophytes are so constituted that they can, without injury, dry up and suspend their vitality for a time when there is a failure of atmospheric precipitation lasting over a long period or when the air itself is very dry. But not every plant which grows upon rocks is to be regarded as a lithophyte in the narrower acceptation of the term. Those that are rooted in earth in the cracks and crevices of the rock must be classed amongst land-plants. To this class indeed more than half the plants now in existence belong. Though surrounded by air as regards a part of their structure they have another part sunk in the soil, and from the soil they take up water and inorganic compounds in aqueous solution. Plants which grow attached to other plants or to animals are called epiphytes.

The majority of plants are during the period of food-absorption connected with the foster-earth and are not capable of locomotion. The plant being fixed to one spot must therefore sooner or later exhaust the ground in its neighbourhood, and must require a further supply of nutritive substances. The parts specially devoted to food-absorption often lengthen out in these circumstances beyond the impoverished region, and thus endeavour to bring areas more and more distant within the range of absorption. Many plants possess the faculty, to which reference has already been made, of alluring animals and of killing and sucking their juices. Not only amongst saprophytes and parasites, but also amongst aquatic plants, instances occur in which certain movements are performed involving the whole body of the organism, with a view to promoting the absorption of nutriment. Particularly striking in this respect are many plasmoid fungi (which we may well refer to here, not on this account alone, but also for the additional reason that they take in nourishment without the intervention of a cell-membrane). The naked protoplasm in these cases, which include in particular the class of Amœbæ, crawls in its search for food over the nourishing substratum, and derives from it immediately the materials needful for growth. Loose bodies are liable to be seized by the radiating processes of the protoplasm, which then closes round them and drains them completely of their juices (see fig. 9, the last figure to the right). These bodies encompassed by the protoplasm, if small, are drawn inwards from the periphery and are regularly digested in the interior. Such parts of foreign bodies as are not serviceable for nutrition are subsequently eliminated or are left behind by the protoplast as it creeps onward. But this method of food-absorption is limited to amœboid forms belonging to the boundary-land of animal and vegetable life. The movements of other naked protoplasts, such as those which are carried about in the water by vibratile cilia, have nothing to do with the search for food or with its absorption, but are connected rather with the processes of distribution and propagation.

## THEORY OF FOOD-ABSORPTION.

In the case of protoplasts inclosed in cell-membranes the food necessary for nourishment must always pass through the cell-membrane and peripheral protoplasmic layer (ectoplasm) into the interior of the protoplasmic bodies. And so, conversely, such of the substances absorbed as are of no use in the construction of the organism or for any other purpose, must be separated and passed out through these envelopes. The cell-membranes of those protoplasts which are employed in absorbing food must accordingly have a special structure: the ultimate particles must be so arranged as to allow of the passage of nutritions material inwards, and of rejected matter outwards, without prejudice to their own stability. The passages in cell-walls used for this purpose are very minute, much smaller at all events than the pore-canals described above as being occupied by fine protoplasmic filaments; the dimensions are in fact so trifling as to be invisible even with the best microscopes. Still we are forced to conclude that they exist by *a posteriori* reasoning from a series of phenomena, and to assume that the cell-membrane, like almost every other kind of body, consists not of continuous matter, but of minute particles, which are termed atoms, and are separated from one another by infinitesimally small spaces. Various processes and appearances have also led physicists and chemists to the conclusion that these atoms are not aggregated in disorder, but are always combined together in groups of two or more, even in the case where all the atoms in a body are of the same kind, *i.e.* are the same element. If a body contains different elements they are not mixed together indiscriminately, but are grouped in conformity to a definite law: every group includes atoms of all the different elements concerned, arranged in a certain invariable manner, not only as regards number, but also as regards relative position. Groups of atoms of this kind are called "molecules," and the spaces between them are supposed to be larger than those between single atoms. Further, it is not improbable that the molecules themselves form groups, each group consisting of molecules conglomerated in a definite manner, and that the passages separating these molecular groups are larger again than those separating the single molecules within each group. These groups of molecules have been called "micellæ" or Tagmata, and they also are supposed to be aggregated together in definite order.

According to this theory the cell-membrane is analogous to a sieve, the pores of which are grouped in a definite manner, the broadest perforations being between

the micellæ or groups of molecules, narrower apertures between the molecules
or groups of atoms in each micelle, and lastly the finest pores between the atoms
themselves in each molecule.   These interspaces are liable to contraction and
expansion, for the union of the molecules is affected by two forces, one of which
manifests itself as a mutual attraction between atoms and atomic groups, whilst
the other tends to drive atoms and molecules asunder.   Of these forces the former,
*i.e.* the attractive force existing in all material particles, is called chemical affinity
when it causes atoms of different kinds to unite to form a molecule; and it is called
cohesion when applied to the mutual attraction of similar molecules, and adhesion
where it holds together masses of molecular groups with their surfaces in contact.
The action of heat is opposed to this attractive force, which is only effective at
infinitesimal distances.   Bodies are all caused to expand by heat, their atoms, molecules, and micellæ being forced apart.   Heat is believed to be a vibratory motion
of these ultimate particles, and it is supposed that the greater the vibrations the
greater is the separation of atoms and atomic groups, the interspaces expanding
and the heated body increasing consequently in volume.   As is well known, the
atoms and molecules may be forced so far apart by increase of temperature that
cohesion is entirely overcome, and solids are converted, first into liquids and at
last into gases.

The interspaces or passages between the molecules and molecular groups composing a cell-membrane are penetrable by molecules of other substances, provided
always, firstly, that the admitted molecules are not larger than the passages; and
secondly, that there exists between the molecules of the cell-wall and those of the
penetrating body that sort of attractive force which has been designated chemical
affinity.   Both premises are satisfied in the case of aqueous molecules, and experiment proves that they are admitted into the inter-molecular spaces of a cell-
membrane with great ease and readiness.   The cell-membrane saturates itself with
water, or, to use the technical phrase, it has the tendency and ability to "imbibe"
water.   The force of attraction between molecules of a cell-membrane and water-
molecules is indeed so intense that the cohesion of the molecules in the membrane
is partially neutralized, and the imbibed water causes them to move apart.   In
consequence of this, the cell-membrane swells up and its dimensions are increased.

It is also supposed that the micellæ of a cell-membrane attract and admit water-
molecules to such an extent as to surround themselves with watery envelopes.
Such a condition would no doubt be nothing but beneficial, promoting, as it would,
the interchange of materials through the cell-membrane, and the mixing of fluid
substances situated on either side of the porous membrane.   At all events this
mixing process must ensue in the interspaces of the cell-membrane; and, in the
particular case out of which this discussion has arisen, viz. food-absorption, the
interacting substances are, on the one hand, the compounds in the soil outside
the cell-membrane, and, on the other, the organic compounds under the control
of the live protoplast within the cell-membrane.   Both the outgoing and the in-
coming substances must be soluble in water, and must, therefore, have an attraction

for water.  But the power of a substance in aqueous solution, whether without or within the cell-membrane, to permeate the saturated pores, and to mix thoroughly there, certainly depends also on the degree of chemical affinity and of adhesion existing between the molecules and micellæ of the cell-membrane on the one hand, and these infiltrating substances on the other.  A very complex interaction of forces takes place which we cannot here investigate any further, as it would take us much too far afield.

Returning to the explanation of food-absorption, attention must be drawn to the fact that the mixing or diffusion which takes place through the cell-membrane differs from the free diffusion which would occur if the cell-membrane were not present.  Experiment has proved that if one side of a cell-membrane is steeped in a saline solution and the other in an equal volume of pure water, the number of saline particles which pass through into the water are many fewer than the number of water-particles which pass into the solution of salt; and, moreover, if an organic compound, such as albumen or dextrin, is on one side, and water on the other, water transfuses to the organic compound, whereas no trace of the albumen or dextrin (as the case may be) passes through to the water.  Now this phenomenon, which is called "osmosis" ("endosmosis and exosmosis"), is of great importance for the conception we have to form of food-absorption.  It is clear that, whilst water and substances dissolved in water are brought under the control of the protoplast within a cell through the cell-membrane, as a consequence of the action of albuminous and other compounds constituting the body of the protoplast, and of the salts dissolved in the so-called cell-sap in the vacuoles, there is no necessity for any part of the cell-content to pass out through the cell-membrane. Thus the protoplasm is able to exercise an absorptive action on aqueous solutions outside the cell-membrane, and to continue to absorb until the cell is filled.  Indeed, the chemical affinity for water possessed by the substances in a cell may occasion so great an absorption of water that, in consequence, the volume of the cell is enlarged and the cell-membrane is subjected to pressure from within.  The cell-membrane is able to yield to this pressure to the extent permitted by its elasticity; but excessive stretching of the cell-membrane is at length counteracted by cohesion, and thus a condition is attained in which the cell-contents and the cell-membrane are subjected to mutual pressure, a state which is called "turgidity."

The process just described, of the absorption of water in large quantities into the precincts of the protoplasm without any simultaneous transmission of matter to the outside, is certainly in no respect an exchange.  But it obviously does not exclude the possibility of a real exchange taking place between substances on either side of a cell-membrane, i.e. between solutions in the soil and those in the cell-sap contained in lacunæ of the protoplasm.  Certain phenomena in fact put it beyond doubt that on occasion a real exchange of this kind does occur.  But it is complicated by the circumstance that substances in process of being exchanged have to pass not only through the cell-membrane but also through the primordial utricle: and the primordial utricle consists of molecules of a kind other than those of the cell-wall, having different chemical affinities, and these molecules again are differently grouped; nor are the passages for aqueous solutions the same. All this cannot but have an important bearing on the permeating capacity of the substances that are being interchanged.

Although all these ideas concerning the molecular structure of cell-membranes and of protoplasm, concerning the intermixture and exchange of materials and the absorption on the part of cells and their swelling up, have only the value of theories, still we have good ground for assuming that they are fairly near the truth. They give us, at all events, an intelligible representation of the interaction which takes place between living protoplasts, with their need for food, and the environment, which supplies the nutriment.

## 2. ABSORPTION OF INORGANIC SUBSTANCES.

Nutrient Gases.—Nutrient Salts.—Absorption of Nutrient Salts by Water-plants, Stone-plants, and Land-plants.—Relations between the position of Foliage-leaves and Absorption-roots.

### NUTRIENT GASES.

One of the most important sources of the nourishment of plants is carbonic acid. The living protoplasts appropriate it from water and from air, in the latter case chiefly by attracting the carbon-dioxide.[1] This gas penetrates a cell-wall saturated with water more readily than the other constituent gases of the atmosphere (nitrogen and oxygen). In the wall it is converted into carbonic acid, and it then passes on into the cell-sap contained in the cavities of the protoplast. Apart from the effects of temperature and atmospheric pressure, the quantity of carbonic acid absorbed is chiefly determined by the requirements of the cells whose nourishment is in question. These requirements, however, vary considerably according to the specific constitution of the protoplasm and with the time of day. During daylight the need of carbon is very great in all green plants. As soon as the carbonic acid reaches the cell-sap it is decomposed and reduced by the action of sunlight, and from it are formed compounds known as carbo-hydrates. The oxygen thus set free is, however, removed from the cell precincts, and expelled into the surrounding air or water. In this way the gas when barely absorbed is withdrawn, as such, from the cell-sap, the carbon alone being retained and the oxygen eliminated, and a renewed attraction of carbon-dioxide from the surrounding medium ensues. The fresh supply again is immediately worked up in the green chlorophyll-bodies, so that there is a constant influx of carbon-dioxide, and therefore indirectly of carbonic acid, from the environment into the interior of green cells to the part where its consumption takes place. Were it possible to see

[1] The atmosphere contains free carbon-dioxide and not carbonic acid. But carbonic acid is formed when the dioxide is absorbed into water.

the molecules of carbon-dioxide in the air, we should observe how much faster they are impelled towards the leaves and other green parts of plants, where the intense craving for carbon is localized, than are the other constituent particles of the air. This impulsion and influx lasts so long as the green cells are under the influence of daylight. The first thing in the morning when the first ray of sunshine falls upon a plant the protoplasts begin work in their little laboratories decomposing carbonic acid, and producing from it sugar, starch, and other similar organic compounds. And it is not till the sun sets that this work is suspended, and the influx of carbon-dioxide stopped till the following morning.

The green plants that spend all their lives under water are supplied with carbonic acid by the water surrounding their cells, which always contains some of that material. In the case of unicellular plants of this class, absorption of carbonic acid takes place through the whole surface of the cell-membrane. Multicellular plants, with their cells arranged in filaments or plates, only take in carbonic acid through those parts of the walls of their cells which are in immediate contact with the water. This applies also to submerged plants composed of several layers of cells and of considerable dimensions. Thus, in plants of this kind, the cells in contact with the water constitute the skin. They are always pressed closely together and squeezed flat, are not thickened on the side exposed to the water, and are united everywhere edge to edge leaving no gaps. But in the interior of these water-plants large lacunæ and cavities are formed from earliest youth, owing to the detachment of single rows of cells, and the spaces so formed are filled with a quantity of nitrogen, oxygen, and carbon-dioxide, that is to say, with a gaseous mixture not essentially different from atmospheric air. Although this organization may have as its primary object the reduction of the plant's weight as a whole, it cannot be without a further importance inasmuch as carbonic acid can be taken up from the air-spaces into adjacent cells. But there is no doubt that, even in this case (of water-plants provided with large internal air-cavities), the chief absorption of carbonic acid is through the epidermis, or more precisely through those walls of the epidermal cells which are in immediate contact with the water.

The carbonic acid taken up by cells, wholly or partially immersed in water, is either contained as such dissolved in the watery medium, or occurs in combination with calcium as bicarbonate of lime. Part of the carbonic acid in this bicarbonate in aqueous solution is susceptible of being withdrawn by water-plants, mono-carbonate of lime, which is insoluble in water, being then precipitated on the cell-wall through which the rest of the carbonic acid has passed into the cell-interior. Accordingly, a large number of water-plants are found incrusted with lime in both fresh and salt water. We shall return to this important phenomenon when we treat of the influence of living plants on that part of the environment which comes within their sphere of action for purposes of nutrition.

Lithophytes obtain carbonic acid from the moisture deposited upon them from the aqueous vapour in the atmosphere, and attract carbon-dioxide direct from the air around them.  The chief members of this class are those mosses, liverworts, and lichens which, though clinging to dry rocks, behave just like water-plants as regards the absorption of carbonic acid.  There is no reason to think that these plants absorb carbonic acid in dry weather; for under the influence of dry air they lose water fast, and meanwhile receive no compensation from the rock to which they are attached, and in a short time they become so dry that they crumble into powder when rubbed between the fingers.  Vitality is suspended for a time, and it is out of the question that there should be any absorption of carbon-dioxide from the atmosphere under such circumstances.  But the moment the plant is moistened by rain or dew, the cell-walls directly exposed to the air become saturated, and are enabled to admit water into the interior.  Then the lithophytes suck up water very fast; the dry, apparently dead, incrustations swell up again, and, together with the rain and dew, carbonic acid is absorbed, it being contained in all depositions of atmospheric moisture.  A tumescent moss tuft can, in addition, absorb carbon-dioxide direct from the atmosphere through its saturated superficial cells; but the quantity of carbonic acid thus acquired by a plant is in any case only secondary.  Many mosses, as for example the widely-distributed *Grimmia apocarpa*, are also able to live just as well under water as in air; nor is any alteration of their leaves necessary in either condition, nor any special contrivance for the absorption of carbonic acid and water.  These substances reach the interior by similar passage through cell-walls of identical construction, whether the *Grimmia* spends its life attached to submerged rocks or in the open air at the top of a mountain; whence we may infer that there is a greater resemblance between lithophytes and water-plants as regards nutrition than between lithophytes and land-plants.

Land-plants satisfy their need of carbon almost exclusively by withdrawing the dioxide from atmospheric air.  For the purpose of this direct appropriation, specially adapted structures are found in them.  Seeing that these plants are not able to endure periodic desiccation in times of drought, as lithophytes are, it is necessary for them to be secured against excessive loss of water.  Accordingly, the cell-walls in immediate contact with the air, that is to say, the outer walls of the epidermis, are thickened by a layer (cuticle) which is impermeable by air or water, and, in general, they are so organized that water cannot readily escape from the interior of the cells.  Obviously, however, a cell-wall which opposes a strong resistance to the extravasation of water will not give easy admittance to an influx either, and the conditions for the passage of gases through a cell-membrane, thickened and cuticularized in this way, would be far from favourable.  As a matter of fact many of the constituent gases of the atmosphere permeate these thickened walls of the epidermal cells only with great difficulty, and others not at all.  Carbon-dioxide alone has the power of penetrating, but even in the case of this gas the quantity is not always sufficient to satisfy the demand.  To ensure that so important a form of plant-food should reach in proper amount those cells lying under the epidermis, which are occupied by protoplasts engaged in the regulation of nutrition, there is an adaptation of structure of the following nature. Among the firmly connected epidermal cells with their thickened outer walls almost impervious to air, other cells are interspersed at intervals. They are always in pairs, are generally rather smaller than the rest, and have a little cleft open between them. Inasmuch as these apertures (stomata) always exist where passages and canals, the so-called intercellular spaces, have arisen from the separation of individual cells of the sub-epidermal tissues, each stoma constitutes the mouth of a system of channels ramifying between the thin-walled cells of the interior. The components of the atmosphere, especially carbon-dioxide, are able to reach these internal passages through the stomata, and in them they travel to the chlorophyll-containing cells. Through the thin, saturated walls of these cells they are able to penetrate with ease, and so they reach the living protoplasts, with their equipment of chlorophyll, whose daily work it is, as already mentioned, to decompose—under the transforming power of light—the carbonic acid as it reaches the chlorophyll-bodies, to work up the carbon and expel by the same path as they entered not only the oxygen but also all other aerial constituents which may have penetrated and for the moment find no employment.

These ventilation-canals, with stomata as orifices at the epidermis, have other uses besides the importation of carbon-dioxide (and therefore of carbonic acid) and the exportation of oxygen. For the same pores, passages, and lacunæ, as serve for the influx and exit of carbon-dioxide and oxygen respectively, are the channels of a plant's respiration. Moreover, they play a very important part also in the escape of aqueous vapour, the process known as "transpiration;" and as the variety in their structure is to be interpreted chiefly as an adaptation to the different conditions under which transpiration occurs, it cannot be profitably discussed until we treat of that process.

Those saprophytes and parasites which contain no chlorophyll or practically none, do not absorb any free carbon-dioxide from the atmosphere, but supply themselves with carbon from the organic compounds in the nutrient substratum on which they grow. But saprophytes and parasites, abundantly furnished with chlorophyll, doubtless do attract free carbon-dioxide in addition. They may do so either after the manner of water-plants and lithophytes, as is the case with Euglenæ, and with mosses growing on the dung of mammalia; or else after the manner of land-plants, as instances of which the cow-wheat, yellow-rattle, and eye-bright may be quoted.

It is a very remarkable fact that no plant is known which takes up carbon-dioxide or carbonic acid from the earth. One might expect that the roots of land-plants at any rate, ramifying as they do in a stratum of earth saturated with water containing carbonic acid in solution, would suck up to some extent so important a food, and that it would be from them conducted to the green-foliage leaves. But so far as experiments have gone, they indicate that this is not the case.

Equally curious is the circumstance that nitrogen, which is an indispensable constituent of protoplasm, and therefore a very important means of subsistence, is not absorbed from the surrounding air, although, as is well known, the atmosphere contains nitrogen to the amount of 79 per cent of its volume. There can be no doubt that though nitrogen permeates the cell-walls of an air-encompassed plant much less readily and quickly than carbon-dioxide, yet it is carried from the atmosphere into the ventilation-spaces of green foliage-leaves, and further through the thin cell-walls into the laboratories of the protoplasts, where one would expect it to be worked up in the same way as carbonic acid. The most careful experiments have determined, however, that it is not turned to account in this form by the protoplasts, but that on the contrary it is given back unused to the air, and only such nitrogen as reaches the interior of plants in combination with other substances is of any service there.

The principal sources of the nitrogen required by plants are nitrates and ammoniacal compounds absorbed from the ground; but nitric acid and ammonia themselves, of which there are traces in the atmosphere and in water, must not be overlooked. The quantity of nitric acid in air is, it is true, even less than that of carbon-dioxide; but just as the small amount of carbon-dioxide can be absorbed from the air with highly productive results, so may also the still smaller proportion of nitric acid be turned to account. The sources of nitric acid are dead organic bodies as they decompose and become oxidized. In many ways the process of formation of nitric acid from decaying bodies may take place so as to produce ammonia in the first place and from it nitric acid. It would seem possible, though it is an unproved assumption, that in places where dead bodies of plants and animals, vegetable mould, manure, and such things are undergoing oxidation, that is to say, in woods and fields, the small quantities of nitric acid that are given off are immediately taken up by the plants growing there. It must be borne in mind that plants behave with reference to what is necessary or useful to them like a chancellor of the exchequer preparing his budget; they take these things where they find them.

The question has been raised, too, as to the source from which the first plants that appeared on the earth were able to obtain nitric acid. We are obliged to assume that, at that time before the existence of nitrogenous organisms to supply nitric acid by oxidation of their dead bodies, all nitric acid, and therefore all the nitrogen used in the nourishment of plants, was generated by thunder-storms. We know that nitric acid is formed in the air on occasion of electric discharges and is deposited on the earth together with rain and dew. This source of nitric acid is not yet exhausted, and even at the present day it no doubt plays the same part as in the ages long past at the commencement of all vegetable life.

If nitric acid is used by protoplasts, in the building up of the highly important albuminous compounds, it is broken up in a manner similar to the decomposition of carbonic acid to form carbohydrates, that is to say, oxygen is separated out. In this case, however, sunlight and, therefore, chlorophyll are not immediately concerned. Moreover, the oxygen that is set free is not eliminated, but is used in the manufacture of other compounds in process of formation in the plant, probably in that of vegetable acids.

Ammonia behaves in relation to plants just in the same way as carbon-dioxide and nitric acid. It is disengaged from dead decomposing organic bodies, and is found in traces, either alone or with equally minute quantities of carbon-dioxide and carbonic and nitric acids in the air, in atmospheric deposits, and in all water wherein animals and plants reproduce their kind, the old individuals dying and making way for the young. Water-plants are all limited to this source for acquisition of nitrogen. As regard lithophytes, it stands to reason that they must derive their nitrogen from the ammonia contained in the air, in atmospheric deposits, and from nitric acid. Whence otherwise could a crustaceous lichen attached to a quartz rock on a mountain supply itself with the nitrogen essential for the growth of its protoplasm? Moreover, some of the larger lithophytes, especially mosses, seem to be capable of absorbing ammonia direct from the air. An observation made in the Tyrolese Alps has some bearing on this question:—The ridges of the Hammerspitze, a peak rising to 2600 meters between the Stubaithal and the Gschnitzthal, is, in favourable weather in the summer, the resting-place of hundreds of sheep, and is consequently covered with an entire crust of the excrements of these animals. A highly offensive and pungent smell of ammonia is evolved, and renders a prolonged stay on this spot anything but pleasant, notwithstanding the beauty of the view. Now, it is worthy of note that the mosses, which are produced in abundance on the rocks above this richly-manured ground, but are not themselves actually amongst the sheep-droppings, exhibit a luxuriance unparalleled on any of the neighbouring summits belonging to the same formation but unfrequented by sheep. The gaily-coloured green carpet extends as far as the ammoniacal odour is perceptible, and it is natural to suppose that this luxuriant growth is stimulated by the absorption of ammonia direct from the air.

Land-plants also can take up ammonia from the air. It has been shown that the glandular hairs of many plants, for instance those on the leaves of *Pelargonium* and of the Chinese Primrose, have the power of absorbing traces of ammonia, and of sucking up carbonate and nitrate of ammonia in water with rapidity. When we consider that a single one of these primroses (*Primula sinensis*) possesses two and a half millions of absorbent glandular hairs so placed as to be able to take up the ammonia brought to the plant by rain, we are unable to look upon this process as of altogether trifling importance. It is highly probable that almost all ammonia, after its formation from decaying substances in the ground, is at once absorbed by the plants growing in the immediate neighbourhood, and that the relatively small quantity of ammonia in the upper atmospheric strata is referrible to this cause. The splendid luxuriance of the pelargoniums, thickly studded with glandular hairs, which one sees in front of cottage windows in mountain villages where a dung heap is close by, and in the windows of stables, frequently excites admiration and surprise. Whether it is due to the fact that in these situations there is the possibility of absorbing an unusually large quantity of ammonia is a question which we will leave undecided.

## NUTRIENT SALTS.

If wood, leaves, seeds, or any other parts of plants are subjected to a high temperature with free access of air, the first changes that occur are in the compounds of nitrogen and of carbon contained in the heated matter. They turn black, are charred and burnt, and ultimately the products of combustion pass into the atmosphere in gaseous condition. The incombustible part which remains behind is called the "ash." The quantity of this ash, as well as its composition, varies very much in different species of plants, and even in different parts of the same plant. Generally the weight of ash is only one or two per cent of the entire weight of the plant in a dry state before burning. The greatest relative proportion of ash is that which is obtained from the combustion of those hydrophytes which live in the sea; and next in quantity is the ash of the family of Oraches which abound on salt-steppes. On the other hand, the smallest quantity is that afforded by fungi and mosses, by *Sphagnum* in particular, and with these must be mentioned the tropical orchids living on the barks of trees. Seeds and wood yield relatively much less ash than leaves. But, as above remarked, some ash is formed upon the combustion of any part of a plant or even of a single cell, and this residue of ash sometimes allows of our recognizing exactly the size, form, and outline of the cells. The universal distribution of ash-forming constituents permits us to conclude with certainty that they do not exist fortuitously in plants, but are essential to them. That these constituents are indispensable may also be proved directly. If an attempt is made to nourish a plant on filtered air and distilled water exclusively, the plant soon dies; but if a small quantity of the constituents of its ash are added to the distilled water in which the roots are immersed, the plant grows visibly in the solution, and develops leaves and flowers and even seeds capable of germination.

Experiments of this kind with cultures have been the means of almost completely establishing the division between those constituents which are indispensable for all plants, and those which are only necessary under certain conditions and to particular species, or, still less, only beneficial. Those elements must be regarded as essential, which are used by plants for the process of construction, and enter into the composition of the protoplasm or of the cell-membrane—such, for instance as are essential constituents of proteid substances, or are in some way necessary to the formation of these products. Amongst these must be included sulphur, phosphorus, potassium, calcium, and magnesium. Some plants, especially those that live in the sea, require sodium, iodine and chlorine, and, for green plants, iron is necessary. Silicon is also very important for most plants in helping them to flourish in the wild state. Most of these elements are taken into a plant, in the course of nutrition, in a condition of extreme oxidation, that is to say in combination with a quantity of oxygen; in fact, as a general rule, they are absorbed in the form of salts, and we may for the sake of brevity include all the mineral food-stuffs under the name of nutrient salts or food-salts.

It is obvious that food-salts can only pass through cell-membranes and reach the interior of a plant in a state of solution. On this account the soluble sulphates, phosphates, nitrates and chlorides of calcium, magnesium, potassium and iron, may pre-eminently be called food-salts. Whether an essential element is absorbed by a plant in the form of one of these compounds or another appears to be unimportant; phosphorus, for example, may be proffered by the soil in the form either of potassium phosphate or of sodium phosphate, with like results. As regards the importance of sulphur to plants, it is at any rate established that it is necessary for the production of proteid substances. Phosphorus appears to be indispensable in the transformation of certain compounds of nitrogen. Potassium is supposed to play a part in the formation of starch. Calcium is introduced into plants in combination with sulphuric acid as calcium sulphate. This salt is decomposed, the lime combining with oxalic acid to form insoluble calcium oxalate, and the sulphur going to form the sulphuric acid which is used in the construction of albuminous substances or proteids. Lime is therefore important, inasmuch as it is a medium of transport for sulphur. Iron certainly participates in the formation of chlorophyll, even if it does not enter into its composition, as was formerly supposed. For, it has been proved, by means of artificial cultures, that plants reared in solutions free from iron were white instead of green, and died at last; whereas, after the addition of a small quantity of a soluble iron salt, such plants became green in a very short time, and were able to continue their development. The utility of most of these elements does not therefore appear to consist necessarily in their entering into the composition of organic compounds, but in the promotion and regulation of the constructive and destructive chemical processes.

Silicic acid, which occurs so plentifully in the ash of many plants as to constitute often more than 50 per cent, has a different function. If the minute unicellular water-plants known as Diatoms are incinerated, or if stems of Equisetum, Juniper-needles, or leaves of grasses, &c., are subjected to a red heat, white skeletons remain behind which consist almost entirely of silicic acid, and exhibit not only the forms of the cells, but even the finest sculpturing of the cell-walls. In particular, the stiff hairs on the leaves of grasses are preserved, and better still the cell-membranes of diatoms. The latter present very beautiful forms with their outlines quite distinct, and many structural properties of the cell-membranes, especially their moulding, striation, and the dots and other excrescences are to be seen much more clearly after than before ignition, when the transparency was less owing to the protoplast occupying the interior of each cell. In order to describe exactly the very varied form of Diatomaceæ, specimens are carefully and thoroughly ignited, and the descriptions and illustrations of these microscopic plants are for the most part made from siliceous skeletons prepared in this way. These skeletons show clearly that silicic acid occurs only in the cell-membrane, and plays no part as constituent of any chemical compound in the protoplasm; nor does it appear to be instrumental in the formation of any such compound. The molecules of silicic acid are so closely packed and so evenly distributed amongst the molecules of cellulose that, even after the removal of the latter, the entire structure is preserved in outline and in detail. They form, therefore, a regular coat of mail which may be looked upon as a means of protection against certain injurious external influences.

For a large number of plants living in the sea, sodium, iodine, and bromine also are of especial importance as food-stuffs. How far fluorine, manganese, lithium, and various other metals, which have been detected in the ash of some plants, are of use is not determined, for our knowledge is particularly incomplete with respect to the various uses subserved in nutrition and growth by the different mineral food-stuffs. It is worthy of note that alumina, which is so widely distributed and easily accessible to plants, is only very rarely absorbed. The ash of *Lycopodium* is the only kind in which this substance has been identified with certainty in any considerable quantities.

Lastly, amongst the sources of elements contained in the food-salts, we must consider the solid crust of the earth. But it is only in the case of comparatively few vegetable organisms that this earth-crust forms the immediate foster-soil. The majority derive the salts that nourish them from the products of the weathering of rocks, from refuse and the decaying remains of dead animals and plants, which, in decomposing, give back their mineral substances to the ground, from underground waters that filter through fissures in rocks and through the interstices of sandy or clayey soils soaking with lye, the adjacent parts of the earth's crust, and, lastly, from the water of springs, streams, ponds, and lakes, which have come to the surface holding salts in solution, as also from sea-water with its rich supply of salts.

The very salts that are needed by most plants are amongst the most widely distributed on the earth's surface. The sulphates of calcium and of magnesium, for example, and salts of iron, potassium, &c., are found almost everywhere in the earth, and in water, whether subterranean or superficial. At the same time it is very striking that these mineral food-salts are not introduced into plants by any means in proportion to the quantity in which they are contained in the soil, but that, on the contrary, plants possess the power of selecting from the abundance of provisions at their disposal only those that are good for them and in such quantity as is serviceable. This selective capacity of plants is manifested in many ways, and we will now briefly consider some of the most important of them.

In the first place we have the fact that plants reared close together in the same soil or medium may yet exhibit an altogether different composition of ash. This is particularly striking in water and bog-plants, which, though rooted in close proximity and immersed in the same water, show very considerable differences in respect of mineral food absorbed. The result, for instance, of testing specimens of the Water-soldier (*Stratiotes aloides*), the White Water-lily (*Nymphæa alba*), a species of Stone-wort (*Chara fœtida*), and the Reed (*Phragmites communis*), all growing close together in a swamp, was as follows as regarded the potash, soda, lime, and silicic acid, held by them respectively:

| | Water-soldier. | Water-lily. | Stone-wort | Reed. |
|---|---|---|---|---|
| Potash, | 30·82 | 14·4 | 0·2 | 8·6 |
| Soda | 2·7 | 29·66 | 0·1 | 0·4 |
| Lime, | 10·7 | 18·9 | 54·8 | 5·9 |
| Silicic Acid, | 1·8 | 0·5 | 0·3 | 71·5 |

The other constituents of the ash of these plants, in particular iron oxide, magnesia, and phosphoric and sulphuric acids, exhibited less marked differences; but the inequality in the amounts of potash, soda, lime and silicic acid are so great, as only to be explicable on the assumption of a power of selection on the part of these plants. Various species of brown and red sea-weeds, which had been attached to the same rock and developed in the same sea-water, showed similar variations in the composition of their ash.

On the mountains of serpentine rock near Gurhof, in Lower Austria, specimens of *Biscutella lævigata* and *Dorycnium decumbens* were collected from plants growing together, and one above the other, upon a declivity which they clothed. Their roots, interlaced here and there, were fixed in the same ground, and drew nourishment from the same store. The following table gives the composition of the ash in these two species:—

| | Biscutella lævigata. | Dorycnium decumbens. | | Biscutella lævigata. | Dorycnium decumbens. |
|---|---|---|---|---|---|
| Potash, | 9·6 | 16·7 | Silicic Acid, | 13·0 | 6·3 |
| Lime, | 14·7 | 20·9 | Sulphur, | 5·2 | 1·6 |
| Magnesia, | 28·0 | 19·6 | Phosphorus, | 15·9 | 22·3 |
| Iron Oxide, | 7·8 | 2·8 | Carbonic Acid, | 5·4 | 9·7 |

The differences here seem to be not so great as in the case of the water-plants previously given, but they are sufficient to prevent our regarding them as merely the result of chance.

If, on the other hand, we compare the composition of the ash of different specimens of the same species, which have been reared on similar soils, but at great distances from one another, the discrepancies are comparatively slight. Foliage from beech-trees growing on the limestone mountains near Regensburg yielded an ash practically identical with that obtained from leaves of beeches on the Bakonyer-Wald hills in Hungary. The ash of different individuals of a single species even exhibits the same constitution, in the main, when those individual plants have obtained their nutriment from soils differing greatly in chemical composition. Only in cases where the quantity of a substance in one soil is more abundant than in the other there is generally a greater or less amount of it to be found in the ash.

That under these circumstances certain substances may replace one another is not improbable. But such substitution must be confined to those nearly allied compounds whose molecules are capable of being used indifferently by the formative protoplasm in construction, and in the storage of materials. The annexed table, which gives side by side analyses of the ash of branches of the Yew (*Taxus baccata*) with their leaves attached, illustrates the replacement of calcium by magnesium:—

| | Serpentine. | Limestone | Gneiss. |
|---|---|---|---|
| | | Ash from branches and leaves of the Yew from | |
| Silicic Acid, | 3·8 | 3·6 | 3·7 |
| Sulphuric Acid, | 1·9 | 1·6 | 1·9 |
| Phosphoric Acid, | 8·3 | 5·5 | 4·2 |
| Iron Oxide, | 2·1 | 1·7 | 0·6 |
| Lime, | 16·1 } 38·8 | 36·1 } 41·2 | 30·6 } 36·3 |
| Magnesia, | 22·7 | 5·1 | 5·7 |
| Potash, | 29·6 | 21·8 | 27·6 |
| Carbonic Acid, | 14·1 | 23·1 | 24·4 |
| Traces of Manganese, Chlorine, &c., | — | — | — |
| Totals, | 99·6 | 98·5 | 98·7 |

The Yew occurs in Central Europe on very various mountain formations, chiefly on limestone, but not infrequently on gneiss, and occasionally on serpentine rocks. On comparing the quantities of calcium and of magnesium in the ash of yews, grown on lime and on gneiss respectively, with those yielded in the case of serpentine formation, we find that magnesia preponderates considerably in weight over lime in a yew from serpentine rocks (which are in the main a compound of magnesia and silicic acid), whilst the proportion between these two salts is reversed in a yew grown upon limestone. The obvious inference from the table is that, in plants from a serpentine ground, lime is to a great extent replaced by magnesia. This is further supported by the circumstance that if lime and magnesia are counted together the resulting numbers are very near one another, namely 41·2 per cent of the ash for limestone, 38·8 per cent for serpentine rock, and 36·3 per cent for gneiss.

But all these phenomena observed in connection with the selection of food-salts are not nearly so surprising as the fact that plants are also capable of singling out from an abundance of other matter particular substances, which are of importance to them, even from a soil containing them in barely perceptible quantities, and of concentrating them to a certain extent. As has been shown above, nearly a third of the ash of the white water-lily is composed of common salt. One might, therefore, suppose that the water in which water-lilies flourish contains a particularly large quantity of common salt. But nothing of the kind is the case. The bog water which bathed the stem and leaves of this specimen only contained 0·335 per cent of common salt, and the mud through which the roots straggled contained only 0·010 per cent.

No less astonishing is it to find Diatomaceæ, with cell-membranes, as above mentioned, sheathed in silicic acid, existing in water which contains no trace of silicic acid. Above the Arzler Alp, in the Solstein chain near Innsbruck, there is a spring of cold water which falls in little cascades between blocks of rock. The water of this spring is hard, and it deposits lime at a little distance from the source. Exactly at the spot where it wells out of a fissure in the rock its bed is entirely filled by a dark-brown flocculent mass which consists of millions of cells of the beautiful *Odontidium hiemale*, a species of diatom with siliceous coating. These cells are ranged together in long rows, and are present in numbers and luxuriance such as are scarcely ever to be observed in other situations. Yet the spring water flowing round contains so little silicic acid that no trace of this substance could be discovered in the residue from the evaporation of 10 litres.

An instance similar to this of silicic acid, is afforded by the iodine in the sea. Most of the sea-wracks inhabiting the North Sea contain iodine, many indeed in considerable quantity, and yet we have not hitherto succeeded in detecting iodine in the water of the North Sea. Similar phenomena, sometimes quite baffling explanation, are exhibited by land-plants. The clefts in the rocks of quartziferous slate in the Central Alps are, in many places, overgrown by saxifrages (*Saxifraga Sturmiana* and *Saxifraga oppositifolia*) with leaves aggregated together in closely-crowded rosettes, which are conspicuous from afar, owing to their pale colouring. On closer inspection one finds that the apices and edges of these rosulate leaves are covered with little incrustations of carbonate of lime, a substance which will be frequently referred to in connection with its importance to plants. But one seeks in vain for any lime compound in the earth which fills the clefts, and the only traces of lime contained in the adjacent rock itself are those occurring in the little scales of mica scattered about, and these are not readily decomposable. Yet the lime incrusting the saxifrage leaves can only be derived from the underlying rock, just as in former instances the silicic acid in the cell-membranes of diatoms must be secreted from the spring described, the iodine in sea-weeds from the sea, and the common salt in water-lilies from the pond where they grow, although in each case the substance concerned is only to be found, if at all, in scarcely ponderable traces in the soil or liquid serving as medium. Facts of this kind have a special interest, because they prove that plants have the power of appropriating a substance, if it is important to them, even when it is only present in extremely minute quantities. Where a plant is surrounded by liquid, we can well imagine that fresh portions of the medium are constantly coming into contact with its surface; for, even in water apparently still, compensating currents are continually being caused by changes of temperature. Thus, in the course of a day, thousands of litres of sea-water may flow over a sea-weed with a surface of one square meter, and, even if only a small portion of the substance, traces of which we are supposing to exist in the water, is wrested from each litre, still, the absorbing plant might collect quite a profitable quantity in a number of days. The volume of water flowing over a plant situated in the source of a spring is still greater, and it is readily conceivable that even the most minute trace of silicic acid may become of account in course of time. There is more difficulty in understanding how plants with roots in the earth set about utilizing substances contained in the soil in scarcely appreciable quantities. These plants must at all events come into contact with as great a mass of nutrient soil as possible, and this is effected by means of a widely-ramifying system of roots; and, in addition, they must assist in making available desirable matter in the soil by the elimination from themselves of certain substances.

In order to explain the remarkable power that plants possess of exercising a choice in the absorption of certain food-stuffs from amongst the whole number presented to them, we must in the first place assume a special structure to exist in the cells which are in immediate contact with the nutrient medium. To reach the interior of a cell, the salts must pass through the cell-membrane and the so-called ectoplasm. We may look upon these walls, that are to be penetrated, as filters, or, to abide by our previous simile, as sieves, which allow only certain kinds of molecules to pass and arrest others. Moreover, just as the structure of a sieve, especially the size and shape of its pores, has its effect in the separation of the particles of the matter sifted, so also may the structure of a cell-wall have a discriminating influence in the absorption of food-salts. It may be supposed that the cell-wall in one species of plant acts as a sieve capable of letting through molecules of potash but none of alumina, whilst the cell-wall in a second species allows molecules of alumina to pass as well, but is impervious to those of chloride of sodium. This hypothesis would also explain why the absorption of food-stuffs by plants generally takes place through cell-walls, and why absorption into the organs concerned by means of open tubes, which would be at all events a much simpler method, is not preferred. It is, however, necessary to investigate first the nature of the force which causes molecules of the various salts to move from the soil to the cell-membranes, which we suppose to be like sieves, and through them into the interior of a plant. A force acting in this sense from without is inconceivable, and we must therefore look for the motive stimulus in the plant itself.

As has been already stated in connection with the absorption of carbonic acid, it is believed that the cause of this movement is the disturbance of the molecular equilibrium in the growing vegetable organism. If at one spot in the protoplasm of a cell a particular substance is altered, and, let us say, converted into an insoluble compound, the previous grouping of molecules appears to be altered, or in other words, the molecular equilibrium is disturbed. To restore equilibrium, there must be a re-introduction of molecules of the material that has been removed; and the attraction of them from the quarter where they occur in a fluid, that is to say in a mobile condition, is the more energetic. Supposing, for instance, gypsum (i.e. sulphate of lime) is being decomposed within a cell, and the lime combines with the oxalic acid (set free in the same cell) to form insoluble oxalate of lime, whilst the sulphur combines with other elements to form insoluble albuminoids, this use of the gypsum occasions a violent attraction of that substance from the environment, or, to put it another way, it causes a movement of gypsum towards the place of consumption. If this latter place is a cell in immediate contact with the nutrient substratum, the absorption of the substance attracted is direct; but if the cell in which the material is used up is separated from the substratum by intervening cells, the attraction must act through all those cells upon it. The substance consumed must be taken in the first place from the cell adjoining the consuming cell on the side towards the periphery; this cell again must take it from its neighbour, which is still nearer the periphery, and so on until the external cells themselves exercise their influence upon the nutrient substratum. Thus, one may regard the growing cells in which substances are used up, as centres of attraction with respect to those substances. This also explains why it is that the influx of food-salts takes place only so long as the plant is growing; and we see, too, that the direction of the current must vary according to the position of the growing cells, and according to the degree of their constructive activity.

But that one plant prefers one substance and another another—that one species attracts iodine, a second sodium, and a third iron—can only be interpreted as a result of the specific constitution of the protoplasm. The protoplasm of a growing cell which contains no iodine does not require that substance either, for the processes of transmutation and storage. A protoplast of this kind will not therefore be a centre of attraction for iodine, but will draw from the environment with great force substances which are its essential constituents. Having gained this conception of the absorption and selection of food-salts, we are able to imagine the possibility of a substance being sought after by one species whilst acting as poison on another. Iodine itself exercises a prejudicial effect on many plants, even when present in very small quantities. Cell-membranes in immediate contact with a medium containing iodine are modified as regards their structure by the iodine; their pores are enlarged, lose their value as orifices adapted to the admittance of certain food-salts in limited quantities, and they no longer prevent the influx of injurious substances. Ultimately they die, and by so doing the entire plant suffers. On the other hand, plants to which iodine is an indispensable constituent are not hurt in any way by the presence of small quantities of this substance in the nutrient medium: their cell-membranes are neither paralysed nor destroyed, and suction is able to take place through them in a perfectly normal manner. But we must in this case specially emphasize the condition of the amount being small, for a larger quantity of this substance is positively injurious even to plants which require iodine.

The general rule for a great number of plants is that they thrive best when the food-salts necessary to them are supplied in very dilute solutions. An increase in the quantity of the salts administered not only fails to promote development, but, on the contrary, arrests it. This is the result even if the salts are such as are absolutely necessary in small quantities to the plants in question. A very minute amount of an iron salt is indispensable to all green plants; but, if a certain measure is exceeded, iron salts have a destructive effect on the cell-membranes and protoplasm, and cause the plant to die. But at what point the boundary lies between salubrious effects and the reverse, where the beneficial action of particular substances ceases and detrimental action begins, is not known more precisely than has been stated. We only know that different plants behave very differently in this respect. Suppose, for example, that we scatter wood-ash over a field which is overgrown by grasses, mosses, and various herbs and shrubs. The result is that the mosses die; in the case of the grasses growth is somewhat increased; whilst some of the herbs and shrubs, notably polygonaceous and cruciferous plants, exhibit a strikingly luxuriant growth. If we scatter gypsum instead, the development of clover is enhanced, and, on the other hand, there are certain ferns and grasses that die earlier when gypsum is supplied, or, at least, are considerably stunted in their growth.

The fact that certain plants predominate on calcareous and others on siliceous ground has been the subject of very thorough investigation: and these researches were regarded as justifying the assumption that particular species require a more or less considerable quantity of lime for food, whilst others require similarly silicic acid. Hereupon was founded a division of plants into those which required and were tolerant of lime, and into such as required and tolerated silica. The explanation given of these facts does not seem, however, to be satisfactory, at any rate in the case of siliceous plants. It is much more probable that the so-called silica-loving plants are produced on ground composed of quartz, granite, or slate, not by reason of the abundance of silicic acid, but because of the absence of lime in any large quantity, such as would be liable to injure plants of the kind; for only traces of lime are found, and its presence to this extent is absolutely necessary for every plant. This is not of course inconsistent with the fact that individual species require larger quantities of particular food-salts and only flourish luxuriantly when these nutritive salts are not meted out too sparingly. In the case of oraches, thrifts, wormwood species, and cruciferous plants, alkalies, in comparatively large quantities, are necessary for hardy development. The proper habitat for these plants, therefore, is on soils which contain an abundance of easily soluble alkaline compounds, in places where the ground is regularly saturated by saline solutions, and where crystals of salt effloresce on the drying surface. Such places are the sea-shore, the salt steppes, and the neighbourhood of salt-mines. The above plants not only flourish in these localities in great abundance and perfection, but they supplant all other species on which the excessive provision of soluble alkaline salts is not beneficial. If the seeds of such plants happen to fall upon the salt ground they germinate, but only drag out a miserable existence for a short time, and in the end are crowded out by the luxuriant oraches and crucifers. Plants which only flourish abundantly on soils rich in alkaline salts are called halophytes. The same name has also been applied to plants which only thrive in sea-water. Most of the species used by us as edible vegetables, as, for instance, cabbages, turnips, cress, &c., are really descended from halophytes, and accordingly require a soil that contains a comparatively rich supply of alkalies. An opportunity will occur, later on, of returning to the question as to how far agriculture has gained by all these discoveries, and of considering what processes, based upon the results of scientific research, have been introduced into practice.    Amongst these processes may be mentioned the rotation of crops, the artificial application of manure to exhausted land, and the restitution of the mineral food-salts which the particular plants last cultivated have withdrawn from the land under tillage.

## ABSORPTION OF FOOD-SALTS BY WATER-PLANTS.

It is usual to designate all plants that grow in water as hydrophytes or water-plants.    But in their narrower sense these names are only applicable to those plants which, during their entire lives, vegetate under water and derive their nutriment, especially carbonic acid, direct from the water.    A number of plants have widely ramifying roots fixed in the earth at the bottom of water, and the lower parts of their stems, either temporarily or throughout life, immersed in water, whilst the upper parts of their stems and their upper leaves are exposed to the air and take carbonic acid direct from the atmosphere, and these should be regarded as marsh-plants and classed with land-plants so far as regards food-absorption.    Reeds and rushes, water-fennel and water-plantain, the yellow water-lily, even the amphibious *Polygonum* and the white water-lily, are marsh-plants and not true hydrophytes. It is characteristic of all these marsh-plants, that. if they are entirely submerged for any length of time they die, whereas they are not injured if the water's level at the place where they grow sinks so as to expose the lower portions of the stem. In places formerly submerged, but from which, in course of time, the water has retreated, so that they have been turned into meadows, one may come across not only clumps of reeds and rushes but even yellow and white water-lilies, flourishing perfectly on the moist earth.

Water-plants, or hydrophytes in the proper acceptation of the term, perish if they are kept for a length of time out of their proper medium and exposed to the air.    In most of them death ensues quickly, for their delicate cell-membranes are not able to prevent the exhalation of water from the interior of their cells; and, there being no provision for a replacement of the evaporated fluid, the whole plant dries up.    If one supplies aquatic plants, thus desiccated, with water, though it is indeed absorbed it no longer has the power of reviving them. Those hydrophytes which occur in the sea, near the shore, are able to stand exposure to the air for a comparatively long time, and they are regularly sub-ject to it during ebb-tide.    Sea-wracks which at high-tide were floating in the water are then seen lying on the dry rocks or sand of the shore.    But the mem-branes of the cells forming the outermost layer in all these sea-wracks is very thick. They retain water staunchly and prevent the plants from drying up, at least until high-tide occurs again, when they are once more submerged.

Amphibious plants in which the lower leaves are like those of aquatics and the upper like those of land-plants so far as desiccation is concerned (*e.g.* several kinds of pond-weed—*Potamogeton heterophyllus* and *P. natans*—and a few white-flowered Ranunculi—*Ranunculus aquatilis* and *R. hololeucus*), exhibit a transition stage from

aquatic plants to land-plants. When the water sinks and they are finally left lying
exposed on the mud or wet sand, to which they appear to be firmly attached by
their abundant roots, it is only the previously submerged leaves that dry up. That
part of the foliage which floated on the surface and was consequently always in
contact with the air continues to thrive, and any fresh leaves that may be developed
adapt themselves completely to the new environment. Similar behaviour is observed in many of the plants which float freely on the surface of water. Such, for
instance, is the case with some species of duckweed (*Lemna minor* and *L.
polyrrhiza*), with *Azolla*, *Pontederia* and *Pistia;* they do not die when the water
sinks, leaving them stranded, but absorb food-stuffs from the wet earth through
their roots, and in this condition are not to be distinguished from land-plants.

Hydrophytes in the narrow sense, *i.e.* plants which are entirely submerged and
die if they are surrounded by air instead of water for any length of time, are for
the most part fixed to some support beneath the water. In many cases the
characteristic method of reproduction consists in the separation of special cells,
which then swim about for a time in the water. Sooner or later, however, they
re-attach themselves to some seemingly suitable spot, and the further phases of their
development are again stationary. Comparatively few permanently submerged
species are freely suspended in the liquid medium in every stage of development.
Such free plants are liable to be shifted by currents in the water, but the extent of
their displacement is never very great, owing to the fact that submerged species of
this kind occur almost exclusively in still water. As instances may be mentioned
the ivy-leaved duckweed (*Lemna trisulca*), the water-violet (*Hottonia palustris*),
the various species of hornwort (*Ceratophyllum*), in all of which roots are absent;
and in addition amongst the lower or cryptogamic plants *Riccia fluitans*, and
many of the Desmidiaceae, Spirogyras and Nostocineae.

Some of these aquatic plants periodically rest on the bottom of the pond or
lake in which they live. An example is afforded by the remarkable plant known
as the water-soldier (*Stratiotes aloides*), which, as is indicated by its Latin name,
is not unlike an aloe in appearance. During the winter, this plant rests at the
bottom of the pond it inhabits. As April draws near, the individual plants rise
almost to the surface and remain floating there, producing fresh sword-shaped
leaves and bunches of roots which arise from the abbreviated axis, and finally flowers
which, when the summer is at its height, float upon the surface. When the time of
flowering is over, the plant sinks again to mature its fruit and seeds, and develop
buds for the production of young daughter-plants. Towards the end of August,
it rises for the second time in one year. The young plants that have meantime
grown up resemble their parent completely, except that their size is smaller.
They grow at the end of long stalks springing from amongst the whorled leaves,
and the stately mother-plant is now surrounded by them like a hen by her chickens.
During the autumn, the shoots connecting the daughter-plants with their parent rot
away, and, thus isolated, each little rosette, as well as the mother-plant, sinks once
more to the bottom of the pond and there hibernates.

Altogether the number of submerged plants which live suspended in water is very small. As has been said before, by far the greater number are attached somewhere. Seed-bearing plants or Phanerogamia, such as *Vallisneria*, *Ouvirandra*, *Myriophyllum*, *Najas*, *Zannichellia*, *Ruppia*, *Zostera*, *Elodea*, *Hydrilla*, and several species of *Potamogeton* (*P. pectinatus*, *P. pusillus*, *P. lucens*, *P. densus*, *P. crispus*); as also Cryptogams, such as the various species of *Isoetes* and *Pilularia* and submerged mosses, are fastened in the mud under water by means of attachment-roots or of rhizoids, whilst the almost illimitable host of brown and red sea-weeds are fixed by special cells or groups of cells, which are often root-like in appearance. The sea-weeds choose rocks and stones, by preference, for their support, but they also make use of animals and plants. The shells of mussels and snails are often completely overgrown by brown and red sea-weeds. Larger kinds of Fucaceæ, especially the species of *Sargassum* and *Cystosira*, which form regular submarine forests, bear upon their branches numerous other small epiphytes, chiefly Florideæ, and these again are themselves covered by minute Diatomaceæ. Many of the huge and lofty brown sea-weeds which raise themselves from the bottom of the sea, remind one forcibly of tropical trees covered with Orchideæ and Bromeliaceæ, whilst the latter are themselves overgrown by Mosses and Lichens. These epiphytes are for the most part, however, neither parasitic nor saprophytic. In general hydrophytes attached by means of single cells or groups of cells derive no nutriment, *i.e.* no food-salts, from the support they rest upon. When loosened from the substratum they continue to live in the water for a long time; they increase in size, and if they come into contact with a solid body are apt to attach themselves to it. In this connection it is well worthy of remark that certain Crustacea have their carapaces entirely covered by hydrophytes of this kind, and that it takes a very short time for the plants to establish themselves upon them. For instance, some species of crabs, such as *Maja verrucosa*, *Pisa tetraodon* and *P. armata*, *Inachus scorpioides* and *Stenorrhyncus longirostris*, cut off bits of Wracks, Florideæ, Ulvæ, &c., with their claws, and place them on the top of their carapaces, securing them on peculiar spiky or hooked hairs. The fragments grow firmly to the crabs' chitinous coats, and far from being harmful to the animals are, on the contrary, an important means of protection. The crabs in question escape pursuit in consequence of this disguise, and it is to be observed that each species chooses the very material which makes it most unrecognizable to plant upon the exterior of its body: those species which live chiefly in regions where Cystosiras are indigenous deck themselves in Cystosiras, whilst those which inhabit the same places as Ulvæ, carry Ulvæ on their backs. This phenomenon has for us a special interest in that it shows that the water-plants we are discussing draw no food-salts from their place of attachment, and that accordingly the chemical composition of the support is a matter of utter indifference to all these Fucaceæ, Florideæ, Ulvæ, &c.

There is no doubt that food-salts are absorbed by these hydrophytes from the surrounding water through their whole surface. Accordingly the structure of their peripheral cells is much simpler than is the case in land-plants. In the latter very complicated adaptations are necessary for the extraction of food-salts from the earth. In particular, the portions which are exposed to the air above ground exhibit a number of special structures connected with this extraction. These structures (cuticle, stomata, &c.) are superfluous in the case of aquatic plants, for there is with them no necessity for raising and conducting food-salts into the parts where they can be used up. Moreover the absorption of nutritious matter is much simpler, inasmuch as it is not necessary for the absorbent parts to search for a perpetual source of the requisite substances. The roots of land-plants have often to range over a wide area in order to find sufficient nourishment in the earth, and frequently they have then to liberate it, i.e. bring it into a state of solution. This is not the case with water-plants. They are completely surrounded by a medium which is itself to a large extent a solution of food-salts, and no sooner are substances withdrawn by the absorbent cells from the layers of water immediately bounding them than those substances are again supplied from the more remote environment. Constant compensating currents occur in water, and there is, therefore, scarcely an aquatic plant towards which there is not a perpetual flow of the food-salts it requires in a form suitable for absorption. In connection with this kind of food-absorption there is also the fact that the parts by which hydrophytes attach themselves to a support are relatively small in area. Fucoids, as large as hazel trees in height and girth, are fixed to submerged rocks by groups of cells perhaps only 1 cm. in diameter.

The quantity of food-salts absorbed by hydrophytes is very considerable compared with the amounts absorbed by other plants. As has been mentioned before, soda and iodine play a very important part in the thousands of different varieties which live in the sea. If Florideæ are transferred from the sea into pure distilled water, common salt and other saline compounds diffuse out of the interior of the cells through the cell-membranes into the fresh water around. The red colouring matter of these Florideæ also passes through the cell-walls into the water, proving that the molecular structure of the membrane is adapted to the agency of salt water in the osmotic processes of food-absorption.

Plants living in fresh, or in brackish water, likewise absorb relatively large quantities of food-salts; and this accounts for the fact that water which is very poorly provided with nutriment of the kind contains only very few vegetable species.

One would expect that exceedingly abundant vegetation would be evolved in running water, provided the latter contained food-salts in solution, however small they might be in quantity. For, in such a situation, it is not necessary to wait for the salts withdrawn by the plants from their immediate environment to be restored by the slow processes of mixture and equilibration; the water which has been drained of nutriment is replaced the next moment by other water bearing fresh food-salts. Experience shows, however, that flowing water is not so favourable to the development of hydrophytes as is the still water of pools, ponds, and lakes. This may partly depend on the fact that running water is always poorer in food-salts, and partly also on the circumstance that mechanical difficulties are opposed to the taking up of saline molecules from water in rapid motion. There are only a few plants that are able to absorb under these conditions, and these choose, by preference, the very spots where they are most exposed to the dash of the water. Thus, certain Nostocineæ (*Zonotrichia*, *Scytonema*) are to be found constantly in waterfalls at the parts where the most violent fall occurs. *Lemanea*, *Hydrurus*, and many mosses and liverworts, grow by preference in the foaming cascades of rapid torrents. Amongst flowering plants we only know of the Podostemaceæ as choosing a habitat of this kind. Podostemaceæ are exceedingly curious little plants, which at first glance one would take for mosses or liverworts without roots. Some of them, *e.g.* the Brazilian species of the genus *Lophogyne* and the various species of *Terniola* growing in Ceylon, exhibit no differentiation into stem and leaves, but are only represented by green fissured and indented lobes attached to stones. They belong without exception to the tropical zone, and occur there in the beds of streams, attached to rocks, over which the foaming water rushes.

## ABSORPTION OF FOOD-SALTS BY LITHOPHYTES.

Nothing would seem more natural, as to the absorption of mineral salts by lithophytes, than that the stone which constitutes their support should yield the salts, and that the attached plants should suck them up; but, generally speaking, the case is not so simple. There are mosses and lichens which cling to the surfaces of rocks on mountain tops. These rocks are sometimes composed of perfectly pure quartz, and yet the plants in question contain very little silica; they contain, on the other hand, a number of substances entirely wanting in the composition of the underlying rock, and which could not, therefore, have been derived from that source. For many of these lithophytes the rock is, in the main, only a substratum for attachment, and in no way a nutrient soil: just as, in the case of many aquatic plants, the stones to which they cling by their discs of attachment are anything but sources of nourishment.

From what source, then, do stone-plants of this kind derive the food-salts which are wanting in their substratum? It may sound paradoxical, but it is nevertheless the fact, that they obtain those salts from the air through the medium of atmospheric precipitation. Rain and snow not only absorb carbon dioxide, sulphuric acid, and ammonia—which occur in air universally, although in extremely minute quantities —but they also collect, as they fall, floating particles of dust. The opinion is widely entertained that although the atmosphere is full of dust in the neighbourhood of cities and human settlements generally, where the soil is laid bare and ploughed up, and roads and paths have been made for purposes of traffic, and perhaps also over steppes and deserts where large areas of ground are destitute of vegetation, yet that there is no dust in the air over land remote from places of that kind or in the air of marshes, lakes, or seas. This notion has certainly some warrant if we regard as dust only the coarser particles which are raised from loose earth and whirled into the air by the wind. Moreover, the quality of the dust will no doubt be characteristically affected by the vicinity of areas of industry. One has only to look at the sooty leaves and branches of trees in parks near manufactories to convince oneself of the reality of this influence. But it would be quite erroneous to suppose that the air in regions far from land that has been cultivated or otherwise opened up is free from dust. It contains dust everywhere. There is dust in the air of the extensive ice-fields of arctic regions and of high mountain glaciers, and there is dust in the air of great forests and over the boundless sea.

If the rays of the setting sun fall obliquely through a gap between two peaks in a wood-clad mountain valley, sun-motes may be seen floating up and down and in circles, just as they do in a room when the last rays before sunset fall through the window. These motes are of course not usually visible, and they are moreover much smaller than the particles of dust which are raised by the wind from roads and then again deposited. Now, when rain falls, it takes the sun-motes from the air and brings them down to earth, and the air is thus washed to a certain degree of purity. This happens still more completely in the event of snow. The latter acts not unlike a mass of gelatine used to purify cloudy liquids, its effect being to drag down with it all the particles to which the turbidity is due, leaving the upper part of the liquid quite clear. Similarly, falling snow-flakes filter the air; and, mixed with fallen snow, there are accordingly innumerable particles of dust. If afterwards the snow gradually melts, it dissolves some of the dust, which then drains away into chinks and depressions; but a portion remains behind undissolved. This portion is gradually consolidated, and then appears lying on the parts of the snow that are still unmelted in the form of dark patches, streaks, and bands; often also it forms a smeary graphitic covering so widely spreading over the last remnants of melting snow that the latter resemble lumps of mud rather than snow. Accordingly we find it everywhere — in regions cultivated and uncultivated, in tilled lowlands and on high grassy plains above forest limits, where no tilled land is to be seen in any direction, and lastly in arctic regions in the middle of glaciers several miles across.

All this snow dust is not invariably deposited as a result of the filtering of the air by falling snow-flakes; an additional supply is brought by the winds which blow across the snow-fields. It is not of rare occurrence in the Alps for snow-fields to exhibit suddenly, after violent storms, an orange-red coloration. On closer inspection one finds that the surface of the snow is strewn with a layer of powder, infinitesimally fine and for the most part brick-red, which has been brought by the gales. Investigation of this "meteoric dust" shows that it is composed chiefly of minute fragments of ferruginous quartz, felspar, and various other minerals. Mixed with these there are, however, sometimes remnants of organic bodies, such as bits of dead insects, siliceous skeletons of diatoms, spores, pollen-grains, tiny fragments of stems, leaves, and fruits, and the like. Once, after a south wind had prevailed for several days, the snow-fields of the Solstein range near Innsbruck were covered, at a height of from two to three thousand meters above the sea-level, with millions of a species of *Micrococcus*, which lent a rosy hue to vast expanses of snow.

Most of the dust in the atmosphere originates, doubtless, from our earth. The air that blows in waves over the earth can carry along with it not only dead and detached portions of plants, but also loose particles of rock, sand, earth, and dried mud. If one draws one's palm across the weather side of a dry rock composed of dolomitic limestone, gneiss, trachyte, or mica-schist, the surface of the stone always feels dusty, and the slightest movement of the hand is sufficient to detach a number of particles which were already separate from the rock and only held in loose connection with it. This dust is liable to be detached and carried away by any strong gust of wind. Larger and heavier particles are not, it is true, lifted much above the ground; they are rolled and pounded along and thereby reduced to a still finer powder. This finer dust may then be scattered afar by gales blowing horizontally, or even ascend into higher atmospheric strata. The finest dust in particular, however, is carried up into the higher layers of the air by the currents which ascend from the earth in calm weather; and this applies not only to the tropics but to the temperate zones as well, and even to the frigid regions of the arctic zone. When, therefore, this dust is brought back by rain or snow from the upper aerial strata to the earth, it but completes a circuit. Indeed it is highly probable that the particles of dust restored to earth by means of atmospheric deposits recommence their aerial travels as soon as they are thoroughly dry again, and that there is thus a circulation of dust analogous to that of water.

There is of course no inconsistency in the fact that meteoric dust, which is often drifted along in surprisingly large quantities, may originate quite suddenly during volcanic eruptions; nay, it is even possible that cosmic dust reaches our atmosphere and thence falls to the earth. Chemical investigation of aerial dust has, no doubt, yielded in most cases only sulphuric and phosphoric acids, lime, magnesia, oxide of iron, alumina, silica, and traces of potash and soda, that is to say, the most widely distributed constituents of the solid crust of our earth: but cobalt and copper have also been found in it, over and over again, and it has hence been inferred that the dust in these cases was of cosmic origin.

In relation to the question which we have here to answer the above is, after all, almost a matter of indifference. The only important facts are that dust in a state of extremely fine division is blown about in the air, that this dust contains the salts required by plants for their food, that it is carried for the most part mechanically by drops of water and flakes of snow, condensed in the atmosphere, and is partially dissolved, that the atmospheric deposits supply lithophytic plants with a sufficient quantity of nutrient salts, and that the aqueous solution so supplied is rapidly absorbed by the whole surface of the plants in question. We must not omit to mention here that the demand of lithophytes for mineral food-salts is not very great. In particular the protonemae and even the leafy shoots of *Grimmia*, *Rhacomitria*, *Andreaceae* and other rock mosses, and the *Collemaceae* and most crustaceous lichens only contain very minute quantities of these substances. Water containing the usual mineral salts in about such proportion as is necessary for the cultivation of cereals in fields has actually an injurious effect on these lithophytes and soon kills them.

At the end of this section we shall consider what happens to dust which is brought to earth from the air by rain and snow but is not dissolved, and the important part it plays in clothing the naked ground and in changes of vegetation. Here, however, it must be noted that most lithophytes are true dust-catchers, that is to say, they are able to retain, mechanically, dust conveyed to them by wind, rain, and snow, and to use it in later stages of development by extracting nutriment from it. Many mosses are completely lithophytic in early stages of development whilst later they figure as land-plants.


## ABSORPTION OF FOOD-SALTS BY LAND-PLANTS.

In no class of plants is the absorption of mineral food-salts accomplished in so complicated a manner as in land-plants. Moreover, this absorption is by no means uniform in different forms of plants, and we must beware of generalizing with regard to processes which have only been traced and studied in isolated groups—perhaps only in the commonly distributed cultivated plants. On the other hand, with a view to synoptical representation, it is not desirable to enter into too great detail or to attempt to describe all the various differences minutely.

At the outset, it is difficult to give an accurate account of the soil which constitutes the source of nutriment in the case of land-plants. From the dark graphitic mass composed of sun-motes, which is deposited in the place of a melted layer of snow, to coarse gravel, there is an unbroken chain of transition stages; loam, sand and gravel are only specially-marked members of this chain. Again, just as earth varies in respect of the size of its component parts, so also it varies in the mineral salts it contains, in the amount of admixture of decaying vegetable and animal remains, in the nature of the union of its constituents, and in its capacity to absorb, to retain, or to yield up water. Compare the sand composed of quartz on the bank of a mountain stream with that of calcareous origin which is found impregnated with salt on the sea-shore, or with the sand at the foot of mountains of trachyte, which has an efflorescence of soda-salts. Or compare the granite bed of a desert, bare of soil, with the loam on the granitic plateaus of northern regions where there is an intermixture of the remains of a vegetation for centuries active. How great is the difference in each case! But whatever the kind of earth, it is only of value as a source of nutriment for a plant when the interstices of its various particles are filled with watery fluid for the time during which the plant is engaged in the construction of organic substances.

But how is the earth supplied with water?

> "Das hat nicht Rast bei Tag und Nacht,
> Ist stets auf Wanderschaft bedacht."

Streams fall into lakes, rivers into the sea, and hence the water ascends into the atmosphere in the form of vapour, and returns once more to earth as snow, rain, and dew. Through porous earth it percolates until it has filled all the interspaces. If its further descent be impeded by impervious strata, it spreads literally as subterranean water, or else comes up at some special spot as a spring. Earth which is richly endowed with decaying vegetable remains is able to absorb vapour in addition from the atmosphere. When this occurs, carbonic and nitric acids are always absorbed along with the aqueous vapour. These are contained, as has been mentioned before, in atmospheric deposits, and another source of these acids is afforded by the decay of dead parts of plants. Water precipitated from the atmosphere, and containing carbonic and nitric acids, is able by their means to decompose the compounds in all the rocks which come in its way as it percolates through the ground, especially when its action is long continued. The siliceous compounds or so-called silicates—felspars, mica, hornblende, and augite in particular—and quartz, the anhydride of silicic acid, which form the preponderant mass of the rocks of the solid crust of our earth, either contain a great quantity of silica, alumina, and alkalies, or if they are relatively poor in silica they may be rich in iron. The former are found chiefly in granite, gneiss, mica-schist, and argillaceous slate; the latter preponderate in serpentine, syenite, melaphyr, dolerite, trachyte and basalt. First the felspars are decomposed by the acid water. Their alkalies combine with the carbonic and nitric acids forming soluble salts, and the alumina and silica remain behind as clay. Iron is also converted into soluble salts. The most difficult substances to decompose are the mica and quartz, and it is on that account that they so often appear in the form of glittering scales and angular nodules mixed with the clay produced from the decomposition of felspar. But, ultimately, even they are unable to withstand the continuous action of the acidulated water. The result of these chemical changes is an earth, which, according to the nature of the parent rock, contains a preponderating amount of clay, of quartzose sand or of mica, which is coloured in various ways by iron compounds. Of substances useful to plants these earths yield generally on analysis the following: potash, soda, lime, magnesia, alumina, ferrous and ferric oxides, manganese, chlorine, sulphuric acid, phosphoric acid, silica, and carbonic acid, sometimes one sometimes another in greater proportion relatively, and traces of many substances often so slight as hardly to be detected.

It is true that limestone and dolomite, which, next to the above-mentioned rocks, enter most largely into the composition of the solid crust of the earth, consist chiefly of carbonate of lime and magnesium carbonate respectively; but wherever they occur in extensive strata and piles, they always contain in addition an admixture of alumina, silicic acid, ferrous oxide, manganese, traces of alkalies in combination with phosphoric and sulphuric acids, &c. Of the carbonates of lime and magnesia a great part is gradually dissolved and carried away upon the invasion of water containing carbonic and nitric acids, and a proportion also of the substances mixed with them, as above mentioned, is lixiviated. What remains behind then consists of an argillaceous, loamy mass, variously coloured by iron and very similar in appearance to the clay formed from the decomposition of felspar. According to the quantity of the substances mixed with the carbonate of lime in the rock, the loamy earth formed from limestone is either abundant or only in restricted layers, bands and pockets lying on, or intercalated within, the undecomposed débris of the stone. Chemical analysis has resulted in the discovery that there are, as a rule, in loamy earth of this kind the same ingredients available for plants as have been identified in earth produced from silicates; and we are led to believe that earths, collected in widely different places and covering rocks of most various kinds, are much more uniform qualitatively than has been supposed. Only, the relative proportions of the substances forming the mixture are usually different. Silica and the alkalies are less conspicuous in earth derived from limestone, and carbonate of lime in that which is formed from silicates. This difference is particularly striking in instances where the rock consisted almost entirely either of quartz and mica or of nearly pure carbonates of lime and magnesium. In these cases the earth formed is not argillaceous, but of loose consistence, very abundant, and composed, according to the kind of rock, of quartzose sand and mica scales or calcareous and dolomitic sand.

The conversion of rocks into earths by the action of water from the atmosphere containing carbonic and nitric acids is, besides, materially modified by the disruptions which ensue from changes of temperature, more particularly by the freezing of water within the pores of rocks. It is also affected, though more remotely, by the mechanical action of water and air in motion, and, lastly, by the plants themselves, which penetrate with their roots into the narrowest crevices and mingle their dead remains with the portions of the rock that are decomposed, broken up, or abraded by chemical and mechanical agencies. The substance produced from a rock in the manner explained is called earth-mould, or simply earth. The matter resulting from the decomposition of plants and animals is designated by the term "humus." Earth which includes an abundance of decomposed fragments of plants, i.e. has a large admixture of humus, is called vegetable mould.

Every kind of earth, but especially earth rich in humus and clay, has the power of retaining gases, and especially water and salts. When water containing salts in solution is poured over a layer of dry vegetable mould, it percolates into the spaces between the particles of earth, and speedily drives out of them the air which has but slight adhesion, and which then ascends in bubbles. It is not till all the interspaces are full of water, whilst a fresh supply is constantly maintained from above, that any of the liquid oozes out from beneath the stratum of earth. The water remaining in the interstices is held there by adhesion to the particles of earth, and we must conceive each of these particles as surrounded by an adherent film of water. The inorganic salts, infiltrating with the water, are held with still greater energy. The water which trickles from the bottom of the earth always contains a much smaller proportion of salts in solution than that which was poured on above, whence we conclude that the latter are in part absorbed by the earth.

The salts are to be regarded as forming an extremely delicate coating round minute particles of earth where they are forcibly retained. If a plant rooted in the earth is to take in these salts it has to overcome the force by which their molecules are detained. This is effected, however, by means of a very powerful attraction exerted by the protoplasts of the plant as they grow, carry on the work of construction, and use up material. What actually happens is an energetic suction by the cells that are in close contact with particles of earth. This suction depends, however, upon the chemical affinity between the substances in the interior of the cells and the salts adhering to the earth-particles, as well as upon the consumption of food-salts for the manufacture of organic compounds within the green cells. It is supposed that whenever salts are abstracted from soil-particles by suction, a restitution of like salts immediately takes place, particles still unresolved in the immediate neighbourhood being dissolved, and a fresh influx taking place from the environment. Consequently the concentration of the solution retained by the earth is always approximately the same, or, at any rate, equilibrium is very quickly restored. One advantage of this is that the cells in immediate contact with particles of earth, and their adherent liquid, can only meet with a saline solution of constant weak concentration, and are therefore secure from injury such as would result in the case of most plants, from contact with a very concentrated solution. In other words, the absorptive power of earth acts as a regulator of the process of absorption of food-salts by plants, and is the means of keeping the saline solution in the earth always at the degree of strength best suited to the plants concerned.

Naturally, the passage of salts from the earth to the interior of a plant is dependent on the aid of water containing both the substances composing cell-contents and the food-salts in solution. The cell-membranes, through which absorption takes place, are saturated with this solution. The aqueous films adhering to the particles of earth, the water saturating the cell-membrane, and the liquid inside the cells are really in unbroken connection, and along this continuous water-way the passage of salt molecules in and out can take place easily.

The absorption of food-salts directly from the earth by green cells occurs very rarely. The protonema of *Polytrichum*, which spreads its threads over loamy earth and wraps it in a delicate green felt, and that of the famous Cavern Moss (*Schistostega*), whose long tubular lower cells penetrate the earth in the recesses of caves, do undoubtedly suck up their necessary food-salts by means of cells containing chlorophyll. A drawing of the latter is given in Plate I., fig. *p.*

The majority of land-plants have, however, special absorptive cells for the taking-up of salts in solution. These cells are imbedded amongst or lodged upon the earth-particles, and are usually in intimate connection with portions of them. Any part of a plant that penetrates into the earth or lies upon it, may, if it performs the function of absorption, be equipped with cells of the kind. *Plagiothecium nekeroideum*, a delicate moss belonging to the flora of Germany, and growing on earth under overhanging rocks, where it is not exposed to rain, and therefore cannot receive any food-salts through that agency, develops absorption-cells on the apices of its green leaflets. So also does *Leucobryum javense*, a species native to Java. Several delicate ferns of the family of the *Hymenophyllaceae* exhibit them on their subterranean stems. Many liverworts and the prothalli of ferns bear them on the under surfaces of their flat thalli which lie outspread on damp earth. But most commonly of all are they to be found close behind the growing tips of roots. Their form does not vary very much. On the roots of plants fringing the sources of cold mountain-springs, as on those of many marsh-plants in low-lying land, they are in the form of comparatively large, oblong, flattened, closely united cells, with thin walls and colourless contents. In some conifers, whilst having in the main the shape just described, they differ in that they are arched outwards so as to form papillae; but in most other phanerogams the external cell-wall projects outwards, and the whole absorptive cell develops into a slender tube, set perpendicularly to the longitudinal axis of the root (fig. 12 ').

Seen with the naked eye, or but slightly magnified, these delicate tubes look like fine hairs, and have received the name of "root-hairs." The end of a root often appears to be covered with velvety pile, and the absorptive cells are then very closely packed; more than four hundred per square millimeter have been occasionally counted. In other cases, however, there are hardly more than ten on a square millimeter. When in such small numbers they are usually elongated and clearly visible to the naked eye. Their length, for the most part, varies from the fraction of a millimeter to three millimeters, and their thickness between 0·008 m.m. and 0·14 m.m. It is only exceptionally that one meets with plants, rooted in mud, possessing root-hairs 5 m.m. or more in length. The absorptive cells of phanerogams are almost always simple epidermal cells of the particular part of the plant that bears them, and are not partitioned by any transverse walls. In mosses and fern prothalli, on the other hand, the absorption-cells are generally segmented by transverse septa and are usually greatly elongated. In those liverworts which belong to the genus *Marchantia* they form a thick felt on the under side of the leaf-like plant, or rather, on such part of it as is turned away from the light, and some of these tangled rhizoids attain a length of nearly 2 c.m. The stems of many mosses also are wrapped in a regular felt. This property is rendered very striking in the species of *Barbula, Dicranum*, and *Mnium*, and especially in such forms as have bright green leaves, by the reddish-brown colour of the cells in question. Sometimes the long capillary cells of which the felt is composed are twisted together spirally like the strands of a rope. A good instance of this is *Polytrichum*. These fine, hair-like, segmented and branched structures, found on mosses, variously matted and intertwisted, are called rhizoids. But only those cells which come into contact with the earth-particles are truly absorbent. The rest do not serve to imbibe from the ground, but to conduct the aqueous solution of food-salts, after it has been taken up by the absorptive cells, to the stem and to the leaves.

The tubular cells resulting from the development of a root's epidermis are placed, as before observed, at right angles to its longitudinal axis. They only grow, however, in earth that is very damp, and even then their course is not always a straight line, for as a rule they describe a spiral as they elongate. Their movement seems as though it were for discovering the most favourable parts of the earth for absorption and attachment. In this manner they penetrate into the interspaces in the earth which are filled with air and water. They also have the power of thrusting aside minute particles of earth, especially if the latter consists of loose sand or mud. If they strike perpendicularly a solid immovable bit of earth, they bend aside and grow round it with their surfaces closely adpressed to that of the obstacle until they reach the opposite point on the other side, when they once more resume their original direction (fig. 12³). When they encounter large grains of earth they

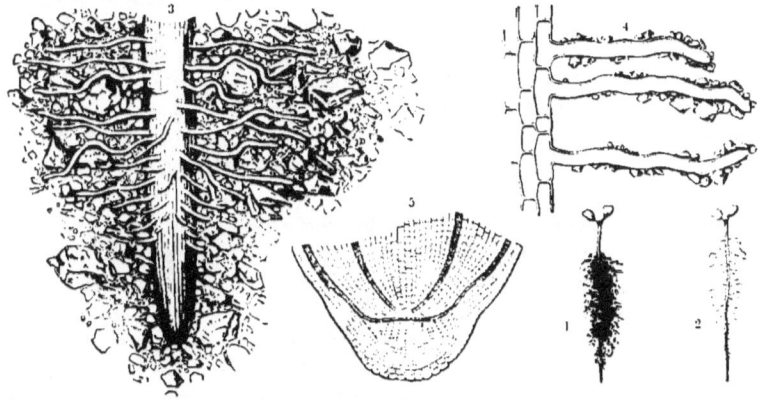

Fig. 12.—Absorptive Cells on Root of *Penstemon*.

¹ Seedling with the long absorptive cells of its root ("root hairs") with sand attached.   ² The same seedling; the sand removed by washing.   ³ Root-tip with absorptive cells; ×10.   ⁴ Absorptive cells with adherent particles of earth.   ⁵ Section through the root-tip; ×60.

sometimes stop and swell up to the shape of a club. The club divides into two or more arms, which grasp and cling to the granule like the fingers of a hand. Many fragments of earth remain thus in the grasp of finger-like processes, whilst others are held fast in the knots and spirals of corkscrew-shaped root-hairs which are often found tangled together. But the retention of most of the earth-particles which adhere to a plant, including fragments of lime, quartz, mica, felspar, &c., as well as plant-residues, is due to the fact that the outermost layer of the absorptive cells is sticky, it being altered into a swollen gelatinous mass which envelops the particles. When this sticky layer becomes dry it contracts and stiffens, and the granules partially imbedded in it are thereby cemented so tightly to the absorptive cells that even violent shaking will not dislodge them.

In the case of most seedlings, and in that of grasses, the absorptive cells which proceed from the roots and which are especially numerous in the latter, are generally thickly covered with particles of earth (see fig. 12⁴). If such a root is pulled out of sandy soil it appears to be completely encased in a regular cylinder of sand (fig. 12¹). A root of *Clusia alba*, taken from coarse gravel, had its root-hairs so tightly adherent to bits of gravel that several little stones, weighing 1·8 grms., were found clinging to it when it was lifted. The gelatinous mass, resulting from the swelling-up of the external coat of the cell, does not in any way hinder absorption or the passage of food-salts in solution. Nor does the inner coat, the thickness of which varies between 0·0006 m.m. and 0·01 m.m., constitute any impediment to imbibition.

In addition to the absorption of nutritive salts by root-hairs, there is also, in many cases, an interchange of materials: that is to say, not only do substances infiltrate from the earth into the absorption-cells, and so onward into the tissues of a plant, but others pass out of the plant through the absorptive cells into the earth. Amongst these eliminated substances, carbonic acid, in particular, plays an important part. A portion of the earth-particles adhering to root-hairs are decomposed by it, and food-salts in immediate proximity to those cells are hereby rendered available and pass into the plant by the shortest way.

Having now seen that land-plants take in food-salts by means of special absorptive cells, it is natural to find that each of these plants develops its absorption-cells, projects them, and sets them to work at a place where there is a source of nutritive matter. The parts that bear absorptive cells will accordingly grow where there are food-salts and water, which is so necessary for their absorption. The Marchantias and fern prothalli spread themselves flat upon the ground, moulding themselves to its contour. From their under-surfaces they send down rhizoids with absorptive cells into the interstices of the soil. Roots provided with root-hairs behave similarly. If a foliage-leaf of the Pepper-plant or of a *Begonia* be cut up, and the pieces laid flat on damp earth, roots are formed from them in a very short time. The roots on each piece of leaf proceed from veins near the edge, which is turned away from the incident light, and grow vertically downwards into the ground.

It is matter of common knowledge that roots which arise upon subterranean parts of stems, like those formed on parts above-ground, grow downward with a force not to be accounted for by their weight alone. This phenomenon, which is called positive geotropism, is looked upon as an effect of gravitation. The idea is that an impetus to growth is given by gravity to the root-tip, and that a transmission of this stimulus ensues to the zone behind the tip where the growth of the root takes place. It is noteworthy that if bits of willow twigs are inserted upside down in the earth, or in damp moss, the roots formed from them, chiefly on the shady side, after bursting through the bark, grow downwards in the moist ground, pushing aside with considerable force the grains of earth which they encounter. The appearance of a willow branch thus reversed in the ground is all the more curious inasmuch as the shoots, which are developed simultaneously with roots from the leaf-buds, do not grow in the general direction of the buds and branches, but turn away immediately and bend upwards. Thus the direction of growth of roots and shoots produced on willow-cuttings remains always the same, whether the base or the top of the twig used as a cutting is inserted in the earth. A similar phenomenon is observed if the leafy rootless shoot of a succulent herb (*e.g Sedum reflexum*) is cut off and suspended in the air by a string. Whether it hangs with the apex uppermost, *i.e.* in the position in which it grew naturally, or with the apex towards the ground, it always, in a short space of time, produces roots which spring from the axis between the fleshy foliage-leaves and bending sharply grow to the earth. Thus in the former case their direction is contrary to the apex of the shoot; in the latter, curiously enough, it is in the same direction. If the height at which the shoot is suspended is only 2 c.m. above the earth, the roots growing towards the ground develop their root-hairs 2 c.m. from their place of origin. But if the shoot is at a distance of 10 c.m., the roots only develop their root-hairs when they have attained a length of 10 c.m. The rule is, therefore, for the roots to grow until they reach the nutrient soil without developing absorption-cells, and only to provide themselves with them when they are in the earth. It is to be observed that these roots are produced on the suspended shoot at places where, under normal conditions (*i.e.*, if the shoot were not cut off and hung up), no roots would be developed. Subject to abnormal conditions and liable to starvation, the plant sends out these roots for self-preservation.

Phenomena of this kind force one to conclude that a plant discerns places which offer a supply of nutriment, and then throws out anchors for safety to those places. This power of detection may, undoubtedly, be explained by the influence which conditions of moisture, in addition to the action of gravitation, have on the direction taken by growing roots. The root-hairs can only obtain food-salts when the ground is thoroughly moist; and whenever roots, or rather their branches, have to choose between two regions, one of which is dry and the other wet, they invariably turn towards the latter. If seeds of the garden-cress are placed on the face of a wall of clay which is kept moist, the rootlets, after bursting out of the seeds, grow at first downwards, but later they enter the wall in a lateral direction. The longitudinal growth of the roots is greater on the dry side than on the wet side, and this results in a bending of the whole towards the source of moisture, in this instance the damp wall. It has been established that the tip of a rootlet is very sensitive to the presence of moisture in the environment. Where there is a moist stratum on one side and a dry stratum on the other, a root-tip receives a stimulus from the unequal conditions in respect of moisture; the stimulus is propagated to the growing part of the root, which lies behind the tip, and the result is a curvature of the root towards the moist side. Thus, the presence of absorbable nutriment, or rather of moisture, in the ground explains the divergence of roots from the direction prescribed by gravity.

The extent to which the direction taken by roots in their search for food is dependent upon the presence of that food, and the fact that roots grow towards places that afford supplies of nutritious material, are strikingly exhibited, also, by epiphytes growing on the bark of trees, such as tropical orchids and *Bromeliaceæ;* and again by plants parasitic on the branches of trees, of which the Mistletoe and other members of the *Loranthaceæ* afford examples. Although the absorption of food by these plants will not be thoroughly discussed till a later stage, this is the proper place to mention the fact that in them positive geotropism appears to be completely neutralized. The growing rootlets which spring from the seed, and the absorptive cells produced from minute tubercles, grow upwards if placed on the under surface of a branch, horizontally if placed on the side, and downwards if on the upper surface. Thus, whatever the direction, they grow towards the moist bark which affords them nourishment.

Positive geotropism seems to be quite abolished also in those marsh-plants which live under water. When, for instance, the seed of the Water-chestnut (*Trapa natans*) germinates under water in a pond, the main root emerges first from the little aperture of the nut and begins by growing upwards. Soon the smaller scale-like cotyledon is put forth, whilst the other, which is much larger, remains within the nut. The whole plant so far is standing on its head, as it were, and is growing upwards with its principal root directed towards the surface of the water. Gradually the leafy stem emerges from the bud between the two cotyledons, and likewise curves upwards and grows towards the surface, whilst an abundance of secondary roots is developed at the same time from the main root. Their function is to absorb nutritive substances from the water around, now that the materials for growth stored in the seed are exhausted. Finding an aqueous solution of food-salts everywhere these roots grow in all directions, upwards, downwards, or horizontally to right or left, forwards or backwards, only they carefully avoid touching one another or interfering with each other's sphere of absorption. It is not till much later that the main root changes the direction of its apex and bends downward. New roots are then produced from the stem; but this subject has no further bearing on the problems at present before us.

The movements of roots, as they grow in earth, suggest that they are seeking for nutriment. The root-tip traces, as it progresses, a spiral course, and this revolving motion has been compared to a constant palpitation or feeling. Spots in the earth which are found to be unfavourable to progression are avoided with care. If the root sustains injury, a stimulus is immediately transmitted to the growing part, and the root bends away from the quarter where the wound was inflicted. When the exploring root-tip comes near a spot where water occurs with food-salts in solution, it at once turns in that direction, and, when it reaches the place, develops such absorptive cells as are adapted to the circumstances.

As has been mentioned before, the roots of most land-plants bear root-hairs on a comparatively restricted zone behind the growing point (see fig. 12[3]), and these hairs have only an ephemeral existence. As the root grows and elongates, new hairs arise (always at the same distance behind the tip), whilst the older ones collapse, turn brown, and perish. In ground which contains on every side food-salts in quantities adequate to the demand, and sufficient water to act as solvent and as medium for the transmission of the salts, the absorptive cells are rarely tubular, but exhibit themselves, as already described, in the form of flat cells destitute of outward curvature. This is the case, for instance, with those Alpine plants which grow in ever-moist hollows and depressions in proximity to springs (*e.g. Saxifraga aizoides* and many others). But wherever the substances to be absorbed are not so easily obtained, the surfaces of the absorptive cells are increased by means of a protrusion of the outer cell-wall, the whole cell being converted into a tube. These tubular absorptive cells are most elongated in mossy forests, where rather large gaps occur not infrequently in the soil. When a root in the course of growth reaches one of these lacunæ, filled with moist air, its root-hairs often lengthen out to an extraordinary extent, and sometimes attain to twice the length of those which are in compact soil. The absorptive cells on the roots of the Water-hemlock (*Cicuta virosa*) and the Sweet Flag (*Acorus Calamus*) do not project at all if the earth in which they grow is muddy; whilst, if the earth is only slightly damp, and an increase of surface is therefore advantageous, the absorptive cells become tubular. Plants which grow in ground liable to periodic drought, and which at these times must secure all the moisture retained by the earth to save their aerial portions from death by desiccation, endeavour to obtain as great an area of absorption as possible by the development of long tubular cells.

The fact must not be overlooked, however, that the form and development of absorptive cells depend partly on the quantity of water that is given off from the aerial parts of the plant, that is to say, by the transpiration of the foliage-leaves. Plants which lose a great deal of water in this way must provide for abundant restitution. They must absorb from as large an area as possible, and enlarge their absorptive surfaces adequately by pushing out the cells into long tubes. For this reason all plants with very thin, delicate, expanded foliage-leaves, which transpire readily and abundantly, have numerous long tubular root-hairs. Examples are afforded by *Viola biflora* and the various species of *Impatiens*. On the other hand, plants with stiff, leathery leaves, being protected by a thick epidermis from excessive transpiration, as, for instance, the Date-palm, exhibit flat, non-protuberant absorptive cells, because there is a very limited amount of evaporation from these plants, and the quantity of water to be absorbed to replace what is lost is therefore small. The same thing holds in the case of evergreen Conifers, in which, owing to the structure of the stiff needles and to the peculiar formation of the wood, water is conducted very slowly from the roots to the transpiring green organs. It has been ascertained that they exhale from six to ten times less vapour than do ashes, birches, maples, and other flat-leaved trees growing on the same ground.

We shall presently return to the question of the substitution for absorptive cells in many coniferous and angiospermic trees and in evergreen *Daphnaceæ, Ericaceæ, Pyrolaceæ, Epacrideæ*, &c., of the mycelium of fungi, and shall treat also of the importance of the form of the absorptive cells, and of the roots which bear them, in relation to the mechanism of striking root in the ground.

## RELATIONS OF THE POSITION OF FOLIAGE-LEAVES TO THAT OF ABSORBENT ROOTS

Anyone who has ever taken refuge from a sudden shower under a tree will remember that the canopy of foliage afforded protection for a considerable time, and that the ground underneath was either not wet at all, or only slightly so. No doubt some of the rain flows down the bark of the trunk, and in many species, as, for instance, the Yew and the Plane-tree, the volume of water conducted down the trunk is considerable; but in the case of most trees the rain-water which reaches the earth in this manner is not abundant, and in comparison with that which drips from the peripheral parts of the foliage its quantity is negligeable. This phenomenon is dependent upon the position of the foliage-leaves relatively to the horizon. In almost all our foliage-trees—in limes and birches, apple and pear trees, planes and maples, ashes, horse-chestnuts, poplars, and alders—these organs slope outwards, and are so placed one above the other that rain falling upon a leaf on one of the highest branches flows along the slanting surface to the apex, collects there in drops, and then falls on to a lower leaf whose surface is also inclined outwards. Here it coalesces with the water fallen directly upon this leaf; and so it goes from one tier to another, lower and lower, and at the same time further and further from the axis, till a number of little cascades are formed all round the tree. From the under and outermost leaves of the entire mass of foliage the water falls in great drops to the ground, and after every shower of rain the dry area at the foot of the tree is surrounded by a circular zone of very wet earth  It is only necessary to dig at these places to convince one's self that the tree's absorptive roots penetrate the earth precisely to the wet zone. When a tree is young, its roots lie in a small circle, and the crown too is not extensive, so that the damp zone is proportionately restricted. But as the latter is enlarged there is a corresponding elongation of the roots in their search for moisture, and thus roots and foliage progress *pari passu* in peripheral increase. It seems not improbable that the custom amongst gardeners and foresters of trimming the foliage and roots of trees when the latter are transplanted is to be attributed to the phenomenon above described. For the rule is observed that the branches of the trunk and those of the root must be about equally shortened, and accordingly the suction-roots, as they develop, reach the zone of drip of the growing crown.

A similar method of carrying off water is to be observed in coniferous trees. Take, for example, the Common Pine. The lateral branches are horizontal near the main trunk: the secondary branches curve upwards like bows  The needles near the tip of each of the latter slant obliquely upwards from the axis, whilst the older needles, situated on the under side of the part of the branch which is almost horizontal and at some distance from its extremity, are directed obliquely downwards and outwards. Rain-drops striking the upturned needles glide down them to the bark of the branch in question, and thence to other needles whose inclination is downwards and outwards. On their apices great drops are gradually formed, which finally detach themselves and fall on to the mass of needles belonging to a lower branch. Thus transmitted, the rain-water travels through the foliage lower and lower and at the same time further from the axis. This is also the case with larches. The drops of rain which fall upon the erect needles of the tufted "short branches" collect and gradually descend to the needles of the drooping "long branches" on lower boughs. Large drops are always to be seen on their drooping apices, whence they drip to the earth. Owing to the pyramidal form of larches, and to the circumstance that the long shoots on each branch are terminal, almost all the water which falls upon one of these trees reaches the long shoots hanging down from the lowest branches, which discharge most of all. Although larches with their tender needles do not look at all as though they would be any protection against rain, the ground underneath them keeps dry nevertheless, the principal part of the water falling upon them being conducted to the periphery. Indeed, the larch belongs to the number of trees which conduct almost all the rain that falls upon them to a certain distance from the axis where the absorbent roots lie, and only allow a little to trickle down the bark of the main trunk.

Many shrubs and perennial herbs also transmit the water, which falls on their upturned laminæ, to parts of the ground where their absorbent roots are embedded; or, rather, the roots send forth their branches bearing absorptive cells to the area which is kept moist by drippings from the leaves. Particularly striking in this respect are the species of the two genera of Aroids *Colocasia* and *Caladium*. A specimen of the latter is figured below (fig. 13[1]). If one digs about individuals of this genus cultivated on open ground, one invariably finds that the tips of the lateral roots, which proceed in a horizontal direction from the bulbous root-stock, are buried under the point of the great leaves which slope obliquely outwards. We must not omit to mention, in addition, that the stalks of leaves which conduct the rain centrifugally are not channelled on the upper surface; they are round, and comparable to wires supporting at their upper extremities the laminæ in an outward and downward direction. As instances we may quote the Horse-chestnut, Maple, and Lime, and many shrubby, suffruticose, and herbaceous plants, such as *Sparmannia*, *Spiræa*, *Aruncus*, and *Corydalis*, and also climbing and trailing plants (*e.g. Menispermum*, *Banisteria*, *Aristolochia*, *Hoya*, *Zanonia*, and *Tropæolum*). Whenever a system of grooves is developed on the surface of an outward sloping leaf, the channels run along the veins and terminate at the apex of the leaf, or at the apices of the leaf's lobes, and invariably cause the water to travel, not to the basal part, but to a spot on the margin whence it will detach itself in the form of a drop, and fall upon the leaves situated immediately below and at a greater distance from the axis.

A striking contrast to these trees and shrubs, climbing and trailing plants, and suffruticose and herbaceous species, with their absorptive roots lying in one plane, and usually spreading at but little depth, is afforded by plants which possess bulbs or short root-stocks with deep-reaching suction-roots, and those which have tap-roots descending vertically in continuation of the main stem, and whose secondary roots are short and travel only a little distance from their places of origin. This other extreme in root-structure, which is represented in fig. 13[2], has its counterpart above-ground in the form and direction of the laminae upon which the rain falls.    In all these plants the surfaces of the leaves are not directed

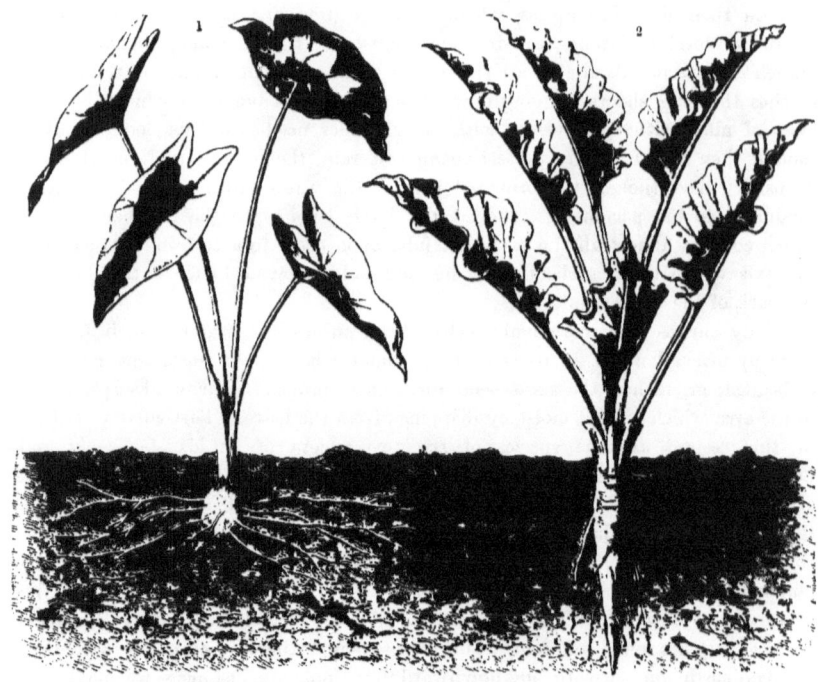

Fig. 13.—Centrifugal and Centripetal Transmission of Water.
[1] By a *Caladium.*    [2] By a Rhubarb plant.

outwards, but slope obliquely towards the central axis.    Their upper sides, moreover, are concave and exhibit a system of grooves, which conveys the water collected by the leaf towards the stem, and therefore also, towards the tap-root and suction-roots.    The leaves of bulbous plants, such as the Hyacinth and Tulip, all stand up obliquely, and their upper surfaces are concave and often deeply channelled. Along the grooves the rain flows centripetally downwards, and so directly reaches the part of the earth where the bulbs and suction-roots, which proceed in a tuft from underneath the bulbs, are situated.    The young leaves of Cannaceæ and of the Lily-of-the-valley are coiled up like a trumpet; and rain, falling from above upon the expanded portion, is led along the coiled surface, describing a helix as it goes, to the earth in the neighbourhood of the absorptive roots, which proceed from the short root-stock. When the leaves of plants furnished with tap-roots are arranged in whorls, and are without internodes, and the rosette rests upon the ground, as is the case in the Mandrake, the Dandelion, and several species of Plantain (*Mandragora officinalis, Taraxacum officinale, Plantago media*), there are always one or more main grooves on the upper surfaces of the leaves, and the leaves have always such form and position as compel the rain which falls upon them to flow centripetally, i.e. towards the tap-root growing vertically beneath the centre. Plants with petiolate leaves, which conduct rain centripetally, always have on the upper side of each leaf-stalk an obvious groove, the depth of which is frequently increased by the development of green or (in many cases) membranous ridges on the two lateral edges. Grooves of this kind are to be seen particularly well on the petioles of the radical leaves of the Rhubarb (see fig. 13 [2]), Beet-root, Funkias, and most Violets.

Far more complicated in structure than the radical leaves just described, are cauline leaves. Leaves proceeding from the stem high above the ground, and forming receptacles for rain-water, like those of the Rhubarb, are best fitted to preserve their proper direction when they have no stalks and the base fits directly on to the stem or passes into it. Cup-shaped laminae, if borne on long erect petioles, necessitate a great expenditure on supporting-cells, and they are, therefore, on the whole, rare. Of the plants we know, only certain Stork's-bills, *Pelargonium zonale, P. heterogamum*, &c., afford examples of cup-shaped, cauline leaves of the kind, borne on long, rigid petioles. In most cases, therefore, cauline leaves which conduct water centripetally are either sessile or very shortly petiolate, have their bases close to the stem, and even extend their edges down it more or less in the form of wings and ridges, or surround it in the form of collars, lobes, and auricles, as in the case of so-called amplexicaul leaves.

When the leaves are in pairs opposite one another and the alternate pairs at right angles, an arrangement known as decussate, the surplus water is usually conveyed through two grooves, which run down the intervening piece of stem from one pair of leaves to the next. Each of these grooves begins in an indentation between the margins of the bases of a pair of leaves, and terminates above the midrib of one of the leaves belonging to the next pair. Now, water trickling down such a groove falls precisely on that part of a lower leaf where the rain retained by the surface of that leaf is collected; and so the stream of water becomes more and more copious as it approaches the ground. These grooves may be seen in many species of ringent *Labiatae, Scrophulariaceae, Primulaceae, Gentianaceae, Rubiaceae*, and Willow-herbs; the best-marked instances are found in the Knotty Fig-wort (*Scrophularia nodosa*), the Yellow-rattle (*Rhinanthus*), the meadow-gentians (*Gentiana germanica, Rhaetica*, &c.), and the Centaury (*Erythraea*). The grooves always possess the property of being wetted by water, whereas the ungrooved parts of the same stem are not wetted. Sometimes the grooves are fringed with hairs which absorb the water like the threads of a wick. By means of both contrivances advantage is ensured in that the water only oozes quite gradually down the moistened grooves, or else is conducted by the hairy fringes to the base of the stem, and does not rebound at any spot in the form of drops. Irregularly bounding drops would be liable to fall on the ground at spots where no absorptive organs awaited them.

In cases where foliage-leaves, adapted to a centripetal conduction of rain, are arranged upon a spiral line down the stem, instead of in pairs opposite one another, the water leaks away along the spiral from one leaf to the next, and finally to the bottom. Then, again, there are often grooves in the stem along which the water trickles, as, for instance, in the Common Whortleberry (*Vaccinium Myrtillus*). The erect leaves of this plant conduct the drops as they fall to the branches, which are deeply furrowed. The water travels through the furrows into those of lower branches, and finally along those of the main stem of the whole bush down to the earth. In *Veratrum album* each of the concave cauline leaves has, on the upper surface, a number of deep longitudinal grooves, which all discharge together at the base of the leaf. The water collected there at length overflows and runs down the round stem in no particular channel.

The descent of rain-water along a spiral line may be very clearly traced in many plants of the Thistle tribe. If tiny shot-grains are substituted for rain-drops in a stiff-leaved plant, the course designed for the drops in that particular species may be followed with ease. When strewn on a mature plant of the Safflower (*Carthamus tinctorius*) or of *Alfredia cernua* (fig. 14[1]), the grains of shot roll down the somewhat channelled surface of the highest cauline leaf, which stands up obliquely, and dash against the stem. The latter is half encompassed by the leaf-base, and the shot then roll over one of the basal lobes of the leaf and travel out of the range of that leaf, falling on to the middle of the one next below. For the amplexicaul foliar bases are so placed that each leaf has one of its basal lobes above a concave part of the next lower leaf. In precisely the same way the shot descend from the second leaf to the third, and so on until they reach the earth quite close to the stem. The descent reminds one of the game in which a little ball is made to roll along a spiral groove on to a board furnished with numbered holes. Rain-drops falling upon thistle-like plants of this kind naturally follow the same course as the shot. Only, the additional fact must be taken into account that not only the highest but all the leaves are adapted as receptacles for the rain as it falls, and that consequently the drops falling from leaf to leaf are augmented by new tributaries, and become greater and greater as they descend.

A somewhat different method of water-conduction from that which occurs in the Safflower and in the nodding *Alfredia* is observed in the Milk Thistle (*Silybum Marianum*), in the Cotton Thistle (*Onopordon*), and in the Mullein (*Verbascum phlomoides*). The upper leaves, which have two semi-amplexicaul lobes, are as nearly erect as those of the Safflower and the nodding *Alfredia*, and lead the rain off in exactly the same way. But the leaves in the middle of the stem are only erect for about three-quarters of their length: the upper-most third, including the apex, is bent obliquely outwards and downwards. Drops of rain falling on this upper third of a leaf would flow in a centrifugal direction, and do, as a matter of fact, drip down from the apex. Now the leaves in all

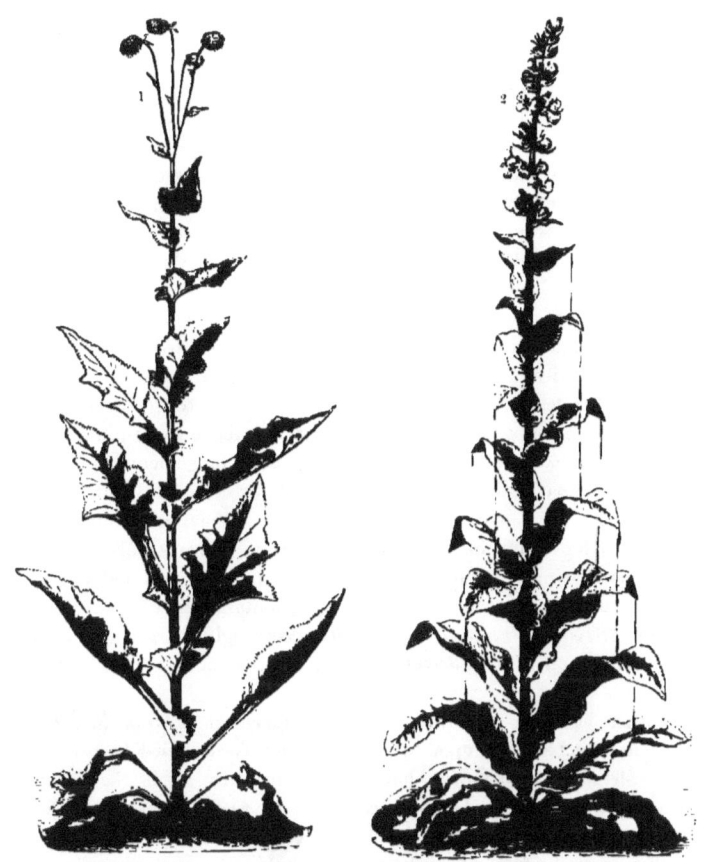

Fig. 14.—Irrigation of Rain-water.
1 In *Alfredia cernua*    2 In a Mullein (*Verbascum phlomoides*).

these plants are shorter the higher their position upon the stem, so that the total contour of the plant may be described as a slender pyramid. In consequence of this, water dropping from the outward-bent and drooping apices of superior leaves is arrested by that part of an inferior leaf which shelves towards the stem, and is thereby conducted centripetally. Thus all the rain-water received by a plant of this kind at last reaches the immediate neighbourhood of the tap-root, and is a source of nutriment to the absorption-roots which proceed from it. In the Milk Thistle (*Silybum Marianum*) the margins of the cauline leaves are very much waved, and, in consequence of this undulation, three or four depressions exist on each side, through which part of the rain, when there is a heavy downpour, flows off sideways. But even this water, falling laterally, drops upon parts of lower leaves, which conduct centripetally, and so coalesces with the streamlets otherwise produced.

It is very rare for plants which convey water centripetally to have their leaves arranged in two rows. The most striking example of this class is the Japanese *Tricyrtis pilosa*. Its leaves are situated on the fully-developed stem very regularly, one above the other, in two series. Each leaf has two lobes embracing the stem, but the base is fixed somewhat obliquely, so that one of the lobes is fixed higher than the other. Moreover, the higher lobe is closely adpressed to the stem, whilst the lower forms a channel which discharges exactly above the concave surface of the next lower leaf belonging to the other side. When rain falls on this plant, the water, collected by one leaf, flows through the broad exit-channel on to the leaf below on the other side. Thence a somewhat augmented stream falls upon a leaf of the first series, and so on, a peculiar cascade resulting, which falls in a zigzag, from leaf to leaf, until it reaches the bottom, close to the stem.

It would, however, be wrong to suppose that the above explanation sets forth the only significance to be assigned to the various arrangements described. To many plants it is a matter of indifference in what direction rain-water falls from the leaves. Such, for instance, is the case with all marsh-plants with roots buried in mud under water, inasmuch as the rain, as it drops, only goes into the water in the pond or marsh, and could not be conveyed to a definite spot for the sake of the absorbent roots. In the Water-plantain, the Flowering-rush, and the Arrow-head (*Alisma, Butomus, Sagittaria*), accordingly, no relationship between the form and direction of the leaves and the position of the absorbent roots is to be discovered.

On the other hand, in arundinaceous plants (*Arundo, Phragmites, Phalaris*) an arrangement has been hit upon which is obviously designed to prevent rain-water from collecting between the haulm and the leaf. As is the general rule with grasses, so also in the above-named kinds of reeds, the stem or haulm is furnished with nodes, and from each node proceeds a leaf the lower part of which encases the haulm in the form of a tube or sheath, whilst the upper part is expanded and presents a flat, strap-shaped or concave surface, standing well away from the stem. The leaves may be folded round the haulm like banners. At the place where the sheath passes into the part of the leaf which stands away from the axis at an obtuse angle, one observes on the edge of the leaf close to the angle, two distinct depressions which represent conduits and convey part of the rain from the lamina. There is also a very neat contrivance here in the form of an erect dry membrane which acts as a dam, the so-called "ligule." This membrane, inserted upon the leaf-sheath, is, like the sheath, in contact with the haulm. When rain-water flows down to this place it is stemmed by the membrane, as by a dam, and diverted right and left into the two grooves. In this way water is prevented from accumulating between the leaf-sheath and haulm, where it might do damage. In many reeds the contrivances for irrigation are even more complete than this. Sometimes hairs depend from the margin of the membrane in the direction of the grooves and, like a wick, lead the water in the proper direction.

An opportunity will occur later on of showing how the conduction of rain to particular spots has an important bearing on the phenomenon of absorption by aerial parts of plants: and also in the regulation of transpiration; and how, by means of the apparatus for water-irrigation, not only absorptive cells at the extremities of roots in the earth, but special organs on the foliage-leaves as well, are often supplied with water.

---

# 3. ABSORPTION OF ORGANIC MATTER FROM DECAYING PLANTS AND ANIMALS.

Saprophytes and their relation to decaying bodies.—Saprophytes in water, on the bark of trees, and on rocks.—Saprophytes in the humus of woods, meadows, and moors.—Special relations between Saprophytes and the nutrient substratum.—Plants with traps or pitfalls for animals.—Insectivorous plants which perform movements for the capture of prey.—Insectivorous plants with adhesive apparatus.

## SAPROPHYTES AND THEIR RELATION TO DECAYING BODIES.

Whenever plants which take up organic compounds formed in the process of decay are the subject of discussion, the first examples that occur to everyone are members of the great family of Fungi, specimens of which make their appearance wherever dead animals or plants are undergoing decomposition. We recall the moulds, plasmodia, puff-balls, and mushrooms, which grow from dead organic bodies, and are associated with the unpleasant mouldy and cadaverous smell always perceptible in their neighbourhood.

Many of these organisms do, in fact, belong to the class of Saprophytes. Indeed, one group of them is itself the cause of the chemical decomposition of dead plants and animals called decay. Their elongated thin-walled cells, the so-called "hyphae", thread themselves through dead bodies, and unite to form strands, bundles, networks, and membranes, the whole constituting a structure to which the term "mycelium" is applied. These mycelia are often to be seen, with the naked eye, covering large areas. For instance, in damp cellars, mines, and railway-tunnels, any old rotten wood-work is clothed with delicate, whitish reticula and membranes. The heaps of grape-skins, stalks, and other refuse piled up in the open air by the side of vineyards after a vintage, are usually so completely overgrown by mycelia that their colour is quite altered. The so-called "mushroom-spawn", used in the cultivation of mushrooms, is also nothing but a mycelium, which entirely invests the manure employed in the cultivation of that fungus, and gives it a white mottled appearance.

In addition to Fungi, however, a number of Mosses, Liverworts, Ferns, Lycopods, and Phanerogams take up organic compounds from the products of decay to serve as their food.

In deciding whether a plant takes up only the mineral substances rendered soluble by the decomposition of the soil, or only organic substances disengaged by the decay of dead plants and animals, we depend generally on the condition and appearance of the nutrient substratum, and, in particular, on its composition, i.e. whether it is exclusively or predominantly organic. But such observations give a very uncertain indication. For, on the one hand, it is possible for plants rooted in a substratum of decaying matter to take nothing but mineral salts (i.e. inorganic compounds) from it; and, on the other hand, it frequently happens that sand or clay, apparently uncontaminated with organic matter, is saturated by water which oozes from a layer of humus in the vicinity, and brings with it organic compounds in solution. The following facts are instructive with reference to the former of these two phenomena. Maize, barley, and other cereals may be reared in fluids, so prepared as to contain a small quantity of mineral food-salts dissolved in distilled water (12 mg. potassium phosphate, 12 mg. sodium phosphate, 27 mg. calcium chloride, 40 mg. potassium chloride, 20 mg. magnesium sulphate, 10 mg. ammonium sulphate, and a few drops of iron chloride in a litre of distilled water), all organic compounds being carefully excluded. When the plants germinate, they develop roots which descend in the liquid and absorb from it mineral salts according to their requirements. They produce stems, leaves, flowers, and, ultimately, seeds capable of germination. Other plants of maize or barley reared simultaneously in richly-manured ground develop likewise leaves, flowers, and fruit. Moreover, analysis of the ash in both cases reveals the fact that the plants which took their nutriment from the manure contain the same salts as those reared in the made-up solution of salts free from organic compounds. Hence, the conclusion may be drawn that a plant of this kind is capable of obtaining an adequate supply of food-salts equally well, either from earth free from humus and manure, or from humus or manure themselves. The experiment further shows that, in the latter case, organic compounds need not necessarily be absorbed, in addition to the mineral constituents of humus or manure which are disengaged during decomposition.

We must next refer to a fact in connection with the second point above mentioned, viz. that plants rooted in sand or loam devoid of humus may yet have organic compounds brought to them by water filtering through a stratum of humus near at hand. The fact in question is, that the very water which one would least expect should contain organic compounds, that, for instance, of cold mountain streams, does very generally include traces of such compounds. On looking through analyses of mineral springs, one finds for the most part, amongst their constituents, combustible bodies arising from the dissolution of organic matter. Even the acid formerly designated by Berzelius by the name of "spring-acid", is doubtless a product of the decay of fragments of plants in the place where the water of the spring collects. So also is humic acid, a compound produced by decay. The nature of this acid is not yet, it is true, thoroughly known, and it may be a mixture of several acids. We know, however, that it is easily soluble in water, and that it forms soluble compounds with alkalies. Brooks running through woods or meadows, small mountain lakes adjoining peat-beds, and pools in actual peat, consist of water, brown in colour, which gives an acid reaction, and contains invariably organic substances in solution.

The following observations are of great interest in connection with this subject. In the salt-mine at Hallstatt (Upper Austria) one of the galleries, which is hewn through rock and contains no wood-work of any kind, exhibited (spread out upon its smooth limestone roof) the mycelium of a fungus (an *Omphalia*), which certainly required organic nutriment. There were no decaying animal or vegetable remains anywhere in the gallery, and the mycelium derived nourishment solely from water oozing from above through a few narrow cracks in the stone whereby the surface of the latter was kept moist. This water came from a meadow lying high above the mine. Between the two was a thick stratum of limestone with a deep layer of earth resting upon it. The water was clear and colourless, and contained a certain amount of lime, but no perceptible trace of organic substances. Yet this water must have brought organic matter from the meadow above into the mine, and the minute quantity so introduced sufficed to enable the fungus mycelium to grow luxuriantly.

In the Volderthal, near Hall, in Tyrol, there is a spring of cold clear water rising out of slate at a height of 1000 metres above the sea-level, which is filled at its source with a dark thick felt. The felt may be lifted out in pieces the size of one's hand, and it is the mycelium of a fungus, probably a *Peziza*. It clings to slabs of slate, between which the water trickles abundantly, and its nutriment can only be derived from this water. There are pine-woods and meadows in the neighbourhood, but no greater amount of vegetation, humus, or rotten timber than is found near other springs.

These instances satisfactorily prove that even the clearest mountain springs contain organic substances in quantities sufficient, however minute, to nourish fungi. When the origin of springs is taken into account, this result is not really surprising. They are fed by deposition from the atmosphere. The water thus deposited percolates into the ground, passing, in the first place, through a layer of earth-mould which is covered by vegetation, and contains more or less humus in its upper strata. A small quantity of the products of decay is inevitably absorbed, and even if they are partially withdrawn again in lower strata of the earth, traces are still retained by the water in its descent to greater depths, and re-ascent to the surface in the form of springs. The characteristics of the great veins of water which ascend in this way are no doubt common to the smaller veins which originate in the vegetable mould saturated by snow and rain on the ground of forests or in the humus covering meadows, and which percolate through into the sand or loam beneath. Plants whose roots ramify in this deeper layer of earth derive thence the organic compounds conveyed by the water, and have the additional advantage of being able to satisfy at the same time their requirements as regards mineral substances. This circumstance is of importance not only to flowering-plants but also to many fungi, as, for instance, to all species of *Phallus*, they having need of a great deal of lime. An explanation is thus afforded of the fact, formerly difficult to understand, that in forests and meadows not only the upper black or brown humus layer, but also the underlying yellow loam, or pale sand, neither of which latter contains any humus, has mycelia of fungi running through it in every direction, and weaving their threads over little fragments of rock. Indeed, it sometimes happens that the lower layer of earth is more abundantly penetrated with plexuses of hyphæ than is the upper layer, consisting of vegetable mould. The greatest number of saprophytes is to be found therefore at places where the humus layer is not too thick and loam or sand occurs at no great depth; but where decaying vegetable remains are piled metres high, as on moors, for example, instead of fungi being produced in extraordinary abundance, as one might expect, only a few occur. Pure peat is by no means a favourable soil for fungi, a circumstance which may be partly due to the antiseptic action of certain compounds developed in it.

It follows from the foregoing observations that a sure conclusion as to the nature of plants rooted in a particular substratum cannot possibly be derived from the mere appearance of the substratum. Moreover, the conditions necessary for the growth of plants requiring organic products of decay as nutriment appear to be of much wider occurrence than one would suppose upon a cursory observation of the conditions existing in fields and forests, or, if one considers exclusively instances of cultivated plants reared on arable land, which is manured and constantly turned over. The great variety of plants produced on a limited area is also now intelligible. From the same soil some absorb organic compounds, others mineral substances only; whilst others again take some organic and some mineral food-salts. The determining factor is not the amount of a given substance present in the substratum, but rather the special needs of each species, and ultimately the specific constitution of the protoplasm in each one of the plants which thus, side by side, nourish themselves in totally different ways.

If, then, neither the appearance of the ground nor its richness in respect of humus affords any certain indication as to whether a particular plant lives on organic products of decay or not, the question may perhaps be solved by the fact of the plant's containing or not containing green chlorophyll-corpuscles. We may take it as proved by many results of investigation, that the decomposition of the carbon-dioxide absorbed by a plant from the air, and the formation of the organic compounds of carbon, hydrogen, and oxygen known as carbohydrates (which play so important a part in vegetable economy), only take place in organs possessing the green pigment known as chlorophyll. We shall return to a discussion of these processes in detail later on, but the fact must be taken into consideration here. One would suppose, accordingly, that plants able to obtain ready-made organic compounds from a nutrient substratum could spare themselves the trouble of building them up, so that the presence of chlorophyll would be superfluous. This conjecture is in fact supported by the absence of chlorophyll in fungi, which are typical instances of saprophytes. But, on the other hand, some plants appear to negative this assumption, or at any rate to deprive it of general application. In mountain districts, where cattle continually pass to and from the meadows and alps, one notices on their halting grounds, and along their tracks, moss of a conspicuous green colour growing on circumscribed spots. On closer examination we find that we have here an example of the remarkable group of the *Splachnaceæ*, and that it has selected the cow-dung to be its nutrient substratum. Each growth of emerald green, *Splachnum ampullaceum*, is strictly limited to the area of a lump of dung; no trace of it is to be seen elsewhere. All the stages of development of this moss follow one another upon the same substratum. First of all the lumps of dirt which are kept moist by rain or by standing water, become enveloped in a web of protonemæ, and their surfaces acquire thereby a characteristic greenish lustre. Later, hundreds of little green stems, thickly clothed with leaves, emerge, and the spore-cases, which resemble tiny antique jars, and are amongst the prettiest exhibited by the world of mosses, become visible as well. Just as *Splachnum ampullaceum* is produced on the dung of cattle, so is *Tetraplodon angustatus* on that of carnivorous animals, and there can be no doubt that these, and in general all *Splachnaceæ*, are true saprophytes. A similar remark holds with regard to the green *Euglenæ* which escape from Hormidium-cells, and fill the foul-smelling liquor in dung-pits and puddles near cattle-stalls in mountain villages, and which multiply to such an extent that in a few days the liquid changes colour from brown to green.

Thus plants do exist containing chlorophyll although absorbing from the substratum organic compounds alone, and containing it, indeed, in such quantities that its presence cannot be looked upon as accidental. It follows, firstly, that absence of chlorophyll is not the distinguishing mark of saprophytic plants; and, secondly, that the organic nutriment of the plants above mentioned cannot be used forthwith unaltered in the building up and extension of their structures, but, like inorganic material, must undergo various changes, that is, must be to a certain extent digested before being used for construction. The probability is that green saprophytes take carbon from their substratum in a form unfitted for the manufacture of cellulose and other carbohydrates. Saprophytes that are not green must obtain carbon from the substratum in the form of a compound, the direct absorption of which could be dispensed with if chlorophyll were present; but it does not necessarily follow that all the organic compounds absorbed by non-green saprophytes are capable of immediate service as materials for construction without any preliminary alteration.

Impartial consideration of the above facts forces us to conclude that there is no well-marked boundary line between plants which absorb organic compounds and those which absorb inorganic compounds from their respective substrata; and that there undoubtedly exist plants capable of taking up both kinds of material at the same time. This conviction is strengthened still further by the circumstance, which has been repeatedly confirmed by experiment, that plants susceptible of being successfully reared in artificial solutions of mineral salts—to the exclusion of organic compounds—do not entirely reject organic compounds when the latter are tendered to them, but unquestionably assimilate some of them (urea, uric acid, glycocoll, &c.) and work them up into constituents of their own frames.

But, in spite of the impossibility of drawing a sharp line of demarcation between the two groups, it is convenient to treat of the absorption of organic compounds separately, because this division of the subject affords the best opportunity of inspecting in detail, and of surveying generally, the conditions of food-absorption, the comprehension of which is otherwise difficult. In order to determine in each individual case whether a given plant lives either exclusively or principally upon organic food, derived from decaying animal or vegetable remains, reliance must be placed on experiments with cultures; and, in the absence of better vantage-ground, the results of the rougher experiments made by gardeners should not be neglected, always providing that they are accepted subject to possible correction by subsequent exact experiment.

## SAPROPHYTES IN WATER, ON THE BARK OF TREES, AND ON ROCKS.

Of the special cases of absorption of organic compounds from decaying bodies, we have first of all to consider those occurring amongst water-plants. In the sea, wherever there is an abundance of animal and vegetable life there is also plenty of refuse, for there death and decay hold a rich harvest. The quantity of organic matter dissolved in the water is naturally greater in these places than where vegetation and animal life are less conspicuous. There is a much more varied flora and fauna to be met with in the sea near its coasts, especially in shallow inlets, than at a greater distance from the shore; and the number of dead organisms is also greater near the coast. A mass of organic remains is thrown up by the tide, and by waves in stormy weather. This mass rots during the ebb. Part of it is dragged out to sea again by the next high tide, and then flung up once more; so that the beach is always strewn with dead remains, and the sea near the shore contains more products of decomposition than in the open.

In the immediate neighbourhood of seaports, moreover, or wherever people live, the volume of refuse is considerably increased, and the water in harbours and stagnant inlets behind breakwaters, and at the mouths of canals and sewers, contains such a large quantity of organic refuse in a state of decomposition that its presence is revealed by the odour emitted. Now it is just at these places that an abundant vegetation of hydrophytes is developed. Not only the bottom of shallows, but stones, stakes, quays, buoys, and even the keels and planks of boats long anchored in harbour, are overgrown by *Ulvæ*, wracks, filamentous algæ, and *Florideæ*. Not a few, as, for instance, the so-called sea-lettuce (*Ulva lactuca*), several species of *Gelidium*, *Bangia*, and *Ceramium*, and the great *Cystosira barbata*, thrive best and in greatest abundance in polluted water of the kind; and there can be no doubt that this is to be accounted for by the presence of a greater quantity of organic compounds in that water.

It is not only in contaminated sea-water, but also in other collections of water which contain products of putrefaction in solution, that we find a characteristic vegetation. We have already alluded to the presence of *Euglenæ* in the liquor of manure-pits. They occur also at the foot of shady walls, in dirty back streets in towns, in the puddles, and on ground which is saturated with urine and impurities of every kind. These places are the home of a number of other minute plants, which stain the polluted ground after rain with the gayest colours. There, side by side with black patches of *Oscillaria antliaria* and verdigris-coloured films of *Oscillaria tenuis*, are blood-red patches of *Palmella cruenta*, and brick-red patches of *Chroococcus cinnamomeus*. Equally characteristic is the vegetation which covers the earth at the mouths of drains, and is bathed by the trickling sewage. Large areas here are overgrown by the green *Hormidium murale*, which weaves itself over the mire, and by the dark, actively-oscillating *Oscillaria limosa*; and, above all, the curious *Beggiatoa versatilis* makes itself conspicuous, sending out from a whitish gelatinous ground mass long oscillating filaments, which emerge after sundown, and next day split up into innumerable little bacteria-rods. The red-snow alga, too (represented in Plate I.), lives at the expense of the pollen-grains, bodies of insects, and other decaying matter blown on to snow-fields; whilst the nearly allied blood-red alga (*Hæmatococcus pluvialis* or *Sphærella pluvialis*) lives in the water in hollow stones where all sorts of animal and vegetable remains collect. Leaves blown into deep pools, and lying rotting at the bottom, are everywhere overgrown by green *Œdogonium*, by *Pleurococcus angulosus*, and by the amethyst-coloured *Protococcus roseo-persicinus*. The bottoms of ditches on peat-bogs, which are full of brownish water containing an abundance of compounds of humic acid in solution, are covered with this amethyst *Protococcus*, whilst a profusion of small filamentous algæ, Oscillariæ and so forth (*Bulbochæte parvula*, *Schizochlamys gelatinosa*, *Sphærozosma vertebrata*, *Micro-cystis ichthyloba*, &c.), as well as a group of dusky mosses (*Hypnum giganteum*, *H. sarmentosum*, *H. cordifolium*), all have their home exclusively in still water richly supplied with organic compounds. When we include also the curious mould-like *Saprolegniæ* produced on dead bodies floating in water—*Saprolegnia ferax* and *Achlya prolifera* on flies and fishes—some idea is obtained of the great variety of saprophytes living in fresh water, as well as of those inhabiting the sea.

A much more agreeable and attractive picture than that of these aquatic sapro-phytes is afforded by plants whose sole habitat is the bark of trees. The dead bark does not constitute the nutrient base of all the plants which grow from trunks and branches, or climb up them in the form of clinging and twining lianas.

Often the trees only serve as supports, by means of which the plants in question raise themselves out of darkness into light. Such food-salts as they require they take, not from their support, but from the earth, into which they send absorptive roots. As years go by, a quantity of inorganic dust collects in the forks of branches and in the little rents and fissures in the bark of old trees, and this dust gets mixed with crumbled particles of bark. The clefts, therefore, are more or less full of vegetable mould, and this forms an excellent foster-soil for a large number of plants. But it is not necessarily the case that all plants rooting in this mould take up organic compounds from it. Thus, one finds not infrequently in the angles of bifurcation of the trunks of old limes and other trees, little gooseberry and elder bushes, and bitter-sweet plants, which have germinated there from fruits brought by black-birds, thrushes, and other frugivora. These shrubs, in the forks of limes and poplars hardly take any organic compounds from the mould in which they are rooted, but confine themselves to the absorption of such mineral salts as they may require.

But, with the exception of instances of that kind, the great majority of plants, nestling in the mould in crevices of bark, do take nutriment from this their substratum in the form of organic compounds. In cold regions the plants living in the mould of bark are for the most part mosses and liverworts. They cover trunks and branches of old ashes, poplars, and oaks, with a thick green mantle, and grow especially on the weather-side of the trees. In the tropics, on the other hand, the fissured bark of trees is a rallying ground not only for delicate mosses and moss-like Lycopodia, but also for a whole host of ferns and vivid flowering plants. The number of small ferns which develop and unroll their fronds from chinks in the bark of trees is so great that old trunks appear wrapped in a regular foliage of fern-fronds. Of Phanerogams, in particular, the *Aroideæ, Orchidaceæ, Bromeliaceæ, Dorsteniæ Begoniaceæ*, and even *Cactuceæ* (species of the genera *Cereus* and *Rhipsalis*) bury their roots in the mould of bark. It is to be remarked that the rosettes of *Bromeliaceæ* ornament chiefly the forks of trunks, whilst *Dorsteniæ, Orchideæ*, and the various species of *Rhipsalis* grow on the upper side of branches that ramify horizontally; whilst, lastly, *Aroideæ* and *Begoniæ* take root, for the most part, on the surfaces of huge erect trunks.

Besides the mould collected in crevices and fissures of bark, the bark itself, that is, the cortical layer, dead but not yet crumbled and mouldered into dust, forms a nutrient substratum for a whole series of plants of most various affinity. Many fungi and lichens penetrate deeply the compact bark, and their hyphal filaments ramify between its dead cells. Other plants, instead of piercing through the substance of the bark, lay themselves flat upon its surface, and grow to it so firmly that if one tries to lift them away from the substratum, either part of the latter breaks off, or the adnate cell-strata are rent, but there is no separation of the one from the other. If a tuft of moss (*e.g. Orthotrichum fallax, O. tenellum*, or *O. pallens*), growing on bark, or a liverwort (*e.g. Frullania dilatata*) closely adherent to a similar basis, is forcibly removed, little fragments of the bark may be always seen torn off with the rhizoids at the places where they issue from the stemlets. The same thing occurs in the case of the roots of tropical orchids growing to the tree-trunks which constitute their habitat. The majority of these tree-orchids nestle, no doubt, in mould-filled crevices of the bark, and nourish them-

Fig. 15. Aerial Roots of a Tropical Orchid (*Sarcanthus rostratus*) assuming the form of straps.

selves, besides, by means of special aerial roots which hang down in white ropes and threads, like a mane, from the places where the plants are situated upon the trees, and which will presently be described in detail. But a small section develops strap-shaped roots as well, which adhere firmly to the bark with their flat surfaces. This phenomenon is most strikingly exhibited by the splendid *Phalænopsis*

*Schilleriana*, a native of the Philippine Islands: its roots are rigid, compressed, and about 1 c.m. in breadth; the surface turned away from the trunk is slightly convex, and has a granular structure and metallic glitter like a lizard's or chameleon's tail. The surface towards the trunk is flat and without metallic glitter, and upon it, close behind the growing point, there is a whitish fur consisting of short, thickly packed, absorptive cells. When the tip of one of these roots comes into contact with the bark it grows so firmly to the substratum by means of the absorption-cells, that it is easier to detach superficial bits of the bark itself than the root. The latter, once fixed, flattens out still more and becomes strap-shaped, whilst creeping outgrowths proceed from it, forming strips which may ultimately attain a length of 1½ metres. The sight of a trunk covered with these long metallic bands is one that never fails to excite wonder even in the midst of the world of orchids, wherein, as is well known, there is much to marvel at.

In other species of tropical orchids, *e.g.* in *Sarcanthus rostratus* (fig. 15), the roots are not flat from the beginning, but become so when they come into contact with the bark. A root is often to be seen which arises as a cylindrical cord from the axis, then lays itself upon the bark in the form of a band, and further on lifts itself once more, resuming at the same time the rope form, as is shown in the illustration. Here also complete coalescence takes place between the bands and the bark, and the union is extremely close. Similar conditions have been observed to hold in many *Aroideæ* living on the bark of trees. The plants in question lie with their stems, leaves, and roots flat against the trunks, so that they suggest a covering of drapery. Taking, for instance, the *Marcgraviæ* (*Marcgravia paradoxa, M. umbellata*), one might at first sight suppose that they adhere to the bark not only by the roots, but also by the large discoid leaves, which are arranged in two rows. A very remarkable fact also, in connection with these plants, is that they only grow on very smooth and firm bark. When transferred to a soft substratum, such as mould or moss, they languish, because their roots are unable to enter into close union with a support of such loose texture. This is also true of most tropical orchids living on bark. When their seeds are transferred to loose earth devoid of humus, they do indeed germinate, but then perish, whereas when sown on the bark of a tree, they not only germinate, but grow up with ease into hardy plants.

Where steep rocks occur near clumps of trees it is not uncommon for the same species of plants to grow on both. Allusion is not here made to kinds which, like ivy, have their roots in the earth at the foot of rocks and trees, and creep up the one or the other indifferently, using both merely for support and not as sources of nutriment, and clinging to them by means of special attachment-roots. The remark is applicable also to plants which live on the products of the decay of organic bodies, for example many tropical *Orchideæ, Dorstoniæ, Begoniæ,* and Ferns: and in cooler parts a number of Mosses and Liverworts. It is not difficult to explain this phenomenon in the case of species which derive their food from vegetable mould. The crannied wall of rock is, in a certain way, analogous to the rugged bark of a tree. The holes in the rock are filled in course of time with black vegetable mould, and plants with foliage, flowers, and fruit of a form adaptable to cracks and holes are able to establish themselves in the mould there, just as well as in that collected in crevices of bark. In one respect, indeed, they are even more favourably situated. For the humus in bark gets quite dry in long periods of drought, because no water is yielded to the bark by the wood of a tree, even though the latter be abundantly supplied with sap; whereas, in the case of rocks the probability is, the clefts being very deep, that even when the top layers of humus filling them yield up their water to the air, a certain restitution of moisture takes place from the deeper parts, which are never quite dry. Moreover, plants growing in the mould of rock crevices are able to send their roots down to much deeper strata than is possible in the case of bark. This is another reason why deep cracks in rocks, filled with humus, exhibit a richer flora, as a rule, than do the much shallower crevices in the bark of trees, although, as has been said before, the two habitats have many plants in common.

It is more difficult to explain how it happens that plants which derive their sustenance, not from the mould in crevices, but from the substance of the bark itself, and which lie flat against its surface, are also found adhering to walls of rock. As an example take *Frullania tamarisci*, a Liverwort with small brown bifurcating stems, which bear double rows of leaves and are of dendritic appearance. This plant grows equally well on the bark of pines or on the face of adjacent gneiss rocks. At first sight it would seem scarcely possible that a plant of this kind, clinging to the unfissured surface of rock, should be in a position to obtain organic compounds from its substratum. This is nevertheless the case. Closer inspection reveals the fact that the Liverwort does not adhere to blank rock, but to a part formerly clothed by rock-lichens. This inconspicuous incrustation of dead lichens is a complete substitute for the superficial layer of bark, and it is into it that the *Frullania tamarisci* sinks its roots. Another way by which food is supplied to plants adherent, like the above, to vertical and unfissured rocks will be discussed later on.

## SAPROPHYTES IN THE HUMUS OF WOODS, MEADOWS, AND MOORS.

Damp shady woods, especially pine woods, are particularly well furnished with saprophytes. Here again we find representatives of the same families as choose the bark of trees for their habitat. On the ground of woods, the most characteristic forms are mosses, fungi, lycopods, ferns, aroids, and orchids. The dark-brown humus, produced from dropped and decaying needles, is first of all covered by a rich carpet of mosses, such as the widely distributed *Hylocomium splendens*, *Hypnum triquetrum*, and *Hypnum Crista-castrensis*. The mouldered dust of dead trees has a clothing of *Tetraphis pellucida* and of *Webera nutans*, and decaying trunks are overgrown by the cushions of species of *Dicranum* (*Dicranum scoparium*, *D. congestum*, *Dicranodontium longirostre*), pale feathery mosses (*Hypnum uncinatum* and *H. reptile*) and various liverworts. Everywhere above the soft, ever-moist carpet of moss rise green fronds belonging to broad-leaved ferns.

Woods are also the special abode of fungi, and the damp ground is covered towards autumn by innumerable quantities of their curious fructifications. Dropped needles and cones, leaves and sticks strewn upon the ground, fallen trunks, and even the dark amorphous dust arising from the mouldering of these bodies and of the numerous roots ramifying in the ground, appear to be perforated by and wrapped in the protoplasmic threads of plasmoid fungi, or similarly invested by a plexus of filaments, the so-called mycelia of other forms of fungi. Amongst the scaly fragments of bark, peeling from the trees, they appear in the form of slimy strings, or as a dark trellis and net-work, inserted between the bark and wood of the rotting tree; on the stripped white trunk they are in dark zigzag lines like those of forked lightning; and between, the white mycelia of huge toadstools and tremellas are woven in all directions. Here and there large areas of the brown decaying soil are flecked and speckled by these mycelia, and even the dead stems of the mosses on the ground are festooned with white fleece, and wrapped round by hyphae.

It is worth while to glance too at the reciprocal relations of these woodland plants. We find mosses, lycopods, and various ferns and phanerogams living upon the fallen twigs and needles, and on the mouldering roots of pines and fir-trees. The dead remains of these plants afford sustenance to the fungi, which lift their fructification above the bed of moss. In their turn the rotting fructifications of the larger fungi form a nutrient substratum for smaller fungi, which cover the decaying caps and stalks with a dark-green velvet. Lastly, these little fungi, too, fall a prey to corrupting bacteria, and are resolved into the same simple inorganic compounds as were absorbed from the air and earth, in the first instance, by the pines and fir-trees. In the depths of forests there is going on, for the most part unseen by us, a mysterious stir and strife, accompanied by an uninterrupted process of exchange between the living and the dead, and a marvellous transformation of those very substances whose secret we have only partially succeeded in solving.

The results of cultivation have proved that in the group of flowering-plants belonging to the woodlands of Central and Northern Europe, which derive sustenance partially or entirely from the organic compounds afforded by the humus, are to be included, amongst others, the various species of coral-wort (*Dentaria bulbifera, D. digitata, D. enneaphyllos*), *Circæa alpina, Galium rotundifolium,* and *Linnæa borealis,* and above all a large number of orchids. Of these, *Dentaria* prefers mould produced from the beech leaves, and *Circæa, Galium,* and *Linnæa* appertain to the mould of pine-woods. Of the orchids some are provided with green leaves, as, for instance, the delicate little *Listera cordata, Goodyera repens* remarkable for its villous petals, and the various species of *Cephalanthera, Epipactis,* and *Platanthera;* others, such as *Limodorum abortivum,* the bird's-nest orchis, the coral-root, and *Epipogium aphyllum* have none. *Limodorum abortivum* belongs rather to the warmer districts of Central Europe. It has fleshy root-fibres, twisted and twined into an inextricable ball, and a slender steel-blue stem, over half a metre in height, bearing a lax spike of fairly large flowers, which subsequently become paler in colour. The bird's-nest orchis (*Neottia Nidus-avis*) is of wide distribution both in forests of pines and in those composed of angiospermous trees. Its stem and flowers are of a light-brown colour, unusual in plants, but somewhat like that of oak-wood. The flowers have no scent, and the numerous roots, issuing from the subterranean part of the stem and imbedded in humus, remind one in form and colour of earth-worms, and together constitute a strange tangled mass as large as a fist. The latter has been thought to resemble a bird's nest, and to this is due the name of the plant. The coral-root (*Corallorhiza innata*), unlike the bird's-nest orchis, has no root at all; but, on the other hand, the subterranean portion of the stem, the so-called rhizome, possesses a distant resemblance to the root-tangle of *Neottia*. Pale-brownish branches of this rhizome, which bifurcate repeatedly at their obtuse and whitish extremities, looking as if they had been subjected to pressure for a time, and all the short lobe-shaped branchlets thereby spread out into one plane, lie closely crowded together, sometimes crossing one another, and so form a body which vividly recalls the appearance of a piece of coral. This underground coral-like stem-structure develops each year pale greenish shoots which rise above the ground and bear small flowers speckled with yellow, white, and violet, and exhaling a scent of vanilla; later, green fruits of a comparatively large size develop, turning brown when they ripen.

The fourth mentioned of these pale wood-orchids, the *Epipogium aphyllum*, is at once the rarest and most curious of them all. Like the coral-root it has no true roots. Its rhizome so closely resembles the latter's that it is easy to mistake the one for the other; but they may be distinguished by the fact that in the case of *Epipogium* the rhizome sends out long filiform shoots, which swell up like tubers at their tips, and may be regarded as subterranean runners. The swollen extremity becomes the point of origin of a new coral-like structure, which develops at about the distance of a span from the old one; whilst the latter, usually exhausted after flowering, gradually perishes. This coral-like stem lives of course underground, and is not visible till one lifts away the moss from the mould on the ground. It is often completely imbedded in sandy loam, lying immediately beneath the black mould. Many years frequently go by without the *Epipogium* producing flowers. The plant meanwhile lives entirely underground. In the course of a summer in which it has not flowered, anyone not having previous exact knowledge of its whereabouts might pass by without dreaming that the bed of moss and humus on his path concealed this strange growth. The flowering stems which at length emerge, when there is a warm summer, are right above the place where they branch off from the subterranean rhizome. They are thickened in a fusiform manner, and have, for the most part on one side, a reddish or purplish tinge. Everything connected with them is tense, smooth, full of sap, and almost opalescent. The few flowers that are borne by the stem are comparatively large, and emit a strong perfume resembling that of the Brazilian genus of orchids *Stanhopea*. The colouring, too, a dull yellowish white with touches of pale red and violet, reminds one of these tropical orchids.

The sight of the pale-coloured plants lifting their heads, at flowering time, from the tumid carpet of moss has all the stranger effect because, as a rule, no other flowering plants are visible in any direction. The flowers are suspended by delicate drooping pedicels, and owing to their peculiar colour, fleshy consistence, and form —the erect concave petal like a Phrygian cap or helmet, and the others stretched out like prehensile limbs—remind one of the opalescent medusæ which float on the blue sea waves. The propriety of the analogy is enhanced by the fact that the form and colour of other saprophytes produced near *Epipogium* in woods have a striking resemblance to the animals and wracks which inhabit the sea-bottom. The fungi, known by the name of club-tops, much-branched, flesh-coloured, yellow or white *Clavariæ*, which often adorn whole tracts of ground in a wood, imitate the structure of corals; *Hydneæ* are like sea-urchins, and *Geaster* like a star-fish, whilst the various species of *Tremella*, *Exidia*, and *Guepinia*, which are flesh-pink, orange, or brownish in colour, and the white translucent *Tremellodon gelatinosum*, resemble gelatinous sponges. The small stiff toad-stools (*Marasmius*), which raise their slender stalks on fallen pine-needles, remind one of the rigid *Acetabularia*. Other toad-stools, with flat or convex caps exhibiting concentric bands and stripes, such as the different species of *Craterellus*, have an appearance similar to the salt-water alga known by the name of *Padina*. Dark species of *Geoglossum* imitate the brown *Fucoideæ*; and one may fancy the red warts of *Lycogala Epidendron*, a plasmoid fungus inhabiting the rotten wood of dead weather-beaten trees, to be red sea-anemones with their tentacles drawn in, clinging to gray rocks. However far-fetched this comparison between the two localities may seem at first sight, everyone who has had an opportunity of thoroughly observing the characteristic forms of vegetable and animal life in woods, and at the bottom of the sea, will inevitably be convinced of its accuracy.

Meadow-land, rich in humus, is much more sparsely occupied by saprophytes than the soil of woods. There is no lack of the strange forms of toad-stools and puff-balls, whose fructifications often spring up in thousands, especially in the autumn, in company with the meadow-saffron: but in numbers they are not to be compared with those which occur in the mould of woods. Amongst ferns and phanerogams, the following species are dependent upon the organic compounds arising from the decomposition of the humus: Moonwort (*Botrychium Lunaria*), numerous orchids, blue and violet-flowered gentians, the famous *Arnica*, Polygalaceæ, and more especially several grasses, chiefly the Matweed (*Nardus stricta*) which, when once it has struck root in the humus, extends in dense masses over large areas. Several plants, too, adorning alpine pastures, and belonging for the most part to the same families as the species mentioned above, are to be regarded as humus-plants. Such are the Alpine Club-moss (*Lycopodium alpinum*), the dark-flowered *Nigritella nigra*, and several other sub-alpine orchids; a number of small, sometimes tiny, gentians (*Gentiana nivalis*, *G. prostrata*, *G. glacialis*, *G. nana*, *Lomatogonium Carinthiacum*), *Valeriana celtica*, the Scottish asphodel (*Tofieldia borealis*) of the north, a few grasses, sedges, and rushes (*e.g. Agrostis alpina, Carex curvula, Juncus trifidus*), various anemones, campions, umbelliferous plants, violets and campanulas (*e.g. Anemone alpina, Silene Pumilio, Meum Mutellina, Viola alpina, Campanula alpina*) and several mosses (*e.g. Dicranum elongatum* and *Polytrichum strictum*) which clothe the humus on stretches of turf and in inclosures.

Many of the plants also that are native on the black graphitic soil in hollows of high mountain ridges take up organic food from their substratum. These include *Meesia alpina* and various other mosses produced exclusively in places of the kind; and, above all, numerous Primulaceæ and Gentianeæ (*Primula glutinosa, Soldanella pusilla, Gentiana Bavarica*). It seems, moreover, to be by no means a matter of indifference to these plants at what temperature, and in what state of the air, in respect of moisture, the decomposition of humus takes place. If species which grow abundantly in these localities are dug up and transferred, together with the black earth in which their roots are imbedded, into a garden, and are there cultivated in such a way that the external conditions are as nearly as possible those of the original habitat; or if young plants are reared from seed in the same black humus-filled earth, they thrive only for a short time, soon begin to fade, and within the space of a year are dead; whereas, alpine plants belonging to the same altitude above the sea, but rooted in loamy or sandy earth, flourish excellently in gardens as well. Various moor-plants (*e.g. Lycopodium inundatum, Eriophorum vaginatum, Trientalis Europæa*) only live a short time in a garden even though the clods of peat, in which their roots are imbedded, are transplanted with them. This fact can scarcely be explained except by supposing that the organic compounds, produced by the decay of vegetable remains on alpine heights and moors, are essentially different from those evolved by similar matter under the changed conditions of temperature and moisture occurring in a garden at a lower level. Gardeners say that the peat and black graphitic soil from the slopes of snowy mountains turn sour in gardens, and they may be to this extent right, that in all probability the humic acids produced under altered circumstances are different.

## SPECIAL RELATIONS OF SAPROPHYTES TO THEIR NUTRIENT SUBSTRATUM.

In the plants under discussion, the cells which absorb organic compounds are, taken all in all, very similar to those which absorb mineral food-salts. Where there is no cell-membrane, as in the case of Plasmodia and Euglenæ, the food diffuses through the so-called ectoplasm, or outer layer of the protoplasm, into the interior of the cell. Saprophytic marine and fresh-water algæ are able to absorb the products of decay in the water around by means of their superficial layers of cells. The mycelia of fungi have the power of taking in nourishment with special rapidity. Each hypha, or more accurately, each long, delicate-walled cell of a mycelium is, to a certain extent, an absorptive cell; its entire surface is capable of exercising the function of suction and of withdrawing from the environment, along with water, the very substances which are needed. The coral-like underground stem of

*Epipogium aphyllum*, as well as that of the "Coral-root", which is entirely destitute of roots, develop fascicles of absorptive cells on their ramifications, and on special little swellings; and the white subterranean stem structures of *Bartsia alpina* are also provided with long absorptive cells. The white, fusiform, tuberously thickened, underground stems of the Alpine Enchanter's Nightshade (*Circæa alpina*) exhibit no roots during autumn and winter, nor until such time as new leafy stems sprout from them and lift themselves into the daylight; they only have scattered club-shaped absorptive cells. Yet it is inconceivable that the few absorptive cells meet the entire requirements of these plants at the season of the development of their aërial stems. Food is absorbed in these cases also by the epidermal cells of the entire tuber, underground stem, or coral-like rhizome, as the case may be. The epidermal cells of these subterranean caulomes which lie immediately in contact with the black mould or humus on the ground of forests, have such thin and tender walls that they are quite as well adapted to the absorption of nutriment as are the projecting absorptive cells; indeed the club-shaped absorptive cells on the small tubers of Enchanter's Nightshade exhibit somewhat thicker walls than those forming the general epidermis of these tubers.

We may compare food-absorption as performed by these coral-like and tuberous structures, imbedded in decaying plant residues, with the action of tape-worms in process of sucking in through their entire epidermis the fluid filling the intestines they inhabit. The epidermal cells of the thick tortuous root-fibres of *Neottia Nidus-avis* are all capable of absorbing nutriment, though they do not project as tubes, but are tabular, and have their outer walls, which are in immediate contact with the nutrient soil, only slightly arched outwards (see fig. 16 [2]). The green leafy orchids rooted in the vegetable mould of woods and meadows are, on the contrary, furnished with very long tubular absorption cells; and these cells do not wither and collapse forthwith when the root elongates, but long retain their vigour and activity. Whereas in the case of land plants adapted to mineral food-salts, the tubular absorption cells ("root-hairs") are limited to a narrow zone behind the growing point of the root and always die comparatively soon; in the case of orchids, having cylindrical roots imbedded in vegetable mould, these structures appear to be beset from end to end with long scattered tubular absorption cells, which are retained even through the drought of summer or the frost of winter right into the next period of vegetative activity; and these cells occur most abundantly in parts of the ground where there happens to be a bed of humus or mouldering remains particularly amenable to their purpose. Similar relations are found to exist in the case of the dichotomously-branched roots of the Club-moss. They are twisted in spirals and bore into the vegetable mould like corkscrews, and their absorption cells form in some places regular tassels, which are completely cemented over with fine black mould. The roots of grasses which, like the Mat-grass, live on the decomposition-products of vegetable mould, are also distinguished by strikingly long absorption cells, which grow in black or brown humus and there undergo the strangest bends and contortions. When, for instance, a fragment of a dead root or underground stem, peculiarly suitable for absorption, is encountered, it is regularly embraced by the suction cells, and as great an absorbent surface as possible is thus brought into contact with the nutritious fragment.    Indeed, the development of suction cells on the roots of many gentians (viz. *Gentiana ciliata*, *G. germanica*, *G. Austriaca*, and *G. Rhatica*) is confined to the parts of the root-branches, which, in the course of their passage through the vegetable mould, have come into contact with a particularly nutritious portion of it.    Wherever there is contact, the root is thickened, and absorption cells project unilaterally from the epidermis and grow into the decaying fragment of wood or bark which is to be drained of its nutrient

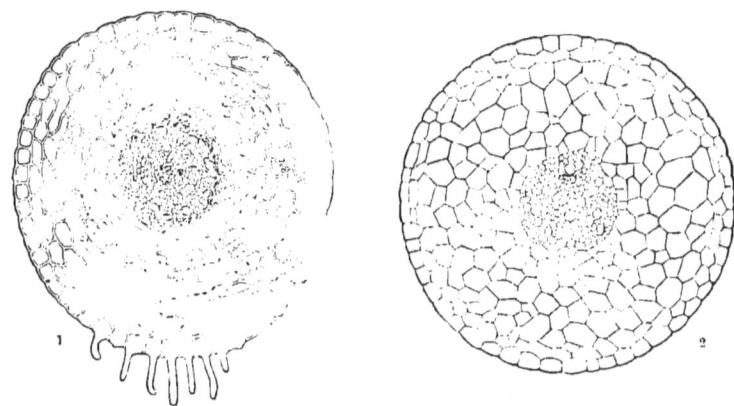

Fig. 16.—Transverse section through absorption-roots of Saprophytes.
ı *Gentiana Rhatica.*        ₂ The Bird's Nest Orchis (*Neottia Nidus-avis*).

material (see fig. 16¹).    Roots of this kind remind one of the root-structures of parasites which are furnished with so-called "haustoria", and which will be discussed more in detail in subsequent pages.    But they are different in that they absorb food not from living but from decaying parts of the nutrient substratum.

Most plants that grow on the vegetable mould of alpine meadows, and the black earth deposited by snow-drifts in mountainous regions, develop flat instead of tubular epidermal cells as suction cells, and in this resemble marsh-plants.    In many of these cases the roots are so abundantly and minutely ramified that they form a plexus investing the humus.    This is likewise true of the absorptive cells on the rhizoids of mosses.

Plants which lie flat against the bark of trees and have no connection with the ground, so that they are unable to derive nutriment from it, have a very peculiar method of maintaining themselves.    Their roots, rhizoids, or hyphæ, as the case may be, either grow straight into the bark or are merely adnate to its surface.    In the latter case they are exposed on one side to the open air, and form more or less projecting lines and ridges ramifying in all directions, often constituting a regular trellis-work cemented to the bark.    Sometimes, too, they are represented by thicker ropes or bands which run longitudinally down or encircle the trunk. These structures certainly serve as instruments of attachment, but at the same time they also absorb nutriment from the substratum, the decaying bark upon which the plant is epiphytic. In periods of drought the absorption of food by plants of this kind is, in general, interrupted and suspended. But when the rainy season commences and there is a long duration of wet weather, water trickling over the surface of boughs and trunks washes the bark, cleanses it as it were, and, falling lower and lower, brings down not only tiny loosened particles of bark but mineral and organic dust which has been blown into it by the wind; it dissolves all the soluble matter it finds on its way, and so reaches the roots, rhizoids, and hyphæ which adhere to the bark, in the form of a solution of mineral and organic compounds, chiefly the latter. The trickling water is in some measure stopped by the projecting ridges of these adnate structures; here and there also it deposits particles mechanically suspended in it, and so it conveys to these curious epiphytes the requisite nourishment.

In the same way, no doubt, epiphytes which grow upon other epiphytes are nourished. In more inclement regions, the green bark, stem, and, less frequently, the green leaves of the mistletoe are found to be beset by mosses and lichens; and, in the tropics it is a common phenomenon for mosses, liverworts, and even small kinds of Bromeliaceæ to settle on the green and still living leaves of Bromeliaceæ, Orchideæ, and Loranthaceæ, although they are certainly not properly parasitic, and only use their absorption cells for the purpose of clinging to the thick epidermis of the living leaves or stems which support them. The principal part of the liquid substances absorbed by these plants is conveyed to them by the rain-water that washes over the substratum.

The species of plants also which have been mentioned as sometimes growing on smooth vertical faces of rock, though the bark of trees is their usual habitat, are able to obtain their food-materials in a similar way. If the summit of a cliff is covered by a continuous carpet of plants, or if ledges and terraces projecting somewhat from its face support sods of grass, tufts of moss, and various small kinds of bushes, it must inevitably happen when there is an abundant fall of rain that the water flowing down the declivity conveys with it organic compounds in solution. First the sods of grass and moss on the ledges and on the top of the cliff are wetted, then the humus, which is their substratum, becomes saturated, and such part of the water as cannot be retained by this humus, or does not percolate into the cracks and crevices of the rock, trickles down from the ledges and moistens the face of the rock as it soaks down to the bottom. A rocky declivity is thus washed in the same way as is the bark of trees, and small fragments of organic and inorganic bodies must of necessity be rinsed out and carried down by the trickling water, and then again be deposited in heaps where projecting obstacles are encountered. It is just in the tracks along which the water flows down steep rocks of the kind that the plants of which we have made mention are situated.

Associated with the above are generally a number of other plants, for the most part microscopic, all of which cannot be classed as saprophytes, but which, in order to be able to thrive in the tracks of trickling water, must have the capacity of surviving desiccation for weeks, and even months, on the barren rock after having been previously supplied with copious moisture for a time. In the case of lichen-growths in particular these are very favourite sites; and when the lichens cover a large area they attract one's attention from afar. In limestone ranges, the light-gray rock of steep declivities, interrupted by ledges covered with grass and low brushwood, is extensively coloured by dark vertical bands and streaks, and the effect is the same as if a dye had flowed from the ledges over the face of the rock. These dark streaks indicate the course of the water which oozes from the humus and renders possible the existence of numberless minute plants on the precipitous face, in particular several dark crustaceous lichens (*Acarospora glaucocarpa, Aspicilia flavida, Lecidea fuscorubens, Opegrapha lithyrga,* &c.).

The quantity of organic compounds brought down in solution by the water which filters from the layers of humus on rocky ledges, and that which trickles down the bark of trees, is, however, very small. Still, it is amply sufficient to meet the requirements of the plants occurring at the spots in question. The claims made by them upon their nutrient source are very moderate. We may here recall the instances previously mentioned of mycelia of fungi which have been found satisfied with the scarcely perceptible quantities of organic compounds in water filtering into the shaft of a mine, and in the pure water of a mountain spring respectively. To these instances must here be added the production of mycelia in the wooden pipes through which the clear water of mountain springs is conveyed. After these pipes, which are made from the trunks of pines, have been used as conduits for years, and their inner layers of wood have long since been washed out, the mycelium of the fungus *Lenzites sepiaria* is not infrequently developed within them, and in such luxuriance, indeed, that it forms great yellowish-gray flocculent masses, which issue from the pipe's inner surface, and float in the stream of running water. In time these flocculent masses increase in the clear spring-water to such a degree that the pipes become completely blocked, and the flow of water is arrested. And yet the water conducted through the pipes is so pure, where it enters into and issues from them, that the residue obtained by the evaporation of hundreds of litres afforded no trace of any organic matter.

Seeing that most saprophytes absorb only such a comparatively small amount of organic matter, one is all the more surprised to notice that a large number of them fall suddenly, at certain times, into the opposite extreme. People speak of things rapidly produced in abundance as "mushroom-growths", and as "shooting up like fungi". The fructifications of many fungi are in fact developed with a rapidity which borders on the miraculous. The various species of *Coprinus* living on dung produce their long-stalked, cap-shaped fructifications during the night, and by the evening of the next day the caps have already fallen to pieces, and are in a state of decomposition, and nothing is to be seen in their place but a black deliquescent mass like a blot of ink. The weight of this fructification, thus matured within twenty-four hours, is certainly many times as great as that of the entire mycelium which produced it; and it is quite incomprehensible how this mycelium, which for weeks only achieves a moderate development, and adds but little to its dimensions, is in a position suddenly, and in so short a time, to supply the amount of water and organic compounds requisite for the building up of the fructification. *Epipogium aphyllum* exhibits a similar property. After producing nothing for two years excepting a few branches on its subterranean stem, it develops all at once and in a very short space of time fleshy stems with large flowers, and one asks with astonishment how the relatively small coral-shaped stock sets about obtaining the quantity of nutrient materials necessary for the construction of these flowering stems. We are here confronted again with the great mystery of periodicity, the solution of which we must for the present forego.

Saprophytes are much more fastidious as regards the quality of their nutriment than one might expect. It is true that certain fungi are produced wherever there are plants in a state of decomposition, and to them it is quite indifferent whether the mouldered dust, which serves as a nutrient soil for their mycelia, has arisen from one species or another. Also in the case of orchids imbedded in vegetable mould, and in that of most of the mosses and liverworts adherent to the barks of trees, it is, as a rule, of no consequence whether the tree constituting the substratum is a conifer or a dicotyledon. But a large number of species are associated with the decaying remains of particular plants or animals only. For example, certain small species of *Marasmius*, belonging to the group of the Agarici, occur only on mouldering pine-needles; another small fungus, *Antennatula pinophila*, is found exclusively on fallen needles of the Silver Fir; *Hypoderma Lauri*, which resembles small black type on rotting laurel leaves, and the tiny *Septoria Menyanthis* on leaves of the Bog-bean (*Menyanthes trifoliata*) lying under water in a state of decay. The cinnamon-coloured receptacles of *Lenzites sepiaria* only grow from prostrate trunks of conifers, and the black fuliginous fructifications of *Bulgaria polymorpha* only on those of oaks. A small discoid fungus named *Poronia punctata*, white with black spots on the top, is only found on cow-dung; another fungus, *Gymnoascus uncinatus* on that of mice, and *Ctenomyces serratus* on decaying goose feathers.

That many mosses are also very fastidious in the selection of their substratum has already been intimated. Just as in the Alps *Splachnum ampullaceum* is only found growing on the putrefying dung of cattle, so in arctic regions the splendid, large-fruited *Splachnum luteum* and *S. rubrum* occur exclusively on that of reindeer. *Tetraplodon urceolatus* is met with on mountains always with decaying excrements of chamois, goats, or sheep for a substratum, whilst *Tetraplodon angustatus* chooses the excrements of carnivorous animals, and *Tayloria serrata* is only seen near cow-chalets on decomposing human faeces. The circumstances of the occurrence of another moss belonging to the Splachnaceae, i.e. *Tayloria Rudolfiana* is also very interesting. It grows usually on the branches of old trees, especially maples in sub-alpine regions, and one is tempted to believe that in respect of its nutrient substratum it is an exception to the rule of the rest of the

Splachnaceæ. But on closer examination there is convincing evidence that this moss also lives only on animal dung undergoing putrefaction. For remains of broken mouse and bird bones are invariably to be discovered in the substratum, and there can be no doubt that the *Tayloria* chooses for its site boughs of old trees upon which birds of prey have dropped their excrements. Of the mosses living on the bark itself, one instance is also worth mentioning. Whereas in the case of most species of the genus *Dicranum*, the mouldering residues of conifers constitute the favourite substratum; there is one species, viz. *Dicranum Sauteri*, which is found only on the bark of the beech. The weather-worn bark of this tree is seen, in sub-alpine districts, covered with the most brilliant emerald-green films of the above-named moss; whilst on adjacent pines and fir-trees no trace of it can be found.

## PLANTS WITH TRAPS AND PITFALLS TO ENSNARE ANIMALS.

A number of plants exhibit contrivances which obviously have for their object the capture and retention of such small creatures as may fly or creep on to their leaves; and it has been ascertained by searching experiments that the majority of these plants use the animals they capture, in one way or another, as sources of nutriment. For the most part the animals that are caught are insects, and hence the term "insectivorous plants" has been applied to the class in question. The flesh of the insect being the part of it principally serviceable for food, the name "carnivorous" or "flesh-eating", or better, perhaps, "flesh-consuming" plants has also been used; and seeing that the most important part of the whole process is really the digestion, or taking in of organic compounds from the captured animals after they are dead, we might call those plants which are furnished with organs for the absorption of the dissolved flesh of animals ensnared by them, "flesh-digesting" plants as well. As will appear from the following discussion of the subject, no one of these names completely covers the wonderful phenomena in question, and it is scarcely possible to find a short and not too cumbrous expression which shall henceforward exclude all misconceptions.

In round numbers we may estimate the plants which capture animals and demolish them for food at five hundred. Within this comparatively small range, however, the variety of the mechanism for seizure and absorption of nutritive matter is so great that in order to give a general picture of them it is necessary to classify them into several sections and groups. In the first section we have a series of plant-forms wherein chambers are developed, which admit of the entrance of small animals, but not of their escape. The organs of capture and digestion of the plants belonging to this section exhibit no external movements of any kind, and are thereby differentiated from the forms belonging to the second section, which perform definite movements, in response to a stimulus caused by the contact of the animals, with the object of covering the prey with as great a quantity of digestive fluid as possible. Lastly, there is a third section wherein the individual forms are neither provided with pitfalls nor capable of performing special movements, but have leaves converted into lime-twigs and on them animals stick and are also digested.

The first and most extensive group included in the first section is that of Utriculariæ or Bladderworts. Their capturing apparatus consists of little bladders with orifices closed in each case by a valve, which permits objects to penetrate into

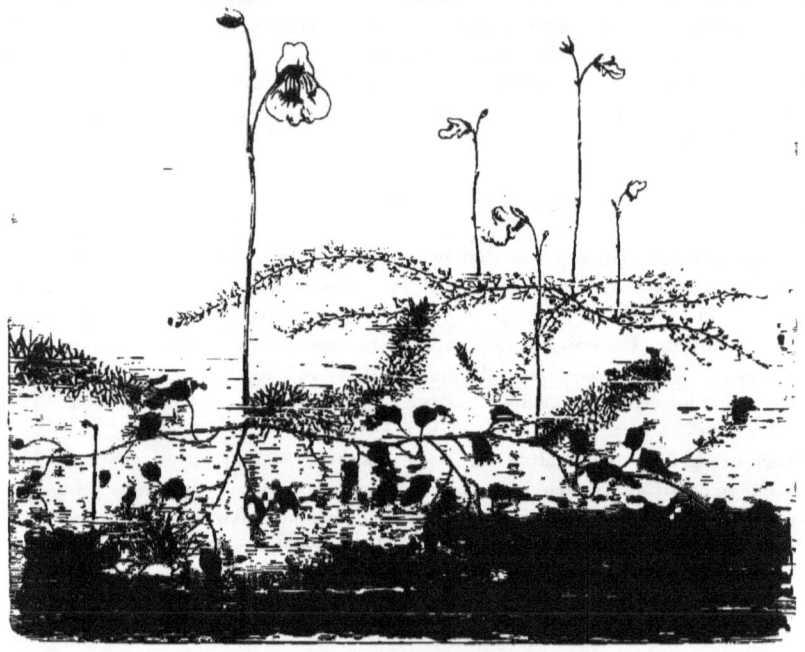

Fig. 17.—Bladderworts.
In the foreground *Utricularia Grafiana*; in the background *Utricularia minor*.

the cavity of the bladder, but not to issue out of it. The Utriculariæ are rootless plants which live suspended in water, and, according to the season of the year, either sink down to the bottom or ascend to just below the surface. Upon the approach of winter, when animal life is gradually disappearing in the chilled and freezing upper layers of water, the leaves at the extremities of the floating stems are enlarged and form spherical winter buds; the older parts of the stems together with the leaves die, their cavities hitherto occupied by air are filled with water, and they sink to the bottom drawing down with them the winter buds. After the winter these buds elongate, detach themselves from the old stems and ascend near the surface, where innumerable little aquatic animals are swimming to and fro, and there develop two rows of lateral branches in rapid succession. Either all of these are thickly covered with leaves which are divided into thread-like, repeatedly bifurcating, segments, or else only half of them are thus clothed with leaves whilst the other half bear the before-mentioned bladders. The former is the case in *Utricularia minor*, the plant represented in the background of the figure on p. 120; and the latter in *Utricularia Grafiana*, which is drawn in the foreground. In instances of the former kind obliquely ellipsoidal bladders are to be seen on short stalks on the principal segments of the leaves, usually quite near their angles of bifurcation. In the smaller species, such as *Utricularia minor*, they have a diameter of about 2 mm. In individuals of the latter kind the bladders have longer stalks, and are about 5 mm. in diameter. They are always pale-green and partially transparent. Each bladder is somewhat flattened at the sides and exhibits a markedly convex dorsal surface and slightly curved lateral surface. An orifice, whose border is fringed with peculiar stiff tapering bristles, leads into the interior of each of these stalked bladders. The aperture has four rounded angles and is framed as it were, by a pair of lips. The under lip is strongly thickened, and is furnished with a solid cushion projecting into the interior of the bladder. From the upper lip hangs a thin transparent, obliquely-

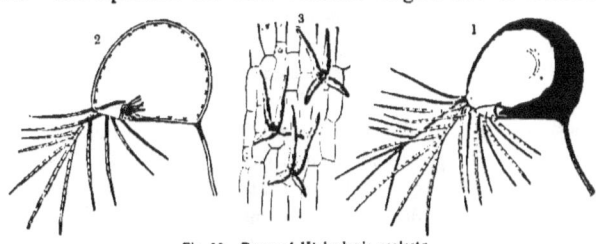

Fig. 18.—Traps of *Utricularia neglecta*.

¹ A bladder magnified (×4).  ² Section of a bladder.  ³ Absorption-cells on the internal surface of the bladder (×250).

placed valve (see fig. 18 ²), the free edge of which rests upon the inner surface of the cushion before referred to, and closes the entire orifice. This valve is very elastic and yields easily to any pressure from outside. A tiny animal is able, by pressing against it, to force a way without difficulty from the nether lip into the interior of the bladder, and to slip in through the opening thus made. But as soon as the animal has got inside, and ceases to press upon the valve, its elasticity brings it back upon the under lip again. It cannot be opened by pressure from within; for, resting as it does ·upon the projecting cushion, it is impossible for the little prisoner to force it over the latter in an outward direction.

The whole apparatus forms a trap for small aquatic animals, they being able, as before observed, to slip into the bladder but not to get out again. Most animals that enter make, it is true, efforts to escape, but they are all in vain. Many perish in a short time—about twenty-four hours—others live from two to three, or, in some cases, even as much as six days. But in the end they must suffer death by suffocation or starvation, and they then decay, and the products of their decomposition are sucked in by special absorption cells developed within the bladder. These absorption cells (see fig. 18 ³) are linear-oblong and somewhat like little rods in shape, and they line the whole internal surface of the cavity of the bladder. They are arranged in fours, each group of four forming a cross and being united by a common basal cell. The basal cells themselves are intercalated amongst the cells lining the bladder. The organic substances from the decaying bodies of captured animals are sucked up by these stellate groups of cells, and from them pass into the basal cells, and later, into the other adjacent cells of the bladder and those of the plant at large.

The majority of the animals caught by the bladders are crustaceans. It is principally larvæ and adult individuals of small species of *Cypris*, *Daphnia*, and *Cyclops* that fall into the trap; but larvæ of gnats, and various other small insects, little worms, and infusoria, are also not infrequently met with imprisoned in the bladders. The number of animals captured is comparatively large. In single bladders the remnants of no less than twenty-four small crustaceans have been observed. The prey secured by *Utricularia minor* (fig. 17), which lives in little pools of still water in peat-bogs, is very abundant. The North American *Utricularia clandestina* seems also to use its capturing apparatus with great success.

What it is that induces the animals to press upon the valves and so fall into the trap is not fully explained. We may suppose that they expect to find food in the bladder-cavity, or that they hope it will afford a shelter where they can rest for a time and be protected from their pursuers. The last suggestion is especially supported by the circumstance that the approach to the valve-covered orifice of the bladder is guarded against the intrusion of larger animals by stiff sharp bristles which stick out from it (fig. 18¹). Only very small animals, which can easily slip in between the relatively large bristles, reach the inside of the bladder, whilst larger creatures, which would injure the whole apparatus, are prevented from coming near it. Thus, the most probable explanation is that lesser animals pursued by greater take refuge in the hiding-places behind the bristles, and so fall into the trap. Another very striking fact is that the bladders of Utriculariæ, living in still water, look delusively like certain Ostracoda, especially species of the genus *Daphnia*. The bladder itself resembles the shell-covered body in size and form, and the bristles the antennæ and swimmerets of one of these crustaceans. Whether there is any significance in this curious similarity of outward appearance must be left undecided.

The majority of Utriculariæ live in pools of water beside foot-tracks on moors and in the little collections of water between clumps of reeds in peat-bogs; and these are precisely the haunts of the little creatures that are to fall into the traps. Every handful of water that one scoops up contains hundreds of midge-larvæ, water-fleas, Ostracoda, and one-eyed Cyclops, which rush about promiscuously, pursuing and seizing one another. One species of these plants lives in the mountains of Brazil in the rain-filled receptacles of *Tillandsia* plants. The *Tillandsia* is allied to the pine-apple, and has rosettes of concave leaves, the latter resting one upon the other in such a way as to form a niche or cavity in front of each leaf which fills with rain like a cistern. Many different kinds of small animals are always swimming about in these little cisterns, and almost every one of the latter is the sphere of activity of an individual *Utricularia nelumbifolia*. This plant is remarkable also from the fact that long runners are thrown out from its stems, which grow across, in wide arches, from its cistern to a neighbouring *Tillandsia*, where it selects one of the reservoirs in the rosettes as a new site and dips down into the water—a fantastic method of propagation of which we shall speak again on another occasion.

A few Utricularieæ do not live in water at all, but grow amongst mosses, liver-worts, and lycopods, in the vegetable mould filling the clefts and crevices of rocks, and the bark-fissures of old trees. Of this habit, for example, is the pretty Brazilian *Utricularia montana*, which, in spite of the difference of its habitat, is provided with an apparatus for capturing animals agreeing in all essential respects with the description already given. The bladders used by these plants for pur-poses of prey are produced on subterranean filiform stems which thread their way in the vegetable mould and wefts of decaying moss-stems, and here and there swell into tubers. The bladders are hyaline and transparent, and are filled with watery liquid, sometimes also with air. They are only 1 millimeter in diameter, but are present in large numbers. The entrance into these bladders is much more con-cealed than in the species that live in water. The dorsal surface of the bladder being still more strongly curved, the position of the orifice is altered so as to be quite close to the little stalk of the bladder. In addition, the orifice is, as it were, roofed over, and thereby protected against the possibility of being stopped up by particles of earth, and the passage leading to it is very narrow. That, in spite of the difficulty of entrance, a number of minute animals do seek a hiding-place here is proved by the circumstance that, besides various infusoria, rhizopoda, and creatures of that kind inhabiting damp earth, species of *Acarus* and larvæ of other animals have been found, both dead and alive, in the bladders.

With this first group of insectivorous plants, wherein the capturing apparatus includes a valve to prevent the egress of such animals as fall into the trap, is associated in the first section a second group, viz. that of the ascidia-bearing or pitcher-plants, in which the foliage-leaves are converted into pitfalls, and the escape of the captured prey prevented by a number of points lining the inner wall of the cavity, and directed from the aperture towards the closed bottom. There is an extraordinary variety in the form of the pitfalls. Sometimes they are tubular, utricular, or funnel-shaped cavities, sometimes mug or pitcher-shaped, or urceolate; in some cases these are straight, in others bowed like sickles, or spirally twisted. They always arise from the part of the petiole upon which the lamina immediately rests. The lamina is always relatively small, being represented in the majority of the traps by a scale or lobe, and it only appears to be an appendage of the large expanded and hollowed-out petiole. In many pitcher-plants the little lamina looks like a lid placed over the orifice to the pitfall, as, for instance, is shown in the illustration (fig. 21⁴), whilst in others (*Nepenthes ampullaria* and *N. vittata*) it has the form of a handle or stalk, and serves as a place for animals visiting the pitchers to alight upon.

In each pitfall there are always three kinds of contrivance to be distinguished: first, a device for the allurement of animals; secondly, an arrangement for entrapping the prey enticed, which at the same time prevents individuals once imprisoned from returning and escaping through the entrance hole; and thirdly, a structure for causing the decay or dissolution of the dead animals at the bottom of the pitfalls, and for rendering possible the absorption of the products of decomposition as nutriment. The means of allurement are similar to those which cause the visits of small creatures to flowers, that is to say, principally honey and bright and varied coloration, whereby the nectar-secreting spots are recognized from afar, especially by flying insects. The escape of animals when they have once entered the cavity of a petiole is prevented, as has been already mentioned, by a fringe of sharp hairs pointed downwards, or by various spinous structures on the inner

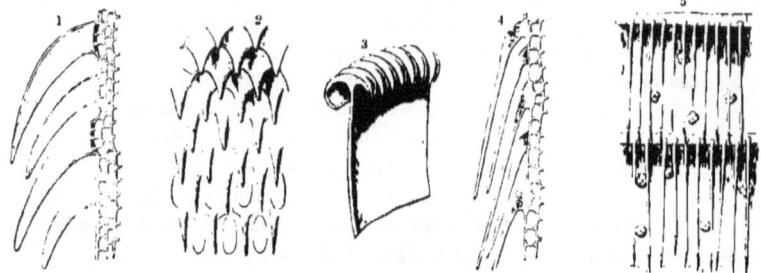

Fig. 19. –Spinous Structures in the Pitfalls of Carnivorous Plants.

1 *Genlisea*; a piece of the tube seen from inside. 2 *Heliamphora nutans*; spines on the walls of pitfalls. 3 *Sarracenia purpurea*; a piece of the lining of the pitcher near the orifice seen from inside. 4 *Sarracenia purpurea*; longitudinal section through the membrane covered with spinous bristles in the lower part of the pitcher. 5 *Nepenthes hybrida*; fringe of spines at the orifice of the pitcher. 1, 2, 4, 5 greatly magnified; 3 slightly magnified.

surface of the cavity. The decomposition and dissolution of the prey are effected by fluids secreted by special cells at the bottom of the utricles and pitchers.

But although in respect of the consecutive and co-ordinate operation of these three kinds of contrivance, all ascidia-bearing and pitcher-plants resemble one another, there are considerable individual divergences as to structure and function that it is well worth while to study in some detail the most noticeable of them.

One of the most noteworthy is the genus *Genlisea*, which is nearly related to Utriculariaceæ in the structure of its flowers and fruit. It is composed of a dozen species growing in water and marshy places. Of these one is a native of tropical and southern Africa, whilst others are found in Brazil and the West Indies. In addition to ordinary leaves, which in them are spatulate, most of the Genliseæ possess leaf-structures metamorphosed so as to constitute pitfalls. Each pitfall consists of a long, narrow, cylindrical utricle, which at its blind end is enlarged into a bladder, whilst at the narrow orifice at the opposite end are placed two peculiar ribbon-shaped processes twisted spirally. The orifice of the utricle is set with very small sharp teeth bent inwards; and the tubular part of the utricle has its inner surface lined throughout with innumerable little bristles, which arise from rows of cells forming inwardly projecting ridges, and have their sharply-pointed tips directed downwards (see fig. 19 [1]). Amongst these needles are also found, scattered over the whole internal surface, roundish wart-like glands or papillæ, composed of four or eight cells. The bottom of the bladder-like cavity in which the utricle terminates is destitute of bristles, and provided only with glands arranged in rows. Small worms, mites, and other segmented animals which enter through the orifice of the utricle can easily reach the enlarged base. But as soon as they try to com-

Fig. 20. *Sarracenia purpurea.*

mence the return journey they are opposed by the points of a thousand bristles. Thus caught they die, and the products arising from the decay of their bodies are absorbed by the glands situated, as above mentioned, at the bottom of the bladder and on the walls of the utricle.

As types of a second series of carnivorous plants belonging to the group of pitcher-plants may be taken *Heliamphora nutans,* a native of moorlands on the mountains of Roraima, on the borders of British Guiana, and *Sarracenia purpurea* (see fig. 20), which is widely distributed in the marshes of eastern North America from Hudson's Bay to Florida. In both instances the leaves metamorphosed into ascidia are arranged in rosettes, rest their bases on damp earth and thence curve upwards. They are somewhat inflated, like bladders, at about their middle, but contract again at the orifice where they pass into the relatively small laminæ. The latter are threaded by red streaks like blood-vessels, have the form of valves, and turn their concave surfaces towards falling rain. They serve, moreover, at least in *Sarracenia purpurea*, to catch the drops of rain, which then flow down into the bottom of the ascidia and fill them more or less with water. There is very little evaporation from the hollow pitchers: and even when there has been no rain for a week, one always finds some of the previously-collected water at the bottom. The inner surface of a pitcher is lined by cells arranged like the scales of enamel on a pike's back (see fig. 19 [2]). The internally-projecting wall of each of these scales is transformed into a stiff decurved point, and the lower the position of the cells the longer do the points become. The shell-like lamina again, above the contracted orifice, bears glandular hairs which exude honey, so that the parts surrounding the aperture are covered by a thin film of sweet juice.

Many animals are attracted by this honey. Some are winged and alight from flying; others, being wingless, make use of a peculiar ridge, which projects on the concave side of the utricle, to help them to creep up the latter. If these honey-eaters happen to travel away from the lamina to that part of the pitcher which is lined with the smooth and slippery decurved cells, they are as good as lost. They slip down over the brink, every attempt to climb up again being rendered futile by the downwardly-pointing needles which clothe the lower part of the wall; and ultimately they fall into the water collected at the bottom, where they are drowned and their bodies putrefy. The products of decay are absorbed as nutriment by the epidermal cells in this region. The number of animals meeting with this fate is often so great that an offensive odour, arising from the decaying bodies, is emitted by the utricles and is noticeable at a considerable distance. In the wild state, the ascidiform utricles are often half-full of drowned animals and it is stated that in these circumstances birds also put in an appearance and pick some of the dead remains out of the utricles.

Whether the liquid filling the bottom of the pitchers consists simply of rain-water, or whether the latter is modified by a secretion originating in the gland-like groups of cells there (see fig. 28 [7]), is still uncertain. A centipede over 4 centimeters long having fallen into a utricle of *Sarracenia purpurea* in the night was found only half immersed in the water. The upper half of the creature projected above the liquid, and made violent efforts to escape; but the lower part had, after a few hours, not only become motionless but had turned white from the effect of the surrounding liquid; it appeared to be macerated, and exhibited alterations which are not produced in so short a time in centipedes immersed in ordinary rain-water. When a number of captured animals are undergoing putre-faction at the same time in a pitfall, the liquid turns brown and has the appearance of manure-liquor.

There is a great difference between the utricles of *Sarracenia purpurea* and the apparatus adapted to the capture of prey in the plants of which we have chosen as examples, *Sarracenia variolaris*, a native of the marshes of Alabama, Florida, and Carolina, and the *Darlingtonia Californica*, found growing at a height of from 300 to 1000 meters above the sea on Californian uplands from the borders of

Oregon to Mount Shasta.   In both of these the liquid with an acid reaction, which fills the bottom of each utricle, is certainly only secreted by the cells in the interior of the cavity itself, and it is quite impossible that a single drop of the rain or dew deposited upon the plant should reach the interior of the cavity.   The hollow petiole is in both plants, above mentioned, utricular or tubular, and only slightly

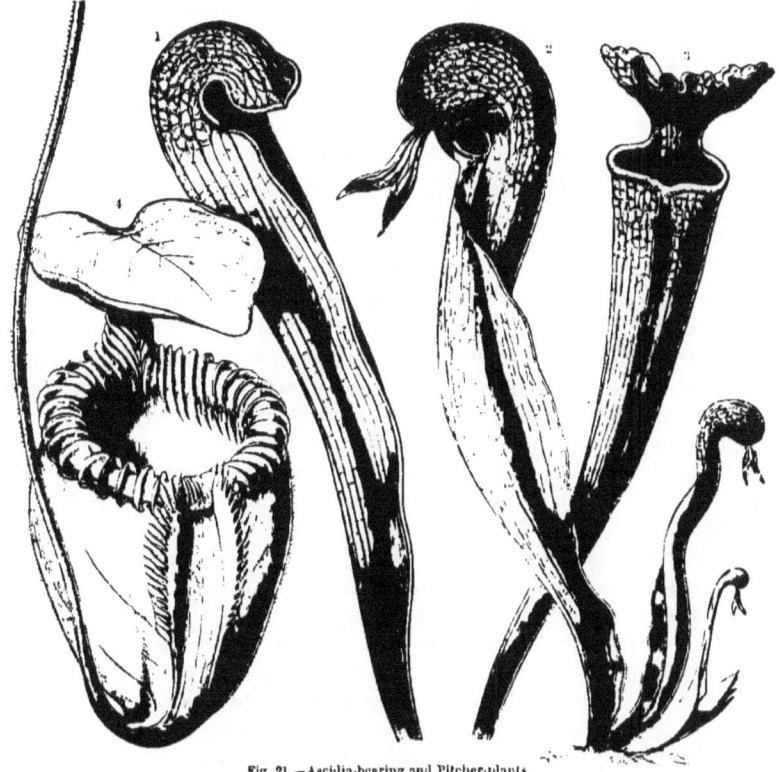

Fig. 21.—Ascidia-bearing and Pitcher-plants.

[1] *Sarracenia variolaris.*   [2] *Darlingtonia Californica.*   [3] *Sarracenia laciniata.*   [4] *Nepenthes villosa,* reduced to one-half natural size.

enlarged towards the top.   The dorsal side of each leaf is, however, at its upper end hollowed out like a cowl or a helmet, and forms a cupola as is shown in fig. 21 [1] and 21 [2].   The orifice or entrance into the utricle is consequently covered over and is reduced to a slit or hole under the hood.   The lamina is transformed into a lobe, which in *Sarracenia variolaris* is small and roofs over the orifice of the utricle, and in *Darlingtonia* is shaped like the tail of a fish, and hangs down in front of the aperture.   The lower part of the utricle is of a uniform green colour, but the upper part (*i.e.* the cupola and lobe-like appendage) has red ribs and veins, and here and there is quite purple.   Between the veins the leaf is thin, translucent, and pale-green or whitish; and these clear translucent patches, framed by purple or green ribs, look as if they were little windows, especially when seen from within the utricle. The mixture of green, red, and white gives the upper parts of the leaves such a gay appearance that, from a distance, they might be mistaken for flowers.

Insects are doubtless attracted by these bright colours, and both round the orifice, and on the inner surface of the cupola, they find exudations of honey which they suck or lick up with avidity. In *Sarracenia variolaris*, honey is to be seen besides, on the edge of a broad free border which is decurrent along the utricle, and extends from the ground to the orifice. This border forms a favourite path for wingless insects, especially ants, which are particularly eager in their quest for honey. For them it is a sure way to destruction, for when they, gradually following the honey-baited pathway, arrive at the orifice to the utricle and pass through it, they inevitably get upon the smooth decurved points of the epidermal cells, constructed just like those in *Sarracenia purpurea*, and then, unable to stop themselves, slip down to the bottom of the pitcher. When small winged insects alight from flying and fall down the slide into the interior, they make use of their wings in the hope of saving themselves, but they never succeed in finding the aperture by which they entered, as it slants downwards and is situated in shadow. They invariably try to escape through the cupola, mistaking the thin portions, through which the light penetrates into the interior, for gaps permitting egress. But just as flies in rooms dash against the windows hoping to pass through them into the open air, so the small insects in the utricles of *Sarracenia variolaris* and *Darlingtonia Californica* knock against these windowed cupolas, in their desire to save themselves by flying through. They always fall down again to the bottom of the utricle as though into a cistern. If they are immersed in the liquid there secreted, or only in partial contact with it, they are stupefied, but not immediately killed. They often live incarcerated for two days, and it would therefore be erroneous to suppose that the fluid in the pitchers acts on the prey as a deadly poison. But it assists the decay and dissolution of the captives as they die of starvation and suffocation, and, as in the case of the utricle-plants previously described, a brown liquor of very unpleasant odour is produced, and there is a residue of solid pieces of skeleton difficult to decompose, such as the wing-cases, claws, and thoraces of various beetles, lice, ants, and other small insects which have shared the same unlucky fate.

The number of animals captured is very considerable. The pitchers of *Sarracenia variolaris*, which attain to a length of 30 cm., are usually found, when growing in their natural habitat, filled to a height of from 8 to 10 cm. with animal remains, and even a heap 15 cm. high has been observed. We must here remark that in the ascidia of *Sarracenia variolaris*, wingless insects, which creep about the earth, are found to predominate, whilst in *Darlingtonia*, on the contrary, most of the insects are winged. The cause of this is easily understood. The former plant has honey exuding on the flap or ridge running down from the orifice to the ground, and many wingless insects are thus induced to climb up the alluring path and to enter the cavity of the pitcher. *Darlingtonia*, on the other hand, is destitute of honey on its decurrent ridge, and only provides the sweet meal at the top in the vicinity of the orifice, where it is available for flying insects, which, as a rule, only visit nectar-secreting flowers. The purplish-red scale, shaped like a fish's tail, and hung out like the sign-board of an inn in front of the entrance to the pitcher, constitutes an instrument for the attraction, from afar, of these winged creatures, which are endowed with a vivid sense of colour; and, as experience shows, it does not fail in its object.

What significance is to be attributed to the spiral torsion of *Darlingtonia* leaves (see fig. 21²) it is difficult to say. Perhaps the escape of animals once imprisoned in the depths of a pitfall is hereby rendered more remote. It would at all events be much more difficult for an insect trying to escape by the use of its wings to ascend a canal which, in addition to being lined with decurved points, was spirally wound, than a similar canal, straight and widened towards the top. We must not omit to mention that a few flies and a small moth have selected as their ordinary habitat the pitchers of both the plants just described, in spite of their being so fatal to most insects. The grubs of a blow-fly (*Sarcophaga Sarraceniae*), in particular, live in large numbers amidst the heaps of decaying insect bodies at the bottom of the pitchers, and are there nourished just as are the grubs of allied species in the rotten flesh of birds and mammals. When mature, the grubs quit the environment of dead remains, passing through holes which they bore in the side wall of the pitcher, and turn into chrysalises in the earth. But the fly itself can without danger pass in and out of the pitfalls, which are so perilous in the case of other insects, and it is enabled to do this by means of the special structure of its feet. On the last joint of each foot it has a long claw and sole-like attachment-lobe, and it is able to push these appendages between the sharp, slippery, decurved hairs lining the inner surface of the pitcher, and so to hook itself to the deeper strata of the wall. This apparatus may be likened to the grapple-like climbing irons of Tyrolese mountaineers, and, thus armed, the fly is in a position to ascend the inner wall of a pitcher unscaleable by other insects. The case of the small moth *Xanthoptera semicrocea* is similar. The tibiae of this insect are armed with long, sharp spurs, one pair on each of the two middle legs, and two pairs on each of the two hindermost legs; and, by the help of these spurs it likewise is able to tread uninjured over the dangerous surface of the wall. Its caterpillars, too, cover the sharp slippery hairs with a web, and so render them harmless.

The presence of these animals in the death-traps of Sarracenias is of special interest, inasmuch as it shows that the animals which perish at the bottom of the pitchers are not exactly digested. If maggoty flesh enters the stomach of a carnivorous animal, not only the flesh itself but the maggots as well (which, indeed, immediately die on reaching the stomach) are speedily dissolved by the action of the gastric juice. Such is also the case with several animal-capturing plants to be described in the next pages. But the fluid secreted in the pitchers of *Darlingtonia* and *Sarracenia variolaris* cannot exercise this digestive action, for if it did the maggots in the heap of rotting insects could not remain alive and well. Its action is limited to the promotion of decay and the formation of a foul liquor, in other words, a liquid manure, which is absorbed as nutriment by the epidermal cells at the bottom of the pitchers.

Another series of pitcher-plants comprises forms in which the petioles are converted into symmetrical sacs with apertures at the top, and the laminæ spread out over them like lids for protection. Most frequently the pitfalls in plants of this kind are shaped like pitchers, jars, urns, cups, or funnels; and the lid over the orifice of each cavity is, for the most part, so placed as to prevent rain-drops from falling in, but not to hinder in any way the entrance of animals. In this series are included, firstly, a few species of *Sarracenia*, viz. *Sarracenia Drummondii* and *S. undulata*, next, the Australian *Cephalotus follicularis*, and lastly, the numerous species of the genus *Nepenthes*, which are designated by gardeners by the name of "pitcher-plants" in the narrow sense.

The leaves in both the Sarracenias just named are heteromorphic. Some of them have acute linear-lanceolate petioles of a uniform green colour, and not hollowed out; and it is only in the case of from three to five leaves in each individual plant that the petioles are transformed into tubes with infundibuliform enlargements at the top. The rim round the mouth of the funnel is somewhat swollen and doubled down externally; but above the orifice the lamina is arched so as to form a cover to the pitcher. The margin of the leaf of *Sarracenia laciniata*, which is shown in fig. 21 [3], is crinkled and sinuously folded. The cover and also the upper funnel-shaped enlargement of the pitcher are very conspicuous on account of the contrast of the colours displayed upon them. The green of the lower part of the pitcher gets paler and paler above, and merges into a pure white, whilst dark-red veins stand out from the green and white ground tints, having the effect of a net-work of blood-vessels. At the mouth of the pitcher, and on the under side of the lid, honey is secreted in such abundance that little drops of it are not infrequently to be seen on the swollen rim, and some oozes down into the infundibuliform portion of the pitcher. But at the very spots where the honey occurs there are also innumerable smooth conical cells with their solid apices directed downwards; and these cells become longer the lower their position in the pitcher. When insects, attracted by the gay-coloured lid, and lured on by the honey, come to the mouth of the pitcher and tread upon the parts covered with the sharp slippery papillæ, they are drawn into the depths as though by an invisible power. After they have once alighted on the perilous area, every movement and every effort to climb up against the points causes them to slide further and further down towards the bottom of the pitcher, where they are hopelessly lost, being killed within a short time and ultimately decomposed.

An instance of an exactly similar kind is afforded by *Cephalotus follicularis*, which has long been known as a plant native on moorlands in eastern Australia. It is allied to saxifrages and currants, and is represented on a scale of half the natural size in fig. 22. This *Cephalotus* also has two kinds of leaves, which are closely crowded in a rosette round the erect flower-stalk. Only the lower leaves of the rosette are transformed into traps for animals, and these are pre-eminently adapted for wingless creatures creeping upon the earth. The tankard-shaped traps all rest on the damp earth, and are furnished externally with borders or winged ridges, which facilitate the ascent of crawling animals to the mouth of the tankard. Flying insects are of course not excluded, and here again they are made aware from afar of the feast of honey provided by the presence of bright colours. The half-open lid is very prettily adorned with white patches and brilliant purple veins, and at a distance is readily mistaken for a flower.

When small animals, whether with or without wings, approach to take the honey, they are so eager in their search that they get upon the inner surface of the mouth of the tankard-pitcher, which, though fluted, is also very smooth and slippery, and thence they easily slide into the interior of the cavity. The pitchers being half-full of liquid, most of the unlucky creatures die there in a short time by drowning. But even if this were not the case, they would never succeed in working their way up to the light of day. For every animal that wishes to save itself from a *Cephalotus* pitcher has three obstacles to overcome: first, a circular ridge projecting inside the pitcher; secondly, a bit of wall thickly covered with

Fig. 22.—*Cephalotus follicularis.*

little papillæ, sharp, ridged, and pointed downward, the whole being comparable to a flax-comb; and, lastly, on the involute rim round the mouth of the pitcher, another fringe composed of hooked, decurved spines which bristle like an impenetrable row of bayonets in front of such animals as may have surmounted the other difficulties. The abundance of the booty found at the bottom of *Cephalotus* pitchers shows how efficiently these contrivances serve to prevent escape. Ants, for instance, sacrifice themselves recklessly in their pursuit of honey, and one often finds great numbers of them drowned in the liquid in the pitchers. The prey is not in this case converted into a putrid liquor, but is partially dissolved by a secretion having an acid reaction. This secretion is separated out by special glandular cells situated on the lining of the pitcher; and the whole process, wherein they are concerned, corresponds to that which obtains in the pitchers of *Nepenthes*, and which will be more thoroughly discussed in the case of these latter plants.

The species of the genus *Nepenthes*, of which we know at the present time thirty-six, are all confined to the tropics. Their area of distribution extends from New Caledonia and New Guinea over tropical Australia to the Seychelles Islands and Madagascar, and over the Sunda Islands, the Philippines, Ceylon, Bengal, and Cochin-China. They only flourish on marshy ground on the margin of small collections of water in damp primeval forests. There the seeds germinate in shallow water. The young plants (see fig. 23), which spring from the boggy

ground, have their leaves arranged in rosettes just like those of Sarracenias (see fig. 20). They are, too, so nearly identical in form with the latter that anyone seeing a young *Nepenthes* plant for the first time, and not knowing the history of its development, would take it for a *Sarracenia*. The leaves, succeeding the cotyledons and forming a circle

Fig. 23.—Young *Nepenthes* plants.

above them, rest their lower portions upon the mud, but their upper parts are curved upwards, and each carries at its extremity a scale resembling a cock's comb, which is, strict speaking, the lamina. This scale roofs over a slit-like aperture, the entrance to a cavity within the swollen petiole. In addition a green lobe with a few coarse projecting points is to be seen on either side of the orifice.

Altogether different from the rosettes of young *Nepenthes* plants are the foliar structures clothing the stems which subsequently arise from the rosettes (see fig. 24). In these leaves the lower part of the petiole is winged and flat, has a linear or lanceolate outline, and resembles the leaf-blade of *Dracæna*; its functions, too, are those of a green lamina. This expanded section of the leaf-stalk passes next into a part which is terete and coiled like a snake, and acts as a tendril. Every stem or branch belonging to a plant, whether living or dead, with which this part of the petiole comes into contact, is seized and encircled by it; and the third portion of the petiole, *i.e.* the pitcher, being situated at the extremity of this clasping portion, is thus slung upon the branch of some other plant growing at the edge of a pool of water. Meanwhile the *Nepenthes* plant rises higher and higher above the wet soil where its seeds germinated and the young rosette rested, becomes entangled with the ramifications of the underwood and with prostrate branches of trees of the primeval forest; in a word, with everything available as a support, and so not infrequently climbs, as a true liane, to the tops of trees of moderate height.

The pitcher must be looked upon as an excavated portion of the petiole, and

Fig. 21.—*Nepenthes destillatoria*

what appears to be the lid of the pitcher is the lamina, as it is in *Cephalotus* and the Sarracenias. In this case also the lamina seems to be but little developed in comparison with the wonderfully metamorphosed petiole. In the majority of the species of *Nepenthes*, the mature pitchers are from 10 cm. to 15 cm. in height. In the graceful *Nepenthes ampullaria* they are only from 4 cm. to 6 cm. high; but, on the other hand, in the species indigenous to the primeval forests of Borneo they reach a height of 30 cm. or even more. The pitchers of *Nepenthes Rajah* have a height of 50 cm., and their orifices are 10 cm. in diameter, whilst below the orifice they expand to 16 cm.; so that if a pigeon were to fly into a pitcher of this kind it would be completely hidden in it. Immature pitchers are still closed by their covers. Often they are hairy outside; and, according to the colour and lustre of the hairs, they may be rusty in tone or glittering like gold; not rarely they look as if they were powdered with flour (*e.g. N. albo-marginata*), and sometimes are even snow-white. Subsequently the lid is raised, and the downy coat disappears either partially or entirely. Having thus become glabrous, the pitchers display a yellowish-green ground colour, for the most part flecked and veined with purple; and many are of a bluish, violet, or rose tint near the orifice, or dark-red as though saturated with blood. The lid is similarly gaily coloured; and the variety of the tints is increased by the fact that a pale-blue zone is visible in the interior, beneath the swollen involute rim of the opening, which is itself brownish, yellowish, or orange-red. Gaily-coloured pitchers of this kind look at a distance just like flowers, and remind one, in particular, of the most brilliant floral forms of the liane-like Aristolochias indigenous to tropical forests. This fact is the more noteworthy, because the genus *Nepenthes* is closely allied to the genus *Aristolochia* in respect of systematic relations.

The bright pitchers of *Nepenthes*, visible from afar, are sought, just as flowers are, by insects, and probably by other winged creatures as well; and this occurs all the more because there is a copious secretion of honey by the epidermal cells upon the under surface of the lid, and on the rim round the mouth of each pitcher. The swollen and often delicately-fluted rim, in particular, drips and glitters with the sugary juice; and it would be permissible in this connection to speak of a honeyed mouth and sweet lips in the most literal sense of the words. Animals which suck honey from the lips of *Nepenthes* pitchers wander, as they do so, only too readily upon the interior surface of the orifice. But the inner face is smooth and precipitous, and rendered so slippery by a bluish coating of wax that not a few of the alighted guests slip down to the bottom of the pitcher and fall into the liquid there collected. Many of them perish in a short time; others try to save themselves by climbing up the internal face of the pitcher, but they always slip again on the polished, wax-coated zone, and tumble back once more to the bottom. In large pitchers the involute rim of the aperture is in addition armed with sharp teeth, which are pointed downwards and bristle in front of such of the unlucky victims in the pitfall as try to emerge (see fig. 19[3]). In a number of species (*N. Rafflesiana, N. echinostoma, N. Rajah, N. Edwardsiana,* and *N. Veitchii,* all natives of Borneo) this fringe of sharp teeth looks like the set of teeth of a beast of prey; and in *Nepenthes villosa*, of which a pitcher is represented in fig. 21 [4], a double row of bigger and smaller teeth directed towards the bottom of the pitcher is developed, and renders the escape of prey, once caught in the trap, impossible.

Most of the creatures that fall into the pitchers are, however, speedily drowned in the large quantity of liquid at the bottom. For a third part or even a half of the cavity is filled with liquid. This liquid originates from special gland-cells on the inner surface of the pitcher, consists mainly of water, and so long as there are no animals in the pitfall, gives only a very weak acid reaction. But as soon as the body of an animal reaches the bottom, more fluid is secreted. This has a distinctly acid taste, possesses the power of dissolving albuminous substances, such as flesh and coagulated blood, and corresponds, not only in respect of this action but also in chemical composition, to the gastric juice. For, in addition to organic acids (malic, citric, and formic acids), an organic body like pepsin has been detected in it, and nitrogenous organic compounds have been brought into solution in it artificially as well. If the liquid from a *Nepenthes* pitcher, which has not yet captured any animal, is poured into a glass vessel containing a small piece of meat, the flesh is at first but little affected; but, if a few drops of formic acid are added, the flesh is dissolved and undergoes the very same changes as it does in the stomach of a mammal. The process going on in the pitchers of *Nepenthes* when animals fall into them is therefore not only analogous to digestion, but may be properly designated digestion.

The digested portions of the bodies are afterwards absorbed by special cells at the bottom, and on the lower parts of the lining wall of the *Nepenthes* pitchers.

The third group included in the first section of carnivorous plants comprises forms with scale-like leaves, within which are peculiar cavities penetrable by minute animals only, on account of the narrowness of the entry. Special contrivances to prevent the escape of the prey are absent. The animals are retained and drained of their juices in the cavities by means of protoplasmic filaments radiating from special cells.

One of the most remarkable of the plants belonging to this group is the Toothwort (*Lathræa Squamaria*), of which we shall repeatedly have occasion to speak. It is nearly allied to the Yellow-Rattle and Cow-wheat, but it is destitute of chlorophyll, and lives underground, parasitic on the roots of arborescent Angiosperms, except during a brief period annually when it sends up above-ground a few short shoots covered with flowers. The subterranean stems are white, have a fleshy, solid, and elastic appearance, and are covered throughout their entire length with thick squamous leaves placed closely one above the other (see fig. 25 [1] and fig. 37). In colour and consistence these leaves are like the stem; in outline they are broadly cordate, and they give the impression of being mounted fairly and squarely upon the stem by means of the highly swollen and notched basal portion. But it is only necessary to detach one of the scales from the stem to convince oneself that this is not the case, and that the part taken at first sight to be the underside or back of the leaf is really a portion of the superior surface. For as a matter of fact each of these thick squamiform leaves is rolled back, and in it the following parts may be distinguished: first, the place of insertion on the stem (fig. 25³) which is relatively small; secondly, the portion taken on cursory examination to be the whole upper surface of the leaf, and consisting of an obliquely ascending blade limited by a sharp edge or border; next, starting from this sharp border, the part, which, owing to its being suddenly bent down at an acute angle and falling away steeply, is usually taken for the lower surface of the leaf, but which belongs, in point of fact, to its upper surface; fourthly, the free extremity of the leaf in the form of an involute limb; and fifthly, the true dorsal (under) part, which is very small relatively to the whole, and is not visible until the involute tip is removed. Owing to the involution of the apex or tip, a canal or rather a recess is formed and runs across beneath the leaf, close under the place where the latter is joined to the stem (see fig. 25²). From five to thirteen (usually ten) chambers open into this recess through a series of little holes. They are excavations in the thickness of the scales and are probably, in this form at any rate, unique in the realm of plants. To solve the problem of their significance in relation to the life of the plant, and to its absorption of nutriment in particular, it is necessary to examine them somewhat more in detail. This we will now proceed to do.

The cavities, varying in number, as has been already mentioned, from five to thirteen, are situated very closely together, but are not connected laterally. They are all deeper than they are broad, and have irregularly undulating walls (see fig. 25³). Two kinds of structures are conspicuous on the internal surfaces of the walls, being raised above the ordinary epidermal cells, and projecting into the cavity. Structures of the first kind are present in large numbers, and each of them consists of a pair of cells in the form of a little head, borne by a short, cylindrical cell serving as a stalk. The other variety, which occurs much more sparsely, is composed of a comparatively large tabular cell, roundish or elliptical in outline, inserted amongst the ordinary epidermal cells and only slightly raised above them, and of two convex cells, forming a low dome, which rests upon this base (fig. 25⁴) as though on a salver. The walls of these cellular structures projecting into the cavity are comparatively thick, and when the protoplasts living in the cells are stimulated, they appear to send out, through pores in the thick walls, delicate filaments exactly like the protoplasmic threads which the coated Infusoria, known by the name of Rhizopoda, stretch forth through the pores of their armour (see fig. 25⁵).

When small animals penetrate into the labyrinthine chambers of a *Lathræa* leaf and touch the organs just described, the protoplasmic filaments are protruded in rays in response to the stimulus, and lay themselves upon the intruders. They act as prehensile arms in holding the smaller prey, chiefly Infusoria, and impede the motion of larger animals so as to cut off their retreat. No special secretion has been observed to be exuded in the foliar chambers of *Lathræa*. But, seeing that some time after the creatures have entered the chambers the only remains of them that one meets with are claws, legs, bristles, and little amorphous lumps, their sarcode, flesh, and blood having vanished and left no trace, we must suppose that the absorption of nutriment from the dead prey here ensues through contact with the extended protoplasmic tentacular filaments as in the case of Rhizopoda, to

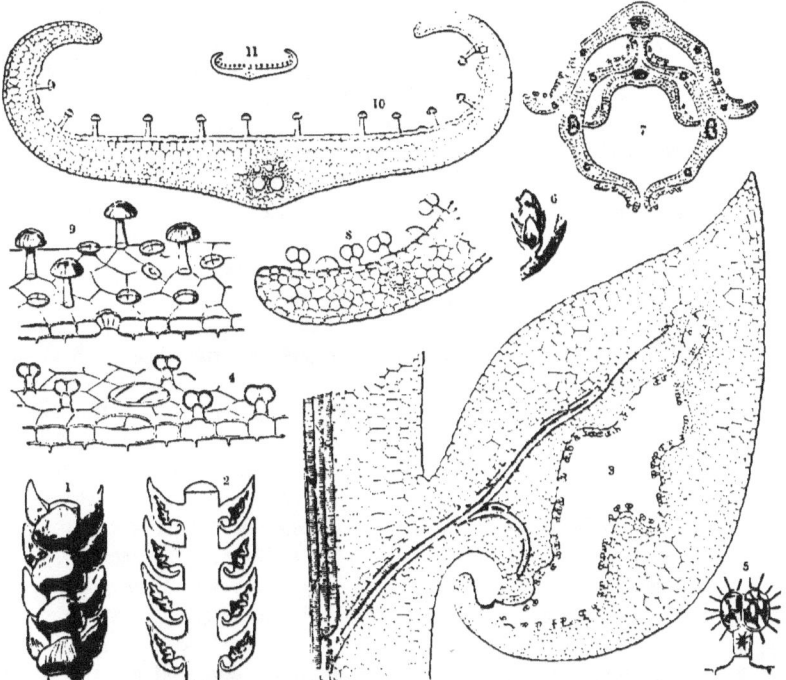

Fig. 25.—Capturing apparatus in the Toothwort, *Bartsia*, and Butterwort.

1 Piece of an underground leaf-shoot of the Toothwort. 2 Longitudinal section through the same; ×2. 3 Longitudinal section through a leaf; ×60. 4 Piece of the wall of a cavity; ×200. 5 Plasmic threads radiating from the cells of the little heads; ×540. 6 Subterranean bud of *Bartsia*; natural size. 7 Cross-section through part of this bud; ×60. 8 The margin of a bud-scale in section; ×200. 9 Piece of the epidermis of a leaf of Butterwort; ×180. 10 Transverse section through the leaf of a Butterwort (*Pinguicula alpina*); ×50. 11 Transverse section through Butterwort leaf; natural size.

which these organs are so strikingly similar. It is not impossible that the sessile organs alone have the function of absorption, and that the stalked capitate structures serve for the retention of the prey; at least, this idea is supported by the circumstance that the former, which, as already stated, are much the scarcer, have vessels running to them connected by a peculiar barrel-shaped cell with the large elliptical tubular cells, whilst this is not the case with the capitate forms of structure.

The openings of the chambers into the recess at the back of a Toothwort leaf being very narrow, only minute animals, such as Infusoria, Amœbæ, Rhizopoda,

Rotifera, small Acarina, species of *Aphis*, Poduridæ, &c., slip in. What it is that prompts them to visit these hidden chambers is as hard to say as it is to give the reason why the various species of *Daphnia* and *Cyclops* make their way into the bladders of Utriculariæ. The most probable explanation is that the tiny creatures push into the cavities in their search for food, and there meet their death.

It has been already stated that *Lathræa* is a parasite. Although we shall not discuss the plant in that capacity until later on, we must point out now that the main part of its nutriment is derived from the roots of deciduous arborescent Angiosperms by means of special suckers. It only grows in regions where the activity of trees and shrubs is interrupted by a winter of considerable duration. As soon as the woody plants on whose roots individuals of *Lathræa* are parasitic acquire their autumn tints and shed their leaves, the suckers invariably perish. When, in the following spring, the ascent of the sap begins in the wood, *Lathræa* sends out new roots, which fasten their suckers underground upon the tree's roots, the latter being turgid with sap. The nutriment supplied in this way to *Lathræa* is not essentially different from that taken up by the roots of the tree or shrub in question from the surrounding earth. It is composed mainly of water holding a small quantity of mineral salts in solution, a mixture which has been termed not unsuitably "crude sap".

Living underground and being destitute of chlorophyll, *Lathræa* has not the power of converting atmospheric carbon dioxide, or crude food-sap absorbed by the suckers from the tree or shrub attacked, into the various organic compounds necessary for further growth. For this reason, and inasmuch as the quantity of nitrogenous compounds in the fluids withdrawn from the roots is but small, every additional supply of organic food, especially of nitrogenous matter, such as is derived from captured animals, must be exceedingly welcome. Although the prey that is caught and digested consists for the most part of minute Infusoria, this addition must not by any means be undervalued. We must take into account the fact that every one of the innumerable leaf-scales of an individual *Lathræa* has an apparatus for capture and digestion, and that this apparatus is active throughout the entire year. The frost in winter does not reach so deep down in the soil as the place where the plant is imbedded, so that there, even at a season when above-ground everything is quiescent, the Infusoria and other little organisms continue their existence and may be captured by *Lathræa*. Thus, the extremely large number of animals secured in the course of a year is nearly sufficient to maintain the size of each individual plant.

It is after all anything but strange that a root-parasite, destitute of chlorophyll and living underground, should make use of traps for animals, besides absorbing crude sap from other plants; but, on the other hand, we are naturally surprised to find plants which actually extract food from the earth by means of absorption-cells, also absorbing through suckers from roots in the capacity of parasites, and, furthermore, preying upon animals. An instance of such a plant is afforded, however, by *Bartsia alpina*. This remarkable organism is distributed in the arctic region and amongst the high mountain flora throughout almost the whole of Europe, and is very striking owing to the colour of its foliage being a mixture of black, violet, and green. The flower, too, is of a sombre dark-violet hue, and the entire plant, by reason of this peculiar colouring, gives a truly funereal impression. We may remark incidentally that the name *Bartsia* was chosen by Linnæus for this sad-hued plant as an expression of his own grief at the death of the zealous naturalist and physician, Bartsch, who was his intimate friend, and who succumbed at a comparatively early age to the climate of Guiana. Damp black earth in the neighbourhood of springs constitutes the favourite habitat of these plants. Upon digging in summer time down to their roots, one sees that a few suckers proceed from them, and fasten upon the sedges and other plants growing in the vicinity; but one also discovers subterranean shoots having "root-hairs" developed near the nodes, at which are inserted the paired white scales; and these "root-hairs" have the function of absorption-cells. Towards the autumn, oval buds, likewise subterranean, are matured, in form not unlike horse-chestnut buds (see fig. 25 $^6$), and composed of etiolated scales arranged in four rows and overlapping one another like tiles, so that only the back of the upper part of each scale is visible, the lower part being covered by the scale next beneath it.

On the visible part of each scale's convex under surface three sharply projecting ribs are noticeable near the middle, whilst the two margins are rolled back so as to form a recess in each case. But, as may be seen in the cross-section of a *Bartsia* bud (see fig. 25 $^7$), one pair of scales lies over the next higher pair in such a way as to convert the recesses into ducts. Owing to this construction the interior of the bud is perforated by twice as many ducts as there are covered leaf-scales, and the orifices of each pair of ducts occur at the spots where the evolute margins of one scale begin to be covered by the middle of the next lower scale. On one wall of the ducts, *i.e.* in the recesses, structures like those which occur in the cavities of *Lathræa* are developed, *i.e.* stalked glands, each composed of two cells borne upon a basal cell; secondly, pairs of hemispherical domed cells; and, lastly, ordinary flat epidermal cells (see fig. 25 $^8$). There can be little doubt that the whole apparatus acts in the same way as in *Lathræa*, and is adapted to the capture of Infusoria.

The subterranean buds of *Bartsia*, just described, are produced late in the summer, and aërial shoots arise from them in the course of the following spring. Seeing that the foliage-leaves on these shoots are richly furnished with chlorophyll, and manufacture organic compounds in the sunlight from the constituents of the air and from the fluids imbibed by absorption-cells from the ground, the question arises whether an additional supply of nutriment from the dead bodies of captured animals can be necessary or even advantageous. We shall, however, taking into account the circumstances of *Bartsia alpina* when growing wild, answer this question with an unconditional affirmative. The plant belongs, as has been said, to an arctic and high alpine flora, and grows in regions where the activity of plants above ground is limited to the short period of two months. After the lapse of this brief vegetative season, the aërial parts of arctic and alpine plants either die altogether, or are buried in the snow, retaining their green colour, but suspending all movement and vital activity for from eight to ten months. The first snow falls in the districts inhabited by *Bartsia* invariably before the ground is frozen, and the wintry covering of snow, which gets deeper and deeper as time goes on, protects the earth so completely from the cold that even in the superficial strata the temperature does not sink below freezing point. In the bed thus kept free from frost neither vegetable nor animal life is quite torpid, and there can be no doubt that it is only beneficial to *Bartsia*, during the long interval, for its subterranean buds to obtain an abundance of food from the bodies of captured Infusoria. The advantage is the more obvious when one considers that the above-ground stem, with its foliage-leaves and flowers, has to be built up in two or three weeks, in the ensuing vegetative period, from the organic compounds stored in the cells of the scales of the subterranean buds, and that both the damp ground in which *Bartsia* grows, and also the roots of the marsh-plants to which it is joined by a few suckers, though yielding water and mineral salts, afford but little material for the production of nitrogenous compounds.

### CARNIVOROUS PLANTS WHICH EXHIBIT MOVEMENTS IN THE CAPTURE OF PREY.

We have taken *Lathræa* and *Bartsia* as types of the last group of that section of carnivorous plants which manifest no external visible movement in the pitfalls for the purpose of capture or digestion. The second section, now to be discussed, includes plants in which movements of the leaves, or parts of leaves, modified as organs of seizure and digestion, take place as a result of the contact of animal bodies—movements which have the common object of bringing about the digestion of the animals, whilst the retention of the latter is effected in very various ways.

Since in *Lathræa* and *Bartsia* the leaves, modified as organs of capture, exhibit no kind of motion themselves, though movements take place in the protoplasm of the capitate pairs of cells in the interior of the cavities, having as their object the holding of the prey, these plants form, to a certain extent, a link between the first and second sections. All these divisions are for that matter merely artificial, and it is not impossible that fresh forms may be discovered and recognized as intermediate between the groups and series here distinguished, obliterating the boundaries which have been adopted by us, simply with a view to obtaining a general survey of the subject.

The first group of carnivorous plants which perform movements for the capture of prey is composed of the various species of the genus *Pinguicula* (Butterwort). Of this stock nearly forty species are known; and they are all much alike. Scarcely any difference would be detected by an ordinary person between *Pinguicula calyptrata* from the mountains of New Granada and *Pinguicula vulgaris* from our own hills. In respect of habitat, too, they exhibit close conformity. In both the Old World and the New they only thrive on damp spots, the neighbourhood of springs, banks of brooks, moorlands, and black peat-bogs. In the equatorial zone they have retired into the cool regions of the higher mountains. The mountain ranges of Mexico are particularly rich in species of *Pinguicula*, but all the forms existing there occupy a circumscribed area. Southern and western Europe also harbour a few native species whose area of distribution is surprisingly limited. The species occurring in the arctic and sub-arctic zones are, on the contrary, exceedingly widely distributed. One species has been found in antarctic regions at the Straits of Magellan.

The species best known and most available for study is *Pinguicula vulgaris*. The area of its distribution extends over the whole of the arctic and sub-arctic regions, over the part of North America which lies to the north of the Mackenzie River, over Labrador, Greenland, Iceland, and Lapland, throughout Siberia down to the Baikal Mountains, and through Europe to the Balkans, Southern Alps, and Pyrenees. This graceful plant is represented on its natural scale and growing on a bog in the annexed Plate II. entitled, "Insectivorous Plants: Sun-dew and Butterwort". It has bilabiate flowers of a violet-blue colour, with palates covered with velvety-white hairs, and with a sharp spur at the back. The flowers are borne singly on slender stalks which rear themselves in an elegant curve from the centre of a rosette of leaves that rests upon the ground. The leaves of the rosette in *Pinguicula vulgaris*, as in all other species of Butterwort, are oblong-ovate or ligulate and of a yellowish-green colour, and rest their under-surfaces upon the wet ground, whilst their upper faces are exposed to the sky and rain. Owing to the lateral margins being somewhat upturned, each leaf is converted into a broad flat-bottomed trough (cf. the section taken right across a leaf in fig. 25 [10] and 25 [11]). The trough is covered with a colourless sticky mucilage which is secreted by glands distributed in large numbers over the entire upper surface of the leaf.

The glands are of two kinds. One variety is distinguishable by the naked eye as consisting of a stalked head, and looks under the microscope like a tiny mushroom (see fig. 25 [9]). Its parts are a swollen disc composed of from eight to sixteen cells grouped radially, and a stalk, consisting of an erect tubular cell supporting this disc. A gland of the other sort is made up of eight cells grouped in the form of a wart or knob supported by a very short stalk-cell, and only slightly raised above the surface of the leaf. For the rest, ordinary flat epidermal cells make up the epidermis, with here and there interspersed the guard-cells of stomata.

It has been calculated that there are 25,000 mucilage-secreting glands on a square centimeter of a butterwort leaf, and that a rosette composed of from six to nine leaves bears about half a million of them. Momentary contact, whether due to rapid brushing by a solid body or to the incidence of drops of rain, causes no kind of movement in them. The long-continued pressure of grains of sand or of solid insoluble bodies in general stimulates the glandular cells to an inconsiderable augmentation of the quantity of mucilage discharged, but does not cause secretion of any acid digestive fluid. But as soon as a nitrogenous organic body is brought into continuous contact with the glands, they are forthwith stimulated not only to a more profuse elimination of mucilage, but also to the secretion of an acid liquid, which has the power of dissolving all bodies of the kind, namely, such as clotted blood, milk, albumen, and even cartilage. It has been experimentally established (for example) that small solid bits of cartilage placed on a leaf of *Pinguicula vulgaris*, whose mucilage shows no sign of an acid reaction, cause, after ten or eleven hours, the secretion of an acid liquid, and after forty-eight hours are almost entirely dissolved by it. At the end of eighty-two hours the bits of cartilage used in the experiment were completely liquefied, the whole secretion was reabsorbed, and the glands had become dry. When small insects such as midges alight from flight on a leaf of *Pinguicula* they remain glued by the mucilage, and their struggles to extricate themselves only cause them to sink deeper into it. Thus they generally perish in a very short time, are digested by the acid juice poured from the glands in response to the stimulus, and are absorbed with the exception of the wings, claws, and other parts of the skeleton.

The acid liquid secreted by the glands is viscous, and when a number of glands are irritated it may exude so copiously as to fill the whole trough of the leaf. If the margin of the leaf alone is stimulated, as when a small creeping insect, or a midge alighting from above, gets upon the slightly up-curved margin of the leaf, not only do the marginal glands, which are comparatively infrequent, discharge their secretion, but in addition the edge curls over; the object of this movement being to cover, if possible, the prey whilst it is held fast by the sticky mucilage, or to push it into the middle of the flat channel, and so, in one way or another, to bring it into contact with as many glands as possible. The marginal glands alone could not produce the requisite quantity of acid liquid to effect solution, and, on this account, the glands on a wider area are summoned to assist in the manner described. The involution of the margin takes place very slowly; it is usually some hours before the animal sticking to the edge is enfolded, or, in the case of the larger specimens, is pushed into the middle of the leaf. After solution and absorption are accomplished, usually by the end of twenty-four hours, the leaf expands again, and its margins assume the position which they had before their involution.

Besides small insects, pieces of plants, such as spores and pollen-grains brought by the wind, not infrequently fall on the viscid surfaces of *Pinguicula* leaves. These are subjected to the same fate as animal organisms, their protoplasts being dissolved and absorbed like the flesh and blood of insects.

The action of the acid juice secreted by the glands of butterwort leaves upon albuminous bodies is identical with that of the gastric juice of animals. We may presume therefore that there are in it, as in the gastric juice, two kinds of substance: firstly, a free acid, and, secondly, a ferment completely analogous to pepsin in its action; for, as is well known, it is by means of this combination that the juice of the animal stomach effects the solution of albuminoid compounds. Inasmuch as the gland-cells of *Pinguicula* absorb all the soluble part of the prey, and re-absorb the solvent previously discharged by them, the action of this plant's leaves

PLATE II.

1. *Drosera rotundifolia.*   2. *Pinguicula vulgaris.*   3. *Sphagnum cymbifolium.*

INSECTIVOROUS PLANTS: SUNDEW AND BUTTERWORT

is exceedingly like that of the animal stomach, and the process may, as in the case of *Nepenthes*, be fairly regarded as digestion. Whether, in carrying out this process, the different forms of glands have also different functions, whether those of one kind serve principally to secrete and those of the other to absorb, or whether, perhaps, the one variety only discharges viscid mucilage to capture the prey, and the other only a liquid containing acid and pepsin, are questions not yet determined with certainty, although such a division of labour is in itself highly probable.

The similarity existing between the leaf of *Pinguicula* and the animal stomach in respect of their action on albuminous substances was turned to a practical application in dairy-farming long before the discovery of the relationship by men of science. The very same changes as are brought about in milk by the addition of the rennet from a calf's stomach can be induced by means of butterwort leaves. If fresh milk, warm from the cow, is poured over these leaves, a peculiar tough mass of close consistence is formed, the "Tätmiölk" or "Sätmiölk" of Laplanders, mentioned by Linnæus a hundred and fifty years ago as constituting a very favourite dish in northern Scandinavia. In particular, the fact that by means of a trifling quantity of Tätmiölk, produced in the manner described, a large amount of fresh sweet milk may be also converted into Tätmiölk is specially worthy of emphasis, for we learn from it that the substance generated by *Pinguicula* behaves in this respect too, like other ferments. The immemorial use of *Pinguicula* leaves by shepherds in the Alps as a cure for sores on the udders of milch cows is also interesting, inasmuch as the curative effect on the sores is to be explained by the antiseptic action of the secretion of the leaves in question; and a method of healing, used empirically two centuries ago, thus finds confirmation and a scientific explanation at the present day.

Since the curling up and unrolling of the leaf-margin in butterwort is accomplished but slowly, the process above described is not at all conspicuous. Moreover, the margin of a young leaf is always incurved, and that of a mature leaf is also somewhat turned up before stimulation has taken place; so that, strictly speaking, we only have to do with a greater or smaller degree of involution, and its nature can only be determined by careful observation.

In the plants which form the second group in this section of carnivorous plants, and of which the best known representatives are the various species of the genus Sun-dew (*Drosera*), the movements, whereby the capture and digestion of small animals is effected, occur much more rapidly and obviously. These species are usually rooted in the damp dark soil of moors. They have also the same habitats as *Pinguiculæ*, and often enough sun-dew and butterwort are to be seen flourishing close together on a patch of boggy ground no larger than one's hand. On Plate II. they are shown thus associated. *Drosera rotundifolia*, together with *Pinguicula vulgaris*, is there represented, life size, growing in a bed of sphagnum amongst sedges on an upland moor. The thing that strikes one most at sight of the round-leaved sun-dew depicted, and in general of all the forty known species of *Drosera*, is the presence of the delicate wine-red filaments, clavate at their free ends and each supporting a glistening droplet of fluid, which stand out from the leaves, and whose function is essentially the same as that of the glands, stalked and sessile, on the leaf of *Pinguicula*. These filaments only proceed from the upper surface and margin of the sun-dew leaf. The under surface is smooth and hairless, and in many species, including the *Drosera rotundifolia* depicted on the plate, it rests upon the damp mossy ground. In this particular, and also in the circumstance that all the leaves of each individual are adpressed to the ground and grouped in a rosette or radially around the central slender flowering-stem, there exists a very obvious analogy between *Drosera*, and not *Pinguicula* alone, but many other carnivorous plants, such as *Sarracenia*, *Heliamphora*, *Cephalotus*, and *Dionæa*, the fly-trap presently to be described.

The filaments or tentacles projecting from the upper surface and margin of the leaf look like pins inserted in a flat cushion and are of unequal size. Those which stand up perpendicularly from the middle are the shortest, and those which radiate from the outermost edge are the longest (see fig. 26 ¹). Between these extremes are intermediate lengths gradually leading from the one to the other. There are on a leaf, in round numbers, about two hundred of these tentacles. The clavate head at the free extremity of each tentacle is really a gland. It secrets a clear, thick, sticky matter which is readily drawn out into threads, and which shines and glitters in the sunlight like a drop of dew, whence the plant has derived its name of sun-dew. Shocks occasioned by wind or the dropping of rain do not excite any kind of movement in the tentacles. If grains of sand are blown upon them by the wind, or if little bits of glass, coal, gum, or sugar, or minute quantities of paste, wine, tea, or any other non-nitrogenous substance are brought by artificial means into contact with the enlarged extremities of the tentacles, the exudation of liquid at the places in question is augmented, and the secretion also becomes acid, but there is no elimination of pepsin, and no change of importance ensues in the direction of the tentacles, or the attitude of the leaf-margin. But the moment a small insect, mistaking the glittering drops on the tentacles for honey as it flies by, alights on the leaf and so touches the glands, or upon the artificial placing of particles of nitrogenous organic matter, such as flesh or albumen, on the tentacle-heads, there ensues, as in the case of *Pinguicula*, an increase in the discharge of acid juice, as well as the addition of a ferment to its composition. The action of this ferment on albuminous compounds is entirely similar to that of pepsin, and we may even go so far as to speak of it as pepsin.

The insects that fly on to the leaves and are caught by the sticky juice try to disencumber themselves by stroking the viscous matter off with their legs, but they only besmear themselves still more, and are soon plastered all over the body, and have their movements greatly impeded by the secretion. Their efforts to save themselves soon cease, the orifices of their respiratory organs are covered with the juice and choked, and after a brief interval they die from suffocation. All these phenomena correspond, in the main, to those occasioned by identical causes in the case of *Pinguicula.* But the leaves of the sun-dew are especially characterized by the movements performed by the tentacles in response to stimulation by animal matter. These movements are exhibited most conspicuously by the longest tentacles, which stand out radially from the edge of a leaf. A few minutes after the gland of one of these marginal tentacles has been excited by a living or dead animal becoming glued to it, a systematic disturbance is set up in the whole fringe of tentacles. First, the tentacle bearing the gland originally irritated with the animal's body attached to it, bends inwards, performing a movement similar to that

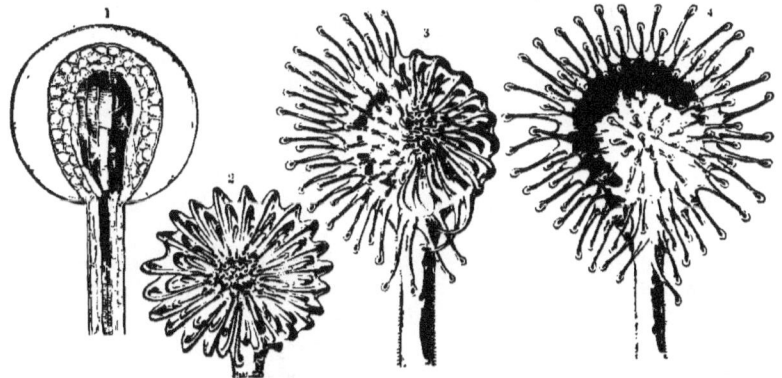

Fig. 26.—Tentacles on leaf of sun-dew.

[1] Glands at the extremity of a tentacle; ×30.   [2] Leaf with all its tentacles inflexed towards the middle.   [3] Leaf with half the tentacles inflected over a captured insect.   [4] Leaf with all the tentacles extended. Figs. 2, 3, and [4] ×4.

of the hand of a watch. Under peculiarly favourable circumstances it describes an angle of 45° in from two to three minutes, and an angle of 90° in ten minutes. A still more intelligible comparison than that of the hand of a watch is afforded by the human hand. Supposing that the foreign body is glued to the tip of a finger it would be moved by the curvature of the finger to the palm in the course of ten minutes. About ten minutes after the first tentacle has been set in motion, those standing near it begin to bend also (see fig. 26[3]). After another ten minutes, tentacles situated further off follow suit; and in the course of from one to three hours all the tentacles are inflected and converge upon the body in question.

We must not omit to mention that this object does not always occupy the same place on the surface of the leaf. Often, no doubt, the prey is exactly in the middle, and the tentacles then swoop down one after the other to that spot; but often also the place is elsewhere and yet the movements never fail in their aim. It may happen that a median tentacle, on repeated excitation, may have to bend now to the right, now to the left. When little bits of meat are placed simultaneously on the right and left halves of the same sun-dew leaf, the two hundred tentacles divide into two groups, and each one of the groups directs its aim to one of the bits of meat. This happens also if two small insects alight at the same moment on a leaf, one on one side and the other on the other. The movement of the tentacles is often accompanied by an inflection of the whole surface of the leaf, the lamina becoming concave like a hollow palm, and when, under these circumstances, the tentacles have converged from the margin on to the concave central part, the leaf resembles a closed fist (see fig. 26 2).

All these movements vary from one case to another and supplement one another according to the needs of the moment and with a view to immediate advantage. The one result that is always attained by the combined action is the covering of the prey with a copious supply of the secretion poured from a number of glands, so that it is dissolved and rendered fit for absorption and for the purposes of nourishment. When an insect is caught by one of the marginal tentacles, the secretion there discharged would not suffice for these purposes. The prey is accordingly transported as far as possible towards the middle of the lamina, where it comes into contact with the digestive juice exuded from a maximum number of glands. It is only when the size of the animal is rather large that the leaf becomes hollow in the middle like a spoon, with the juice of more than fifty glands concentrated in the depression. In a case of this kind the tentacles remain inflected much longer, because the solution of the prey requires more time. If the captive is very small, its solution and absorption are completed in a couple of days. Afterwards, the tentacles lift, straighten themselves, and resume their original positions. The jaws, wings, compound eyes, leg-bones, claws, &c., of the captured animals are left behind undigested; but the flesh and blood are totally absorbed, and the liquid poured out by the glands to effect solution is also re-imbibed by them. The undigested remnants being now suspended on dry tentacles are easily blown away from the sun-dew leaves by the wind. After an interval of a day or two the glands at the ends of the tentacles, now occupying their original positions, again separate out a viscid fluid in the form of tiny dewdrops, and the leaf is once more furnished with the means of securing insects, and is able to repeat the movements above described.

Amongst the animals which fall victims to the sun-dew the most predominant are little midges; but rather larger flies, too, ants both with and without wings, beetles, small butterflies, and even dragon-flies, as they run, creep, or fly past, adhere to the extended gland-bearing tentacles as though they were limed-twigs. The larger animals, such as dragon-flies, are secured by the co-operation of two or three adjacent leaves. Some idea of the large number of captives made by a sun-dew is given by the fact that once upon a single leaf were found the remains of thirteen different insects.

In order to place in a true light the vast significance of the movements of the tentacles belonging to *Drosera* leaves in relation, not only to the nourishment of that plant, but to plant-life in general, it is necessary to direct attention to the facts that these movements are accomplished not in the cell directly excited, but in others, *i.e.* in adjacent cells belonging to the same community; that a propagation of the stimulus takes place from one protoplast to a second, thence to a third, fourth, tenth, and so on, to a hundredth, and that the speed of transmission is susceptible of measurement. The movements occasioned in protoplasts situated at a distance from the seat of irritation by the stimulus propagated from its vicinity are, according to the position of the stimulating object, sometimes in one direction, sometimes in another, but in every case they are purposeful and for the benefit of the whole organism.

Investigations with a view to determining the degree of sensitiveness of *Drosera* leaves yielded the following results. A particle of a woman's hair, 0·2 mm. long and weighing 0·000822 mg., when placed upon a gland of *Drosera rotundifolia*, caused a movement of the tentacle belonging to the excited gland, which manifested itself externally as an inflection. If so minute a body of the kind is placed on the human tongue, its presence is not perceived, so that the sensitiveness of the protoplasts in the glands of the sun-dew is greater than that of the nerve extremities in the tip of the tongue, though the latter are well known to be the most sensitive in the human body. A four-thousandth part of a milligram of ammonium carbonate sufficed to induce motion, as also did $\frac{1}{50000}$ mg. of ammonium phosphate. It would lead us too far to consider all the experiments in detail, but they point to the conclusion that liquid substances stimulate more strongly than solid bodies, and that the more nutritious to the plant the material placed upon the gland, the more quickly does the inflection of the tentacles ensue.

The propagation or conduction of a stimulus from cell to cell, as it takes place in the cell-community constituting a sun-dew leaf, may be compared to the conduction of stimulus by nerves from a sense-organ to the central organ, and of the force of will from the brain to the muscles. This transmission is conceived to be a progressive movement affecting the ultimate particles of the nerves, and comparable to the conduction of sound, light, and electricity; but no one has yet succeeded in making these movements visible. So much the more interesting is it to be able to see and follow in the glands and tentacles, by the aid of very slight magnifying power or even with the naked eye, the material change which occurs in the protoplasts of the sun-dew leaf when they are receiving or transmitting a stimulus. The pedicel of a tentacle is penetrated by one or two vessels with fine spiral sculpturing on the inner surface, and around these are parenchymatous cells. The gland has in the middle a group of oblong cells sculptured internally with very delicate spiral thickenings ("spiroids"), and the vessel or pair of vessels running down the middle of the tentacle (see fig. 26[1]) merge into these spiroids. A parenchyma composed of two or three layers surrounds the median group of spiroids. In each parenchymatous cell the protoplast is discerned forming a thick lining to the wall, and having a continuous streaming motion: whilst within the vacuole is contained a homogeneous liquid of a purple colour. If the minutest fragment of animal matter, such as flesh or albumen, be placed on these cells it acts as a stimulant on the contents of the cell-cavities, and the impulse manifests itself in a division of the hitherto homogeneous purple liquid into dark, roundish, club-shaped and vermiform lumps, cloudy spheres, and an almost colourless liquid.

This change, known as "aggregation", is propagated from the spot irritated down from one cell to another through the tentacle, across the leaf surface to adjoining tentacles, up to the heads of these, and so further and further radiating, so to speak, in all directions. Accompanying this visible sign of conduction, we have the bending of all tentacles in which the purple fluid is altered in the way described. When the source of excitation, the piece of flesh, is dissolved and digested, and the tentacles resume their original position, the dark lumps and spheres in the cavities

Fig. 27.—Venus's Fly-trap (*Dionæa muscipula*).

of the protoplasts disappear, and the homogeneous purple colour is restored as it existed before the stimulation.

The various species of the Sun-dew genus are distributed over all parts of the world, and are more numerous than those of any other genus of the family of Droseraceæ. Most of the other genera belonging to this order (*Dionæa, Aldrovandia, Byblis, Roridula, Drosophyllum*) are by no means rich in members. Each is represented merely by a single or few species, and is found exclusively in a very limited district. Like *Drosera*, they are all insectivorous plants, and all have the power of dissolving, absorbing, and using as supplementary nutriment, nitrogenous compounds from dead animals. The most striking of them are *Dionæa* and *Aldrovandia*. They form the very small third group of animal-captors, in which movements are performed for the purpose of prey, and their apparatus for seizure and digestion is one of the most curious adaptations displayed by the vegetable world.

The Venus's Fly-trap (*Dionæa muscipula*), represented opposite (fig. 27), in half its natural size, grows wild only in a narrow strip of country in the east of North America (from Long Island to Florida) in the vicinity of peat-bogs. The leaves, like those of many other carnivorous plants, are grouped in rosettes round the flowering axes, and for the most part rest their under surfaces either entirely or partially upon the ground. Each leaf consists, first, of a flat, spatulate petiole, which is, as it were, truncated in front and suddenly contracted to the midrib, and, secondly, of a roundish lamina. The latter is divided by the midrib into two symmetrical halves, inclined to one another at an angle of from 60° to 90° like the leaves of a half-open book. Both margins of the lamina run out into from twelve to twenty long, sharp teeth, which, however, do not carry either glands or any other special structures on their tips.

On the central part of each half of the leaf there are three very stiff and sharp spines, which are always shorter than the marginal teeth, and which stand up obliquely. They are composed of elongated cells whose protoplasm throughout life is in very active circulation. At the base of each spinous process is a short cylindrical pad of tissue formed of small parenchymatous cells, and this pad allows the spine to be deflected. The spines themselves are rigid and do not bend in response to pressure; they are forced down on to the surface of the leaf, the pad of tissue referred to acting as a hinge. In addition to these processes, glands are scattered over the whole upper surface of the lamina. They look like the shortly-stalked glands of a butterwort leaf, are composed of some twenty-eight small cells, are purple in colour, and capable of secreting a mucilaginous liquid. Little trichomes, stellate hairs, are also borne on the edge of the leaf between the sharp teeth, and also on the under-surface.

No visible change is produced by a blow or shock or by pressure affecting the whole plant or leaf, as might be caused by wind or falling drops of rain, nor even by injuries to the petiole or back of the lamina. But as soon as the upper surface of the lamina is touched, the two lobes, hitherto at right angles, approach one another until the sharp marginal teeth are interlocked, and the body touching the leaf is inclosed within two walls (fig. 28²). When the places beset with purple glands are alone excited by contact with the object, this inflection and closing follows very slowly; but if one of the six spines projecting in trios from the two foliar lobes is ever so lightly touched, the leaf shuts up within 10–30 seconds, *i.e.* quickly and steadily; an action best compared to the closing of a half-open book. The teeth standing at the edge of the leaf lock into one another on these occasions like the fingers of clasped hands. The lobes, however, whose surfaces were hitherto plane, become at the moment of closing somewhat concave, so that when contracted they do not lie flat against one another but inclose a cavity, the contour of which nearly corresponds with that of a bean.

The further changes and processes now ensuing depend upon whether the sensitive part of the leaf was subjected to prolonged or only momentary contact, and also upon the nature of the body touching it, whether inorganic or organic, non-nitrogenous or nitrogenous. When rapidly touched or stroked, the leaf folds together, but only remains closed for a short time. The lobes soon begin to re-open, and can be stimulated afresh immediately and caused to shut again. This is also the case when the disturbance was due to the impact of a grain of sand or any other inorganic body, and likewise when the stimulus proceeded from an organic but non-nitrogenous object. But if, on the other hand, the body upon the upper surface of the lamina was nitrogenous and the contact not too hasty, the two lobes of the leaf remain closed over the object for a longer period. They also

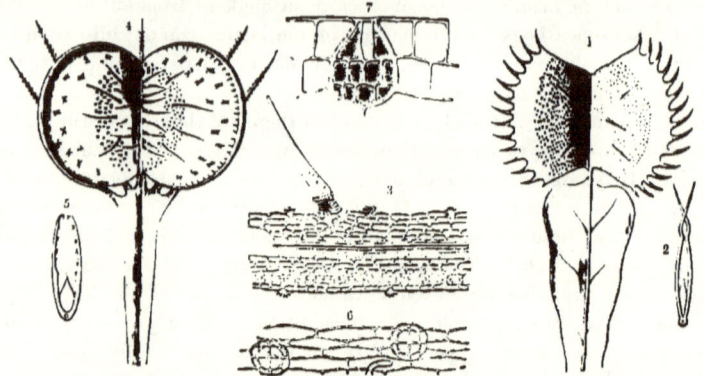

Fig. 2s.—Capturing apparatus of the leaves of *Aldrovandia* and Venus's Fly-trap.

¹ Expanded leaf of a Venus's Fly-trap.    ² Section of a closed leaf.    ³ One of the sensitive bristles on the surface of the leaf.    ⁴ Expanded leaf of *Aldrovandia*.    ⁵ Section of a closed leaf.    ⁶ Glands on the surface of leaf of *Aldrovandia*.    ⁷ Gland from the wall of a *Sarracenia* pitcher.

become flat and even again, and are pressed together so tightly that intervening bodies, if soft, are squeezed and crushed to pieces. In addition, the glands, dry till then, begin to secrete a slimy, colourless, highly acid juice; and this is true even of those glands which are not at all in contact with the nitrogenous bodies inclosed. The secretion flows so copiously that it can be seen in the form of drops if the shut lobes be forcibly separated. It covers the imprisoned body and gradually dissolves the albuminous compounds therein contained. Afterwards, the secretion and the matter dissolved in it are re-absorbed by the same glands as previously discharged the acid liquid, containing pepsin, in response to the stimulus; and when the trap reopens, the glands are dry. The soluble part of the prey has now vanished: the six little spinous processes, which were bent in the closed leaf like the blades of a pocket-knife and lay pressed down upon the surface, stand up; and the leaf is once more equipped for making fresh captures.

The time requisite for the digestion of a nitrogenous body resting upon the surface of a leaf varies according to the size of the body. The leaf usually remains closed for from eight to fourteen days, but often even for twenty days. Although the larger live articulated animals—earwigs, millipedes, and dragon-flies—caught upon the upper surface of the leaf, cause the lobes to slam together, they are able to slip out if part of their bodies projects beyond the toothed margin, for the teeth are flexible and yield to strong pressure.   But small creatures are hopelessly lost when the lobes have closed over them.   They are at once suffocated in the liquid which is poured out copiously by the glands and are then dissolved and absorbed with the exception of their claws, leg-bones, chitinous rings, &c., which are incapable of being digested.

In spite of the identity of aim and of result, the mechanism of a *Dionæa* leaf differs very materially from that of the sun-dew leaf described above.   Division of labour is carried much further in the Fly-trap.   The pre-eminently sensitive structures, viz., the six filaments situated upon the upper surface of the leaf,

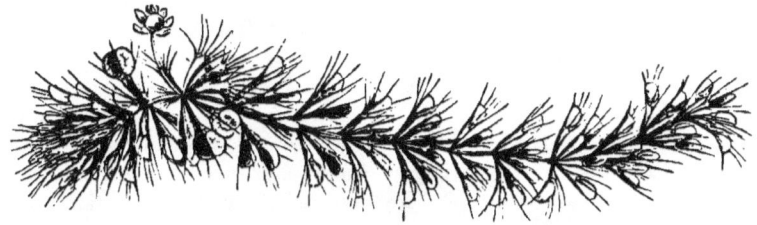

Fig. 20.—*Aldrovandia vesiculosa.*

do not act also as digestive glands.   Again, the long sharp teeth at the edge of the leaf, which correspond in position to the marginal tentacles of a sun-dew leaf, carry no glands, and only serve to close the trap securely when an animal has been caught.   Accordingly in *Dionæa* there exist special structures for three different functions, namely, stimulation, seizure, and digestion, whilst in the case of *Drosera* all these functions belong to the gland-bearing tentacles alone.   The stimulus acting on the sensitive filaments on the leaf of the Fly-trap is liberated in the form of a rapid motion of the lobes and a discharge of digestive fluid from the glands, and this discharge of secretion ensues therefore through the mediation of cells which have not themselves been directly excited.   The process here again is much more striking than in the sun-dew leaf.   The transmission of stimulus, though as a fact identical in the two plants we are comparing, proceeds at any rate with much greater rapidity in *Dionæa* than in *Drosera*.

The analogy existing between these processes, especially the conduction and liberation of stimulus, and similar phenomena of the muscles and nerves in an animal organism, has already been brought out in discussing the sun-dew.   It is a noteworthy fact that, in the fly-traps, actual electric currents have been observed, which shows that the greatest resemblance exists to muscles and nerves as regards electro-motor action also.   A positive current runs from the base to the apex of the lamina; another current running in the opposite direction is demonstrable in the petiole; and the upper layers of cells in the lamina and the midrib are ascertained to be the seat of origin of this phenomenon. A great alteration in the intensity of the current ensues upon each excitation of the leaf; and, inasmuch as this fluctuation of the electric current precedes the movement of the leaf caused by the stimulus, it is natural to assume that it depends upon the conduction and liberation of the stimulus.

*Aldrovandia*, the plant nearest allied to the Fly-trap in the structure of its leaf, is a water-plant, which occurs scattered over the southern and central parts of Europe. It only flourishes in shallow ditches, pools, and small ponds inclosed by banks of reeds and rushes, where the plants are immersed in clear, so-called soft water, attaining in summer to a temperature of 30° C., and are exempt from any incrustation of carbonate of lime, whereby the tender parts of the leaves might be hindered in their movements. On cursory inspection, one might take *Aldro-vandia vesiculosa*, which is represented in fig. 29 full size and in its natural position, for a *Utricularia* (cf. fig. 17). It lives, like the latter, floating in water; is destitute of roots, and has a slender filiform stem with leaves arranged in whorls and ter-minating in bristles. In proportion as it grows at the apex, the hinder part dies away and decays. The development of hibernating buds takes place also in precisely the same manner as in *Utricularia*. Towards autumn, the stem ceases to elongate, and the two hundred small and young leaves, which adorn the ex-tremity of the stem and whose cells are quite full of starch, remain lying closely wrapped one upon another and form a dark, oval, bristly ball, which sinks at the commencement of winter to the bottom of the pool or pond and hibernates there lying upon the mud.

It is not till very late in the following spring, when little midge-larvæ and other animals begin to move about in the water, that fresh life is awakened in these structures. The starch-grains in the leaves are brought into solution and used for building-material; the axis elongates, and lacunæ filled with air are developed, whereupon the plant becomes lighter, ascends, and remains throughout the summer and autumn floating just below the surface of the water. Although the little leaves of the winter-buds generally admit of the recognition of their future form, the apparatus adapted to the capture of animals is but little developed on them. But when once the leaves are mature, they bear laminæ, which are extremely like those of *Dionæa* in shape, and serve, as do the latter, for the capture of small animals. Each leaf is differentiated, as in *Dionæa*, into a strong, dark-green petiole expanded and anteriorly clavate, and into a roundish lamina with a delicate epidermis and with two lobes connected by the midrib and inclined nearly at right angles to one another (see fig. 28 ⁴). The midrib projects beyond the apex of the delicate lamina in the form of a bristle. In addition, comparatively long, rigid bristles, tipped with extremely fine spines, proceed from the petiole close to where the latter is joined to the lamina; and these bristles, which are directed forwards, give the whole leaf-structure a spiky appearance and prevent the approach of such animals as are not suitable for prey. The two margins of the lamina are bent inwards, and their rims are studded with small conical points. On the surface of the lamina, especially along the midrib, there are pointed hairs, whilst a great number of glands, some larger and some smaller, occur from the midrib to nearly the middle of each lobe. The larger glands are discoid, and not unlike the sessile glands on the leaves of *Pinguicula*. They consist of four median cells with twelve others grouped round about them, and are borne upon a very short stalk. The small glands are few-celled, being usually composed simply of a capitate-cell resting upon a short foot-cell (see fig. 28 [6]). Towards the incurved margin of the lamina are displayed scattered stellate hairs, *i.e.* groups of cells so arranged as to present the appearance of a St. Andrew's cross when seen from above.

If minute animals or Diatomaceæ, especially species of *Navicula*, whilst swimming about in the water, touch the upper surfaces of the lobes set at right-angles—in particular, if the hairs in the middle are stroked as they creep by—the two lobes shut together quickly in the same way as those of *Dionæa*, and the animal or *Navicula*, as the case may be, is then enclosed in a cage between two somewhat inflated walls. The possibility of an attempt on the part of the captive to escape by the place where the margins of the lamina meet is met by the circumstance that the edges of the incurved margins are furnished with sharp indentations turned towards the interior of the cavity enclosed between the lobes (see fig. 28 [5]).

Amongst the prisoners we find the same company as in the traps of *Utricularia*, namely, small species of *Cyclops*, *Daphnia*, and *Cypris*, larvæ of aquatic insects, and not infrequently also species of *Navicula* and other free and solitary Diatomaceæ.

How the prey is killed and digested has not yet been ascertained. It does not in any case take place so quickly as in *Dionæa*, for instances have been seen of animals still living in their prison six days after being caught. But, at last, movements and vital actions cease, and if after a couple of weeks the two lobes of the lamina are pulled apart, the only contents to be found are shells, bristles, rings, and siliceous skeletons, whilst everything soluble has vanished, having evidently been absorbed.

Very similar to the species distributed through Southern and Central Europe are *Aldrovandia australis*, a native of Australia, and *Aldrovandia verticillata*, inhabiting tropical India. The fact that the remains of small aquatic beetles and other creatures have been found within their closed laminæ, leads us to the conclusion that they act as entrappers of animals in the same way as *Aldrovandia vesiculosa*.

## CARNIVOROUS PLANTS WITH ADHESIVE APPARATUS.

The forms constituting the third section of carnivorous plants neither have pit-falls nor move in response to the contact of animal matter, but the leaves act as motionless limed twigs, their glands having the power of pouring out sticky substances to capture prey and juices to digest it, being able besides to re-absorb the albuminoid compounds dissolved. The most striking representative of this section, and the one most accurately studied, is the Fly-catcher (*Drosophyllum lusitanicum*), which is indigenous to Portugal and Morocco, and is shown in the illustration on p. 155. This plant differs from all the carnivorous kinds hitherto discussed in respect of habitat, inasmuch as it does not grow under water or even in swampy places but on sandy ground and dry rocky mountains. The stem in robust specimens is nearly 9 inches high, and bears, on a few short branches at the top, flowers from 2 to 3 cm. in diameter. The leaves are very numerous and particularly crowded round the base of the stem. Their shape is linear and much attenuated towards the filiform tip, whilst the upper surface is somewhat hollowed so as to form a groove. With the exception of these grooves, the leaves are entirely covered with beads, which glisten in the sunshine like dewdrops; and it is to this circumstance that the plant owes its name of *Drosophyllum*, *i.e.* Dew-leaf. The glittering drops are the secretion of glands, which in form remind one in some respects of the long-stalked glands of the butterwort, and in others of those of the Sun-dew (*Drosera*). They resemble the latter in their red coloration, in the fact that the pedicel bearing the gland contains vessels whilst the glands themselves have oblong cells with internal walls thickened by fine spiral ridges, and further, in the circumstance that the secretion covers the gland with a colourless film in the form of a drop. But in shape they especially resemble the glands of the butterwort, being just like little mushrooms.

Besides these glands, which are borne on stalks of unequal lengths and are plainly to be distinguished with the naked eye, there are also very small sessile glands. These latter are colourless, and in particular differ from the stalked variety in the fact that they discharge an acid liquid only when they come into contact with nitrogenous animal matter, whereas the production of drops on the stalked glands is accomplished without any such contact. This secretion is acid and extremely viscid. It has the property of adhering immediately to foreign bodies coming into contact with it, though it is readily withdrawn from the gland itself. When an insect alights on the leaf, its legs, abdomen, and wings instantly stick to the drop touched by them. The insect, however, is not held fast by the gland which secreted that drop, but, being able to move, drags the drop off the gland. Its movements bring it into contact with other drops, which thereupon are similarly detached from the glands; and so, in a very short time, the insect is smeared with the secretion from a number of glands. Thus clogged and overwhelmed, it is no longer able to crawl along, but, suffocating, sinks down to the sessile glands which cover the surface of the leaf at a lower level. All the soluble parts of its body are then dissolved by means of the secretion of these glands and are afterwards absorbed.

The glands renew the drops of secretion of which they are despoiled with great rapidity. The quantity of acid liquid secreted is, in general, very great, so that it is not surprising to find *Drosophyllum* covered at the same time with remains of besmeared dead bodies drained of their juices, and with still struggling insects which have recently alighted and become clogged. The number of animals caught by the leaves of a single plant is very great; and even people who are not otherwise interested in the vegetable world are impressed by the sight of a plant with its leaves covered with a number of insects adhering to them as though they were limed twigs. In the neighbourhood of Oporto, where *Drosophyllum* grows abundantly, the peasants use these plants instead of limed twigs, hanging them up

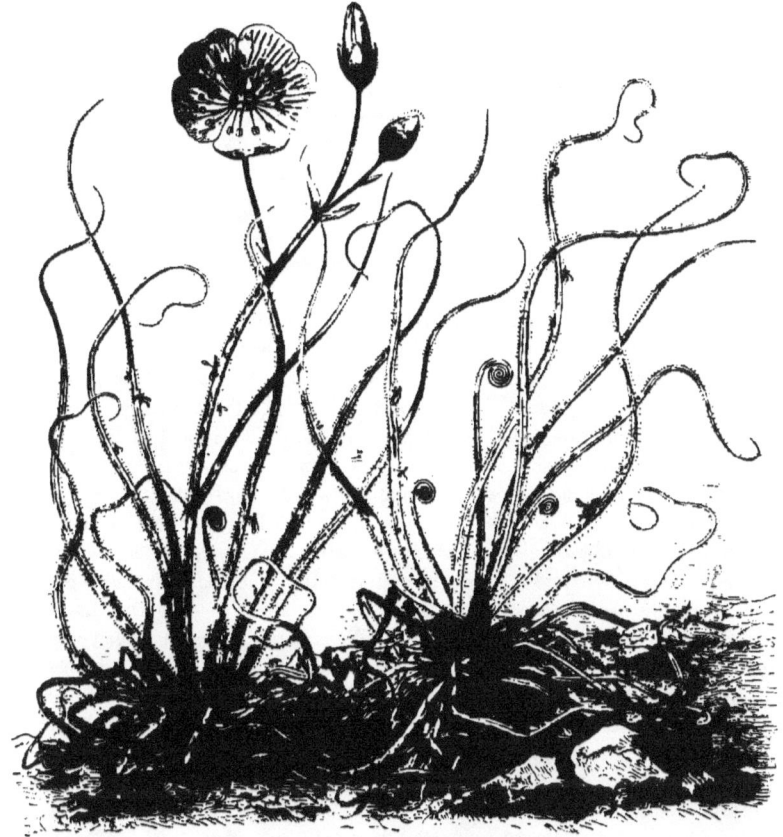

Fig. 30.—The Fly-catcher (*Drosophyllum lusitanicum*).

in their rooms, and so getting rid of numbers of troublesome flies which stick to them and are killed.

A number of other plants have the power, though in a less conspicuous degree than *Drosophyllum*, of obtaining additional nitrogenous food out of adherent animals by means of secretory and absorptive glands. Such are many species of primulas, saxifrages, and house-leeks, which bury their roots in cracks and crevices of rock (*e.g. Primula viscosa, P. villosa, P. hirsuta, Saxifraga luteo-viridis, S. bulbifera, S. tridactylites, Sempervivum montanum*), secondly, caryophyllaceous plants and species of the caper order (*e.g.* *Saponaria viscosa*, *Silene viscosa*, *Cleome ornithopodioides*, *Bonchea cohiteoides*), and lastly, a series of plants which flourish in peat-bogs and upon deep beds of humus, such as *Sedum villosum*, *Roridula dentata*, *Byblis gigantea*, and many others besides.

It would, however, be erroneous to suppose that in all cases where a sticky coating occurs on leaves and stem a solution and digestion of the insects adhering to the viscid parts is necessarily denoted. In many instances structures of this kind, which are analogous to limed twigs, are a means of protecting honey-bearing flowers against unwelcome guests belonging to the world of insects, as will be explained in greater detail later on. Glands secreting a viscid substance may, no doubt, often possess two kinds of function—they may, on the one hand, prevent unbidden animals from approaching the honey, and, on the other, by dissolving their flesh and blood with the aid of the secretion and then absorbing them, turn to advantage such insects as are tempted by immoderate craving to step upon the perilous path leading to the honey-receptacles and adhere there and die.

Many plants have structures on the epidermis of their leaves corresponding in form to the glands of insectivorous plants, but which do not discharge secretions either spontaneously or when irritated. On the other hand, these structures have the power of imbibing water, and are, in this relation, of the greatest importance to the plants in question. Although the more detailed treatment of them is postponed until we have occasion to deal with the absorption of water by aërial organs, it is advisable to refer now to the fact that chemically pure water only very rarely reaches the interior of a plant by means of the absorptive organs mentioned. Sulphuric acid is almost always introduced with atmospheric water, and in some circumstances ammonia also. However trivial the amount of the nitrogen conveyed to plants in this way, it must not be undervalued, at all events in the case of those which are only able to acquire small quantities of nitrogenous compounds from the ground by means of their roots. Now, it is very probable that plants of this kind do not reject even other nitrogenous compounds which are brought with the water from the atmosphere to their aërial leaves. The foliage-leaves of many plants display contrivances whereby rain-water is often retained for a considerable time in special hollows. In these depressions there is invariably a collection of dust-particles, small dead animals, pollen-grains, &c., which have been blown in by the wind, whilst rain trickling down the stem brings very various objects with it from higher up and washes them into these reservoirs in the leaves. Sometimes too a few animals are drowned in the water-receptacles. As a matter of fact, the water in the hollows of the leaves of the Peltate Saxifrage and of Bromeliads, in the inflated vaginæ of many umbelliferous plants, and in the cups formed by the coalescence of opposite leaves in many Gentianeæ, Compositæ, and Dipsaceæ, is always brown-coloured, and contains nitrogenous compounds in solution, derived from the decaying bodies of dead animals which have fallen into these receptacles.

If absorbent organs are present in the reservoirs in question, the water, together with the nitrogenous compounds dissolved therein, is absorbed without delay. Hollows of this kind occurring in foliage-leaves only differ from those above described as developed on sarracenias in being destitute of special contrivances for decoying animals into the traps, and for rendering their escape from the latter impossible. It cannot be denied that through forms of this kind a gradual transition has been proved to exist between plants which absorb nearly pure water by means of their foliage-leaves and those which capture animals. And, further, amongst the latter we find all gradations of mechanism from *Drosophyllum* and the Primulas with their epiphyllous secretory glands up to the Fly-trap (*Dionæa*), which exhibits the most complex apparatus of all for capturing and digesting prey, and in which division of labour is carried to its highest development by the communities of cells constituting the foliage-leaves.

It is not surprising that the first apparatus for capturing and digesting insects to be noticed, to have its functions recognized and to be described, was that of *Dionæa*. But it strikes one as all the more strange that of late the question has repeatedly been mooted in the very case of *Dionæa*, as to whether the capture and digestion of insects is not injurious instead of beneficial to these plants. Gardeners, who have cultivated *Dionæa* in greenhouses, have made the observation that individuals protected from the visits of insects thrived at least as well as those whose leaves were covered with bits of meat, &c., or, to employ the usual phrase, were fed with meat. It has also been found that a leaf cannot stand more than three meals; indeed, it often happens that even after the first occasion of digesting a bit of meat, the leaf concerned shows signs of having been injured by the repast. That is to say, a long time elapses before leaves which have digested a largish albuminoid mass regain their normal irritability; and often they wither and die. If cheese is placed on *Dionæa*, it is true the leaf closes over it, and there is a commencement of the process of solution, but before this is accomplished the leaf turns brown and perishes. Yet if *Dionæa* were obliged to lose a leaf after every meal, the result would be very disadvantageous.

As against these considerations, we have first of all to remark that the absorption of nutriment takes place in nature in a manner differing materially from the phenomenon in greenhouses. A leaf of *Dionæa* in the wild state is protected against the possibility of receiving too plentiful a dose of albuminoid substances at a time. Insects so large as not to allow the lobes to close together over them slip out again, and only small ones are caught and retained. When, in the latter case, one deducts the chitinous coat, and in general all parts not susceptible of being digested, such a small quantity of albuminoid compounds is left that, compared with it, the little cubes of meat used in the experiments made in greenhouses must be looked upon as an exceedingly sumptuous repast. But that so small an amount of nitrogenous food as is to be derived from a tiny captured insect does not act injuriously, follows from the fact that dionæas growing wild flourish excellently, and do not exhibit the brown discoloration of the leaves which is caused in a greenhouse by placing bits of cheese upon them. If the absorption of nitrogenous aliment from prey were injurious to *Dionœa*, the plant would certainly have died out long ago. If, therefore, cultivated specimens of *Dionœa* have suffered from being fed with meat, fibrin, cheese, and other such materials, only this much is proved, that the nutriment in question was not beneficial to them owing to its quality or to its being too concentrated.

As regards the other point, that *Dionœa* thrives well under cultivation, even when all visits from insects are excluded, we must, on the other hand, bear in mind that the successful growth of *Dionœa*, like that of *Drosera*, *Pinguicula*, &c., is not conceivable unless in some way or another the nitrogen indispensable for the construction of the protoplasm is conveyed to the individuals in question. The source from which it is taken varies according to the site. If the roots are buried in deep sods of bog-moss upon a flat expanse of moorland, the supply of nitrogen from the ground, and also from the air, will be extremely limited, and probably insufficient; under these circumstances the nutriment derived from the dead bodies of captured insects would be not only useful and beneficial, but may be even essential. If, on the contrary, the place where the plants have been reared or have grown up spontaneously is such that they can obtain the requisite nitrogen from the ground or air, they are able without harm to dispense with the available source of nitrogen afforded by the capture of insects. It is worthy of notice that insectivorous plants always grow wild only in places that are poorly supplied with nitrogenous food. The majority occur in pools fed by subterranean water, whose course lies through layers of peat, or in the spongy peat itself, or in the sods of *Sphagnum*. Others are rooted in deep chinks in the stone on the declivities of rocky mountains, whilst yet others occur in the sand of steppes. The water available in such situations for absorption by the suction-cells is, to say the least, very poorly furnished with nitrogenous compounds; and the quantity of these compounds passing from the ground into the air at the places mentioned is extremely minute and inconstant. Under these circumstances, the acquirement of nitrogen from the albuminoid compounds of dead animals is certainly of benefit, and all the various pitfalls, traps, and limed twigs are explained as contrivances by means of which this advantage is secured.

# 4. ABSORPTION OF NUTRIMENT BY PARASITIC PLANTS.

Classification of parasites.—Bacteria.—Fungi.—Twining parasites.—Green-leaved parasites.—Tooth-wort.— Broom-rapes, Balanophoreæ and Rafflesiaceæ.—Mistletoe and Loranthus.—Grafting and budding.

## CLASSIFICATION OF PARASITES.

The ancients understood by parasites people who intruded uninvited into the houses of the rich in order to obtain a free meal. The designation was first applied to plants by an eighteenth - century botanist, named Micheli, in his work "De Orobanche" (1720) wherein are described amongst others, many kinds of "plantæ secundariæ aut parasiticæ". Micheli included under this term plants which with-draw organic compounds from living plants or animals, thus sparing themselves the labour of forming those compounds out of water, salts, and constituents of the air. For a long time all epiphytes, including mosses and lichens growing on the bark of trees, and indeed even many climbing plants, were held to be parasites. Thus, it is not long ago that *Clusia rosea*, which occurs in the Antilles, was described as a regular vampire, in whose embraces other plants met their death; and it has been asserted respecting a whole series of other plants of the tropical zone, including, for instance, several species of fig, that they attach their stems and branches to other trees, divest themselves of their bark, and cause the death of that of the neighbour attacked as a consequence of the pressure which they exert. The young wood of the invader would then come into direct connection with the young wood of the plant assailed, and the possibility would thus be afforded of draining the latter of all its juices.

These assumptions, at least as regards the exhaustion of juices, have not been confirmed. When individuals of species of *Clusia* or *Ficus*, which have roots buried in the earth, and are themselves already grown up into stately leaf-bearing plants, attach their flattened stems and branches to other plants, investing them so completely as to interfere with the process of respiration, this constitutes, at all events, an invasion of one of the most important of the vital functions of the plant attacked, and may ultimately cause its death; but the killing is not under these circumstances due to drainage of juices, but is brought about by suffocation. Lichens, too, when they cover the bark of trees with a close-fitting mantle, may possibly restrict the process of respiration through particular parts of the cortex, and thereby injure the development of the tree in question; but they are not on that account to be looked upon as parasites any more than the fructifications of the species of *Telephora*, and other Basidiomycetes, which grow up rapidly from the ground, and, spreading out like plastic doughy masses, envelop all objects which come in their way, and ultimately stifle such as are living, namely, grass haulms, bilberry bushes, &c. Even creepers, which impose woody stems upon the trunks of young trees, winding round them like serpents, and restricting their circumferential growth at the parts in contact with the coils, so that ultimately the latter lie imbedded in regular grooves in the cortex, ought not to be considered as parasites. The *Lonicera ciliosa* of North America, represented in fig. 31, may be taken as an example of creepers of this kind. They only interfere with the conduction of the constructive materials generated in the green foliage, preventing, in particular, the

Fig. 31.—*Lonicera ciliosa* in South Carolina.

part of the axis below the strangulating coils from being supplied with those materials; and so at last they cause the whole trunk, which serves as their support, to dry up. The assertion may then be made that the young tree assailed has been strangled or throttled by the creeper, but not that the latter has drained it of juices and adapted them to its own use. Still less would the statement be applicable to the numerous brown and red sea-weeds, which settle upon the ramifications of the great species of *Sargassum*, or of the innumerable Diatomaceæ, which often entirely cover both fresh and salt-water plants. In still inlets of the sea it is not rare to see the larger sea-wracks with smaller specimens clinging to them, whilst Florideæ are fastened to the latter, and minute siliceous-coated diatoms to the Florideæ. Even in fresh water, e.g. in cold and rapid mountain streams, we find little tufts of *Chantransia* or *Batrachospermum* developed as epiphytes upon the black-green filaments of *Lemanea*, and on the former, again, Diatomaceæ. One of these Diatomaceæ, which, from its resemblance to a scale insect, has received the name of *Cocconeis Pediculus*, is especially conspicuous, and is often found by the score upon the green filaments of Algæ. Such a connection does, no doubt, suggest the idea that the *Cocconeis* drains the green algal cells of nutriment; nevertheless, such an assumption is not well founded, and if algæ, beset by *Cocconeis*, derive injury at all from their presence, it is chiefly owing to a restriction of their absorption of nutrient substances from the surrounding water and to interference with their respiration.

The distinctive property of true parasites does not lie, therefore, in the habit of growing upon other plants and animals, or even in the fact of killing their living supports, but resides exclusively in the withdrawal of nutrient substances from the living vegetable or animal bodies which they invest.

The plants and animals attacked and drained of their juices by parasites are called hosts.

From the point of view of food absorption, true parasites may be classified in three groups. The first group includes generally all microscopic forms which live in the interior of human beings and animals, chiefly in the blood; the second comprehends fungi possessing mycelia, which have the power of withdrawing by the entire surface of their filamentous cells, or by clavate outgrowths of the same, nutritive material from the tissues of the host invaded by them; and the third group comprises flowering plants wherein the seedling, upon emerging from the seed, penetrates into the host, by means of suction-roots or some other part which subserves the function of a suction-root, so as to absorb juices from the host.

## BACTERIA. FUNGI.

In treating of parasites of the first group, we must, in the first place, refer to several of the unwelcome visitors known by the name of Bacteria. They appear to be invariably unicellular, sometimes spherical, sometimes shortly cylindrical or rod-shaped; some are straight, and others curved in arcs or spirals; a few are non-motile, whilst some are actively motile. The largest forms have a diameter of $\frac{1}{500}$ mm.; the smallest do not measure more than $\frac{1}{50000}$ mm., and are reckoned amongst the minutest organisms hitherto revealed by the aid of the best micro-scopes. In liquids of suitable chemical composition and temperature, they multiply with extraordinary rapidity, reproduction being effected by division. The rod-shaped cells elongate somewhat and divide into two equal halves, each half, when grown to a certain size, divides once more into two, and so on without limit.

The process is of the nature of a repeated splitting of the cells, and this is the origin of the name of Fission-fungi (Schizomycetes) used to designate these organisms. It has been observed that within 20 minutes a bacterium-cell grows enough to be able to divide or split into two, and hence it has been calculated that from a single cell, under favourable external conditions, upwards of 16 millions of similar cells are produced in 8 hours; and in 24 hours many millions of millions.

It is this very capacity for rapid multiplication that gives so great an importance to Bacteria as parasites. For multiplication can only take place at the expense of the juices and nutrient substratum in which they live. If this nutrient substratum is to afford materials for constructing the millions of millions of cells produced within two periods of 24 hours, a far-reaching transformation is inevitable. Now, for certain bacteria, the blood, with its albuminoid compounds and carbo-hydrates, is an extremely favourable medium of nutrition; moreover, the tempera-ture of the blood of men and other mammals (35°–37° C.) could not be more suitable for the development of bacteria. Hence, it is readily intelligible that if a single parasitic bacterium-cell gets into the blood, it may be the origin of innumer-able other cells, and that these are in a position, in a comparatively short time, to alter and decompose the whole mass of the blood. Owing to their extraordinary minuteness, bacteria are able to penetrate from outside into the channels of the blood by a number of spots; every abrasion, pin-prick, and sore place, may become an entrance-door; so, too, through all the external orifices of the various canals in the bodies of men and animals, the bacteria can enter, especially through the pas-sages to the respiratory organs—and it becomes more and more probable that bacteria, diffused in the air, are in the main introduced into the respiratory organs by the process of breathing, thence penetrating into the finest blood-vessels, the so-called capillaries, and so pass into the current of the blood.

As regards the parasitic action of bacteria when they have penetrated into the bodies of men and animals, the supposition is that the protoplasm of each bacterium works as a ferment upon the environment, splitting up the chemical compounds in immediate proximity to it, and attracting and incorporating such products of the decomposition as are necessary for its own growth. Parasites with this method of operation act, at all events, much more destructively than those which, although they too absorb part of the host's juices, yet do not enter upon the necessary decompositions until the juices have passed into the cavities of their own bodies, and, therefore, do not alter the constitution of the unabsorbed residue. When the component parts of the blood are split up and resolved by bacteria, the nutrition of the host must be especially disturbed, and so must all the functions of the organs through which the blood perpetually circulates. Ultimately it may culminate in the organs ceasing to exercise their functions, and in the death of the host. When one remembers how fast the blood is pumped by the heart's action into every part of the body, it becomes intelligible how bacteria, possessing the power of decom-posing the blood, may also cause the death of the host at very short notice, as we have occasion to observe whenever there is an epidemic of cholera.

That numerous diseases affecting men and animals are caused by bacteria is established beyond question. Indeed, the conviction is gradually gaining ground that all infectious illnesses are occasioned by bacteria, and that the contagious matter which used to be called virus or miasma, but as to the nature of which people formerly had only very confused notions, consists of parasitic bacteria. Different phenomena in organisms in which illness has been induced by infection point to differences in the decompositions effected by the bacteria. But a particular kind of parasitic cell can only set up the same decomposition in any given liquid. If, therefore, the products of separation or decomposition vary in one and the same liquid, this can only be attributed to a difference in the impetus causing decomposition, and therefore to a difference in the parasitic cells; in other words, we are justified in assuming that every distinct infectious disease is due to a special kind of parasitic bacterium. This assumption is believed to be warranted even when no difference in the form of the bacteria is to be discovered which is discernible to sight or demonstrable by the expedients of research.

Most of the parasitic bacteria regarded as causes of diseases in man and beast are moreover capable of being very clearly distinguished from one another by the shape of their cells. The bacterium supposed to be the cause of diphtheria (*Micrococcus diphthericus*) presents itself in the form of minute spherical cells crowded together in close masses. The bacterium which causes anthrax in cattle (*Bacterium Anthracis*) has straight rod-like stationary cells. In the blood of people suffering from relapsing typhus, infinitesimally fine spiral filaments (*Spirochaete Obermeieri*) are found during the fever, whilst in the intestines of cholera patients, the comma-bacilli, so frequently described, occur: and in these cases, likewise, the organisms are brought into causal connection with the illnesses mentioned respectively. The answer to the question as to whether parasitic bacteria are developed and propagated in dead bodies also, thus becoming saprophytic, and, in general, the detailed description of the organisms, which are so important a factor for the weal or woe of humanity, are reserved for another section.

The second group of parasitic plants, according to the classification above given, includes several thousands of different kinds of moulds, toad-stools, and Discomycetes, which, notwithstanding great diversity in the conditions of life, dissimilarity in the history of their development, and endless variety in the form of their fructifications, yet exhibit great uniformity in respect of food-absorption and in their methods of attacking and draining their hosts. Spores, conveyed by currents of air or carried by animals, germinate under the influence of atmospheric moisture wherever they happen to come to rest. Tubular thin-walled cells, called hyphae, emerge from them and endeavour to grow into the stems, branches, leaves, or fruits of the host, sometimes horizontally, sometimes from above downward, sometimes up in the opposite direction. Many select spots where the resistance offered is nil or only very weak: they grope about on the surface of the host until they find a stoma, and then use it as an entrance, and so enter the passages and lacunae, of which the stomata are the orifices. Others seek out places where the

surface of the plant serving as host has become broken—wounds occasioned by
animals, violent wind, hailstones, or the weight of superincumbent snow—and use
these as means of ingress.  Yet others adopt the shortest route by breaking through
the wall and so effecting an entrance for themselves.  The tips of the hyphae and
also of the outgrowths developed by them have the power of decomposing and
destroying the membrane of cells in the living plant serving as their host.  At the
spots to which they apply themselves, little gaps are shortly produced in the cell-
membranes, and through them the hyphae penetrate, either in their entirety
or by means of special processes, into the interior of the cells attacked.  In
this operation it does not matter whether the hypha concerned has just emerged
from a germinating spore or is a ramification of a mycelium several years old,
which has been quiescent for a time and then begun to germinate again vigorously;
the power of perforating cell-walls is a property possessed by the one as much as
the other.

The aspect of the host's epidermal cells at the places where the hypha comes
into contact with its victim is, on the other hand, not quite such a matter of
indifference.  For plants liable to become hosts are not without contrivances for
protecting themselves against intruders.  Thus their epidermal cells have their
external walls greatly thickened and invested with cuticle.  Although the main
object of this is merely to afford protection against excessive transpiration and
desiccation of cells filled with sap, a thickening of the kind constitutes also a coat
of armour which is not liable to be broken through by every hypha.  Still greater
security is afforded by a double or triple layer of thick-walled cells destitute of
sap, such as a solid corky bark.  Coats of this kind are not penetrated even by the
most vigorous hyphae.  In order to gain admittance notwithstanding, many force
their conical tips into the fissures and crannies of the bark, push the peeling scales
apart or even burst them, and so succeed ultimately in reaching parts which are
susceptible of being pierced and allow the hyphae to conduct their mining operations
with effect.  In the majority of cases the parasite is not content with perforating
and exhausting the superficial cells alone of the host; its hyphae grow faster as
they penetrate deeper, a process generally accomplished irrespective of the number
or direction of the partition walls in their way.  Thus the hyphae of Polyporeæ,
which are parasitic in the wood of living trees, penetrate whole series of cells, now
growing through a bordered-pit, now piercing the uniformly thickened part of the
wall of a wood-cell (see fig. 32 [3]).  Others, as, for instance, the Peronosporeæ, prefer
to bury themselves in the passages between individual cells, i.e. in the so-called
intercellular spaces.  The hyphae imbedded in this way then develop lateral outgrowths which perforate the walls of the cells adjoining the intercellular space, and
upon entering the interior of the cells swell up to the shape of a club (see fig. 32 [1]).
By means of these clavate or almost spherical excrescences, which are named
haustoria, the parasite sucks the substances required for its own nourishment from
the living substance of the penetrated cells.

The hyphae of the above-mentioned parasitic fungi have the peculiarity that in proportion as the one end elongates the other dies away. Hence the same effect is produced as if the progressive motion of these hyphæ were like that of ship-worms. This impression is particularly strong in cases wherein one part of the mass of wood attacked exhibits hyphæ occupied with their mining operations and growing through partition walls, whilst the other part has been the scene of past activity, and exhibits numbers of drilled holes, but no longer any trace of hyphæ. The fact that a plant is thus invaded internally by the parasitic mycelia of fungi is not always betrayed by its external appearance. Sometimes the hosts remain somewhat backward in development, but this circumstance might be just as well due to other causes, perhaps to unsuitability of situation. It is not till the mycelia need once

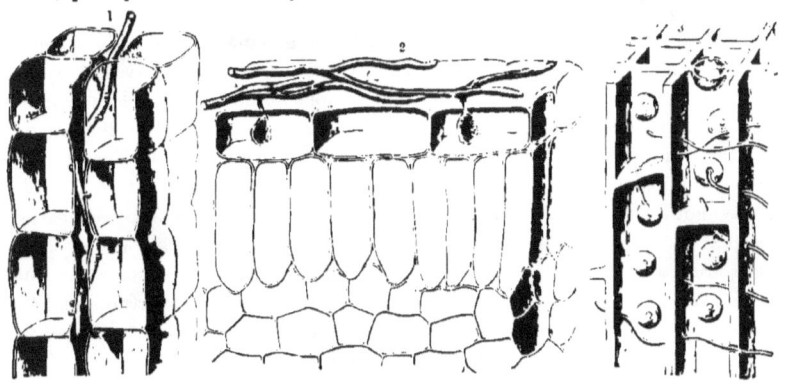

Fig. 32  Hyphæ of Parasitic Fungi.
1 Of one of the Peronosporeæ,  2 Of a Mildew,  3 Of one of the Polyporeæ.

more to multiply and distribute their kind that they emerge partially from the host; they then lift their spore-forming hyphæ above the surface, leaving it to the wind to distribute the spores as they are detached.

This process vividly recalls the similar behaviour of those water-plants which, in a similar manner, vegetate submerged for months, and only come to the surface at the flowering and fruiting seasons, in order to expose their flowers to insects, and their seeds to the breeze. We are also reminded of the saprophytic orchids already described, which nourish themselves and grow for years imbedded in the humus of woods, and then seize the opportunity afforded by a favourable summer to raise up in a few weeks flowering stems above the bed of the forest. As a rule the spore-bearing hyphæ, emerging from the hosts of parasitic fungi, are highly conspicuous both in form and colour. As well-known instances we may here mention the powdery, rust-coloured, chocolate-brown, or coal-black masses of spores, known by the names of rust and smut; the mealy, orange-coloured masses which make their appearance on the green stems and fruits of roses (Æcidium stage of *Phragmidium subcorticum*), and the discomycetous *Peziza Willkommii*, which is parasitic in the branches of green larches, and exposes its fructifications beyond the bark in the form of small scarlet shields. Again, we have the yellow *Poly-porus sulfureus* with its immense yolk-coloured, bracket-like fructifications, which in the space of a week grow out from the trunks of larches, although the outward appearance of the host gives no indication of its being completely occupied internally by a mycelium. *Polyporus betulinus* and *P. fomentarius* likewise grow to a considerable size, and in both cases it is specially deserving of notice that the colour and structure of the surface of the fructification is surprisingly like the bark of the trees upon which they are respectively parasitic; that is to say, the fructification of *Polyporus betulinus* strongly resembles the whitish bark of the birch, and that of *Polyporus fomentarius*, parasitic on old beech-trees, exhibits the same pale gray as does the trunk of a beech.

Mildews form in some respects a contrast to these parasites whose hyphæ pene-trate into the interior of their hosts. They attack tender green leaves, stems, and young fruits, and accomplish their entire development upon the epidermal cells of the hosts. At first sight the parts assailed appear to be strewn with flour or dust from the road. But on closer inspection a delicate weft is to be distinguished, composed of filaments ramifying extensively upon the green substratum, intersect-ing one another, uniting to form reticula, and in parts a regular felt-work covered at certain spots with the small dark spheres of the sporocarps. Individual hyphæ of this weft adhere closely to the epidermal cells of the host, dissolve the outer walls of these cells at the points of contact, so as to make little apertures, and then develop processes which grow into the interior of the epidermal cells in question, assume a club-like form, and exhaust the cell-contents. The mycelia of mildews do not penetrate into the host beyond the epidermal cells. Fig. 32 [2] shows a piece of a leaf of *Acanthus mollis* attacked by mildew, with hyphal suckers penetrating into the epidermal cells of the leaf. One of the best-known mildew fungi is the Vine-mildew (*Erysiphe Tuckeri*), which weaves itself over the epidermis of still green and unripe grapes, and has frequently manifested itself through the districts where the vine is cultivated in southern and central Europe in the form of a ravaging disease.

The protuberances sent by the hyphæ, in the form of clavate swellings, or more rarely winding tubes, into the cells of the host-plants, correspond to the absorption-cells of land plants, and the conditions under which suction takes place are essentially analogous in the two cases. The absorption-cells on the roots of land plants do not take in all the substances in their nutrient substratum, and similarly the hyphæ only appropriate by means of their organs of suction a portion of the contents of the cells invaded. They begin by dissolving and breaking up for this purpose the substances in the infested cells of the host. What compounds they then select from among the products of decomposition, and what they leave behind, cannot certainly be specified in detail. It is believed that, in many cases, tannin is appropriated first of all by parasites. The wood of a healthy oak, for instance, has a characteristic smell due to the abundance of tannin it contains, whereas this odour is not emitted by wood attacked by the mycelia of fungi, and this decayed wood is destitute of tannin. It is natural to suppose, therefore, that the mycelium takes away and uses up the tannin. It has also been observed that wherever the hyphæ of the Pine-blister (*Peridermium Pini*) ensconce themselves, the nitrogenous parts of the protoplasm and the starch vanish, whilst turpentine remains behind, clinging in drops to the inner walls of the cells. These are, to be sure, very sparse data; but they show that the entire cell-contents are not absorbed by the parasite unaltered, or used in that condition as material for the building up of its own body.

Not only the contents of the cells preyed upon, but the walls as well, are partially used as food by the hyphæ which penetrate into the woody axes of arborescent angiosperms and gymnosperms. The mycelium of several species of *Polyporus* and *Trametes* begins by bringing the lignin in the cell-walls into solution, leaving nothing but a pale-coloured cellulose wall. Soon afterwards, the so-called middle lamella, which connects adjoining wood-cells, is also dissolved, and the colourless wood-cells, now almost like asbestos-fibres in appearance, fall apart at the slightest touch. When the wood of a larch has been infested by the mycelium of *Polyporus sulfureus*, there are always deep furrows running obliquely on the internal walls of the wood-cells; this loss of substance, too, can only arise from the solution, and absorption as nutriment, of parts of the walls by the action of the hyphæ.

All decompositions and alterations of structure of the above kind within the precincts of the host's cells are naturally followed by a disturbance of function, and ultimately by death. The entire plant is, however, but rarely killed by parasites belonging to this group. The decomposition by bacteria of a mammal's blood, though at first confined to a particular part of the body, spreads in a moment throughout the whole organism, owing to the heart's action and the circulation of the blood. But the decomposition taking place in the manner just described, through the intervention of hyphæ, propagates itself, on the contrary, only very gradually from the cells immediately attacked to their neighbours, and it gets weaker and weaker as the distance from the site of the invasion increases, a circumstance to which we shall recur later on when discussing the phenomena of fermentation and decay. The nature of the parasite and the power of resistance of the host have an undoubted influence on the rate of distribution. In many cases alteration is limited to the cells attacked and those immediately adjoining, so that the area destroyed is circumscribed. It is manifested on fresh green leaves, often merely in the form of small, isolated, yellow, brown, or black spots and patches, which only slightly interfere with the activity of the leaf, and do not cause it to change colour, wither, or fall off any earlier. In other instances, however, the entire leaves and stem do undoubtedly become flaccid and shrivelled and dried up into a black mass, looking as though they had been carbonized; or else putrefaction, such as that which is excited by bacteria, invades the whole mass.

As above stated, when the wood in the trunks of trees is perforated and consumed by hyphæ it is resolved into fragments. It becomes rotten, takes the form of an asbestos-like or crumbling and pulverulent mass, and is then obviously no longer capable of fulfilling its various functions in the living plant. If the invasion is limited in extent, and the host succeeds in surrounding the area of infection with a rampart of cells capable of resistance, and not liable to be pierced by the hyphæ, then the tree may live for years although its trunk is infested, and in parts rotten.    Such is also the case when particular branches of a tree are alone attacked by the mycelium of a fungus.    When, for example, the branch of a larch is assailed by the mycelium of the Discomycete, *Peziza Willkommii*, the fact is first manifested externally by the fascicles of needles on the branch in question becoming discoloured in the summer, and acquiring, prematurely, an autumnal appearance, so that, among the fresh green shoots, individual branches are to be seen bearing golden-yellow needles.    Towards autumn, scarlet cup-shaped fructifications make their appearance upon the surface of the bark on the branch; in the course of the next few years the whole branch as a rule dries up, withers, and dies.    It is then broken by the first violent shock of wind and falls to the ground; but the tree, disembarrassed of the dead bough, continues to grow unharmed, and to put forth green shoots.    It is only when almost all the branches of the larch are infested by the mycelium of this fungus that the whole tree perishes as a result of the invasion.

Certain groups of plants are specially liable to be attacked by parasitic fungi, and there are some conifers and angiospermous trees in which the same stem is colonized by three, four, or five kinds of parasite.    The green foliage leaves of large numbers of flowering plants are also apt to be selected by parasites, as also are their roots, tubers, and bulbous structures.    Many parasites only attack the anthers in flowers; others, as for instance the ergot, only the young ovaries.    Parasitic fungi are rarely found on mosses or ferns; whereas a considerable number of parasites settle upon lichens and even on the fructifications of fungi, moulds even being infested by other fungi; for example, a fungus named *Piptocephalis Freseniana* is parasitic upon the very common mould, *Mucor Mucedo*.

A fungus known by the name of *Cordiceps militaris* is parasitic in the caterpillars and pupæ of butterflies and other insects, and its relatively very large fructification at length bursts out of the body infested by the mycelium in the form of a club nearly 6 cm. long.    This clavate structure, built up at the expense of the insect's flesh and blood, produces tubular cells in special receptacles, and, inside these, little rod-like spores, which afterwards fall out and infect other caterpillars, developing within the bodies of these animals into a hoary mycelium and ultimately causing their death.    The disease of silk-worms, known as muscardine, is likewise occasioned by a species of *Cordiceps*.    We must also refer here to the widely-distributed *Empusa Muscæ*, a mould which attacks flies and causes every autumn a regular epidemic amongst house-flies.    The flies so often seen at that season adhering stiff and dead to window-panes are surrounded by a whitish halo, and this is composed of a conglomerate of spores thrown off by the mould which is parasitic upon the flies and causes their death.    Parasitic fungi have also been observed in the human skin, and recognized as the causes of skin-diseases.    For instance, to the mould *Achorion Schoenleinii* is due the disease of the skin popularly known as "honey-combed ringworm", and named *Favus* by doctors; dandruff (*Pityriasis versicolor*) is produced by *Microsporon furfur*, and *Herpes tonsurans* by *Tricophyton tonsurans*. The latter has a remarkable effect on the hair, causing it to fall out and leave the part of the skin affected bald.

Water-plants are attacked by parasitic fungi comparatively rarely, which is the more noteworthy because such large numbers of non-parasitic epiphytes settle upon the filaments of green algæ, and on the brown Fucoideæ, and red Florideæ. Minute

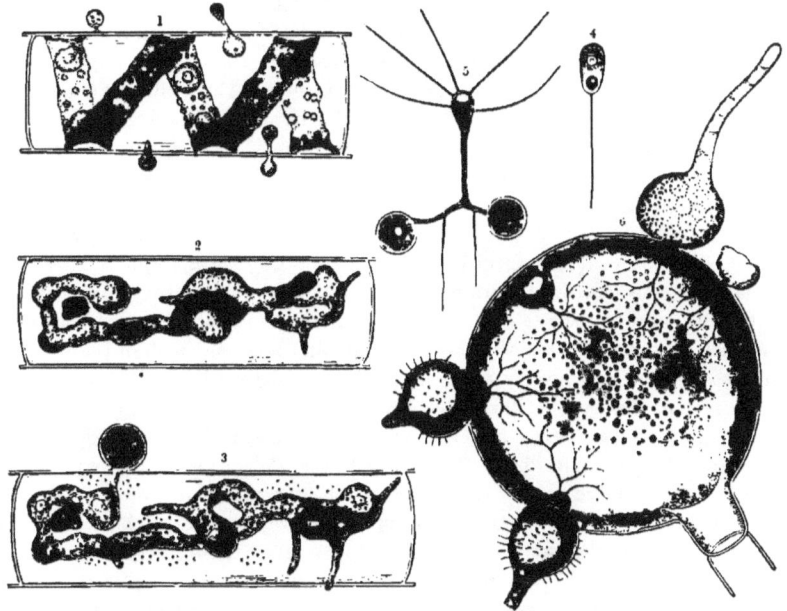

Fig. 33—Parasites on Hydrophytes.
1, 2, and 3 *Lagenidium Rabenhorstii*. 4, 5 *Polyphagus Euglenæ*. 6 *Rhizidiomyces apophysatus*.

forms of fungi, invisible to the naked eye, and belonging to the Chytrideæ and Saprolegniæ, are parasitic upon green algal filaments, especially on the fresh-water species of the genera *Œdogonium*, *Spirogyra*, and *Mesocarpus*. One of these microscopic parasites is represented in fig. 33 [1, 2, 3], and bears the name *Lagenidium Rabenhorstii*. It develops non-ciliated, spherical swarm-spores, which lay themselves upon the walls of Spirogyra-cells, perforate them, and insert a club-like process. The protuberance forthwith becomes a tube, which increases rapidly in size in the interior of the cell, ramifying and completely destroying the bands of chlorophyll. The branched tubes of *Lagenidium* reproduce themselves in two ways at the expense of the host's cells infested by them: they form on the one hand so-called oospores by means of fertilization, and on the other sporangia. The latter process is clearly shown in fig. 33 [1, 2, 3]. In this case, one of the tubular processes of the parasite fungus pushes out of the cell-cavity of the invaded *Spirogyra* into the surrounding water again and there swells up into a spherical vesicle, within which the protoplasm divides into eight spores.   These spores are then set free as swarm-spores and attack new healthy Spirogyra-cells.

Materially different is the behaviour of the parasite *Chytridium Ola*, which attacks the green cells of fresh-water Œdogoniæ.   Its roundish swarm-spores are furnished each with one long cilium, and swim, searching about in the water until they meet with an Œdogonium-cell to their taste just occupied in the formation of oospores.   When they find one, they fasten upon it and send infinitesimally fine hair-like tubes (which have been called rhizoids) into the interior.   By means of these tubes they derive their nutriment from the host.   The body of the parasite, which remains outside the invaded cell, increases in size, and at length grows out into a sporangium; the latter opens at the top by a lid and once more sets free swarm-spores into the surrounding water.

*Polyphagus Euglenæ*, a member of the Chytrideæ, is parasitic on the green cells of Euglenæ living in water.   The swarm spores of this microscopic fungus (see fig. 33[4]) are oval and furnished, like those of *Chytridium Ola*, with a long cilium.   They swim about the water with the non-ciliate extremity leading, so that the cilium appears to be a tail at the posterior end.   As soon as these swarm-spores have come to rest, they assume a spherical form and send out in all directions thin, hair-like tubes, which search for a host.   When a tube reaches an Euglena-cell, it penetrates into the body of the latter, drains it, and, continuing to grow, produces fresh hair-like tubes, which attack other green Euglenæ, often linking together dozens of them (see fig. 33[5]).   In this way the *Polyphagus* grows apace and becomes a comparative large oblong vesicle, whilst the protoplasm within it divides into a number of parts.   These, again, turn into swarm spores, with long ciliary filaments, and they slip out of the vesicle and may attack fresh Euglenæ.

Curiously enough, even saprophytic water-plants destitute of chlorophyll are sometimes attacked by parasites, and that, indeed, by species belonging to the same group.   Thus, for instance, the species of *Achlya* growing on the dead bodies of fishes and other animals which have perished in the water, are themselves infested by small parasitic Saprolegniaceæ and Chytrideæ.   The example of these minute parasites represented in fig. 33[6] is named *Rhizidiomyces apophysatus*, and its host is *Achlya racemosa*.   The swarming spores of the parasite lay themselves, in the manner described in previous instances, upon the spherical oogonia of *Achlya*, and insert extremely fine hair-like tubes into the interior of the cells attacked. These ramify like roots in the Achlya-cells, exhaust them of nutriment, grow perceptibly, and at length form spherical swellings, which, after reaching a certain size, break through the walls of the host-cells, project from the opening, and, lastly, push out in each case a sporangium.   The latter produces a number of swarm-spores, which escape into the water and are able to seek fresh prey.

We cannot here enter into details respecting the other kinds of reproduction occurring in the minute fungi parasitic upon hydrophytes.   This is the right place,

however, to mention the fact that the various species of Chytrideæ and Saprolegniaceæ do not content themselves with plants that are second-rate hosts, but
exercise a selection amongst the different green algæ living in the water. It is
astonishing to find that the swarm-spores invariably swim to cells whose protoplasm
affords the most suitable nutrient basis for them, and attach themselves to those
cells only, and never on other species unadapted to their requirements.

## CLIMBING PARASITES. GREEN-LEAVED PARASITES. TOOTHWORT.

The third group into which parasites were divided at the beginning of this
chapter is composed of flowering plants throughout. According to their method of
attacking the host for the purpose of absorbing nutriment from it, they range
themselves in six series. In the following pages we shall discuss the characteristics of each series as manifested in the most remarkable forms belonging
to it.

The first series includes plants destitute of green leaves and of chlorophyll in
general, whose seeds germinate on the ground and send forth each a filiform stem,
which brings itself, by means of peculiar movements, into contact with the host-
plant, coils round it, and develops organs of suction whereby it takes nutriment
from the plant assailed.

To this series belong the genera *Cassytha* and *Cuscuta*. The former includes
some thirty species, all of which appertain to warm climates. Most of the Cassythæ inhabit Australia, where they attack, in particular, the copses of Casuarinæ
and Melaleucæ, fastening their wart-shaped, or, in many cases, shield-like or discoid
suckers upon the young green shoots of those plants. Several species also are
indigenous to New Zealand, others to Borneo, Java, Ceylon, the Philippines, and
the Moluccas. South Africa, too, is the home of a few Cassythæ, and one species
(*C. Americana*) is distributed over the West Indies, Mexico, and Brazil. A
European, seeing these parasites with their twining, thread-like, leafless stems, and
their flowers aggregated in capitula, umbels, or spikes, takes them at first to be
species of the genus *Cuscuta*, popularly called Dodder. That these plants should
be most nearly related to laurel-trees is the last thing one would expect. Examination of the flowers and fruit reveals, it is true, a close resemblance to those of
laurel and cinnamon trees, and, therefore, these Cassythæ are rightly placed by
systematic botanists among the Lauraceæ. But in respect of food-absorption, as in
general aspect, they are entirely analogous to the various species of the genus
*Cuscuta*, which belong to the family of Bindweeds (Convolvulaceæ). The last-
named genus is even more variously differentiated than the genus *Cassytha*, and
includes about fifty species dispersed pretty evenly over the whole world. Every
part of the world has its own characteristic forms. One group occurs in California,
Carolina, Indiana, Missouri, and Mexico, another in the West Indies, Brazil, Peru, and
Chili, a third at the Cape of Good Hope. Other species are natives of China, the
East Indies, the steppes of Central Asia, Persia, Syria, the Caucasus, and Egypt.

A comparatively large number of species, i.e. twenty-five, are distributed through central and southern Europe.   A few have been introduced recently for the first time with seeds from the New World, as, for instance, *C. corymbosa*, which was accidentally conveyed with lucerne seeds from South America to Belgium, and has latterly begun to range over central Europe.

The various species of *Cuscuta* attack chiefly small herbaceous, suffruticose, and shrubby plants; but a few American species coil themselves round branches growing at the top of the highest trees.   Notice has been especially drawn to certain European species on account of their disastrous effects upon cultivated plants.   The most famous is *Cuscuta Trifolii*, known as the Clover-Dodder, the appearance of which in clover-fields causes so much anxiety to farmers, and which is so difficult to exterminate.   Another unwelcome visitor is *Cuscuta Epilinum*, which coils round flax stems and hinders their growth, and a third species, *Cuscuta Europaea*, sometimes ravages hop-plantations.   This last is, indeed, the most widely distributed of all the Cuscutas, and extends from England over central Europe and Asia to Japan, and southwards as far as Algiers.   It is parasitic not only on hops, but also on elder, ash, and various other shrubs and herbs; in particular it exhibits a preference for nettles.

The seeds of this species, and of Dodders in general, germinate on damp earth, on wet foliage undergoing putrefaction, or on the weathered bark of old trunks.   The seedling, which in the seed lies imbedded in a cellular mass full of reserve-food, is filiform and spirally coiled.   It is twisted once, or once and a half, and is thickened at one end like a club.   In true Cuscutas, no trace of cotyledons is to be perceived, nor does one find vessels in the interior of the seedling; but chains of cells arranged with great regularity are noticed in the axis of the filiform body, and are easily distinguished from the surrounding cells.   In nature, the seeds, after falling to the ground and lying there through the winter, do not germinate till very late in the following year, i.e. at least a month later than the majority of the other seeds reaching the same ground simultaneously with them. Perennial herbs, also, have, by the time that germination takes place, already developed shoots from their subterranean roots or rhizomes above the surface of the ground, later a circumstance of great importance to the parasites.   If a *Cuscuta* were to germinate early in the spring, it would not readily find close by a support up which to twine; whereas later, there is seldom any lack of annual stems or shoots of perennial plants in the immediate neighbourhood.

When the twisted embryo germinates, it stretches and at the same time revolves from right to left, assuming the shape of a screw and pushing its lower clavate extremity out beyond the coat of the seed (see fig. 34[1, 2, 3, 4, 5, 6]).   This extremity forthwith grows into the earth and fastens tightly on to particles of the soil, withered foliage, and other objects of the sort.   The other, attenuated extremity of the filiform seedling, which is still wrapped in the seed-coat and the mass of reserve-food, lifts itself up in the opposite direction, avoiding such solid bodies as it may happen to encounter, and grows in a curve round them.   Further growth does not take place at either extremity, but always in the median part of the filament. It is so rapid that by the fifth day after the commencement of germination the entire seedling has increased fourfold in length. As early as the third day after the emergence of the tip that fastens itself in the earth, the integument of the seed, which until then continues to envelop the opposite extremity, is thrown off and the seedling's apex is exposed. The reserve-food, given by the parent-plant to the seedling as provision for the journey, has meanwhile been absorbed and consumed, so that the seedling is now thrown entirely upon its own resources, and depends for sustenance upon the earth, to which it is firmly attached, and upon the surrounding air. Having no chlorophyll, it is not in a position to take up

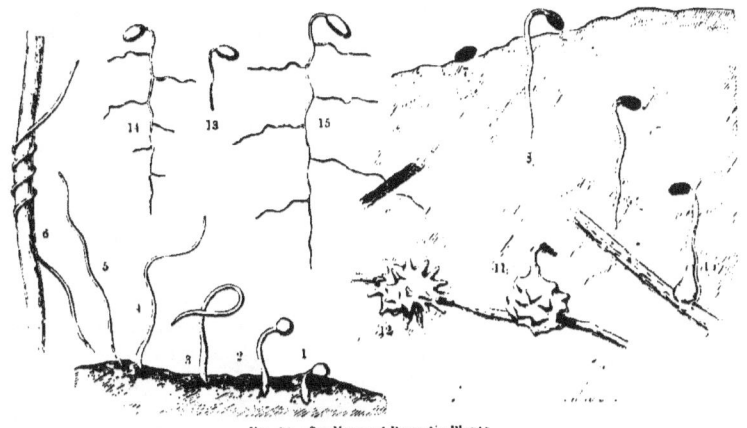

Fig. 34.—Seedlings of Parasitic Plants.

1. 2. 3. 4. 5. 6 The Great Dodder (*Cuscuta Europæa*). 7. 8. 9. 10. 11. 12 A Broom-rape (*Orobanche Epithymum*). 13. 14. 15 Wood Cow-wheat (*Melampyrum sylvaticum*)

materials from the air; nor can it derive sufficient nutriment from the earth, even supposing that water is imbibed by the cells of the clavate extremity. There is no doubt that it now grows at the expense of the substances contained in the cells of this club-shaped end. The latter at once begins to shrivel and soon dies, whilst the upper part of the filament elongates conspicuously. Should this portion of the seedling meantime come into contact with a neighbouring plant, a rigid haulm, or anything else that will serve as a support, it straightway coils itself round the object in question, and its future is then, as a rule, assured.

Failing such a support, the seedling, after the death of the clavate extremity, falls down and sinks to the ground. In doing so, it almost invariably touches an adjoining object, whereupon it immediately winds tendril-like round the support thus afforded. But if there is nothing anywhere around to serve as a prop, and the young seedling, by this time from 1 to 2 centimeters long, comes to rest upon the bare earth, all further growth is stopped. It preserves its vitality, however, for a surprisingly long time, and may remain almost unaltered, lying on the damp earth for four or five weeks waiting for something to turn up. Not infrequently something of the sort happens, for another plant may germinate close by or extend a growing shoot from the vicinity and touch the Cuscuta seedling. In this event, the latter at once seizes the anchor thus thrown out, and winds round it. But if no support of the kind is to be had, the seedling must ultimately perish. It is, to say the least, a very remarkable thing that a filament, capable of developing suckers when adherent to a living plant, is not able in damp earth to produce any absorbent organs whatsoever.

If the thread-like Dodder plantlet succeeds in seizing a support of any kind, either during the existence of the swollen extremity, or later, after it has been absorbed, it makes a single, or from two to three, coils round the prop, raises its growing point from the substratum, and moves it round in a circle like the hand of a watch. By means of these manœuvres, which look exactly like a process of feeling or seeking, the filament is brought into contact with fresh haulms twigs, and petioles belonging to other plants. To these it adheres, making once more two or three tight coils round them. Throughout, it is obvious that the growing point of the young Dodder rejects dead props, as far as is practicable, and shows a striking preference for living parts of plants.

At each place where the Dodder is pressed in a coil against the support, the filament becomes somewhat swollen, and wart-like suckers are developed, which are usually situated close together in rows of three, four, or five (see fig. 35 [1]).

A piece of stem thus furnished with suckers or haustoria resembles a small caterpillar creeping up the supporting stem. These haustoria, arranged close together in rows, and corresponding in origin entirely to rudimentary roots, are at first smooth, but acquire soon a finely-granulated aspect owing to the walls of the epidermal cells projecting outwards. With the help of the papillæ thus formed, and especially through the action of a juice secreted by them, the suckers fasten themselves to the host. If the plant has been obliged to clasp a dead object for support, the wart-like processes flatten themselves against it and assume the form of a kind of disc, which exhibits no further development, and only serves as an organ of attachment; but, if the substratum is a living plant, a bundle of cells forces its way out from the middle of the haustorium and grows into the substratum direct. The phenomenon here manifested is altogether characteristic. Each sucker from the time of its production exhibits a kind of core composed of cells arranged in regular rows, which, together with a few spirally-thickened vessels, constitute a bundle standing at right angles to the axis of the Dodder's stem. This bundle now breaks through the coat formed by the rest of the cells of the sucker and penetrates into the living tissue of the plant attacked (see fig. 35 [2]). Great force is exerted in the penetrating process. The closely-joined cells of the epidermis, and not infrequently a cortex of considerable density are pierced, and the bundle of cells often penetrates right into the body of the wood. Having once reached the interior of the host, the cells, till then bound together in a bundle, diverge a little, insert themselves singly between the cells of the host.

and energetically absorb food-materials. They withdraw organic compounds from the host and convey them by a short route to the strands developed meantime in the axis of the Cuscuta-stem. When once a union of this kind between the parasite and the host has been established, the portion of the Cuscuta situated below the first haustorium gradually dies. The lowest extremity, *i.e.* the clavate tip, has already perished, so that the Cuscuta-plant is now no longer in any connection with the ground whereon it germinated, but only remains rooted to its living host by means of the suckers. If it has had the good fortune to cling to a host with green foliage, which generates an abundance of organic compounds, such as the luxuriant juicy stems of the Hop, or the Nettle, with its

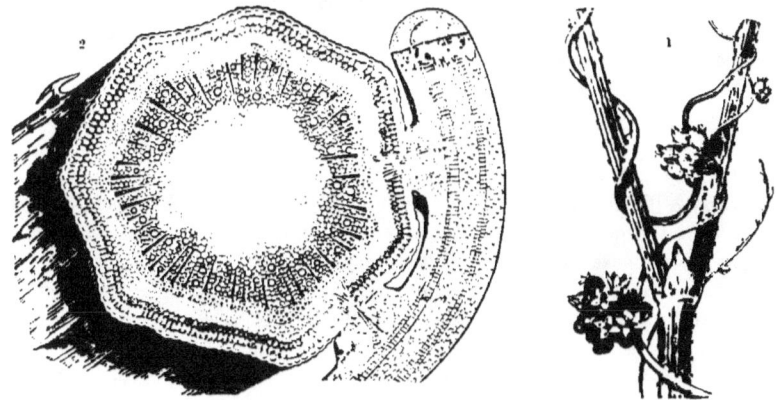

Fig. 35 —*Cuscuta Europæa* parasitic on a Hop-stem.
1 Natural size. 2 Section; ×40.

plentiful dark green leaves, which are shunned and spared by grazing animals on account of their unpalatable stinging hairs, the parasite continues to grow with extraordinary rapidity, and puts forth a number of branches immediately above the lowest group of haustoria. All these again feel around with their tips, develop tendrils and suckers, sometimes intertwining and becoming entangled together, cover an ever-increasing area of the host with their network, and in this condition fully deserve the name of "Hell-bind", sometimes popularly applied to this plant. Little spheres of rose-coloured flowers are then formed on individual threads of this tangle, and from them balls of small capsular fruits, which dehisce by means of lids and have their seeds shaken out by the wind.

The European species of *Cuscuta* are all annuals. Even when their haustoria are attached to perennial plants, as, for instance, on young branches of woody plants, they wither after the seeds have ripened, and nothing is to be seen of them in the following spring except a few dried tendrils coiled round branches of ash or willow. But under a tropical sun, perennial species flourish as well. The suckers of *Cuscuta verrucosa*, for example, continue to exercise their function throughout the year wherever they have once attacked the host.  If the woody branches of the host, with haustoria fastened in them, grow in thickness and superimpose new wood-cells upon the wood, down to which the absorbent cells of the haustoria have penetrated, these suction-cells of the Dodder are likewise inclosed by the wood-cells, and, in proportion to the augmentation of the circumference of the wood in the branch in question, they also lengthen out so that the bundle of absorption-cells proceeding from a sucker may, in such cases, be seen imbedded in the wood to a depth of several annual rings.

The Cassythæ, referred to above, behave exactly like the Dodders.  In them also the seedling which issues from the seed is filiform, and lives originally at the expense of reserve-food stored up within the coat of the seed.  So, too, it grows upward, ramifies, and endeavours, by means of revolving movements of the apex, to reach a living support, coils round the latter when found, and uses it as a nutrient substratum.  Here, again, at the parts where the tendrils of the filiform stem are firmly appressed to the living support, rows of wart-like suckers are developed, and a bundle of absorption-cells grows from each into the host.  As in the Dodder, the lower extremity of the filiform stem then dries up at once, and connection with the earth is thus cut off.  The parasite, once attached by its haustoria to the host, is able to branch repeatedly, to weave its thread-like stems over all the branches and to climb to the top of the host, even should the latter be a tall bush.  At some spots everything is entangled to such an extent that one would think there were birds' nests amongst the boughs.

The second series of parasitic Phanerogams consists of herbs bearing green foliage-leaves, whilst the seed contains an embryo furnished with seed-leaves (cotyledons) and root.  The seeds germinate in the earth and there develop seedlings without the support of a host; it is branches of the root that first attach themselves by means of suckers upon the roots of other plants.  To this series belong about a hundred Santalaceæ, mainly of the genus *Thesium*, and many more than two hundred Rhinanthaceæ besides.  The chief examples of this latter family are the various species of the Eyebright (*Euphrasia*), the Yellow-rattle (*Rhinanthus*), Cow-wheat (*Melampyrum*) and Lousewort (*Pedicularis*), and also *Bartsia*, *Tozzia*, *Trixago*, and *Odontites*.  The most extensive genera are *Euphrasia* and *Pedicularis*, the species of which, with few exceptions, are found in the northern hemisphere, adorning grassy meadows with their pretty flowers, especially in the arctic zone, and the high mountain regions of the Himalaya, the Altai and Caucasus, the Alps and the Pyrenees.

Little suggestion of parasitic habit is given in the first stages of development of any of these plants.  A seedling of the Cow-wheat within a week puts forth a primary root 4 cm. long, from which half a dozen lateral roots ramify at right angles without there being any attachment to a host to be noted (see fig. 34 [13, 14, 15]).  Suckers are never developed until the secondary roots have attained a length of from 12 to 24 mm., and then only if the latter come into contact with other living plants to their taste, a circumstance which doubtless is almost certain to happen, seeing that the lateral roots are numerous and are sent out in all directions from the main root, and therefore must inevitably come across the root-systems of other plants.

The seedling in perennial species of *Thesium* develops comparatively slowly. It reaches a length of from 3 to 4 cm. in the first year, sends a tap-root into the earth, and puts forth a few branchlets, which do not fasten upon the roots of other plants by means of suckers until several weeks after germination. These suckers are relatively large in all species of *Thesium*, and they catch one's eye the moment the roots of a plant are carefully divested of earth. They are then recognized, as may be seen in fig. 36 [1], as little white knobs, which stand out clearly from the dark earth and are always inserted laterally upon the secondary roots. They are

Fig. 36 —Bastard Toad-flax (*Thesium alpinum*)
[1] Root with suckers; natural size. [2] Piece of a root with sucker in section; ×35.

constricted near their insertion, and the strangulated portion often gives the impression of being a pedicel upon which the knob is seated. This knob is differentiated into a central core and a multicellular, cortical coat enveloping it. The cellular coat rests upon the root of the host attacked, and does not merely adhere to one limited spot, but spreads itself out over the root like a plastic mass, and forms a cushion surrounding about a fourth or fifth part of the circumference (see fig. 36 [2]) without, however, penetrating into the substance of the root. There are in the core two strands or bundles of vessels, and between them small cells arranged in rows, from which absorption-cells arise at the spot where the sucker first applied itself to the nutrient root. These absorption-cells grow out beyond the rind-like envelope round the core, perforate the cortex of the host, penetrate into the wood at the centre of the invaded root, and there diverge like the hairs of a dry paint-brush.

The suckers of the green-leaved Rhinanthaceæ are on the whole similarly constructed; only they are relatively smaller and more delicate, being sometimes almost translucent, and they are either not at all or only slightly constricted at the base.  Whereas in *Thesium* they never issue otherwise than laterally from the ramifications of the roots, in Rhinanthaceæ they are often terminal.  A differentiation into core and rind-like envelope is never clearly marked; a vascular bundle runs through the middle of the sucker and is surrounded by thick-walled cells.  The absorbent cells are, moreover, shorter than in the Santalaceæ.  The individual genera of the Rhinanthaceæ exhibit amongst themselves only very slight differences in respect of their suckers.  On the roots of Eyebright (*Euphrasia*), the haustoria are tiny roundish nodules which rest upon the host's root without encompassing it.  The absorption-cells are very short, and only just penetrate into the host.  The vascular bundle is either entirely wanting within the sucker, or its place is taken by a single, comparatively large vessel.  On the roots of the Yellow-rattle (*Rhinanthus*) the suckers are spherical and of considerable size (up to 3 mm. in diameter); their margins are swollen and often encompass more than half the circumference of the roots attacked.  The absorbent cells are short but very numerous.  In the Cow-wheat (*Melampyrum*) the suckers resemble those of the Yellow-rattle in size and shape and in the shortness of the absorption-cells; but in the former the margins of the suckers not only embrace the roots of the host, but cling to them in such a way as to penetrate their substance and form circular grooves upon them.

All the Rhinanthaceæ mentioned are herbaceous annuals.  Their suckers are few in number, and therefore easily escape observation.  By the time these plants ripen their seeds any piece of a root that has been attacked has for the most part already turned brown and been killed, and is in a state of decay.  But shortly afterwards the parasite itself withers.  The comparatively large seeds, well-furnished with reserve-material for the nourishment of the embryo, fall out of the dry capsules, and generally reach the ground at no great distance from the mother-plant and germinate there.  In the autumn, close to Cow-wheat plants, which are still green but have already let fall the seeds from their lowest capsules, individual examples of those seeds may be seen already sprouting in the damp moss and mould on the ground of woods.  If they fall to earth not very far from the parent-plant, the seedlings may happen to attack the host which has already had one of the branches of its root sucked and killed by the latter in the previous summer.

Nearly all these annual green-leaved parasites make their appearance in numbers close together.  If, for instance, a species of Cow-wheat has taken up its quarters in a particular part of a wood, there are always collections of hundreds and thousands of specimens to be found together.  The small-flowered Yellow-rattle often grows so abundantly in damp meadows that one might suppose it to have been sown by the bushel.  The large-flowered, hairy Yellow-rattle is similarly exuberant in ploughed fields, and the Eyebright, with its large number of species, is produced in such abundance in mountainous districts that, at the season when its little milk-white flowers are open, regular milky ways seem to stretch across the green meadows.  Millions of them are situated together rooted in the grass-covered ground, and one would suppose that in course of time the growth of grass at such places would be injured. This conclusion appears to be supported by the assertion of the country folk that after the season when the Eyebright is in full bloom, the cows yield less milk, a fact which explains the German name of "Milchdieb" (milk-thief) popularly given to the plant. The diminution in the quantity of milk yielded is, however, certainly connected with other circumstances. It depends especially upon the universal abatement of the growth of grasses in early autumn and the consequent curtailment of the food afforded by the pastures. The injury done by the Eyebright to its hosts by the withdrawal of nutriment and destruction of rootlets cannot be very considerable, for the appearance of the grasses and other host-plants, which are affected, is not noticeably different from that of the plants of the same kind which escape invasion.

The same statement is true in the case of the various species of Lousewort (*Pedicularis*), almost all of which are meadow-plants; that is to say, they are present in great abundance in upland and alpine pastures without apparently injuring the species growing in their company and used by them as hosts. Unlike the species of Cow-wheat, Yellow-rattle, and Eyebright, however, nearly all the Louseworts are perennial, and accordingly differ from them also in the construction of their suckers. There is, it is true, no difference in shape between the suckers of the Cow-wheat and those of *Pedicularis*, but they are dissimilar in respect of size and place of origin. The suckers of the perennial Louseworts are barely more than half the size, and are only developed near the attenuated extremity of a rootlet. They are very few in number; each of the long, thick, fleshy rootlets, proceeding from the base of the stem usually produces a single sucker only which settles upon the root of a suitable host-plant in the same way as the suckers of Cow-wheat. By the time that the parasite's fruit ripens, the piece of root which has been invaded has usually already turned brown and fallen into decay. Now in the case of Cow-wheat it may undoubtedly be immaterial whether the piece of root attacked by it is living or not when its fruit is ripening, inasmuch as its own annual root rots as soon as the seeds have been produced from the flowers above ground. But with *Pedicularis* it is different. The perennial roots of this plant require a host to nourish them next year, and when the piece of a host's root which has been attacked and sucked as a nutrient substratum one year dies, the sucker belonging to the root parasitic upon it is no longer in a position to fulfil its function by continuing to absorb fresh juices. Suckers thus reduced to a state of quiescence soon perish, and only leave little scars to indicate the places where they existed. The perennial root of the *Pedicularis* has now to seek a new source of nutriment, and this is effected by the elongation of its tip, which continues to grow until it reaches the living root of another plant suitable as host, whereupon it develops a fresh sucker upon that root. This elongation doubtless requires a large quantity of plastic materials; but these are found stored in abundance in the older parts of the parasitic root.

These circumstances explain, at anyrate in part, the characteristic structure and disproportionate length of the roots of *Pedicularis*. From all round the short erect root-stock, which is generally only from $\frac{1}{2}$ cm. to 2 cm. long, issue fleshy rootlets of the thickness of a quill, but, in many species, as long and thick as a little finger. These rootlets are abundantly supplied with starch, and, in course of time, elongate till they measure 20 cm.   They radiate in all directions in the black soil of the meadow, wherein are buried the root-systems of grasses, sedges, and various other plants, and fasten on to suitable hosts by means of one or two suckers yearly, and repeating this process until at length their tips travel into earth devoid of roots, where no more prey is to be found, and there growth ceases.   This explains also why these long Pedicularis-roots never descend vertically in the earth, but remain only in the upper strata of soil on a meadow, where a number of other roots are interwoven together, and where it is most likely that the tapering growing-point will meet with the root of some new host or other.

The Alpine Bartsia (*Bartsia alpina*), one of the perennial Rhinanthaceæ prevailing in the arctic regions as well as in mountainous parts of Europe on damp, marshy, grass-covered spots, is distinguished by the sombre dusky violet colouring of its leaves, and has already been noticed amongst carnivorous plants.   On the secondary roots are suckers exactly like those of the Yellow-rattle (*Rhinanthus*), and by means of these organs it clings to the fibrous roots of sedges and grasses, and sucks their juices.   The long, subterranean, runner-like stems, which are covered with small, whitish scales, also bear, however, elongated absorption-cells (root-hairs), which are distinctly differentiated, and take up nutriment from the vegetable mould around.   This *Bartsia* is, therefore, half-parasitic and half-saprophytic, and it is not improbable that many other perennial Rhinanthaceæ behave in the same way.

The species of *Pedicularis* which constitute the most extensive group of perennial green-leaved and parasitic Rhinanthaceæ are, it is true, destitute of tubular absorption-cells (root-hairs) whether on the subterranean stem-structures or on the root-tip, with the exception of those which develop in the middle of the suckers.   But the construction of the epidermal cells on the roots, and the circumstance that these epidermal cells are always in intimate connection with dark particles of humus, would favour the idea that these plants are capable of taking up organic compounds from the mould of meadows in addition to the food acquired by means of suckers from their hosts.   This supposition is further supported by the fact that I succeeded in rearing a species belonging to the Rhinanthaceæ, namely, *Odontites lutea*, from a soil composed of a mixture of sand and humus, in which no other plants were rooted, so that the possibility of a withdrawal of nutritive matter from hosts was excluded.   It is true that the plants thus reared remained comparatively small and poor, and only developed few flowers and fruits.   But at anyrate they may be considered to prove that plants exist, which, though normally parasitic, are yet on occasion able to subsist in vegetable mould without the assistance of hosts.

The third series of parasitic flowering-plants is very restricted, contrasting in this respect with the second series, composed of the numerous green-leaved Santalaceæ and Rhinanthaceæ.   The species belonging to it differ from those of the second series chiefly in their lack of chlorophyll. They all live underground on the roots of trees and shrubs, develop deep down in the earth a number of flowerless perennial shoots thickly covered with scales, and, in addition, push up annually into the light temporary axes bearing flowers, which ripen their fruits and die after the fall of the seed.

As the best known representative of this series, we may take the Toothwort (*Lathræa Squamaria*), which is represented in fig. 37, and has been already described on a previous occasion as an instance of a plant nourished by capturing

Fig. 37.—Toothwort (*Lathræa Squamaria*) with suckers upon the roots of a Poplar.

and digesting infusoria in special receptacles. Like *Bartsia*, it is a remarkable example of a plant living on juices in part derived from animals killed by itself and partly from living hosts. Formerly, the Toothwort used to be included in the family of Broom-rapes (Orobancheæ) on account of the structure of its capsules, but it is entirely different as regards the form of its seedling. For, whereas the seedling of a Broom-rape is a thread without any trace of cotyledons, as will be seen when we study its development and mode of attachment to the host in the next few pages, that of the Toothwort is clearly differentiated into radicle, cotyledons, and rudimentary stem, corresponding in this respect entirely with the Rhinanthaceæ. Moreover, the Toothwort resembles Rhinanthaceæ much more than Broom-rapes in the manner in which it attacks its hosts and withdraws nutriment from them.

The seed of *Lathræa* germinates on damp earth.  The young root of the seedling grows at first at the expense of reserve material stored in the seed, penetrates vertically into the earth and sends out lateral branches, which, like the main root, follow a serpentine course and search in the loose damp earth for a suitable nutrient substratum.  If one of these meets with a living root belonging to an ash, poplar, hornbeam, hazel, or other angiospermous tree, it fastens on to it at once and develops suckers at the points of contact; these suckers are at first shaped like spherical buttons, but soon acquire, as their size increases, the form of discs adherent to the host's root by the flattened side and with the convex hemispherical side turned towards the rootlet of the parasite.  These discoid suckers cling to the root attacked by means of a viscid substance produced by the outermost layer of cells.  As in the case of the parasites already described, a bundle of absorption-cells grows out of the core of each sucker into the root of the plant serving as host, and the tips of the absorbent cells reach to the wood of the root.  The shoot extremity of the seedling, thus nourished by the juices of the host, now develops very quickly, elongating and producing thick, white, fleshy, scale-like leaves which overlap one another closely, the whole thus acquiring the appearance of an open fir-cone.  The scaly stems also branch underground, and thus a curious structure is gradually produced, consisting of crossed and entangled cone-like shoots covered with white scales, and this structure fills entirely the nooks and corners between the woody roots on which it preys.  Individual plants extending over a square meter and weighing 5 kilograms are by no means rare.  Later on, inflorescences raise themselves above the surface from the extremities of the scaly subterranean shoots.  Their axes are at first curved like crooks, but straighten themselves out by the time the fruit ripens.  Whereas the subterranean portions are white as ivory, the flowers and bracts pushed up above the earth are of a purplish tinge.  The roots, which issued originally from the seedling, and their suckers have long since ceased to meet the requirements in respect of nourishment of so greatly augmented a structure, and therefore additional adventitious roots are produced every year, springing from the stem and growing towards living woody branches of the thickness of a finger, belonging to the root of the tree or shrub that serves as host.  When there, they bifurcate, forming numerous thickish filiform arms, which lay themselves upon the bark of the nutrient root and weave a regular web over it.  Sometimes two or three of these root-filaments of the parasite coalesce, forming tendrils, and the resemblance to a lace-work or braid is then all the more pronounced.  Suckers such as have been described are developed by these root-filaments laterally, and more especially on the ends of the branches.

*Lathræa* is interesting in so many different connections that we shall again return to this plant later on.  As has been stated before, it affords a type of a series of parasites which resembles the species of *Cassytha* and *Cuscuta* in the absence of chlorophyll, Rhinanthaceæ in the shape and development of the seedling and the form of the suckers, and the Balanophoreæ, presently to be described, in being parasitic upon the roots of woody plants.  *Lathræa Squamaria*, the species represented in fig. 37, is indigenous to Europe and Asia, its area of distribution extending from England eastwards to the Himalayas, and from Sweden southwards to Sicily. Two species are confined to the East, the Crimea and the Balkans, and another Toothwort (*Lathraea clandestina*), distinguished by large flowers, but slightly raised above the earth, extends in western and southern Europe from Flanders over France to Spain and Italy. This last has the distinctive feature that the discoid suckers developed on its yellow roots, which latter are of the thickness of a quill, are as large as lentils and the biggest hitherto discovered on any plant.

## BROOM-RAPES, BALANOPHOREÆ, RAFFLESIACEÆ.

The fourth series of parasitic Phanerogamia is composed of plants destitute of chlorophyll, whose seed contains an amorphous embryo without cotyledons or radicle. The seed germinates on the earth, and the embryo grows as a filiform body into the ground and there fastens upon the root of a host-plant, penetrates into and coalesces with it in growth, forming a tuberous stock, from which, later on, flowering stems are projected above the earth.

To this series belong the Broom-rapes or Orobancheœ and the Balanophoreœ. Of the genus *Orobanche* about 180 species are recognized, which, exhibiting great uniformity in floral structure and in their general development, can only be distinguished by minute characteristics. The flowering stem growing up from the subterranean tuber is, in all the species, rigid, erect, thick, fleshy, and covered at the top with dry scales. The open flowers, ringent in shape, are crowded together in a terminal spike, and often emit a strong scent like that of pinks or sometimes of violets. The colour of the flowers is in one group (*Phelypaea*) mostly blue or violet; in the rest it is waxen yellow, yellowish-brown, dark-brown, rose-red, flesh-tint, or whitish. *Orobanche violacea* and *O. lutea*, both natives of Northern Africa, have stems which grow to a height of half a meter and become almost as thick as an arm. The best-known species is the Branched Broom-rape (*Orobanche ramosa*), which is parasitic on the roots of hemp and tobacco plants, and is very widely distributed. The greatest number of species belong to the East and to Southern Europe. The extreme north of America harbours one species which bears a single flower at the end of its stem. In all the species the stem projects only partially above the earth. The subterranean portion, adherent to the root of a host, is often greatly swollen and thickened above the place of attachment; in the case of *Striga orobanchoides*, which is prevalent in the Nile basin, it is irregularly lobed above the host's root. The root of the nutrient plant also is usually somewhat swollen wherever a parasitic *Orobanche* has settled upon it, and sometimes it exhibits an irregular outgrowth inclosing the spot whereto the *Orobanche* is adnate like a cup. Beyond the place of attachment of the parasite the root has often the appearance of having been bitten off, and this is owing to the fact that the particular piece of root has been killed and demolished by the attack of the parasite. From the base of the stem, near the point of adhesion to the host, spring short, thick, fleshy fibres, and one or other of these bends its tip towards the root of the foster-plant and clings to it. These fibres are, in many species, very numerous, and are interlaced and entangled so as to form a reticulate mass, which vividly recalls that of the Bird's-nest, and is an instance of the general resemblance existing between Orobancheæ and the Orchideæ destitute of green leaves (*Neottia, Corallorhiza, Epipogum, Limodorum*), which have already been discussed.

The establishment of parasitic Orobancheæ upon the roots of host-plants takes place in the following manner. The embryo imbedded in the small seed shows no trace of differentiation into root and stem, possesses no cotyledons, and indeed consists only of a group of cells; it is surrounded by other cells filled with reserve-nutriment. When this embryo grows forth from the seed, during which process it consumes the reserve-food, it exhibits no distinction between root, stem, and leaf, but is a spiral filament consisting of delicate cells. One extremity, the shoot end, of this filiform seedling, remains covered by the seed-coat, which looks like a dark cap (fig. 34[8]); the opposite extremity is the root.

The seedling Broom-rape stretches downwards just as the Dodder (*Cuscuta*) extends upwards. In so doing the descending tip traces a spiral line, and so, as it were, seeks in the earth for the root of a plant suitable as host. If the search is fruitless, and if the reserve-material in the seed has meantime been altogether consumed, the seedling begins to wither and gradually shrivels, turns brown, and dries up. It lacks the power of nourishing itself by means of the surrounding earth. But, if the lower, foraging extremity of the seedling succeeds in finding a live root belonging to a plant able to serve as host, it not only adheres closely to it, but swells in such a way as to give the young plantlet a flask-shaped appearance (fig. 34[9] and fig. 34[10]). The upper end is still inclosed by the seed-coat, but in proportion as the lower part thickens, the upper shrivels till no trace of it is left. The thickened part, on the other hand, which has become attached to the root of the host, becomes nodulated and papillose. Some of the papillæ develop into elongated conical pegs, and the young Broom-rape now rests upon the nutrient root in the shape of the head of a fighting-club (see fig. 34[12]). At the place of attachment one of the conical pegs has meanwhile penetrated the cortex of the root, and there it continues to grow energetically, forcing the cortical tissue apart, until it reaches the wood. Vessels now arise in the body of the young club-like plant, and, passing through the middle of the plug, wedged in the nutrient root, are brought into connection with the vessels of the latter. At the point of union between host and parasite, a bud is formed, clothed with abundant scales, which may best be likened to the bulb of the Martagon Lily. Lastly, out of this bud grows a strong, thick stem, which breaks through the earth and lifts a spike of flowers into the sunlight.

That portion of the Broom-rape which is buried in the root of the host-plant is so intimately associated with the separate parts of that root in the development of a tuber that it is usually difficult to determine which cells belong to the parasite and which to the host. The degree of union is such that one cannot even state with certainty where the epidermis of the nutrient root ceases, and that of the Broom-rape begins. The latter looks as if it were a branch growing out of the root it preys upon, and this apparent fusion gave some colour to the view of the earlier botanists, who, ignorant of the life-history of these parasites, believed that they did not arise from seeds, but were pathological outgrowths of the roots, produced from their tainted juices; in other words, that they were "pseudomorphs" sprouting from diseased roots in the place of leafy branches.

It is also deserving of mention that some of the thick, fleshy fibres issuing laterally from the nodulated seedlings curve towards the host's root, bury their tips in the cortex, and thenceforth behave exactly like the peg which was inserted at the point where the seedling first became attached. We must leave undecided the questions as to whether the other fibres, which terminate freely in the earth, are capable of taking up food-materials from that source, whether these fibres are only present in perennial species and become the starting-points of new individuals, and lastly, whether they should be looked upon as root-structures or as stem-structures.

In addition, it is noteworthy that in many Orobancheæ only those embryos continue to develop which meet with a plant suitable to be their host. Although it is not the case that every species of *Orobanche* adopts one particular species of plant as foster-parent, yet thus much is certain, that most of them only thrive on members of a limited circle of species; one lives exclusively on kinds of Wormwood, a second on species of Butter-bur, and a third on those of Germander. For example, *Orobanche Teucrii* prevails on *Teucrium Chamædrys*, *Teucrium montanum*, &c., the hosts being invariably species of the genus *Teucrium*. Suppose a hill thickly covered with plants comprising *Teucrium montanum* growing in company with thyme, rock-roses, globe-flowers, sedges, and grasses, but no great abundance of the *Teucrium*, a plant belonging to the species named occurring only here and there, and let *Orobanche Teucrii* have established itself at one particular spot, have attained to flowering and developed fruits, the tiny seeds of which have been shaken by the wind out of the ripe capsules. Owing to the exceptional minuteness and lightness of its seeds, every gust of wind will scatter them in innumerable quantities over the entire hillside and beyond it. The next step is germination. Filiform embryos emerge from the seeds, in the manner described above, and penetrate into the earth. *Teucrium montanum* being only sparsely present on the hill in question, comparatively few seedlings will meet with the roots of that plant, whereas thousands will fall in with the roots of the thymes, rock-roses, globe-flowers, sedges, and grasses. But, curious to relate, only those seedlings of *Orobanche Teucrii* which come into contact with the roots of *Teucrium montanum* establish themselves firmly, penetrate into them, and continue their development; whilst the numerous individuals which touch the roots of the thyme and other plants perish. This phenomenon can scarcely be explained in any other way than by the supposition that the roots of *Teucrium montanum* alone, by virtue of their special structure and quality, afford a suitable nutrient substratum, and therefore constitute centres of attraction for seedlings of *Orobanche Teucrii*;

and that the roots of the thyme, rock-roses, and other plants growing upon the hill side by side with *Teucrium montanum* do not share this property.

Whereas the Broom-rapes constitute a family of plants, the species of which, though very numerous, are so similar in the structure of flowers and fruit, in the history of their development and in the general impression they convey, that it is necessary to discover minute distinctive marks in order to be able to classify them with tolerable completeness, the *Balanophoreæ*, which, together with these Oro-lancheæ, belong to the fourth series of parasitic Phanerogams, are related to one another in a manner quite the reverse. Only forty species of them are known, but they are so various that, on the basis of the obvious differences, no less than fourteen genera have been distinguished, among which the forty species are fairly equally divided. In respect of distribution and occurrence they also contrast strikingly with both Broom-rapes and Rhinanthaceæ. The Orobancheæ belong in particular to the Mediterranean flora, and to the East, and the Rhinanthaceæ, as has been already stated, adorn chiefly sunny pastures in arctic regions and in mountain districts of the northern hemisphere. Balanophoreæ, on the other hand, are only found within a belt encircling the Old and New Worlds, which stretches little beyond the equatorial zone to the north or south, and they almost all inhabit the dark bed of primeval forests, where they are parasitic on the roots of woody plants, beneath a covering of vegetable mould.

The genus of Balanophoreæ named *Langsdorffia* is confined exclusively to tropical America. One of its species (*Langsdorffia Moritziana*) is found native in the damp forests of Venezuela and New Granada, where it is parasitic on the roots of palms and fig-trees; a second species (*Langsdorffia rubiginosa*) occurs in Guiana and Brazil in the region of the sources of the Orinoco, and a third, the most common of all (*Langsdorffia hypogæa*) represented in fig. 38, has an area of distribution extending from Mexico to the south of Brazil. They all avoid the hottest districts, remaining rather in cool regions; indeed the species first named has been found at an elevation of from 2000 to 3000 meters. Unlike all the rest of the Balanophoreæ, *Langsdorffia* exhibits a branched, cylindrical stock ascending from the place of attachment to the nutrient root, more or less felted externally, and before putting forth any flowers has a remote resemblance to a doe's antlers with their winter covering of downy skin. These stems are almost as thick as a little finger, have a fleshy consistence, and exhibit a clavate expansion at the base where they rest upon the root of the host. Many of those stems which bear the male flowers are 30 cm. long; those which bear the female flowers are usually somewhat shorter. They are all of a pale-yellowish colour; the thickly tomentose *Langsdorffia rubiginosa* looks as if it were covered with a yellowish velvet. At the extremity of each of the ramifications of the stem, which are often extremely short, having then the form of lobes or knobs, a bud is developed sooner or later in the lower cortical layer. This bud swells, bursts the outer layer of cortex, uplifts itself and grows out as an inflorescence between the four lobes formed by the cruciform rupture of the bark. The inflorescence is surrounded, like the capitulum of a composite, by a whorl of imbricating scales, of which the lower are shorter and broader, and the upper longer, narrower, and pointed at the apex. These scales being stiff, somewhat shiny, and varying in colour from a waxen yellow to orange or red—in the case of *Langsdorffia Moritziana* brown-red,—the whole inflorescence has a vivid resemblance to certain immortelles, namely, the large species of *Helichrysum* occurring at the Cape. The inflorescences bearing male flowers are elongated and egg-shaped, those possessing only female flowers are shorter and capitulate. The seeds dropped from the nut-like fruits, which are pulpy internally, have no special integument. The embryo exhibits no trace of

Fig. 38 — *Langsdorffia hypogæa*, from Central America.

cotyledons or radicle, but consists of an undifferentiated group of cells which may be likened to a tiny bulbil.

Seeds of this kind germinate like those of *Lathræa*, and upon meeting with the root of a tree or shrub suitable for prey, develop into larger tubercles and have a remarkable effect upon the substratum. The cortex of the host-root is destroyed at the place of adhesion of the tubercle, and its wood is laid open, lacerated, and unravelled. The woody bundles are diverted from their previous direction, ascend towards the parasitic tubercle, which meantime has grown into a full-sized tuber, and spread out like fans. The cells and vessels of the parasite penetrate between the ascending wood-fibres, and this results in the formation of a zone at the place of union of the parasite and root, where cells and vessels belonging to both inter-lace, traverse, and join one another, coalescing completely in exactly the same way as happens in the case of the species of Toothwort. A similar phenomenon occurs also when one of the wavy stems of *Langsdorffia* comes into contact with a root adapted to the purpose. The cortex of the root is demolished at the place of contact; the wood is exposed, split open, and unravelled, whilst the tissue of the parasitic stem fills up all the interspaces in the upcurved and sundered woody bundles and fibres, and so intimate is the union thus effected that the stem of the *Langsdorffia* might be taken to be a branch of the root of the host-plant which sustains it. At the point of connection of an already adult *Langsdorffia* stem, the hypertrophy of the tissue is not very striking; but the base of each stem of an individual produced from a seed presents a highly swollen and clavate appearance. At first the parasite is only fastened by one side of this thickened base to the nutrient root, but later on it wraps both sides round the root, and rests upon the latter like a saddle on the back of a horse.

Between the bundles of a *Langsdorffia* stem there are passages filled with a peculiar wax-like matter named balanophorin. The quantity of this substance is so great that if one end of a stem of Langsdorffia is lighted, it burns like a wax-taper, and in the region of the Bogota these Langsdorffias are collected and sold under the name of "siejos", and are used for illuminating purposes on festive occasions. In New Granada they have also been employed in the making of candles; and, although this source of wax is not sufficiently abundant for us to be able to believe in its consumption and conversion on a large scale, the fact of its application in this manner shows that the parasite we are discussing must occur in great exuberance in many tracts of country in Central America.

Much rarer than the parasitic Langsdorffias are the species belonging to the genus *Scybalium*. Like the former these are confined to the equatorial zone of America. Two species, viz. *Scybalium Glaziovii* and *S. depressum*, flourish in mountainous districts, one of them indeed occurring only on the mountains of New Granada; two other species (*Scybalium jamaicense* and *S. fungiforme*) live in the woods and savannahs of lower-lying regions. The aspect of the last-named species when seen growing on the ground of a primeval forest, tempts one to suppose it to be a fungus, and it is easily understood why the first discoverer selected the term *fungiforme* to apply to it. Figure 39[1], representing this rare and marvellous plant, is taken from the original specimens discovered in the year 1820 by Schott in the Sierra d'Estrella of Brazil, and brought thence by him to Vienna. We see that, in this case, instead of the elongated, wavy, branched stem characteristic of Langs-dorffias, a lumpy, tuberous mass rests upon the root of the host-plant. This tuber is sometimes rounded and sometimes compressed and discoid; it is nodulated and often irregularly lobed also, and grows to the size of a fist. It is developed from a seed which, as is the case in all Balanophoreæ, is a cellular structure without integument containing an embryo destitute of cotyledons and radicle, and is best described as a minute tubercle. The embryo, after emerging from the seed and finding the living root of a woody plant, increases in volume, and, in the form of a little knob the size of a pea, exercises the same influence on the plant preyed upon as has been noted in the case of *Langsdorffia*. The root attacked is stripped of bark at the place where the tubercle is attached; the wood is then resolved into a fringe of fibres which stand straight up, and, diverging like the spokes of a fan.

distribute themselves in the tissue of the parasite, the latter having in the meantime developed into a tuberous stock as large as a nut. These radiating bundles, issuing from the wood of the nutrient root, come then into such intimate connection with the vessels formed in the tuber of the parasite, that the one appears to be a continuation of the other. They are, besides, entangled together, and between them is intercalated a mass of small parenchymatous cells which also adheres to the yet unfrayed portion of the foster-root's wood, and coalesces with it. The tuberous body of the parasite, which in the first instance is only adnate to the host on one

Fig. 39 — Parasitic Balanophoreæ.

1 *Scybalium fungiforme*, from Brazil.     2 *Balanophora Hildenbrandtii*, from the Comoro Islands.

side, gradually encompasses it entirely, and the nutritive root then appears to perforate this irregular tuber. The inflorescences are produced direct from buds, which are formed under the bark at projecting spots of the brown tuberous stem, the cortex bursting open and allowing a thick flesh-coloured shoot, closely beset by ovoid pointed scales, to emerge and grow up into a form resembling a mortar-pestle. At the summit this shoot expands into a disc, and upon this are borne little capitulate groups of flowers, which are inserted amongst innumerable quantities of scales and hairs. The pistillate and staminate flowers are separated in different inflorescences, whilst the entire structure has an undeniable resemblance when in bloom to the inflorescence of an artichoke gone to seed, and later on to a toad-stool.

In the eastern hemisphere we find the various species of the genus *Balanophora* replacing the Langsdorffias and Scybalia. One of these, *Balanophora Hilden-*

*brandtii*, which is represented on the left side of the figure 39, occurs in the Comoro Islands off the east coast of Africa; seven species inhabit the islands of Java, Ceylon, Borneo, Hong-Kong, and the Philippines, and three species the East Indies. *Balanophora fungosa*, first discovered by Forster, is parasitic on the roots of *Eucalyptus* and *Ficus*, and is indigenous to Australia and the New Hebrides. The more elevated regions of Java and the Himalaya abound especially in these singular organisms. *Balanophora elongata* is so prevalent in Java on mountains of between 2000 and 3000 metres, that it is collected in quantities for the sake of the wax-like matter obtained from it. In that island candles are made from Balanophoras as they are from Langsdorffias in New Granada, or else rods of bamboo are smeared with the viscid substance, as they are then found to burn quite quietly and slowly. In the Himalaya, *Balanophora dioica* or *B. polyandra* are the commonest and most widely distributed species, and *Balanophora involucrata* is there met with upon the roots of oaks, maples, and araliads even at a height of from 2300 to 2500 metres above the sea-level. They possess in almost all cases very vivid and conspicuous colouring—deep-yellow, purple, red-brown or flesh-tint, thus resembling the Gastromycetes, Clavarieæ, and Toad-stools, in whose company they grow, and with which they manifest an additional uniformity in being all of fleshy consistence and containing no trace of chlorophyll. At a certain distance, moreover, the inflorescences rising from the dark ground in a wood, have the appearance of fungi, and all the early observers describe these Balanophoreæ with one accord as truly abnormal growths, viz. as fungi which by some marvellous accident bear flowers. They were also the object of the boldest speculations and most exuberant imagery on the part of the botanists belonging to the school of the " nature philosophers " of the first decades of this century. Even as late as the forties a famous German botanist says of them: "They are in the position of a hiero-glyphic key between two worlds, which intercept and evade one another in an infinite variety of ways, like dreaming and waking moments", and the worthy Junghuhn, who discovered several of these plants in Java, writes: "Those are words which we may hope will be rightly interpreted thousands of years hence. Their sublime truth affected me deeply. There, flowerless and leafless, stood the mysterious plants which afford an instance of the combination of special vessels in a stalk like that of Balanophoreæ with the fructification of imperfect Hypho-mycetes!"

A young *Balanophora* not in flower is not unlike a *Scybalium* in appearance at the corresponding stage of its development. It consists of an irregular tuberous stem, which rests upon the creeping root of a tree or shrub. The exterior of this structure, which sometimes attains to the size of a man's head, is uneven, and in some cases convoluted like the human brain, or it may project in humps and knobs, or be divided into lobes or short branches like a coral-stem. The resemblance to the latter is heightened by the fact that the surface is covered by little papillæ shaped like stars or forget-me-nots, which distinguish the genus *Balanophora* from all allied genera.

The seeds settle upon the roots of trees, develop into tuberous axes, and unite with the nutrient root in the same manner as the Balanophoreæ already described. Also the inception of the rudimentary inflorescence beneath the cortex of the tuber and its eruption are similarly accomplished. In this genus the cortical layer thus broken through and forced outward always forms a large cup-shaped or crateriform sheath with an irregularly-lobed margin surrounding the base of the inflorescence.

Fig. 40 – Parasitic Balanophoreæ.

[1] *Rhopaloenemis phalloides*, from Java.          [2] *Helosis gujanensis*, from Mexico.

The inflorescence itself is spadiciform, and is borne by a thick shaft beset with large squamous leaves. The spadices growing from a tuber-stock are, for the most part, only as long as a little finger, but occasionally they reach a height of 30 cm., as, for example, is the case in the *Balanophora elongata* of Java, which is parasitic on the roots of *Thibaudia*.

The species of the American genus *Helosis*, whereof the most common (*Helosis gujanensis*) is represented above, resemble those of the genus *Balanophora* in the shape of the inflorescence. There is, however, considerable difference in the method adopted by these *Helosis* species of settling upon the roots of host-plants and in the whole mode of growth. The phenomena of the swelling of the embryo into a tubercle after it has chanced upon a nutritive root, the destruction of the cortex, the exposure of the wood at that part of the root where the tubercle is adnate, and the derangement of the course of the woody bundles ensue, it is true, in the same manner as in the other Balanophoreæ; but the frayed wood-bundles of the foster-root only form quite short lobules which penetrate but a short distance into the parasitic tuber-stock, whilst the vascular bundles, formed meantime in the latter, adhere to them in such a manner that they might be mistaken for direct continuations of them.

When once the parasitic tubers have thus become adnate to a root, and by means of this union are provided with food, they grow round the nutrient roots in such a way that the latter appear to perforate or actually to issue from the tubers. They are always roundish, brown outside, and warty, but without scales, and they never produce inflorescences directly, but put forth in the first place several whitish or yellowish runners varying in thickness from a quill to a finger, which creep along horizontally under the ground, bifurcating, and becoming interlaced with other ramifications. At the places of contact they coalesce, and so occasionally form a net-work which is almost inextricably entangled with the root-system of the plant preyed upon. Whenever a runner of this kind comes into contact with a living root belonging to the host-plant, the surface of contact at once swells up. The part affected is converted into a tuberous mass and becomes adnate to the root, the process being the same as occurs in the case of the tubercle produced from seed. A net-work of runners thus connected with the root-system of the nutrient plant at several spots by means of tubers as large as peas might be compared to the reticulum woven by *Lathræa* round the roots of its hosts; but, apart from the size, there is the essential difference that inflorescences are never produced from the white threads of the ramifying and sucker-bearing roots of *Lathræa*, whereas the runners of *Helosis* afford points of origin for new inflorescences. Warts are produced on the surfaces of the thicker cylindrical runners, and within these are developed the buds of the inflorescences. The outer coat of the warts is then rent open at the top and constitutes a little cup, out of which grows a naked, scaleless shaft terminated by an oval spadix. Seeing that the runners rest horizontally under the earth whilst the shafts ascend bolt upright from the ground, the latter are always at right angles to the runners, of which they are to be regarded as branches.

The flowers are grouped in capitula, presenting in the spadix a dense mass. They are protected by peculiar bract-scales, each of which by itself is like a nail with a facetted head. These heads are in close contact with one another, so that the young inflorescence seems to be inclosed in a panelled coat of mail, and resembles to a certain extent a closed fir-cone. By degrees, however, these bract-scales detach themselves and fall off, and thus the flowers, till then roofed over by them, become visible. When the seeds are mature, the whole runner concerned in the production of the inflorescence, and usually also the tuber which served as the starting-point of that runner, perishes, and another tuber belonging to the net-work above described, or rather the system of runners proceeding from it, becomes the basis for the development of new inflorescences.   To this extent we may regard these *Helosis* species as perennial plants, whereas the majority of the other Balanophoreæ can lay no claim to this distinction, inasmuch as in their case the whole plant dies after it has flowered and ripened its seeds.   The floral spadices in *Helosis* have a purple or blood-red colour, and in Brazil are called "Espigo de sangue". Only three species of *Helosis* have been discovered up to the present time, and those are distributed over equatorial America, in the Antilles, and from Mexico to Brazil.

Nearly allied to *Helosis* is the genus *Corynæa*, which resembles it in having facetted bract-scales like nails and a cone-like inflorescence, but differs entirely in other respects in its mode of growth, especially in being without runners.   Four species of this genus have been discovered in the Andes of South America, in Peru, Ecuador, and New Granada, where they are parasitic, like the rest of the Balanophoreæ, upon the roots of trees.   One of them, *Corynæa Turdici*, is worthy of notice as living on the roots of Peruvian-bark trees, and is rendered conspicuous by its purple spadix, borne on a white shaft.   *Rhopalocnemis phalloides* (see fig. 40 [1]) is another root-parasite related to *Helosis*, and the single representative in Asia of these pre-eminently American groups.   It is found preying upon the roots of fig-trees, oaks, and various lianes, in mountainous parts of Java and the eastern Himalayas, and is one of the biggest of all the Balanophoreæ.   The fleshy, yellowish or reddish-brown tuber-stock attains to the size of a man's head; the inflorescences, which burst from the protuberances of this lumpy mass and are from two to six in number, are over 30 cm. long and from 4 to 6 cm. thick.   The protuberances are light-brown in colour, and resemble in form a cycad-cone. *Rhopalocnemis*, a drawing of which is given in fig. 40 [1] on a scale of one-half the natural size, is distinguished, like *Corynæa*, from *Helosis* by having no runners issuing from the tuberous axes.

The Lophophyteæ are set apart as a further group of parasitic Balanophoreæ, and differ from all the groups hitherto described in having their flowers arranged in separate roundish capitula upon a fleshy rachis springing from the tuberous-stock. They, again, belong to Central America, and are divided into three genera (*Lophophytum*, *Ombrophytum*, and *Lathrophytum*) into particulars of which we cannot enter without exceeding our limits.   Only the genus *Lophophytum*, which is in many respects different from other Balanophoreæ, and in particular has been more thoroughly studied with reference to its peculiar mode of connection with the host-plant, demands special consideration.   The *Lophophytum mirabile* (see fig. 41 [1]) found in the primeval forests of Brazil adhering to the roots of Mimoseæ, to those of Inga-trees especially, occurs at some places in such profusion that areas of ground, occupied by Inga-roots, from twenty to thirty paces in circumference appear to be entirely overgrown by the parasite.   Hundreds of tubers, some large, some small, rest upon the roots of the trees, covered by fallen leaves and a light stratum of vegetable mould. Most of them are the size of a fist, but a few are as big as a head, and then weigh 15 kilogr. and more. The tubercles formed directly by the germinating seeds which chance upon the roots are, by the time they attain to about the size of a pea, already in connection with the wood of the attacked root. The cortex and a portion of the wood at the place where the parasite is adnate are absorbed by this root. The tissue of the small tuber-stock is squarely and firmly inserted into the superficial notch thus made in the root, and short, peg-shaped bundles, isolated by the loosening of the wood of the nutrient root, appear to grow into the substance of the parasite. As the tuber increases in size vascular bundles are developed in it also, and these grow towards the said bundles of the host and unite with them.

No boundary can then any longer be certainly recognized between host and parasite, and the strangest fact of all is that we find, in these bundles, cells concerning which we are not able to decide, even by reference to their shape, whether they belong to the one or to the other. The cells which belong undoubtedly to the wood of the nutrient root have dotted walls; the bundles unquestionably developed in the parasitic tuber exhibit, on the other hand, cells with reticulate thickening, which, when slightly magnified, look as if they were transversely striated. Wherever these pitted and reticulate cells meet, cells are intercalated which do not altogether correspond either to the pitted variety belonging to the host or to the reticulate cells of the parasite, but display a form intermediate between the two. Here and there, too, cell-groups belonging to the parasite are entirely buried in the wood of the foster-root in its growth, and in the older tubers the cellular elements of the two plants there bound together are so involved that it is, as has been stated, impossible to establish any line of demarcation between the two.

By the time the tubers have reached the size of a fist their cortical layer is always solid, corky, and areolated; each of the areas being more or less uniformly angled, as is shown in the illustration below. Some of the more protuberant portions elongate and grow out into short, thick stumps bearing scales all round, each of the little areas having a triangular-pointed scale situated in the middle of it. At this stage of development the entire Lophophytum plant has an extraordinary resemblance to the squamigerous rhizome of a fern, or to a dwarf cycad-tree, stripped of its green leaves; and this likeness is enhanced by the fact that the bark and scales of *Lophophytum* are dark-brown in colour. From the centre of each of these thick stumps, which often reach a height of 15 cm., there now arises a spadiciform inflorescence. At first it is so thickly covered with ovate lanceolate scales possessing dark-brown, quasi-horny tips, overlapping one another like tiles, that the spadix as a whole looks extremely like an erect cycad-cone. Imagine the surprise of a traveller, who chances upon a spot in the depths of a primeval forest where the ground is occupied by *Lophophytum*, upon seeing hundreds of these brown, scaly cones grow up suddenly, in the course of a night following some days of rain, from the subterranean roots of the trees. A day or two later, this garden of Lophophyta presents an altogether different picture. The brown scales have detached themselves from the rachis, first those at the base of cone, then also those on the upper parts. They fall off almost simultaneously, and with them the envelope which up to that time has concealed the flowers. The erect, fleshy, white, or reddish rachis bearing the flowers then becomes visible. The female flowers are

Fig. 41 – Parasitic Balanophoreæ.

[1] *Lophophytum mirabile*, from Brazil.  [2] *Sarcophyte sanguinea*, from the Cape of Good Hope.

on the lower part, and arranged in spherical, deep yellow or orange-coloured capitula which are packed close together; the male flowers are situated above the lowermost third of the spadix, and are arranged in looser and less crowded capitula of a pale yellow colour.

However striking the phenomenon presented by these flowering cones of *Lophophytum mirabile*, it is surpassed by another native of Brazilian forests, the *Lophophytum Leandri*. The colouring of the inflorescence in this species cannot be exceeded in variety, its rachis being pale reddish-violet, the bract-scales gamboge, the ovaries yellowish, the styles red, and the stigmas white. It is not surprising that even in Brazil, where there is certainly no lack of curious plant-forms, they have attracted attention, and that they are used there, as is the case with all rare plants, for purposes of healing and magic. The tubers of *Lopho-phytum mirabile*, which have a disagreeable, bitter, resinous taste, and bear the popular name of "Fel de terra", or earth-gall, are employed by quacks against jaundice, and a belief also prevails that by secretly eating the blossoms youths are enabled to win the affection of the maidens they admire. The same may be said of *Lophophytum Leandri*, and, in addition, there is a tradition that the eating of it brings luck and agility in hunting, fishing, fighting, and dancing, and for this reason the Indian youth collect the plants secretly and eat them on particular days.

Of the other parasitic Balanophoreæ most nearly allied to *Lophophytum* we will here only mention in passing the species of *Ombrophytum*, known in Peru by the name of "Mays del monte", which has a yellowish inflorescence over 30 cm high, and from 6 to 7 cm thick, somewhat resembling a spike of maize, and lastly, the *Lathrophytum Peckoltii* of Brazil, to which a special interest attaches inasmuch as it is the sole instance of a flowering plant entirely destitute of all structures of the nature of leaves, with the exception of the stamens and ovaries. *Langsdorffia*, *Scybalium*, *Lophophytum*, and even *Balanophora*, *Helosis*, and *Rhopalocnemis* exhibit scales, which, though transformed in various ways, are yet always in point of position and form recognizable as leaves; but neither on the tuber, shaft, nor spadix of this *Lathrophytum* is any trace of a scale to be seen, nor even a swelling or rim that might be looked upon as a degenerate leaf.

In comparison with equatorial America with its wealth of parasitic Balano-phoreæ the corresponding zone of Africa must be called poor so far as these plants are concerned. Possibly further explorations may bring to light a few more of these wonderful vegetable parasites, but it is hardly to be expected that such a variety as is presented in Brazil, the Peruvian Andes, New Granada, and Bolivia will be found. Only three Balanophoreæ have been discovered in the Cape regions, where the flora is well known. One of these, which is represented on the right-hand side of fig. 41, bears the name of *Sarcophyte sanguinea* (i.e. blood-red flesh-plant), whilst the name of *Icthyosoma* (i.e. fish-carcase) has also been applied to it because it smells of rotten fish. These names imply that the plant resembles an animal rather than a vegetable organism. The host-plants adapted to this *Sarcophyte* are various Mimoseæ, especially *Acacia caffra*, *Acacia capensis*, &c. In the first place, as is the case with all Balanophoreæ, small tubers are formed on the roots of the above-mentioned woody hosts, and enter into connection with the wood of the nutrient roots in the manner already described more than once. An inflorescence then emerges from a bud originating beneath the cortex of the tuber, and rapidly grows up from out of the cortex, which is rent and pushed up in the process. The axis of this inflorescence resolves itself into a number of thick, repeatedly ramifying, fleshy branches, differing in this respect from every other

Fig. 42 —*Cytinus Hypocistus* on the left; *Cynomorium coccineum* on the right

example of the Balanophoreæ. The flowers are arranged side by side on the branches, staminate flowers on one plant, and pistillate flowers on another, the latter always grouped in spherical capitula, as is shown in fig. 41 [2]. Reddish-brown scale-like leaves are situated at the points of origin of the branches, and also at the base of the entire inflorescence. The general aspect is that of a bunch of verrucose grapes ascending from the root, or of the fruiting axis of *Ricinus*, and is very striking owing to the blood-red colouring of all the parts.

As a final instance of the Balanophoreæ we may take the genus *Cynomorium*, which was so highly valued in olden times, and is the sole species belonging to this family of plants indigenous in the south of Europe. A drawing of it is given on the right-hand side of fig. 42.

Whilst other Balanophoreæ are parasitic on the roots of trees and lianes in the shade of lofty woods, this *Cynomorium* thrives most luxuriantly upon plants near the sea-coast, on the roots of Pistacias and Myrtles, and even on actual salt-loving maritime plants, the various Tamarisks, Salicorniæ, Salsolaceæ, and Oraches, which are sprinkled with foam whenever the breakers are high. The seed is like that of other Balanophoreæ and those of the Orobanche species, and germinates in the same way as they do. From the group of cells in the seed which represent the embryo, a filiform body emerges, and then grows downwards, its upper part remaining for some time in connection with the other cells in the seed, which are richly furnished with food-materials. The filiform embryo continues to grow deeper and deeper at the expense of this nutritive store, and as soon as it reaches a living root, swells into an oval or irregularly-lobed tubercle, which unites with the wood of the nutrient root in the manner already described. These tubercles swell, and from the summit of each a spadix is produced, as in *Lophophytum*, which is raised above the surface of the earth. The spadix is clothed with pointed scales, and is clearly differentiated into a lower stalk-like support, and a fleshy inflorescence resembling a cone. The small scales are separated from one another by the process of elongation of the spadix, and some fall off. Others of them, situated about the middle of the inflorescence, persist, however, until the time when the entire spadix dries up. The whole of the structure standing above the ground has a blood-red colour, and when it is injured a red fluid exudes, which was at one time supposed to be blood. At an age when the peculiar properties of extraordinary plants were looked upon as an indication given by higher powers that they were to be used for curative purposes, it was believed that the spadices of *Cynomorium*, being blood-red in colour, and bleeding when wounded, had styptic properties. In those days they were even collected for the sake of this property, and sold in apothecaries' shops under the name of the Maltese fungus (*Fungus melitensis*). Various miraculous virtues were also attributed to this plant, and the demand for it was so great that it became a regular article of commerce, its main source being the Island of Malta, whence is derived the name above referred to.

Of the Hydnoreæ, which are most properly included in the same series as

Balanophoreæ in consideration of their coalescence with the roots of their hosts, only three species are known. Two of them (*Hydnora Africana* and *H. triceps*) belong to South Africa, the third (*Hydnora Americana = Prosopanche Burmeisteri*) to South Brazil. The tuber is represented by a prismatic body with from four to six angles furnished with papillæ along the edges. The flower-buds which burst from it have at first the form of spherical Gasteromycetes, but gradually elongate and assume the form of a large fig or upright club. This structure opens at the thickened upper extremity by three stout fleshy valves representing petals. At the base of this curious flower no appendage is to be seen that could be interpreted as a bract or leaf. The fleshy mass of flowers evolves a disagreeable putrid odour, and in this property the Hydnoreæ resemble the Rafflesiæ, which belong to the next group of parasitic Phanerogams.

The fifth series of flowering parasites is composed of the Rafflesiaceæ, plants connected with Balanophoreæ and Hydnoreæ by their general aspect, the absence of chlorophyll, and the undifferentiated embryo which consists merely of a group of cells. They used all to be classed together under the name of Rhizantheæ; but the Rafflesiaceæ are now treated as a separate family on account of the characteristic structure of their flowers and fruit. The formation of these organs will again come up for discussion later on when we treat of the wonderful structure of the famous giant-flower *Rafflesia*; at present we are only concerned with the relationship of the parasite to the food-providing host-plant. This is, if possible, even more remarkable than in the case of Balanophoreæ and Hydnoreæ. In the latter the union is effected within a structure like a tuber or a rhizome, the vessels and cells of the parasite coalescing with the exfoliated and disordered wood-cells belonging to the root or stem of the host-plant; whereas in Rafflesiaceæ the embryo, having penetrated beneath the cortex of the host, produces a more or less definite hollow cylinder which surrounds the wood of the host's root or stem (as the case may be), and constitutes a sort of vestment intercalated between the wood and the cortex of the host. There is no production of tuberous enlargements as in the Balanophoreæ. The stem or root attacked by the parasite only exhibits a moderate thickening at the place where the parasite dwells beneath the cortex, and the cortex itself is only destroyed at the spot where the embryo pierces through it, and where subsequently the flowers emerge. When roots constitute the substratum whereupon the parasite has established itself, they are always of a kind that run throughout upon the surface of the ground; when stems are chosen for attack, they are either the branches of trees or shrubs, shoots clothed with dead foliage belonging to dwarf suffruticose bushes, or else woody lianes of tropical forests. The seeds are conveyed to the host-plants through the intervention of animals.

Rafflesias are found in the haunts of elephants and along the tracks followed by those beasts. The Rafflesia-fruits are accordingly no doubt trampled upon and crushed, and the little seeds imbedded in the pulpy mass of the fruit thus have an opportunity of adhering to the elephants' feet. The seeds are afterwards rubbed off by projecting roots at places more or less remote from the original locality, and if the root upon which they are detained belongs to a *Cissus* plant, they germinate. On the other hand, such Rafflesiaceæ as occur on the woody branches of trees, shrubs, and undergrowths, or on lianes, develop succulent fruits, which are eaten by animals. Their seeds are protected by a horny coat, and preserve their power of germination unimpaired as they pass through the animals' alimentary canals and are deposited with the excrements on the stems of fresh host-plants; or the seeds may stick to some part of an animal that happens to rub against them, and be brushed off later on as being an uncomfortable appendage, and in this way also they may fall upon the stem of a host-plant. Those Rafflesiaceæ which occur in Venezuela on the woody lianes (*Caulotretus*), known by the name of "monkey-ladders", owe their dispersion for the most part probably to monkeys.

Now, if a seed has been deposited in one way or another upon a woody root, creeping along the surface of the ground, or upon the stem of a woody plant, the filiform embryo emerging from the seed finds a suitable nutrient substratum present and it pierces the cortex of the root, and develops beneath it a tissue, which incloses the wood like a sheath. In *Rafflesia* and in the *Pilostyles* parasitic on the suffruticose shrubs of Tragacanth (*P. Haussknechtii*, see fig. 43[1]), this tissue consists of rows of cells, which to the naked eye look like threads. Some are simple and greatly elongated, others branched, and they are united together to form a net-work, so closely resembling the mycelium of a fungus as to be readily mistaken for one. The most complete similarity to these vegetative bodies living beneath the cortex of a host-plant is exhibited by the mycelia of the toad-stools which spread themselves in the form of nets and webs between the wood and the cortex of old trunks of trees. The vegetative bodies of the other species of *Pilostyles* consist, in each case, of a tissue composed of many layers of cells forming a parenchyma imbedded between wood and cortex in the host-plant and including some vessels and rows of cells capable of being interpreted as vascular bundles. Only in rare instances does this tissue of the parasite form an unbroken hollow cylinder encompassing the wood of the host; usually the elements of the host's tissues penetrate into it and permeate and split up the cylindrical soma (vegetative body) in the form of bands, ribs, and fibres. Many elements of the tissues, which the imbedded parasite has displaced from the living wood, and carries, as it were, on its back, perish; but sometimes these discarded layers remain in connection with other living tissues and so preserve their own vitality and power of expansion, and develop layers of wood-cells covering the parasite. There is then a general confusion and entanglement, and it is difficult to say what part belongs to the parasite and what to the host.

When the somatic tissue of the parasite has accomplished its connections with the host-plant in the manner just described, the latter is unable to rid itself of its occupant. A portion of the juices of the host-plant passes into the parasite's cells and the unwelcome guest augments in volume, and endeavours forthwith to reproduce and distribute its kind by the formation of fruit and seeds. For this purpose buds are developed at suitable spots in the reticular body of the parasite, each of which is manifested as a parenchyma of pulvinate appearance, and is

termed a floral cushion. The cells in this cushion, however, now group themselves in a definite way; ducts and vessels are produced, and, at the same time,
a differentiation into axis and flowers is exhibited. These members continue their
development, increase in size, and finally the enlarged bud breaks through the
cortex of the host-plant under shelter of which it has been evolved.

In the genus *Cytinus* alone do we find a stem richly furnished with leaves and
bearing at the top a flattened symmetrical tuft of flowers (see fig. 42, left-hand
side) developed from this bud; in the rest of the Rafflesiaceæ, the bud, which has

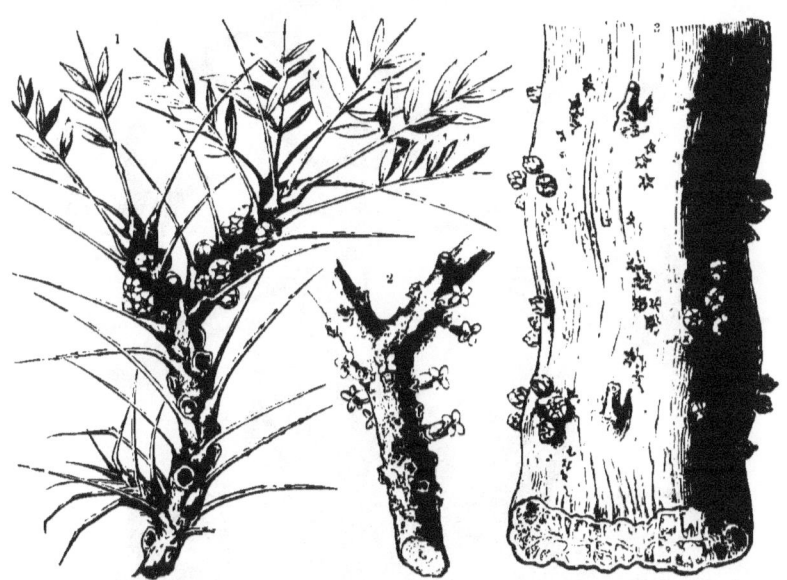

Fig. 43.—Rafflesiaceæ parasitic on trunks and branches.

¹ *Pilostyles Hausknechtii.*        ² *Apodanthes Flacourtiana.*        ³ *Pilostyles Caulotreti.*

emerged from beneath the cortex of the host, is the flower-bud itself. The axis
supporting the bud is extremely abbreviated and clothed merely by a few scales,
and the flowers are sessile directly upon the root or stem of the host (see fig. 43).
In the case of roots creeping upon the ground, the buds always emerge only on the
side turned towards the light; on lianes, also, they are only formed on the side more
exposed to light where subsequently the opened flowers are easily accessible to
flying insects (see fig. 43 ³); on upright shrubs and under-shrubs, on the other hand,
they burst forth on all sides upon the branches. Branches of this kind bearing
ubiquitously extruded flowers of a parasite such as *Apodanthes Flacourtiana* (see
fig. 43 ²) look delusively like the Mezereon (*Daphne Mezereum*) when the latter is
in bloom in the early spring before the development of foliage-leaves, its woody
branches being similarly studded all round with flowers, which stand out horizontally

from them; but, in the one case the flowers belong to a foreign parasite living under the cortex and have broken through it, whereas in Mezereon it is the flowers of the plant itself that have unfolded. In the case of *Pilostyles Haussknechtii*, which is parasitic on the low bushy tragacanth shrubs of the Persian plateaus, the buds are formed regularly on both sides of the leaf-bases of the host, so that at the insertion of every one of the older foliage-leaves, one finds a pair of buds, which subsequently expand into flowers (see fig. 43 [1]).

Fig. 44.—Parasitic Rafflesiacea (*Brugmansia Zipellii*) upon a Cissus-root.

Throughout the species of *Apodanthes* and *Pilostyles* the flowers are small—about the size of elder, jasmine, or winter-green blossoms—and by no means conspicuous. But this is not the case in the genera *Brugmansia* and *Rafflesia*. The Brugmansias, indigenous to Borneo and Java, have very handsome flowers, as may be seen in the above drawing, which represents on the natural scale *Brugmansia Zipellii* parasitic upon the root of a *Cissus*. But in magnitude they are far surpassed by the flowers of the Rafflesiæ, one of which, viz.: *Rafflesia Arnoldii*, may be described as actually the largest flower in the world. When open it has a diameter of 1 meter, a dimension exceeding even that of the gigantic blooms of South American aristolochias. At the period of emergence of the buds of *Rafflesia Arnoldii* from the roots of the vines which serve them as hosts, they are only as large as a walnut and give scarcely any indication of their future magnitude; but they gradually increase in size, and before opening are curiously like a cabbage.    Up to this time the bracts still inclose the flower proper, and to them is due the above-mentioned resemblance.    They now open back, and the flower, which, to the last, grows rapidly, unfolds and displays five immense lobes around a central bowl or cup-shaped portion.    The form of the giant-flower when open is best likened to that of a forget-me-not blossom.    The semicircular outline of the lobes, at least, is similar, and the very short throat of the flower also exhibits a distant resemblance.    At the part where the bowl-shaped centre, which

Fig. 45.  *Rafflesia Padma*, parasitic on roots upon the surface of the ground.

has the stamens and styles inserted in it, passes into the lobes there is a thick, fleshy ring like a corona.    The upper surface of the lobes is covered with numbers of papillæ.    The lobes themselves, the hollow central bowl, and the ring, are all fleshy, and the flower, as a whole, emits an unpleasant putrescent smell.    This floral prodigy was first discovered in the year 1818 in the interior of Sumatra at Pulo Lebbas on the river Manna, where it occurs parasitic on the roots of wild vines in places where the ground is strewn with the dung of elephants.    It has never yet been seen anywhere outside Sumatra.    Four other Rafflesiæ have, however, been discovered, but all in the islands of the Indian Ocean—Java, Borneo, and the Philippines.    In mode of growth, as also in the form of the flowers, they resemble the species above described, but their flowers are rather smaller. *Rafflesia Padma*, which occurs in Java, and is represented in fig. 45, possesses flowers with a diameter of half a meter.    The hollow, somewhat ventricose centre and the ring bordering the floral receptacle are in this *Rafflesia* of a dirty blood-red, whilst the verrucose lobes have almost the colour of the human skin. The flowers are sessile upon roots which wind about upon the dark forest ground, and a cadaverous smell, anything but pleasant, issues from them.    All these peculiarities explain the uncanny impression made by the organisms in question upon their original discoverers and upon all subsequent observers.

Whilst the Rafflesiæ, as well as the genera *Brugmansia* and *Sapria*, belong to the tropical and sub-tropical regions of Asia, and to the world of islands adjacent thereto on the south side, the genus *Apodanthes* is confined to tropical America. Most of the species of *Pilostyles* also appertain to tropical America, especially to Brazil, Chili, Venezuela, and New Granada.   One species alone—*Pilostyles Æthiopica*—has been observed in the mountains of Angola, and another, as has been mentioned before, in Persia.

The only European representative of the remarkable group of Rafflesiaceæ is *Cytinus Hypocistus*, represented on the left side of fig. 42, but its distribution is coincident with the entire range of the Mediterranean flora.   The roots of cistus shrubs, plants which are characteristic of the vegetation belonging to the basin of the Mediterranean, constitute the nutrient substratum in the case of *Cytinus*.   It is especially where the layer of earth-mould is not deep, and consequently the roots of the shrubs in question are exposed, that *Cytinus* is met with growing in abundance amongst the under-wood of the cistus plants.   The squamous leaves clothing the stem of this parasite being scarlet, and the plants not solitary but in large numbers, one sees here and there a flaming red colour glowing in the gaps in the cistus-groves, and one is thus from far off made aware of the presence of the parasite. The flowers themselves, which open between the red scale-like bracts, are yellow. The combination of colour thus afforded is a rare phenomenon in the vegetable world, and gives a very strange appearance to the plant.   Besides the species of *Cytinus* distributed over the area of the Mediterranean flora, there are two other species in Mexico, and one also at the Cape, which, although not parasitic on *Cistus* shrubs but on other woody plants, especially *Eriocephalus*, yet do not differ from *Cytinus Hypocistus* in floral structure or in mode of connection with their host.


## MISTLETOES AND LORANTHUSES.

The sixth and last series of parasitic phanerogams includes epiphytes of bushy appearance with much bifurcated branches, green cortex, green leaves, and berries containing large seeds, which germinate whilst resting immediately upon the branches of such trees as are adapted to act as host-plants, and will surrender to the invader a portion of their nutriment.   To this series belong a dozen different species of the genus *Henslowia*, belonging to the family of Santalaceæ, and indigenous to the South of Asia—chiefly the East Indian Archipelago—and, in addition, upwards of 300 species included in the family Loranthaceæ.   Amongst the latter, the plant that is best known and most widely distributed is the European Mistletoe (*Viscum album*) represented in fig. 46, and as it is also fitted, in respect of its life-history, to serve as type of the entire series, we will describe it first of all.

As is well known, the Mistletoe is parasitic upon trees, and these may be either Angiosperms or Gymnosperms. Most frequently it establishes itself upon trees the branches of which are coated by a soft sappy cortex—an extremely delicate and tender cork-tissue in particular — as is the case with silver-firs, apple-trees, and poplars. The Mistletoe's favourite tree is certainly the Black Poplar (*Populus nigra*). It flourishes with astonishing luxuriance on the branches of that tree, and wherever there is a small plantation of Black Poplars, the Mistletoe takes up its abode.

Along the shores of the Baltic and by the Danube near Vienna—especially in the celebrated Prater from which fig. 47 is taken, one finds, on many of the Black Poplars, tufts of Mistletoe measuring 4 meters in circumference, and with axes of a thickness of 5 cm. Birds use their most crowded branches, by preference, to nest in. In the forests of Karst, in Carniola, and in the Black Forest, where poplar trees play merely a subordinate part, whilst on the other hand, quantities of silver firs shade the ground, large numbers of these conifers have their tops covered with Mistletoe; and in the Rhine districts and the valley of the Inn in Tyrol, the same parasite occurs as a troublesome visitor upon apple-trees in the neighbourhood of the peasants' farms. In localities destitute of these three kinds of trees, which are pre-eminently the Mistletoe's favourite host-plants, it puts up with other trees, and is then usually found on whatever species happens to be the most common in each particular country. Thus, in the Black Pine district of the Wiener Wald, it occurs upon the Corsican Pine, whilst on the heaths of the sandy lowlands of the March, it settles upon the Scotch Pine. Much less frequently it has been observed on walnut-trees, limes, elms, robinias, willows, ashes, white-thorns, pear-trees, medlars, damsons, almond-trees, and on the various species of Sorbus. Mistletoe has also been found by way of exception upon the oak and the maple, and upon old vines. On one occasion, in the district of Verona, it has been seen established upon the parasitic shrubs of *Loranthus Europæus*, that is to say, one member of the Loranthaceæ was found parasitic upon another. The birch, the beech, and the plane, are avoided by the Mistletoe, a fact which no doubt depends upon the special structure of the cortex in those trees.

The dissemination of the European Mistletoe is effected, as in all the other Loranthaceæ, through the agency of birds—thrushes in particular—which feed upon the berries and deposit the undigested seeds with their excrement upon the branches of trees. That a preliminary passage through the alimentary canal of birds is essential to the germination of these seeds is no doubt a delusion, this assumption of former times being easily refuted by the fact that one can readily induce the seeds of berries, taken fresh from a tree, and stuck into fissures in the bark of moderately suitable trees, to germinate; it is, however, true, that in nature, mistletoe-seeds are dispersed exclusively by birds in the manner above mentioned. To this method of dissemination must be attributed the phenomenon, which, at first sight, is surprising, that Mistletoe-plants are rarely seated upon the upper surface of branches, but very frequently on the sides. For the dung of thrushes, which live upon Mistletoe-berries, is in the form of a semi-fluid, highly viscid mass, ductile like bird-lime; and, even when it is deposited upon the upper surface of slanting branches, it immediately runs down the sides, sometimes extending in ropes 20 or 30 centimeters in length. Owing to the viscous mass thus following the law of gravity, the Mistletoe-seeds imbedded in it are conveyed to the sides, and even to the under surface of the bark, and there remain cemented.

Fig. 46.—The European Mistletoe (*Viscum album*).

It may be a long time before a seed of the kind germinates, especially if it does not become attached until the autumn. The embryo is completely surrounded in the seed by reserve food. It is club-shaped and comparatively large, and is distinguished by the fact that the two oblong cotyledons, which are closely pressed together, but often somewhat wavy at the margins, are coloured dark green by chlorophyll, like the environing cellular mass filled with reserve materials. In the process of germination the axis of the embryo, especially the part lying beneath the cotyledons, and passing into the hemispherical radicle, lengthens out; the white seed-coat is pierced, and the radicle makes its appearance through the breach. Under all circumstances the emergent radicle is directed towards the bark of the branch to which the seed is adherent. This is the case even when the seed chances to stick with the radicle of the seedling pointing away from the branch; the whole axis of the embryo curving towards the surface of the bark in a very striking manner. Thus the radicle always reaches the bark, and having done so it becomes adpressed and cemented to its surface, spreads itself out in the form of a doughy mass, and so develops into a regular attachment-disc. From its centre a slender process now grows into the bark of the host-plant, piercing the latter and penetrating as far as the wood, but not growing into that tissue. This penetrating process has been termed a "sinker", and must be looked upon as a specially modified root.

Fig. 47 – Bushes of Mistletoe upon the Black Poplar in winter.

The development of the first year ends with the formation of this sinker. When the winter is over, the branch, into which the sinker is inserted so as just to reach the wood with its point, grows in thickness, a new layer of wood-cells—a so-called annual ring—being superimposed upon the wood of the previous year. The increasing mass of wood first surrounds the tip of the sinker with wood-cells, then forms a rampart all round it, pushing the cortical tissue, wherein that organ has hitherto been wedged, in front of it in an outward direction, and in this way the sinker is at length fixed deep within the woody cylinder. The process of inclosure by the wood-layers, as they are built up, may be compared to the gradual surrounding of a stake on the sea-shore by the rising tide; the lowermost extremity is first immersed and then higher and higher parts until the whole is enveloped. The sinker itself remains, strictly speaking, stationary; it does not grow into the wood, but the wood overgrows it. But what happens in the following season when a fresh annual ring is once more added to the wood? If the sinker had entirely ceased growing it would of necessity be ultimately completely closed by the layers of wood, as they develop with ever-increasing energy and add to the thickness of the branch, and at last it would be quite buried. To prevent this result, which would be fatal to the Mistletoe, a zone of cells is provided near the base of the sinker, which zone, at the time when the rampart of wood is being raised, adds in an equal degree to its own height, and causes, of course, an elongation of the sinker in a peripheral direction. The length of the piece thus intercalated in the haustorium is exactly equal to the thickness of the corresponding annual ring in the surrounding wood of the branch. Thus at length the Mistletoe-sinker is found imbedded in a number of annual rings, although it has not grown into the latter, but has been banked up by them year by year.

That zone of the sinker which possesses the capacity for growth, and which is always to be sought, in accordance with what has been said above, at the outside limit of the wood of the branch, in the so-called "bast" layer situated on the inner face of the cortex, produces, in the second year after the adhesion of the Mistletoe-embryo, lateral ramifications which are called cortical roots. They are thick, cylindrical, or somewhat compressed filaments, and all run close together under the cortex in the bast layer of the invaded branch. These rootlets issuing from the sinkers pursue a course parallel to the longitudinal axis of the branch, whilst the sinkers themselves are at right angles to the axis (see fig. 48 [3]). If a rootlet springs from the sinker in a direction transverse to the longitudinal axis it bends immediately afterwards so as to be parallel to the long axis, and adopts the same direction as the rest, or else it bifurcates just above its place of origin into two branches which separate suddenly, and in their further course follow the axis of the branch. Thus it comes to pass that all the rootlets of a Mistletoe run up and down in the infested branch of the host-plant in the form of thick green parallel strands, but that none of them ever encircle the branch in the form of an annular coil. Each of these cortical roots may now develop from behind the growing-point new sinkers, which are formed in the same way as the first one above described as proceeding from the actual seedling. They, too, penetrate into the branch perpendicularly to the axis, and as far as the solid wood are then encompassed by the growing mass of wood, but maintain the power of growth in the part close to their insertions, and in their growth keep pace with the thickening of the wood of the branch. The fact of the yearly recurrence of this formation of sinkers explains how it is that those situated nearest the growing-points of the cortical roots are the shortest, they being the youngest, whilst those which arise near the first sinker are the longest and oldest. It also accounts for the former being only inclosed by one annual ring of the host's wood, and the others being surrounded by an increasing number of rings the nearer they are to the spot where the Mistletoe-plant first struck root.

The root-system of the Mistletoe taken as a whole may be described as like a jaw-bone in shape, or, still better, a rake. The cross-beam of the rake corresponds to the cortical root, whilst the teeth are analogous to the sinkers; the cross-piece must be supposed to be parallel to the axis of the branch and lying under the bark, and the spokes must be thought of as perpendicular to the axis and driven into the wood.

Whilst the roots of the Mistletoe-plant are spreading in the interior of the branch in the manner described, the stem is developed outside. At the time when the process, subsequently to be the first sinker, emerges from the attachment-disc of

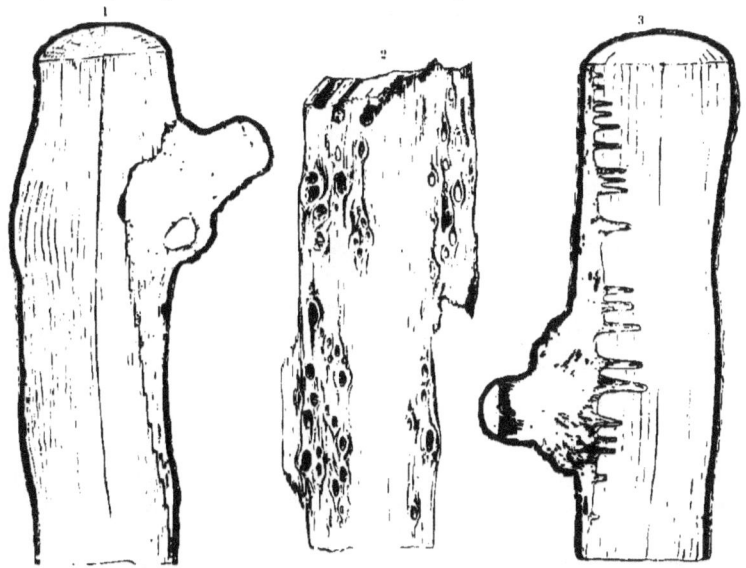

Fig. 48.—1 *Loranthus Europæus*, and 3 Mistletoe (*Viscum album*) - both parasitic on branches of trees, and seen in section. 2 A piece of the wood of a Fir-tree perforated by the sinkers of a Mistletoe.

the embryo and pierces through the bark, the cotyledons are still covered by the white seed-coat, which rests upon them like a cap. But when once this first sinker is firmly fixed and in a position to take up nutritive juices from the wood of the host, the seed-coat is thrown off; the apex of the stem, which is still very short, is raised; the cotyledons are detached, whilst close above them is produced a pair of green leaves. Thenceforward the development of the visible portion of the Mistletoe-plant outside the bark keeps pace with that of the roots underneath the cortex, and is moreover dependent upon the quantity of food taken up by the sinkers from the wood. Where there is an abundant supply of nutriment, as in the case of poplars, the growth of the Mistletoe is correspondingly exuberant; where the flow of juices is scarce, the parasite is stunted in its growth, and often develops only small yellowish sickly-looking tufts. If the foster-plant is of a lavish nature, adven-

titious buds are produced regularly by the cortical roots to which the absorbed
nutriment is first of all conveyed from the sinkers. These buds occur on the side
of the rootlets nearest the exterior of the bark, and later they burst through the
rind, and develop into new Mistletoe-plants.

These outgrowths are analogous to the adventitious shoots produced from the
subterranean roots of the Aspen, and this comparison is rendered all the more
appropriate by the fact that the removal of the tuft of Mistletoe encourages the
sprouting of adventitious root-buds just as in the case of the Aspen, the growth of
shoots from the roots is promoted by the felling of the trees to which those roots
belong. If a large Mistletoe-bush, growing in solitude on a Black Poplar, is removed
from the tree with the intention of freeing the latter from its parasite, the hopes
entertained by the operator are disappointed; for, an outgrowth of shoots from the
cortical roots ensues at a number of different spots, and in a few years' time the
poplar in question is the prey of a dozen Mistletoe-bushes instead of one. Inasmuch
as these bushes, produced from offshoots, are able, under favourable conditions, to
send out fresh roots, and these again may develop shoots, a good host of the kind
will at last have all its boughs from top to bottom overgrown by Mistletoes. In
the Prater at Vienna there are poplars beset by at least thirty large Mistletoe-
shrubs, and double that number of small ones, and if one catches sight of such a tree
at some distance in winter-time when the branches have lost their leaves, one takes
it to be a Mistletoe-tree, for almost the entire system of branches is mantled in a
continuous tangle of evergreen bushes of Mistletoe, which are in a state of parasitism
upon it.

Sinkers of the Mistletoe, 10 cm. in length, and inclosed in forty annual rings,
have been found in the wood of the Silver Fir, whence we may conclude that the
Mistletoe may live for forty years. A greater age could scarcely be attained
by one and the same bush of the parasite. If the Mistletoe dies, the rootlets and
haustoria survive for a time, but at length moulder and fall to pieces, whilst the
wood in which they were imbedded remains unaltered. The affected parts of the
wood exhibit in that case numerous perforations, and look just like the wood of a
target which has been fired at and struck by shot or small bullets (see fig. 48 [2]).

A small plant belonging to the Loranthaceæ and named Juniper-Mistletoe
(*Viscum Oxycedri* or *Arceuthobium Oxycedri*) occurs on the red-berried juniper
bushes (*Juniper Oxycedrus*) of the Mediterranean flora. It is very different from
the common European Mistletoe, as is obvious at first sight, its foliage-leaves being
reduced to little scales, which gives a characteristic jointed appearance to the ramifications. A whole series of leafless forms allied to this species is found to exist in
India, Japan, Java, Bourbon, Mexico, Brazil, and at the Cape. They are nearly all
small bushes which project from the boughs of host-plants and sometimes clothe
the latter so thickly that the boughs in question serving as nutrient substratum are
entirely enshrouded by the parasitic growth. The Juniper-Mistletoe is only from
3 cm. to 5 cm. tall, and the branchlets are not woody, but soft and herbaceous;
the fruits are blue oblong berries, almost destitute of succulence. The latter are

dispersed by birds like the berries of the common Mistletoe, and the way in which the parasite settles upon and clings to branches of the host-plant is the same as in that species. It also develops sinkers and cortical roots, but these root-structures are not by any means so regularly arranged as in *Viscum album*, but form an inextricable web of strands and filaments pervading the internal layers of cortex, and resolving itself into finer and finer groups of cells, which end by looking not unlike a mycelium, and also remind one of the suction-apparatus possessed by Rafflesiaceae. Such of these strands and cellular filaments as are imbedded in the wood of the juniper do undoubtedly play the part of suction-organs. They are present in large numbers, and some of them are occasionally encompassed by several annual rings. They possess no special zone of growth. The elongation necessary to prevent their being enveloped and overwhelmed by the wood, as it adds to its thickness, is effected by the division of individual cells and groups of cells. The outgrowth of shoots from the root is much more exuberant than in the common Mistletoe; but the death of the original plant takes place much earlier, and close to yellowish-green bushes of various degrees of smallness, one finds very regularly dead or dying shrublets already turned brown, all growing promiscuously over the somewhat swollen branches of the red-berried Juniper.

The behaviour of *Loranthus Europaeus*, which is parasitic on oaks and chestnuts in the east and south of Europe, is altogether unique. The mode of its attack upon the branches of oaks is, it is true, similar to that of the two other Loranthaceae just described. The yellow berries, which are grouped in graceful biseriate racemes, are eaten with avidity by thrushes in the autumn and winter, and the undigested seeds are deposited with the dung of those birds upon the branches of trees. The embryo, on emerging from the seed, bends towards the bark and sticks to it, at the bottom of little rifts and crevices, for the most part, by means of the radicle, which becomes an attachment-disc. A process now arises from the centre of the attachment-disc, and pierces through all the cortical layers of the oak-branch as far as to the zone of young wood, just as if it were a small nail driven in. This process increases in thickness at the expense of the nutriment it withdraws from the young wood, and from it are developed one, two, or three branches, which, however, invariably run downwards beneath the bark, that is to say, in the direction opposed to that of the stream of sap ascending in the oak-wood, and never produce the sinkers so characteristic of the Mistletoe. Each of these roots is shaped like a wedge, even from the rudimentary stage, and acts, too, in the manner of a wedge, penetrating between the yet soft and delicate cells of the cambium, which were formed in the spring at the periphery of the solid older wood of the previous year, and were destined to constitute a new annual ring, splitting and tearing in the process that cell-tissue. Such of these tender cells as lie outside the wedge die, those situated within become lignified and altered into solid wood, to which the wedge-shaped root firmly adheres. Beneath the apex of the wedge, the lignification of cambium cells naturally extends much further towards the exterior, because there it is not at all broken or dead. In front of the apex of the wedge, therefore, there

is, presently, solid resisting wood. The root being no longer able to split the tissue
with its point, is stopped in its growth at this spot. But there is nothing to prevent its continuing to grow along a course somewhat nearer the periphery, and
outside the limit of the new annual ring of solid wood, where a fresh development
of soft and tender cells has taken place in the cambium, and this indeed actually
happens.

Thus, every addition to the length of the Loranthus-root, as it grows onward
between the wood and the cortex of the oak-branch, is further removed from the
axis of the branch; or, in other words, the surface of contact between root and
wood has the conformation of a flight of stairs, of which the lowest step constitutes
the base, and the uppermost the apex of the root (see fig. 48[1]). These steps are
very small, their height varying from about 5 mm. to 7 mm., but they may be
distinguished quite clearly in longitudinal sections, on account of the darker colour
of these roots contrasting with the lighter oak-wood. Nutritive fluids are imbibed
by the Loranthus-root from the wood of the oak at the surface of contact, and it
is probable that this absorption takes place especially at the notches forming the
steps. The root can only elongate, naturally, during the period when there is a
young and fragile cell-layer superimposed upon the solid wood, whence it follows
that in Loranthus the continuation of the root's growth is more dependent upon a
particular season and upon the annual progress of development of the host than is
the case with the Mistletoe. There may be some connection between this circumstance and the fact that the Mistletoe possesses evergreen leaves, whilst *Loranthus*
is green only in summer, acquiring fresh green foliage in the spring in the very
same week as the oak does, and casting its leaves in the autumn simultaneously
with the tree it infests.

The stem which issues from the embryo of a Loranthus-seed grows away from
the oak-branch into the open air, and develops with great rapidity at the expense
of the nutriment absorbed from the host's wood, and conveyed to it by the root
above described, into a dense, dichotomously-branched bush. In summer it is not
unlike a Mistletoe-bush, but in autumn, when it has cast its leaves, it acquires a
totally different aspect owing to the dark-brown branches and the conspicuous
yellow clusters of berries.

Bushes of *Loranthus* grow to a greater size even than those of the Mistletoe;
their stems attain not infrequently a thickness of 4 cm., and clothe themselves with
a blackish, rugged bark, the older stems of this kind being then usually studded by
an abundance of lichens. At the spots where stems of *Loranthus* spring from an
oak-branch they are always surrounded by a great rampart of wood belonging to
the oak, and the base of the stem is often fixed in a deep symmetrically-rounded
bowl reminding one vividly of the similar structures out of which the stems of
Balanophoreæ arise. But whereas in Balanophoreæ this bowl-shaped rampart
appertains to the parasite, in Loranthus it is formed from the wood of the host-
plant, *i.e.* the oak. It must, in the case we are considering, be interpreted as an
exuberant growth of wood-cells and compared to the hypertrophies called galls,

which will be treated of in detail in a subsequent part of this book. On old oaks in the east of Europe these growths round the bases of Loranthus-plants sometimes reach the size of a man's head. In the case of a bush of *Loranthus* nearly 100 years old, from the Ernstbrunner Wald, in Lower Austria, which had reached a height of 1·2 m. and a circumference of 5·5 m., the hypertrophy in question measured 70 cm. round. It is not only the base of a bush that is overgrown by wood-cells, but the older portions of the roots described above are frequently walled in and partially inclosed by the wood of the branch as it becomes thicker. They may often be seen fixed deep in the wood, yet still preserving their freshness and vitality, and this is to be explained by the fact that they retain connection with other parts of the roots by means of isolated ledges and bridges. Indeed an adventitious shoot may develop from a piece of a root thus deeply wedged in the wood of the oak, and this shoot then grows so outwards and breaks through all the layers lying above it and originates a young bush, which pushes roots under the host's bark and afterwards behaves in exactly the same manner as a plant produced from a seed cemented to the oak-branch.

The Loranthus chosen here for description (*L. Europæus*) has only small inconspicuous yellowish flowers; on the other hand, under the tropical sun of Africa, Asia, and, above all, Central America, the parasitic species of this genus are amongst the most splendid-flowered of plants. There are species in the tropics—*e.g. Loranthus formosus, L. grandiflorus,* and *L. Mutisii*—whose flowers attain a diameter of 10, 15, or even 20 centimeters, and are besides clothed in the most gorgeous purple and orange colours. Many Loranthi are like small trees grafted upon other trees. The host-plants of these Loranthi are principally angiospermous trees; members of the genus have also repeatedly been met with parasitic upon one another—as, for instance, *Loranthus buxifolius* upon *L. tetrandrus* in Chili. The fact has been already mentioned that the European Mistletoe has been observed near Verona parasitic upon *Loranthus.* It is also worth noticing, in order to complete the account of the complex relationships between parasites, that one species of *Viscum* has been found in India parasitic upon another, viz.:—*Viscum moniliforme* on *V. orientale.*

## GRAFTING AND BUDDING.

Parasitism of one woody plant upon another, such as occurs in the case of Loranthaceæ, calls to mind certain modes of organic union between woody plants that are artificially effected by gardeners. From ancient times gardeners have performed special operations which are known as processes of "ennobling", and consist in the transference of the branch or bud of one plant on to another plant as substratum, and the inducement of organic union between the two. The plant from which the branch or bud is taken is perhaps a valuable variety of fruit-tree, or a handsome specimen of an ornamental shrub, whilst for the purpose of a substratum a robustly-growing individual belonging to a wild species of shrub or tree is selected as a rule, and constitutes the so-called wild "stock". The branch which yields the bud for the operation or which is itself transferred in its entirety to the wild stock is named, in the terminology of horticulture, the noble "scion".

The process of ennobling is effected either by grafting or by budding. In grafting the stem of the stock is cut off transversely, an excision is made at the periphery of the surface of the section and the scion is inserted in this opening. The scion must be previously trimmed to fit: in preparing it care must be taken that it bears a pair of healthy buds, and that the end to be inserted is cut so as to correspond to the form of the tissue made in the stock. In inserting it one must see that, as far as possible, the bark, bast, and wood of the one come into contact with the corresponding parts of the other. The wounds of the stock caused by the operation are then covered by a mass of putty, wax, or some other protective medium, and the chances are that the branch thus introduced will contract an organic union with the substratum, that nutritive matter will be supplied it by the substratum, and that new branches will sprout from its buds. In this case therefore the nutriment taken from the ground by the stock passes into the grafted scion, and the scion, which develops branches from its buds, and ultimately may become a densely ramifying tree-top, behaves as a parasite, whilst the stock plays the part of host.

It not infrequently happens that a substratum supporting at its summit the branches of a grafted scion develops subsequently branches of its own lower down as well, and the curious sight is then afforded of a tree or shrub bearing different foliage, flowers, and fruit on its inferior parts from those of its upper regions. If, for example, the stem of a Quince is used as substratum, and Medlar branches are grafted upon it, the result may be a bush or tree which exhibits below branches with the round leaves, rose-coloured flowers, and golden "pomes" of the Quince, and above branches with the oblong leaves, white flowers, and brown fruit of the Medlar. Gardeners, of course, do not willingly allow this to happen, but carefully remove the branches belonging to the stock in order that all the food materials may fall to the lot of the grafted plant, and the latter thrive as vigorously and luxuriantly as possible.

The same result is obtained by budding as by grafting; but here a single bud of the scion, instead of an entire branch, is transferred to the stock. This is accomplished in the following manner:—Two incisions at right angles forming a T, are made in a branch of not too great age belonging to the plant employed as substratum. These cuts are carried through the bark as far as the wood. The two lobes of bark, formed by the T-shaped incision, are then carefully raised from the wood, and the bud to be transplanted is pushed in under them. The bud which has previously been taken away from the scion must have retained in that process a portion of bark, and usually the bit of bark peeled off is given the shape of a little shield. This shield, carrying the bud that is to be transferred upon it, is now introduced between the two lobes above mentioned, and the lobes are folded over it in such a manner as to allow the bud to project freely from the slit between the lobes. Besides this, the whole is held together by a bandage, the shield in particular with its bud being pressed firmly on to the new substratum, and thereupon, as a rule, coalescence takes place at once, and the inserted bud grows out into a branch which stands in exactly the same relation to the stock as a *Loranthus* to the oak whereon it is parasitic. All the branches belonging to the substratum, that is to say, to the wild stock, may then be removed, leaving only the one branch that has sprung from the stranger-bud, the result being that all the juices absorbed from the ground by the substratum are concentrated in this branch and cause it to grow with the greatest exuberance.

There is between this process of budding and the settling of a parasite a further resemblance in that shrubs and trees cannot all be made to unite at pleasure one with the other. A successful result of grafting or budding can only be counted upon when nearly allied species, belonging to the same genus or family, are employed for the purpose. Almonds, peaches, apricots, and plums can be grafted the one upon the other; so also can quinces, apples, pears, medlars, and white-thorns. But we must relegate to the realms of fiction such assertions as that peaches might be successfully grafted upon willow stocks, or that the Siberian Crab (*Pyrus salicifolia*) has sprung from the grafting of branches of the Pear upon the Willow and other tales of the sort. Whether it is possible by grafting or budding to produce new forms, or at least hybrids, is a question which will claim our attention in connection with the problem of the origin of new species. The only additional remark to be made here is that notwithstanding the undeniable similarity between grafted or budded plants and the parasitic Loranthaceæ, a very essential difference exists in the circumstance that the latter develops roots which continue to grow year by year, and are always penetrating into new layers of the host's tissues, whereas this is never observed in the case of grafted or budded plants. When the branch of a Peach is grafted on an Almond-tree, there is, it is true, an organic union of the two at the place of contact, and the juices from the wood of the Almond stock are conducted direct into the grafted Peach-branch: but neither roots nor sinkers ever arise from the base of the adnate branch or penetrate into the stem of the Almond-tree.

## 5. ABSORPTION OF WATER.

Importance of water to the life of a plant—Absorption of water by Lichens and Mosses, and by Epiphytes furnished with aërial roots—Absorption of rain and dew by foliage-leaves—Development of absorptive cells in special cavities and grooves in the leaves.

### IMPORTANCE OF WATER TO THE LIFE OF A PLANT.

In the building up of the molecules of sugar, starch, cellulose, fats, and acids, of proteids, and, in short, of all the important substances of which a plant is composed, atoms of water have to be incorporated as constructive material, and without water no growth or addition to the mass of a plant whatsoever could take place. From this point of view water must be considered just as indispensable an item in the food of plants as the carbon-dioxide of the air. But water plays, in addition, another important part in plant-life. The mineral salts which serve to nourish hydrophytes, land-plants, and lithophytes, as also the organic compounds which are the food of saprophytes and parasites, can only reach the interior of plants in the form of aqueous solutions. They can only pass through a cell-wall when it is saturated with water, and, having reached the interior of a plant, they can only be conveyed to the places where they are worked up through the medium of water. In connection with the discharge of these functions in a living plant, water must be regarded as a dynamic agent. Just as a mill on a stream only works so long as its wheels are kept in motion by the water, and stops at once if the latter fails, or flows by in insufficient quantity, so the living plant, as it nourishes itself, grows and multiplies, needs a continuous and abundant supply of available water to render possible the performance of the complicated vital processes within it. This available or organizing water is not in chemical combination like that which is present as food-material, and is, in general, not permanently retained. On the contrary, we must conceive it as perpetually streaming through the living plant. In the course of a summer, quantities of water, weighing many times as much as the plant itself, pass through it. The total amount of water in chemical combination in the organic compounds of a plant is very trifling compared with this, though it often happens that the weight of the latter in a particular plant is greater than that of all the other substances put together.

Inasmuch as this water evaporates from plants in dry air, and that it may also easily be withdrawn by alcohol or other means, very simple experiments suffice to give an idea of the great bulk of free water in any plant. Berries, fleshy fungi, succulent leaves, and things of that kind, if left in alcohol, are reduced in a short time to barely half their size in the fresh state. The Nostocineæ, which are gelatinous when alive, and many fungi (e.g. Guepinia, Phallus, Spathularia, Dacryomyces) shrivel up so stringently in drying, that a piece possessing an area of 1 square centimeter when fresh leaves only a dry crumbling mass covering scarcely 3 square millimeters. A Nostoc, which weighed 2·224 grms. in the fresh state only weighed 0·126 grm. after desiccation, so that when alive it must have contained 94 per cent. of water. Bog-moss, weighing 25·067 grms. before the abstraction of the water was reduced to 2·535 grms. afterwards, showing that the percentage of water was 90. Similar results are obtained in the cases of succulent leaves and stems of flowering plants, *Cucurbita*, and other fruits. The least proportion of water is contained by mature seeds, solid stony seed-coats, wood, and bark; but even in these an average proportion of 10 per cent of water has been detected. We shall not go wrong in assuming, on the evidence of the weights determined, that most parts of plants, when fresh, consist of dry substance only as regards a third, and as regards two-thirds, of water of imbibition, which passes over into the surrounding air in the form of vapour when desiccation takes place.

From all this it follows that water is absolutely necessary to plants as food-material, that it is indispensable as a medium of transport of other substances, and that the demand for water on the part of all plants is very great. Further, we may infer that the importation and exportation of water must be regulated with exacti-tude if the nutrition is not to be disturbed and development hindered.

Water-absorption is at its simplest in hydrophytes. In this case it coincides with the absorption of the rest of the food-materials, and there is therefore nothing material to add to the statements already made on that subject.

As regards land-plants, lithophytes, and epiphytes, we may likewise refer to what has been already said in so far as these plants suck up water at the same time as food-salts, by means of absorption-cells, from the substratum to which they are attached, or the earth in which they are rooted; but to the extent that they take also water direct from the atmosphere, and have the power of absorbing that water immediately they require it, must be discussed in the following pages.

## ABSORPTION OF WATER BY LICHENS AND MOSSES, AND BY EPIPHYTES FURNISHED WITH AËRIAL ROOTS.

The plants which absorb water direct from the atmosphere may be classified in several groups with reference to the contrivances adapted to the purpose. Of all plants lichens are most dependent on atmospheric moisture. Many of them, especially the Old Man's Beard Lichens, which hang down from dried branches of trees, and the gelatinous, crustaceous, and fruticose lichens, which cling to dead wood, and on the surface of rocks and blocks of stone, do in fact derive their necessary supply of water entirely from the atmosphere, and that by absorbing it, not in a liquid but in a gaseous form. The latter circumstance is of the greatest importance to those species in particular which occur on receding rocks, or on the under face of overhanging slabs of stone. Rain and dew cannot reach such places directly, but only by some of the water trickling down from the wet top and sides of the rocks on to the receding wall, and this happens but seldom. Accordingly, lichens occurring in situations of the kind are entirely dependent upon the water contained in the air in the form of vapour. Lichens, however, are also, of all plants, the best adapted for the absorption of aqueous vapour from the air. If living lichens, which have become dry in the air, are left in a place saturated with moisture, they take up 35 per cent of water in two days, and as much as 56 per cent in six days. Water in the liquid form is naturally absorbed much more rapidly still. When Gyrophoras, which project in the form of cups after a long continuance of dry weather, are moistened by a fall of rain, they swell up completely within ten minutes, and spread themselves flat upon the rocks, having in that short space of time absorbed 50 per cent of water. The saying, " Light come, light go," is no doubt true in these cases. When dry weather sets in, evaporation from the masses of lichens goes on at a pace corresponding to the previous absorption. In the Tundra, the lichens, which form a soft tumid carpet when moistened by rain, are liable to be so powerfully desiccated in the course of a few hours of sunshine, that they split and crackle under one's feet, so that every step is accompanied by a crunching noise.

In the power of condensing and absorbing the aqueous vapour of the atmosphere, lichens are most analogous to mosses and liverworts, and to those preeminently which live on the bark of dry branches of trees or on surfaces of rock, covering places of the kind with a carpet which is often enough interspersed and interwoven with lichens. Like the latter these mosses and liverworts are able to remain as though dead in a state of desiccation for weeks together, but as soon as rain or dew falls upon them they resume their vitality; and similarly if the air is so damp as to enable them to derive sufficient water of imbibition from that source. A specimen of *Hypnum molluscum*, a moss which covers blocks of limestone in the form of soft sods, was after a few rainless days detached from the dry rock and placed in a chamber saturated with vapour, and it was found that after two days it had absorbed water from the air to the extent of 20 per cent, after six days 38 per cent, and after ten days 44 per cent. Many mosses condense and absorb water with the whole surfaces of their leaflets, others—as, for example, the gray rock-mosses clinging to slate formations (Rhacomitriæ and Grimmiæ)—do so especially with the long hair-like cells at the apices of the leaflets, whilst others again only use the cells situated on the upper saucer-shaped or canaliculate leaf-surface.

In some bearded mosses (*Barbula aloides, B. rigida,* and *B. ambigua*) chains of barrel-shaped cells occur closely packed together upon the upper surface of the leaf and at right angles to it, which to the naked eye have the appearance of a spongy dark-green pad. The terminal cells of these short moniliform chains have their upturned walls strongly thickened, but the other cells have very thin walls and take up water rapidly. It is the same with the various species of *Polytrichum,* which are provided on their upper leaf-surfaces with parallel longitudinal ridges likewise composed of thin-walled, highly-absorbent cells. The rhizoids also play an important part in these processes. These brown, elongated, thin-walled cells entirely clothe the moss stems, usually in the form of a dense felt, and often project from the under surface of the leaves, whilst in a few tropical species they make their appearance, strangely enough, in the form of little tufts at the apices of the leaflets. In many instances this felt of rhizoids does not come into contact at all with the soil, rock, or bark (as the case may be), but is surrounded by air alone, and is able to condense or attract, to use a common expression, the aqueous vapour of the air like a piece of cloth or blotting-paper. In dry weather, it is true, mosses, like lichens, lose their water, but they part with it much more slowly than the latter. This is chiefly due to the fact that the moss-leaflets at the commencement of a drought wrinkle, curl up, become concave, and lay themselves one above the other, so that the water is retained at the bottom for a longer period.

A very remarkable contrivance for the absorption of water from the atmosphere is also exhibited by the white-leaved Fork-mosses (*Leucobryum*) and Bog-mosses (Sphagnaceæ). Although they possess chlorophyll, and assimilate under the

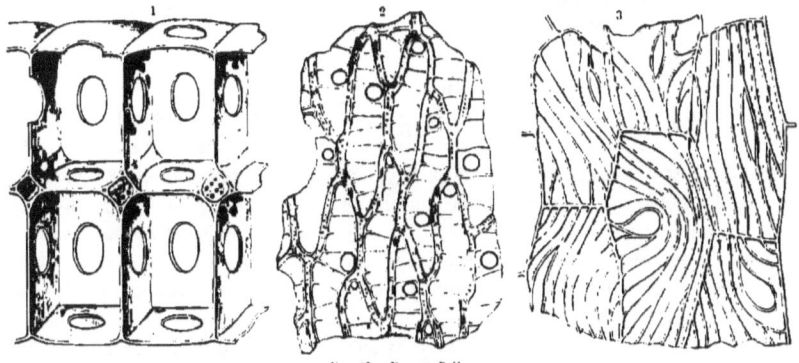

Fig. 40.—Porous Cells.

1 Of the white-leaved Fork-moss (*Leucobryum*); ×550.   2 Of the Bog-moss (*Sphagnum*); ×230   3 Of the root of an Orchid
(*Lælia gracilis*); ×310.

influence of sunlight, yet they look like parasitic and saprophytic plants destitute of chlorophyll. They are of a whitish colour and always grow in great cushion-like sods, so that the spots where they grow are deficient in verdure, and stand out conspicuously from their surroundings in consequence of their pale tint. Microscopic investigation at once explains this appearance. The cells containing chlorophyll and living active protoplasts are relatively small, and, as it were, wedged and hidden between other cells many times as great, which have entirely lost their protoplasm by the time they are mature, and then cause the paleness of colour appertaining to the plant as a whole. The walls of these large colourless cells are very thin, and in the Bog-mosses have spiral thickening-bands running round them, being thus secured against collapse. After remaining for a time in a dry environment they are full of air only; but the moment they are moistened they fill with water. If there were an actively absorbent protoplast at work in the interior, the water would be able to pass into the cell-cavity through this easily moistened wall, as in the case of other mosses, owing to the delicacy of the cell-membrane. But the air which fills the cells is not absorptive, and in the case of *Leucobryum* and Bog-mosses the water reaches the interior, not in consequence of a chemical affinity on the part of the cell-contents, but solely by capillary action. All the cell-walls are perforated and furnished with pores, and through these the water rushes into the interior with lightning rapidity.

This extremely rapid influx of water into an air-filled cavity leads us necessarily to the conclusion that each cell has a number of pores in its walls, and that in proportion as water enters through one of the small apertures the air can escape equally fast through another. This is in fact the case. The large cells not only have pores on their external walls, but communicate one with another by similar holes, and the water soaks in from the one side as it does into a bath-sponge, whilst the air is at the same time forced out on the other. This absorptive apparatus is exceptionally elegant in *Leucobryum*, which grows abundantly in many woods. In it, as is shown in the illustration above (fig. 49 ¹), the adjacent prismatic cells communicate by highly symmetrical, circular gaps made in the middle of the partition-walls, whilst in the Bog-mosses (the various species of *Sphagnum*), they are to be seen scattered here and there between the thickening bands on the cell-walls (see fig. 49 ²). Now these porous groups of cells possess not only the power of taking up water in the liquid state, but also that of condensing it when in the form of vapour. There is no need of any more proximate proof of the fact that the cells previously mentioned as containing chlorophyll, and lying imbedded between the large perforated cells, take up water supplied by the latter, or perhaps it is better to say that the large perforated cells suck in the water for the living green cells. We have only to ask why it is, then, that these small green cells do not absorb water themselves direct from the environment, as is done in the case of so many other mosses and liverworts. It is difficult to answer this quite satisfactorily, but thus much seems certain, that the large porous cells, when full of air, afford a means of protecting the small living cells from too excessive desiccation, and that they are in addition preservative of the chlorophyll in the small cells, a matter to which we shall return presently.

A certain resemblance to these Leucobryums and Sphagnums, in respect of water-absorption, is exhibited by a few Aroideæ, and more especially by a whole host of Orchidaceæ. Of the 8000 different orchids hitherto discovered, a good proportion, it is true, are rooted in the earth. But more than half these wonderful plants flourish only on the bark of old trees, and most of them would quickly perish if they were detached from that substratum and planted with their roots buried in earth. A double function appertains to the roots of these Orchideæ which inhabit trees. On the one hand they have to fix the entire orchid-plant to the bark, and, on the other, to supply it with nutriment. When the growing tip of an orchid's root comes into contact with a solid body, it adheres closely to it, flattens out more or less, sometimes even becoming strap-shaped (see fig. 15), and develops papilliform or tubular cells, which grow into organic union with the substratum, and might conveniently be termed clamp-cells. In many cases these cells creep over the bark, divide, interlace, and form regular wefts. The organic connection with the substratum is so intimate that an attempt to separate the two usually results in a detachment of the most superficial parts of the bark, but not of the tubular cells. Now, if a root, after having sent out cells of this kind which contract an organic union with the substratum, reaches into the open, beyond the limit of the

Fig 50.—Aerial Roots of an Orchid epiphytic upon the bark of the branch of a tree.

substratum, it immediately ceases to develop clamp-cells, loses its ligulate shape, and hangs down from the tree in the form of a sinuous white filament. A few root-fibres are as a rule sufficient to fix the plant to its substratum, the bark of the tree, and the rest of the roots put forth by the orchid grow from beginning to end

freely in the air.   They are not infrequently to be seen crowded together in great
numbers at the base of the plant, forming regular tassels suspended from the dark
bark of the branches as may be seen in fig. 50, where an *Oncidium* is represented.

Each of these aërial roots is invested externally by a white membranous or
papery envelope, and it is the cells of this covering that own the resemblance, above
referred to, to the cells of *Leucobryum* and Bog-mosses.   Their walls are furnished
with narrow, projecting spiral thickenings and therefore do not collapse, notwithstanding their delicacy or the circumstance of their inclosing at times an air-filled
cavity; they are further abundantly perforated, two kinds of apertures indeed
being found.   The one variety arises in consequence of the tearing of the portions
of the cell-wall situated between the rib-like projections and consisting of extremely
thin and delicate membranes (see fig. 49 [3]); the existence of the other variety is due
to the detachment of the cells which protrude in the form of papillæ, the result
being, in this latter case, the formation of circular holes very similar to those
already described as occurring in *Leucobryum*.   The cells resembling papillæ have
the peculiarity that they roll off when they get old in the form of spiral bands.
The holes, of course, can only occur on the external walls of the outermost cells
which border upon the open air, whilst in the interior the communication between
the cells themselves is established by means of the rents previously referred to.
The entire covering thus composed of perforated cells may be compared to an
ordinary sponge, and, indeed, acts after the manner of a sponge.   When it comes
into contact with water in the liquid state, or more especially when it is moistened
by atmospheric deposits, it imbibes instantaneously its fill of water.   The deeper-
lying living green cells of the root are then surrounded by a fluid envelope and are
able to obtain from it as much water as they require.

But these roots also possess the power of condensing the aqueous vapour
contained in the air.   They act upon the moist air in which they are immersed in
exactly the same way as spongy platinum or any other porous body.   If the aërial
roots of *Oncidium sphacelatum* are transferred from a chamber full of dry air to
one full of moist air, they take up in 24 hours somewhat more than 8 per cent of
their weight of water, those of *Epidendron elongatum* absorb 11 per cent, whilst in
the case of many other tropical orchids the amount thus imbibed is doubtless much
more considerable still.

The power of condensing aqueous vapour, and other gases as well, is of the
greatest importance to these plants.   The tree-bark serving as their substratum, to
which they are fastened merely by a few fibres, is anything but a permanent
source of water.   Such water as the bark does contain reaches it, not from the
interior of the trunk and indirectly from the soil in which the trunk has its roots,
but from the atmosphere; that is to say, from the very source whence the
epiphytes upon the bark must also derive their supply.   Now, when on the occasion of a long-enduring uniform aërial temperature, there is a failure of atmospheric deposits, which is a regularly recurring circumstance in the habitat of the
orchids in question, the sole source of water left is the vapour in the air, and the

PLATE III.

1. *Saccolobium guttatum.*     2. *Dendrobium nobile.*     3. *Phajus Wallichii.*

only possible method of acquiring that vapour is the condensation of it by the porous tissue investing the roots. In the event of the air around the orchid-plant containing temporarily but very little moisture, the porous tissue dries up, it is true, very quickly; its cells fill with air and their function as condensers is interrupted. But these air-filled cellular layers then form a medium of protection against excessive evaporation from the deeper strata of the root's tissues, which might be very dangerous in the case of this kind of epiphyte. There is a wide-spread impression that the tropical orchids grow in a perpetually moist atmosphere in the dark shade of primeval forests, and this preconception is fostered by pictures of tropical orchids representing these plants as living in the most obscure depths of woods. In reality, however, the orchids of the tropics are children of light. They thrive best in sunny spots in open country. Those species in particular which have their aërial roots invested each by a thick, white, papery, porous covering belong to regions where a long period of drought occurs regularly every year, and where, in consequence, vegetative activity is subject to periodical interruption, as it is in the cold winter season of the more inclement zones.

For epiphytes inhabiting these regions of the tropics a more expedient structure of root cannot easily be imagined. In the dry season the papery covering reinforces the safeguards against too profuse transpiration on the part of the living cells in the interior of the root, and in the wet season it provides for the continuous supply of the requisite quantity of water. In this sense the porous layer is to a certain extent a substitute for wet soil, or, in other words, the concealment of the living part of an aërial root in the saturated envelope is analogous to that of the root-fibres of land-plants in the damp earth. The manner in which the water reaches the inner cells of an aërial root from the saturated envelope is also quite characteristic. Under the porous tissue lies a layer composed of two kinds of cells of different sizes. The larger cells are elongated and have their external walls, which are adjacent to the porous tissue, thickened and hardly permeable by water. Between these lie smaller, thin-walled, succulent cells, which admit the water from the porous envelope, and should therefore be regarded as absorption-cells. It is also noteworthy that the porous, paper-like covering is discarded as soon as an aërial root is placed in earth. Most orchids with aërial roots perish, it is true, when they are treated like land-plants and planted in soil; but a few species, on occasion, bury their aërial roots spontaneously in the earth and push off their envelopes, and then the imbedded parts exercise the same functions as in the case of land-plants.

We have already mentioned that, in addition to thousands of orchids, several Aroideæ exhibit the porous, papery covering on their aërial roots. But still more frequently the air-roots of Aroids, which live as epiphytes upon trees, are furnished with a dense fringe of so-called root-hairs in a broad zone behind the growing-point. The hairs project on all sides from the roots, which are surrounded by air; they are crowded very closely together and give the parts affected a velvety appearance. Besides several Aroideæ, one of which (*Philodendron Lindeni*) is drawn on the left side of fig. 51, many other epiphytes, such as the South

American *Campelia Zanonia*, belonging to the Commelynaceæ, represented on the right side of the same figure, and also several tree-ferns, display this velvety

Fig. 51.—Aerial Roots with root-hairs; on the left *Philodendron Lindeni*, on the right *Campelia Zanonia*.

coating on their aerial roots. The roots of the tree-ferns are short, but spring in thousands from the thick stem, and are so closely packed that the whole surface is clothed as it were by a woven mantle of rootlets. After some time these aërial roots turn deep brown, whilst the hairs collapse and die, and both are converted into a mouldering mass. But as soon as they perish other new air-roots, covered with golden-brown velvet, make their appearance and take their place. These aërial roots never reach the ground or adhere to any substratum, so that their hairs cannot contract an organic connection with a solid body. It is consequently also impossible in this case for the root-hairs to draw moisture from the soil in the capacity of absorption-cells.

These root-hairs, however, are scarcely ever in a position to take up even the atmospheric deposits. The various species of *Philodendron* and the other epiphytes referred to, have large leaves which cover the air-roots hanging from the stem like umbrellas, and every tree-fern also bears at the top of its stem a tuft of great fronds, which prevents falling rain from wetting the aërial roots. Moreover, the very plants whose air-roots exhibit a velvety coating occur in woods where the tops of the trees arch over the ground in lofty domes, and form a sheltering roof against deposits from the atmosphere. On the other hand, the air within these forests is saturated with aqueous vapour, and it is certain that the velvety roots have the power of condensing vapour, and that the root-hairs instantly suck up the condensed water and convey it to the deeper-lying layers of cells. The truth of this has been established by the results of repeated experiments. Thus, air-roots of the tree-fern *Todea barbata*, after being transferred from moderately damp air into a chamber full of vapour, condensed and absorbed in the space of twenty-four hours water amounting to 6·4 per cent of their weight. There is, therefore, no doubt that water may be acquired in this way also by plants, even though the instances may not be very numerous. All plants in which this kind of water-absorption has been hitherto observed grow in places where the air is very moist the whole year round, and where there is also no risk of the temperature falling below freezing-point. Under other conditions, especially in places where the air is periodically very dry, these plants would not be able to survive; for, although they possess organs for the condensation and absorption of water, they have no means of protection against the desiccation of these organs.

## ABSORPTION OF RAIN AND DEW BY THE FOLIAGE-LEAVES.

The idea that plants absorb with their roots such water as they require is so intimately associated with our whole conception of plant-life, that this process is commonly adduced for the purpose of analogies of the most various kinds, and one looks upon the water-absorption effected by aërial roots in the manner just described really as a thing to be expected, notwithstanding the fact that in this case, as the above account shows, the phenomenon is not so simple as is usually supposed. We now turn to the consideration of land-plants. If the leaves of plants cultivated in pots become flaccid, water is poured as quickly as possible upon the dry soil with a view of supplying the roots which ramify in it with moisture. Nor does the result fail to be produced. In a short time the foliage becomes fresh and elastic again, the roots having discharged their function. Even in the open air, it is especially the soil in which the roots are imbedded that a gardener waters on dry days, although incidentally he may pour the water over the aërial parts of the plants. He sees, however, that the water which falls in the form of rain or dew upon the foliage and stems normally runs off them at once, or else collects in drops, which trickle down whenever the plant is shaken by the wind, and are sucked up by the thirsty ground. This phenomenon must be due to the possession by the leaves of special contrivances to prevent their being wetted. It does not in any case support the idea that foliage is as well adapted for the absorption of water as experience has proved subterranean roots to be. This train of thought, which forces itself upon every unbiassed observer of the processes as they take place in nature, is certainly warranted in the majority of cases. Each absorption-cell on the roots buried in the earth has an easily permeable membrane, and, as is well known, water passes from damp earth through the cell-membranes into the interior of a plant with great rapidity. The water in the interior of the plant would be equally easily withdrawn through these cell-membranes by dry surroundings, but, as it is, this scarcely ever happens, in consequence of the roots being situated underground. In the case of aërial parts, especially the foliage-leaves, the circumstances are quite different. The leaves have to yield up to the air a portion at least of the water conducted from the roots, because, as will be more thoroughly explained later on, it is only by means of this evaporation that the entire machinery in the interior of the plant can be kept in motion. But this evaporation must not go too far; it must be in proper relation to the absorption of water by the subterranean roots, and be regulated to that end if the plant is not to run the risk of drying up altogether at times—an occurrence which flowering plants are unable to survive, although the mosses described in former pages have that power. Accordingly, in the case of the foliage-leaves of flowering plants, evaporation is confined to certain cells and groups of cells, and these, in addition, have contrivances by means of which evaporation can be entirely stopped on occasion of great drought. It stands to reason that all contrivances which make it impossible for water to pass from the interior of the leaves through the walls of the superficial cells into the surrounding air also hinder the entrance of water into the leaves from the atmosphere.

It would be altogether inconsistent with the system of arrangement of the subject adopted in this book if we were to discuss here all the contrivances serving to regulate the exhalation of water by leaves, and we must, therefore, confine ourselves to referring, by way of introduction, quite briefly, to the following facts, namely, that those pores on the surface of leaves which are known by the name of stomata, and are used as doors of egress by the exhaled water, do not admit rain or dew, or in general, any water in the liquid state; that the so-called cuticle covering the external walls of the epidermal cells in leaves is an additional barrier to both egress and ingress of water; that when, in particular, this cuticle is furnished with a wax-like coating, water does not adhere to the surface of cells so protected; and, lastly, that atmospheric moisture can only penetrate into the interior of the plant at parts of the leaves where the waxen incrustations are absent, where water remains adherent to the leaf-surfaces, and they are distinctly wetted. But even cells and groups of cells of this kind usually act but for a short time as absorption-cells, and only when the necessity and craving for water is very great, or when there is an opportunity of acquiring nitrogenous compounds at the same time as the water; and here, again, special contrivances are always present which regulate this kind of water-absorption, and render it impossible whenever it is not truly advantageous.

At first one would suppose that amongst the cells composing the epidermis of foliage-leaves, those are best adapted to the absorption of water from the atmosphere which take the form of hairs. The superficial area being as great as possible, and the contained matter relatively little, one can scarcely in fact conceive a conformation better suited to the purpose of water-absorption. As, moreover, the area of contact between the cells of the leaf and of a hair is small, there would afterwards be but very little evaporation through the surface of the hair of the water once sucked up by it and conducted into the interior of the leaf. In a word, these hairs on the surface of a leaf appear to be peculiarly adapted to the taking up of water, and not at all favourable to its exhalation. The hypothesis based on these observations is indeed entirely applicable to the case of hairs occurring on the leaflets of mosses, as has been already stated. But it does not hold in the case of the hair-like structures which spring from the leaf-surfaces of flowering plants. These are frequently not wetted at all by water; rain and dew roll off them in drops, and cannot, therefore, be absorbed by them. This is true even of many soft trichomes (hair-structures) which form investments upon leaves, and which seem to be more than any fitted for the absorption of water. For instance, experiments upon the woolly leaves of the Great Mullein (*Verbascum Thapsus*) have shown that they neither condense aqueous vapour nor take up water in liquid drops. Small importance must be attributed to the thickness of the cuticle, for sometimes it is the very cells which are equipped with a cuticle of considerable stoutness that are adapted to admit water, under certain circumstances, through their walls. On the other hand, much depends upon the presence of wax in the cuticle and upon the contents of the cells; that is to say, upon whether those contents in particular have a strong or weak affinity for water. If the cells of the hairs are full of air they are not adapted to the absorption of water.

If a hair is septate, *i.e.* consists of a simple series of cells, only the undermost or else only the uppermost cells of the series absorb water. Instances wherein it has been observed that the lowest cells alone in hairs of the kind become absorption-cells are afforded by the *Alfredia*, represented in fig. 14, by *Salvia argentea*, and several other steppe-plants. The same statement is made concerning the widely-distributed *Stellaria media*, the common Chickweed. This last has hairs on the internodes of the stem, running down in ridges from node to node. Usually only one side of the stem exhibits a ridge of hairs of the kind, and the ridge always terminates at the thickened node, whence springs a pair of opposite leaves. The stalks of these leaves are somewhat hollowed out and have their edges beset with hairs like lashes. The hairy ridges on the segments of the stem are readily wetted by rain and retain a considerable quantity of water. The water that they cannot hold they conduct downwards to the ciliate axils of the next lower pair of leaves, where it is drawn through the lash-like hairs in due course and collected into a ring of water surrounding the node (see fig. 52 [3]). If this accumulation of water becomes so voluminous and heavy that it cannot any longer be retained by the fringe of lashes, the surplus glides on to the unilateral ridge of hairs on the adjacent internode down to the pair of leaves below. Accordingly, after a shower every node from which leaves arise is seen to be inclosed in a water-bath, and the hairy

Fig. 52.—Hairs and Leaves which retain Dew and Rain.
[1] Dwarf Gentian (*Gentiana acaulis*).     [2] Lady's Mantle (*Alchemilla vulgaris*).     [3] Chickweed (*Stellaria media*).

ridges also are so soaked with water that they look like edgings of glass. All the individual cells in each of the hairs are full of protoplasm and cell-sap, but only the lowest, which are very short, really act as absorption-cells. When these cells become at all relaxed in dry air, the fact is indicated by the appearance on the external cell-wall of fine striæ (see fig. 53 [1] and 53 [2]). The protoplasts inhabiting them attract water, and after being relaxed in the manner referred to the cells regain their turgidity on being wetted, whilst the fine wrinkles on the outer membrane are in consequence immediately smoothed out. Although the upper cells of the hair possess a less thick cuticle, they, on the other hand, seem not to absorb any water, but to serve rather to conduct it by their surfaces.

This case is, as we have said, comparatively rare, and the corresponding absorption of water is not very considerable. But it often happens that the uppermost cells of a septate hair are developed into absorption-cells. The terminal cell is then usually spherical or ellipsoidal and larger than the rest, or else this cell is divided into two, four, or a greater number of cells, which together form a little head, whilst the lower cells constitute a stalk supporting it (see fig. 53 [3] and 53 [4]). In botanical terminology structures of this kind are named capitate or glandular hairs. The protoplasm in the cells of the head is, for the most part, of a dark colour, and the

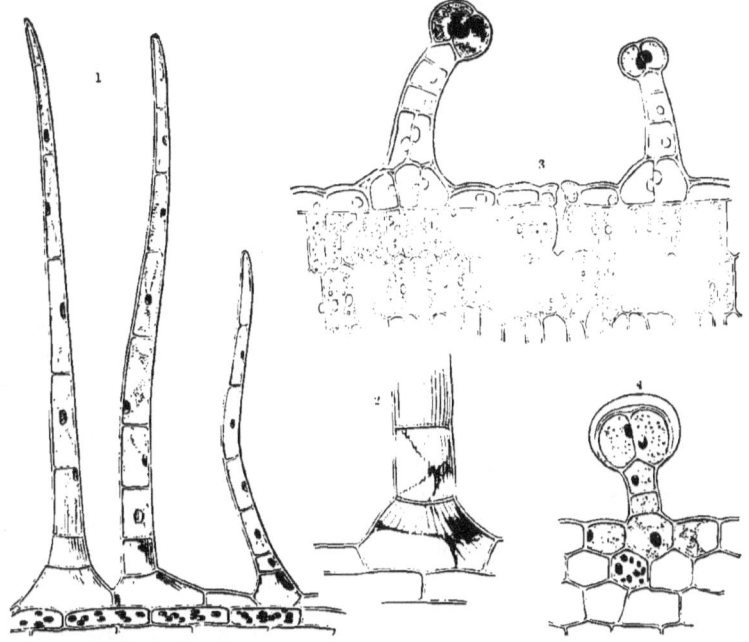

Fig. 53.—[1] Hairs from stem of *Stellaria media*; ×110. [2] Lowest cells of the same hairs; ×200. [3] Capitate hairs of *Centaurea Balsamita*; ×150. [4] Capitate hairs of *Pelargonium lividum*; ×150.

cell-membranes are readily permeable by water, which is attracted with great energy by the cell-contents. The cell-membrane is often very thick, it is true, but as soon as water comes into contact with it the outer layer is discarded, the inner layers swell up and the water passes through these swollen layers into the interior of the cell. This happens, for instance, in many pelargoniums and geraniums, wherein the capitate cells go through a process of excoriation on every occasion of the imbibition of water (see fig. 53 [4]). In other plants the walls of the capitate cells are everywhere thin, and not only do the cell-contents consist of a viscid gum-like mass, but the external surface of the wall is also covered by a layer of viscid excretion. In many cases the viscid matter excreted by the glands spreads over the entire surface of the leaf, so that the latter feels sticky and looks as if it were coated with varnish. Many plants which have their roots buried in crevices of rock and no small number of herbaceous steppe-plants are quite thickly covered with glandular hairs of the kind. *Centaurea Balsamita* (see fig. 53³), a plant occurring on the elevated steppes of Persia, may be selected as an example of the latter group. The advantage of the structure of capitate hairs is not far to seek. In dry weather the thick cuticle (*Pelargonium*) or the varnish coating (*Centaurea Balsamita*), as the case may be, prevents desiccation of the cells and groups of cells in question. But as soon as rain or dew falls, the cuticle and the coat of varnish take up water, and it is by their instrumentality that water reaches the interior of the cells. Thus, whilst the exhalation of water is hindered, its absorption is not.

Other epidermal cells of foliage-leaves besides trichomes are capable of acting as absorption-cells, although this action, for reasons already given, is very restricted, and is only had recourse to when the turgidity of the cells of the foliage-leaves has diminished, and the water exhaled by those cells is not being restored by the ordinary apparatus of conduction from the roots. If branches are cut from plants which bear no glandular or other form of hair on their leaves or stems—as, for instance, the leafy stem of *Thesium alpinum*—and the cut ends are closed with sealing-wax, and the branches left to wither, and, when quite withered, are immersed in water, they freshen up speedily and the leaves become tense again, the cells having recovered their turgidity. Here, then, decidedly absorption has taken place through the ordinary cuticularized epidermal cells. Certainly these epidermal cells in *Thesium* are not protected against wetting. Wherever the epidermal cells are not susceptible of being wetted owing to a coating of wax or any other contrivance there could naturally be no question of water being absorbed. This very circumstance, however, leads to the supposition that an important part in water absorption is to be attributed to the alternation of wettable and non-wettable parts on one and the same leaf. In the case of many foliage-leaves one can see that only those cells of the epidermis which lie above the veins of the leaf retain the water which comes upon them, that is to say, are wetted by it, whilst the water rolls off the intervening areas of the lamina. Indeed, there are in many instances contrivances obviously designed for the purpose of conducting water from parts of the epidermis not liable to be wetted to parts that can be moistened.

## DEVELOPMENT OF ABSORPTION-CELLS IN SPECIAL CAVITIES AND GROOVES IN THE LEAVES.

The contrivances last described are all only adapted to rather a casual appropriation of water from the atmosphere. But besides these we find a number of other contrivances, which render it possible for every rolling dewdrop and every passing shower to be made of use to the utmost extent. These contrivances consist of a variety of depressions and excavations, in which rain and dew are collected and protected against rapid evaporation. Some species have deep hollows or channels, others little pits, whilst others again have basins, vesicular or bowl-shaped structures, to collect and absorb the water; and the construction of the protective apparatus, which prevents too rapid evaporation into the air of water that has once flowed into the depressions, is as various as the form of the depressions themselves. A short account of the most striking of these structures will now be given.

Such water-collecting grooves as are closed, so as to form ducts, occur principally in petioles and in the rachises of compound leaves. For instance, in the Ash the leaf rachis, from which the leaflets arise, is furnished with a groove on its upper surface. Owing to the fact that the edges of this groove, which are strengthened by a so-called collenchymatous tissue, are bent up and curved over the groove, a duct or conduit pipe is produced, and this duct only gapes open at the places where the leaflets are inserted upon the rachis, and where, therefore, the drops of rain to which the leaflets are exposed flow off into the groove (see fig. 54 [1]). The simple hairs and peltate groups of cells developed in the grooves and ducts (fig. 54 [2] and 54 [3]) are not merely transiently moistened, but inasmuch as the water is retained there for several days after a fall of rain, they are during that time immersed in a regular bath of water, and are able to absorb the moisture very gradually.

In many Gentianeæ—most conspicuously in the large-flowered Dwarf Gentian (*Gentiana acaulis*)—the decussate pairs of radical leaves form a loose rosette (see fig. 52 [1]). The larger dark-green blade of each leaf is flat and even, and only the pale-coloured base is fashioned into a groove. This groove is made deeper by the tissue of the leaf being puffed up round it, and as all the leaves of the rosette arise close together, the groove of each leaf is covered by the lamina above it. The rain or dew accumulated from the blade remains standing in this concealed nook for some time without evaporating, so that absorptive apparatus with the power of taking up water has plenty of time for the purpose. In this case the absorptive apparatus is in the hindmost extremity of the groove, and consists of long, club-shaped structures composed of extremely thin-walled cells (see fig. 54 [4]), and these act so energetically that if leaves are cut off and left to fade, and if the cut surfaces are stopped with sealing-wax, and the whole then bathed with rain-water, they take up in twenty-four hours about 40 per cent of their weight of water. A similar phenomenon occurs in the case of a number of Bromeliaceæ which adhere by a few roots to the bark of trees in the tropics, and have grooved rosetted leaves, the latter covering one another, and being arranged in such a manner as to form a regular system of cisterns. At the bottom of each cistern there are special groups of thin-walled cells which suck up any water that flows in when rain falls.

On the under surface of the leaves of the Cow-berry (*Vaccinium Vitis-Idæa*) little depressions are formed, and in the middle of each depression there is a club-shaped structure composed of small thin-walled cells, which contain slimy, viscid substances and act as absorbent organs. The rain which falls upon the upper surface of the leaf gets drawn over the edges on to the under surface, fills the small depressions occurring there, and is taken up by the absorptive apparatus. A similar contrivance is also exhibited by the leaves of alpine roses and those of the American *Bacharis.* For instance, on the under surface of the leaves of the Alpine Rose (*Rhododendron hirsutum*) there is a large number of discoid glands (fig. 54 ⁵), each of which is supported on a short stalk and sunk in a little hollow (fig. 54 ⁶) The cells composing the gland are arranged radially, and contain slimy, resinous matters capable of swelling up. These contents are also excreted, and then cover the entire glandular disc, and often even the whole surface of the leaf in the form

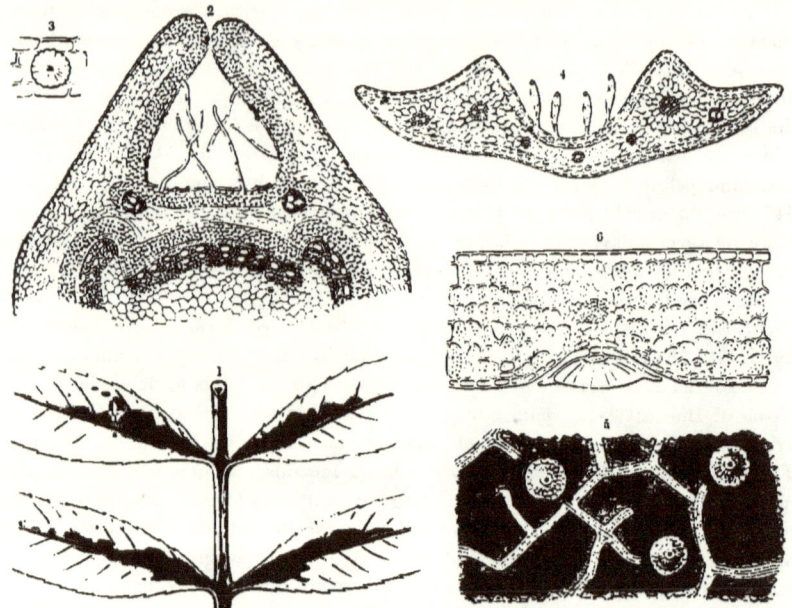

Fig. 54.—Absorption of Water by Foliage-leaves.

¹ Grooved rachis of the ash-leaf.    ² Section through the same; ×30.    ³ Peltate group of cells from the groove.    ⁴ Section through the base of a leaf of the Dwarf Gentian; ×20.    ⁵ Under side of a leaf of *Rhododendron hirsutum*; ×30.    ⁶ Section through a leaf of *Rhododendron hirsutum.*

of a light-brown crumbly crust. When drops of rain fall upon Alpine Rose leaves, the whole of the upper surfaces, in each case, is in the first place moistened; but without delay, and partly through the action of the hairs fringing the margin, the water soaks on to the under side of the leaf. As soon as it reaches the glands it is taken up by the crumbly incrustation mentioned above, which swells up in consequence. The little cavities in which the glands are situated also fill with water, and each gland is then immersed, as it were, in a bath, and able to absorb as much moisture as is required. Owing to the glands being invariably developed above the vascular bundles of the leaf (see fig. 54 ⁶), the water that is absorbed can be conducted without delay by them to the places where it is required. As soon as the leaves of alpine roses become dry again, the mass of resinous mucilage again forms a dry crust over the glands and protects their tender-walled cells from too great evaporation.

Very remarkable also are the structures adapted to absorption on the leaves of saxifrages belonging to the group *Aizoon*, and on those of a large proportion of the Plumbagineæ. The saxifrages in question have little depressions visible to the naked eye upon the upper surface of the leaves behind the apex, and along the margins. When the margin is dentate or crenate, as, for instance, in *Saxifraga*

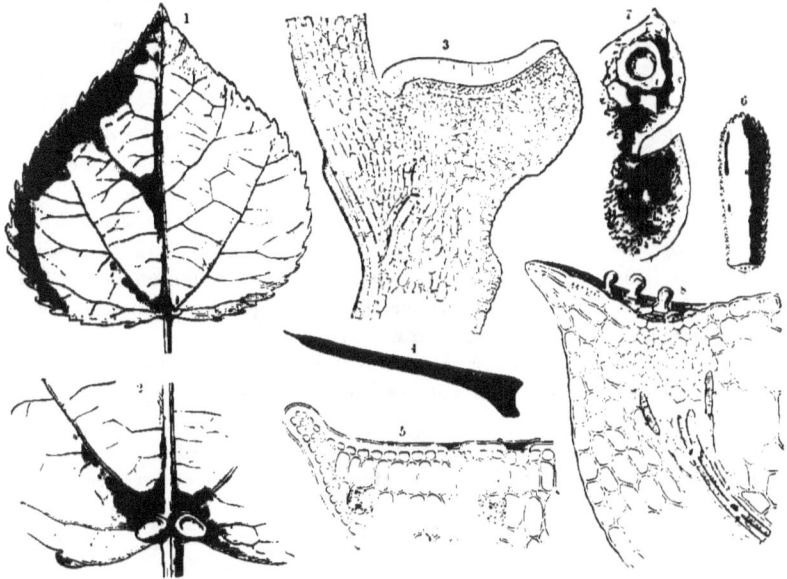

Fig. 55.—Absorptive Cavities and Cups on Foliage-leaves.

1 Leaf from a shoot of the Aspen.  2 The base of this leaf; ×3.  3 Section through an absorption-cup; ×25.  4 Leaf of *Acantholimon Senganense.*  5 Section through part of this leaf; ×110.  6 Leaf of the Evergreen Saxifrage (*Saxifraga Aizoon*).  7 Two teeth from the margin of this leaf. The absorptive cavity in the upper tooth incrusted with lime; the lower one with the incrustation removed.  8 Section through a tooth from the leaf and its absorptive cavity; ×110.

*Aizoon* (see fig. 55⁶), one of these cavities occurs in the middle of each tooth. The cells forming the outer edge of the tooth or scallop are always much thickened, firm, and rigid; but the median portion of the leaf as a whole is fleshy, and composed of a bulky large-celled parenchyma. The vascular bundle, after entering the leaf at its base, divides into a number of lateral bundles which either run towards the margin without further ramification (as in *Saxicæsia*), or else form a net-work by uniting one with another in their course (as in *Saxifraga Aizoon*). These lateral bundles terminate in the marginal teeth of the leaf and immediately beneath the little cavities which occur there, whilst the extremity of each bundle swells into a knob or pear-shaped enlargement strongly resembling the roundish groups of spirally-thickened cells in the tentacles of the Sun-dew (cf. fig. 26 [1]). The bottom of each depression is made up of cells with very thin external walls, and the function of these cells is to suck up the water that flows into the cavity. It is obvious that the absorbed water passes thence into the enlarged extremities of the branches of the vascular bundles, and may then be conducted to other parts of the leaf. Seeing that all these saxifrages have their habitat in crevices of rocks on sunny declivities, they are much exposed to desiccation in times of drought. The epidermal cells of the medial area and those of the extreme edge are no doubt protected by a very thick cuticle (see fig. 55 [8]); but in the case of the thin-walled cells at the bottom of the depression there is the danger of as much or even more water escaping through them, in the form of vapour, than has been previously taken in during the prevalence of rain.

In order to prevent this loss of moisture recourse is had to a very remarkable contrivance for closing the cavity, viz., an incrustation of carbonate of lime. In many saxifrages this crust covers the whole face of the leaf, in others only the margin, or the spot where the depression occurs. In the latter case it looks like a lid over the cavity. At that spot the crust is always thickened, and sometimes it forms a regular stopper which fills up the entire cavity. It rests upon the epidermis of the leaf, but is not adnate thereto, and may be removed with a needle. When a leaf is bent the crust is ruptured and breaks up into irregular plates and scales, and a strong gust of wind would then easily strip off the fragments and blow them away. In species subject to this danger, as, for instance, *Saxifraga Aizoon*, in which the rosetted leaves curl strongly upwards and inwards in dry weather, the crust of lime is held fast by peculiar plugs which arise from individual epidermal cells projecting above the rest in the form of papillæ (see fig. 55 [8]). These plugs are found principally on the side walls of the cavities, but are also scattered everywhere on the epidermis of the margin of the leaf. They are so incrusted with the lime that the latter cannot easily fall off, and a comparatively strong pressure must be applied with the needle to detach it from the substratum. The calcium carbonate of which these crusts consist is excreted in solution by the plant from pores occurring at the bottom of the depressions. The pores are constructed like ordinary stomata, but are, as a rule, somewhat bigger, and it is not improbable that, when once the lime crust has formed from the excreted solution, they take part in the function of transpiration.

There is scarcely any need for further explanation of the manner in which the apparatus here described acts. When rain or dew falls on a saxifrage leaf the whole upper surface is moistened directly, whilst the water soaks under the crust of lime, and, diffusing itself there, fills in a moment the depressions, and is taken up by the absorption-cells situated at the bottom of the latter. The calcareous stopper imbedded in each cavity is only upheaved by this process to a trifling extent. In dry weather the crust is appressed closely to the epidermal cells, and the stopper descends again and impedes the evaporation of water from the thin-walled cells within the cavities.

The absorptive organs on the leaves of *Acantholimon, Goniolimon*, and a few

other Plumbagineæ, resemble in an extraordinary degree those pertaining to saxifrages. The depressions are here found uniformly distributed over the entire surface of a leaf, and when they are closed by a crust or scale composed of calcium
carbonate, the leaves are dotted with white spots, as may be seen in the drawing
of a leaf of *Acantholimon Senganense* given in fig. 55 [4]. Upon the calcareous scale
being removed, a little cavity is revealed beneath, and one observes that the floor of
this cavity is composed of from four to eight cells, separated by radial partition-
walls, and with exceedingly thin and delicate outer walls. The other epidermal
cells adjoining the cavity are, on the contrary, always furnished with a thick cuticle
(see fig. 55 [5]). Whenever water is being copiously supplied to the roots, and the
turgidity of the cells in the leaves is great, the cells forming the floor of the cavity
excrete bicarbonate of lime in solution. Part of the carbonic acid escapes into the
air, and the insoluble mono-carbonate of lime in the water then forms a crust, which
fills and covers the cavity, and often even spreads over the whole leaf, constituting a
coherent calcareous coat.

All Plumbagineæ which exhibit this contrivance—that is to say, the various
species of *Acantholimon*, *Goniolimon*, and *Statice*—inhabit steppes and deserts,
where in summer no rain falls for months together, and the soil becomes dry to a considerable depth, so that extremely little water is available for the roots. Although
the rigid leaves are protected by a thick cuticle, and by crusts and scales of lime
against excessive evaporation of their aqueous contents, still it is difficult to avoid
some slight loss of water, especially when the noon-day sun beats down upon the
steppe, and, owing to the extremely arid nature of the soil, it is scarcely possible to
replace this loss, however small it may be, by absorption from the earth on the part
of the suction-cells on the roots. All the more welcome to plants of the kind is the
dew which sometimes falls copiously on steppes and in deserts in the course of the
night; it wets the rigid leaves, and, soaking immediately underneath the crusts and
scales of lime to the thin-walled cells at the bottom of the cavities, is absorbed with
avidity by them. When drought returns with the day, the scales of lime close
tightly down like lids on the epidermis beneath, and, so far as possible, prevent
evaporation. In particular, they impede the exhalation of water from the thin-
walled cells at the bottom of the cavities—a loss which would otherwise be quite
inevitable, and would be followed by a rapid desiccation of the entire plant. To
prevent the calcareous lids from dropping off, there are either, as in *Saxifraga
Aizoon*, papilliform or conical projections from cells in the immediate vicinity of
the cavities, which projections often have hooked ends and confine the crust of
lime, or else each cavity is somewhat contracted at the top and enlarged below, so
that the lime stopper, being shaped according to the contour of the cavity, cannot
fall out.

A significance similar to that attributed to calcium carbonate excretions belongs
also to the saline crusts which are found covering the leaves of a few plants growing on the arid ground of steppes and deserts in the neighbourhood of salt lakes
and on the dry tracts of land near the seashore. Owing to the fact that in these

situations crystals of salt are sometimes to be seen separated out from the soil, and lying as a white efflorescence upon the ground, it used formerly to be believed that the salt incrusting leaves and stems was derived, not from the plants in question, but from the soil around, and had only spread from there over the various plant-members. But this is not the case. As a matter of fact, the salt observed on the leaves and stems of *Frankenia, Reaumuria, Hypericopsis persica*, and a few species of *Tamarix* and *Statice*, is produced from the substance of the leaves. It is excreted in just the same way as the crust of lime, above described, is from the leaves of saxifrages. To the naked eye the surfaces of the leaves in all the plants enumerated have a punctate appearance. On closer inspection, it is evident that, corresponding to each dot, there is a little cavity, the deepest part of which is constructed of cells with extremely delicate external walls. In quite young leaves only a single thin-walled cell of the kind is to be seen at the bottom of each shallow depression. But this divides, and, by the time the leaf is full-grown, from two to four cells are seen to have arisen by division of the one cell. Stomata are, in addition, intercalated in the membrane in the neighbourhood of these thin-walled cells, and, in the rainy season, when there is no lack of water in the habitats of the plants in question, a watery juice, containing a large amount of salts in solution, exudes from these stomata. The saline solution soaks over the whole surface of the leaf, and in a dry atmosphere crystals form from it and adhere to the leaf in the form of little gland-like patches or continuous crusts.

If these tamarisks, frankenias, and reaumurias are observed during a rainless season, the crystals of salt are seen under the noon-day sun glittering on the leaves and stems, and may be detached in the form of a fine crystalline powder. But if the same place is visited after a clear night, no trace of crystals is to be seen; the little leaflets have a green appearance, but they are covered with a liquid with a bitter salt taste,[1] and are damp and greasy to the touch. The crystals have attracted moisture from the air during the night, and have deliquesced, and the saline solution not only covers the whole of the leaf, but also fills the little cavities visible as dots to the naked eye. The thin-walled cells at the bottom of the cavities differ from the rest of the epidermal cells and the guard-cells of the stomata, in that they are susceptible of being wetted, and they may act as absorption-cells, and allow the water, attracted by the salts from the air, to pass through their thin walls into the interior of the leaves.

When the air dries under the rising sun, crystals are again formed from the solution of salts, and, covering the leaves once more in the form of crusts, fill up the depressions and protect the plants during the hot hours of the day from excessive evaporation. Whilst, therefore, in the dewy night these plants are indebted to their salt crusts for water, they are in the day-time preserved from desiccation by the action of the same contrivance.

---

[1] The salt incrustations which were removed from plants of *Frankenia hispida*, collected on a Persian salt-steppe, consisted principally of common salt (chloride of sodium). They contained in smaller quantities, gypsum, magnesium sulphate, calcium chloride, and magnesium chloride.

It is also worthy of mention that papillæ are developed near the absorption-cells, with a view to the retention of the salt crystals, similar to those which hold the calcareous incrustations on the leaves of saxifrages and *Acantholimon*.    The leaves of plants covered with crystals of salt are also for the most part furnished with little bristles, to which the salt adheres so firmly that it is not readily detached, even by violent shaking.

But however striking the analogy may be between the development and significance of lime crusts and salt crusts, there is the essential difference that the former have not, like the latter, the power of attracting moisture from the air. And on this particular stress must be laid.  In the broken and hillocky tracts on the shores of salt-lakes or of the sea, where tamarisks and frankenias are especially wont to live, the sandy ground dries up to such an extent in the height of summer that it is scarcely conceivable how plants growing in it are able to preserve their vitality.  The proximity of the sea has no immediate effect on the moisture of the ground in such situations.  The sea-water does not penetrate into the ground far beyond the high-water line, and it is out of the question that the layers of soil serving as substratum to the frankenias and tamarisks should be irrigated by subterranean water.  When in summer there is an absence of rain for months together, these plants—even though in close proximity to the sea—would necessarily perish of drought.  Only the circumstance that they turn to account the moisture of the atmosphere by means of the excreted salts renders it possible for them to flourish in these most inhospitable of all inhospitable sites.

Many plants which are periodically exposed to great dryness have the tips of the teeth on the leaf-margins thickened into little cones or warts.  They also glitter somewhat and at times are sticky.  The glitter and viscidity are due to a resinous slimy substance, which often contains sugar and tastes sweet.  This substance covers the teeth and sometimes spreads from the teeth inwards to a great distance over the face of the leaf in the form of a delicate film-like varnish.  The greatest resemblance exists between this varnish (sometimes known as "balsam") and the secretions of the glands on the leaves of the Alpine Rose and of the glandular hairs on those of *Centaurea Balsamita*.  It is excreted by special cells, which are intercalated in the epidermis of the foliar teeth, and are at once marked out from the other cells of the epidermis by the facts that their protoplasm is of a brownish colour and that their external walls are easily permeable by water.  The excretion of the varnish-like layer takes place at a time when the entire plant is distended with sap, chiefly, therefore, in the spring.  When summer is at its height the varnish dries and thenceforward affords an excellent preservative from the risk of too much evaporation from the cells it covers, and especially from those situated on the teeth of the leaves by which it was excreted.  But if this dried film of varnish is wetted it saturates itself quickly with water and renders moisture accessible to the cells beneath it.  Thus its value is similar to that of the crusts of lime and salt on the leaves of the plants above described.  When moist it effects the absorption of water, when dry it guards against desiccation.

The reason for the contrivance just described being exhibited especially by the marginal teeth of the leaf, lies in the fact that dew is deposited particularly at those spots. If one looks at the leaves of the dwarf almond and plum trees in the steppe-districts, after clear summer nights, one finds a dew-drop suspended to every tooth on the margins; but by noon all the teeth are dry again and protected from loss of water by the coat of varnish. Moreover, not steppe-plants alone, but very many plants which grow in poor sandy soil on the banks of streams and rivers, exhibit this contrivance for the direct absorption of water from the atmosphere. Instances are afforded by the Sweet Willow, the Crack-willow, Poplars, the Guelder-rose, the Bird-cherry, and many others. It is at once evident that this contrivance is observed chiefly on the leaves of trees, shrubs, and tall herbs, whilst incrustations of lime occur only on shorter plants with rosulate leaves spread out on the ground, or with rigid acicular leaf-structures. The grounds of this distinction may well reside in the fact that the weight of a crust of lime is many times as great as that of the dry film of varnish. A load capable of being borne without hazard by the leaves of a *Statice* plant, they being spread out on the ground, or by the rosettes of *Saxifraga Aizoon*, would be unfit for the leaves of a Cherry or Apricot tree, or for those of the Sweet Willow, or the Crack-willow; indeed the branches of these trees would break down under the burden if their leaves were incrusted with lime.

In many cases only a few of the marginal teeth of the leaf are transformed into absorbent apparatus, and special contrivances then always exist to convey rain and dew to those teeth. The Aspen (*Populus tremula*) serves as a very good example of this. This tree has, as is generally known, two kinds of leaves. Those arising from the branches of the crown have long petioles and laminæ of roundish outline and with somewhat sinuate margins; those which are borne by the radical shoots have shorter stalks and larger sub-triangular laminæ sloping outwards; and the whole leaf is so placed and its margin so curved as to oblige the rain which strikes the upper surface in its descent to flow down towards the petiole (see fig. 55 [1]). Now, situated exactly on the boundary of lamina and petiole are two cup-shaped structures (fig. 55 [2]) originating from the lowest teeth of the leaf, and so arranged that every drop of rain descending from the lamina must encounter their shallow cavities and fill them with water. These cups are brown in colour and the size of a grain of millet; and the cells of their epidermis are furnished with a thick cuticle. Only the cells lining the shallow depression of each cup have thin walls, and they excrete a sweet-tasting, slimy, resinous substance which in dry weather films over the cavity like a varnish, and protects, at all events, the cells lying beneath it against an injurious desiccation. When, however, this coat is itself in contact with water it swells up, and the moisture is then absorbed by the cells in the pit-like depression and is transmitted to the vessels running underneath the cups (see fig. 55 [3]).

A number of tall herbs, principally of the group of Compositæ, have, like the Aspen, leaf-teeth which are developed at the part where petiole and lamina join and act as organs of absorption. In some, besides, the margin of the green lamina extends in the form of a narrow ridge down the pale canaliculate petiole; and, when this is the case, teeth of the kind are found on this narrow green ridge which runs along the groove. In *Telekia*, a handsome herbaceous plant of wide distribution in the south-east of Europe, these teeth—conical or club-shaped—springing from the margin of the petiole-groove are incurved, and are in general so placed that their blunt apices project into the groove. But precisely on these obtuse tips of the teeth are situated cells with very thin outer walls easily permeable to water, and having contents with a strong attraction for it. Thus, as soon as the groove of the

Fig. 56.—Water-receptacles.

¹ In a Teasel, *Dipsacus laciniatus.* ² In the American *Silphium perfoliatum.*

petiole is filled with rain, collected from the surface of the leaf, the tips of the conical teeth are moistened, and they suck up the water.

Lastly, we have to mention the curious receptacles appertaining to foliage-leaves in which water from the atmosphere accumulates and continues to stand for weeks without being protected from evaporation by the excretion of special substances. Any region or portion of the leaf may participate in their construction. In *Saxifraga peltata* the lamina is shaped like a shield and forms a shallow plate with the concave surface turned to the sky. In the Cloud-berry (*Rubus Chamæmorus*) the formation of basins is brought about by the margins of the reniform lamina being superimposed over one another as if to make a spathe. In the various species of Winter-green, especially in *Pyrola uniflora*, the pale cauline leaves, inserted above to the green leaves, are metamorphosed into little saucers. In one species of Teasel, *Dipsacus laciniatus* (see fig. 56 [1]), and in the North American *Silphium perfoliatum* (fig. 56 [2]) the two sheathing portions (vaginæ) of every pair of opposite leaves are connate and form comparatively large and deep funnel-shaped basins, from the middle of which rises the next higher internode of the stem. In several Meadow-rues (*Thalictrum galioides* and *T. simplex*) the secondary leaflets, which are opposite one another and shut close, almost like the valves of a mussel, are moulded so as to form cavities for the retention of water, and in many Umbelliferæ, such as *Heracleum* and *Angelica*, the vagina of each individual leaf is ventricose or inflated, thus forming a sac enveloping the segment of the stem which stands above it.

These basins, saucers, and dishes are always so placed, relatively to their surroundings, that the water derived from rain and dew is directed into them from the surfaces of the leaves, or by the segment of the stem which rises from their centres, and thus it is that the depressions are filled. Whether in all cases much of the water accumulated is absorbed is certainly open to doubt. In the case of the leaves of the *Alchemilla* (fig. 52 [2]), which exhibit the phenomenon so conspicuously that the plant has received the popular name of Dew-cup; the absorption of water is, at anyrate, very inconsiderable, and here the retention of the dew secures advantages of a different kind to which we shall presently have occasion to return. On the other hand, it is established that in the case of basins belonging to tall herbaceous plants, particularly such as grow on steppes and prairies where often no rain falls for a long interval, the water collected is absorbed by the glandular hairs and thin-walled epidermal cells developed within them. The fact of this absorption may be proved by a very simple experiment. Let a stem of the *Silphium*, represented in fig. 56[2], be cut off beneath the pair of connate leaves, which form a basin by their union, and let the cut surface 1 c closed with sealing-wax, so that no water can be taken up by the stem from below. If the water accumulated in the basin is now emptied out, the leaves shortly become flaccid and droop; but if the basin is left full of water, the leaves preserve their freshness a long while and do not begin to wither until all the water has evaporated and disappeared from the basin. If oil is poured upon the collection of water in the basin, so that evaporation from the latter is impeded, a constant diminution of the water in the basin is observed notwithstanding; this leads to the conclusion that the water in question is really taken up by the absorption-cells at the bottom of the basin and conveyed to the tissue of the leaf.

The first thing that strikes one on surveying once more all the plants possessing on their aërial organs special contrivances for water-absorption is that a large proportion of them have taken up their abode in swamps and on the banks of rivers and streams, or if not there, at all events in situations where no danger exists of the ground being thoroughly dried up. No doubt this appears to be inconsistent. How are we to explain the fact that Gentianeæ, ashes, willows, alpine roses, bog-mosses, &c., are still in need of water from the atmosphere, when they all grow either in damp meadows, peat-bogs, on the borders of never-failing springs, or in ever-moist ravines, where their requirements in respect of nutrient water and imbibitious water can be supplied all around by means of the roots? A glance at the company in which these plants occur may perhaps lead to a solution of the problem. In the damp meadows and along the margins of springs where gentians, the Sweet-willow, and plants of that kind are found, the Butterwort (*Pinguicula*), which has been described in earlier pages amongst carnivorous plants, is never absent; whilst wherever the pale cushions of the Bog-moss spring, there also the Sun-dew is certain to spread out its tentacles for the capture of prey.

With reference to community of site the assumption is warranted that all these plants which flourish under identical conditions of life endeavour to acquire the same material by means of their aërial parts. Now, this material cannot well be other than nitrogen, of which they do not find a sufficient store in the substratum. What then is more natural than that those plants, which are not adapted to the capture of animals, should use their aërial organs, when these are moistened with rain or dew, to take up direct nitric acid and ammonia, which are contained— though in small traces only—in the atmospheric deposits, instead of waiting till compounds of such great importance to them penetrate into the ground where they may chance to be detained at spots whence the roots could only obtain them after long delay and by a highly complicated process? When one considers that plants, growing amid the sand and detritus of steppes, on ledges, and in crevices of steep rocks, or epiphytic on the bark of trees, are also able to acquire little or no nitrogenous food from the substratum by means of their roots, their especial equip- ment with apparatus for the absorption of atmospheric water becomes explicable on the ground of the latter being the medium of solution and transport of nitrogenous compounds. In the case of epiphytes and of plants growing on steppes or rocks, there is the additional consideration that a supply of pure water, supplemental to that which can be withdrawn from the substratum, must be very welcome to them in dry weather, and that at such times it is a great advantage for the atmospheric water to be absorbed directly by the aërial organs instead of reaching them in a roundabout manner through the substratum.

If this idea is justified, the atmospheric moisture taken up by the aërial organs with the help of the above-described contrivances, would be of value to the plant chiefly in being a carrier of nitrogenous compounds, and in this acceptation would have to be looked upon as water of imbibition. Whether it is also used, at least in part, as food-material can neither be asserted nor controverted. A separate absorp- tion of water which serves only for motive power, and of that which is in addition employed in the construction of organic compounds does not take place in a plant, it is not possible to make any *a priori* statement concerning the moisture taken up, as to which part it has to play in the plant. Most probably the allotment of functions is not at all uniform, but varies considerably according to conditions of time, place, and requirement.

On a former occasion it has been mentioned that small animals are not infrequently killed accidentally in the water filling the larger kinds of basins formed as parts of foliage-leaves, that pollen, spores, and particles of earth also are blown by the wind into these basins, and that, after the ensuing solution and decomposition of the organic and mineral bodies in question, the water exhibits a brownish colour and contains organic compounds as well as food-salts in solution. It is not necessary to repeat that these compounds are able to pass into the interior of the plant with the water through the action of the absorption-cells which are never absent from the bottom of the basins; but it seems proper to consider specially in this connection the most conspicuous cases of the phenomenon which have been observed. The greatest quantity of matter, dissolved and undissolved, is found in the flat, saucer-shaped laminæ of *Saxifraga peltata*, which grows on the sites of springs in the Sierra Nevada of North America. The water in these saucers is sometimes coloured quite a dark brown by the presence of decayed beetles, wasps, centipedes, fallen leaves, and animal excreta; and when it evaporates a regular crust is left behind at the bottom of the reservoir. Three days after rain I still found in the inflated vagina of *Heracleum palmatum*, a species of cow-parsnip, a pool of brown water 2 cm. deep, and at the bottom a deposit of blackish, oily mud in which the remains of decayed earwigs, beetles, and spiders, were still recognizable. The same thing is observed in the cisterns of Bromeliaceæ and in the water-basins of *Dipsacus laciniatus* and *Silphium perfoliatum* (fig. 56), and it is interesting to find there are cells also at the bottom of the basins of the *Dipsacus* in question from which protoplasmic threads radiate forth, as in the case of the chambers of the Toothwort, and that numberless putrefactive bacteria always make their appearance in the water in these basins. The quantity of organic residue is less considerable in the saucer-shaped leaves of pelargoniums, but, on the other hand, earthy particles are frequently met with in them to such an extent that, when the water has evaporated, the concave surface of the leaf is covered with an ashen-gray layer of earth.

Observations of this nature establish the conviction that no sharp line of demarcation exists in respect of the absorption of water either between carnivorous plants and land plants, or between land plants and saprophytes, or between saprophytes and carnivorous plants; and they lead further to the conclusion that water, mineral food-salts, and organic compounds are susceptible of being taken up not only by subterranean but also by aërial absorptive apparatus.

## 6. SYMBIOSIS.

Lichens.—Cases of symbiosis of Flowering Plants having green leaves with the mycelia of Fungi destitute of chlorophyll.—Monotropa.—Plants and Animals considered as a vast symbiotic community.

### LICHENS.

In describing the vegetation of a limited area botanical writers are apt to designate the various species of plants as "denizens" of the country in question. The conditions under which the plants live are likened to political institutions, and the relations existing amongst the plants themselves are compared to the life and strife of human society. By no means the least important factor in the suggestion of these analogies is the circumstance that often as a matter of fact one has opportunities of seeing how the species of plants which live together in a locality are dependent in various ways upon one another; how they exist in continual conflict for the food, the ground, for light and air; how some are preyed upon and oppressed by others, whilst others are supported and protected by their neighbours; and how, not infrequently, quite different species join together in order to attain some mutual advantage.

As regards the preying of one upon another the subject has been treated in detail in a previous chapter, and it was also stated then that the term parasite can only be applied to those plants which withdraw materials from the living parts of other organisms without rendering a reciprocal service in return. The host attacked by a parasite supplies food and drink without being in any way compensated. One might suppose that nothing would be simpler and easier than to ascertain the existence of this relationship, and yet many difficulties are encountered in the determination of parasitism in individual cases. The main difficulty is due to the fact that one cannot always say with certainty whether the host does not perhaps get some advantage from the parasite which drains its juices. Should this be the case, however, the latter would be no longer a parasite, and the relationship between the two would rather be that of simple commerce and mutual assistance, an amicable association for the benefit of both.

Whilst discussing the second series of parasites, the fact was mentioned that the plants upon which the various species of Eyebright fasten their suckers suffer no apparent injury as a consequence of this connection. The rootlet organically united to the suckers does, it is true, die away in the autumn: but the Eyebright also withers at that season, and it is not inconceivable that the useful substances existing in the green leaves of the Eyebright may be transferred, shortly before the latter withers, to the host-plant and deposited there at a convenient time in the permanent part of the root as reserve-material, and that in this way the host-plant ultimately derives benefit from the so-called parasite. The idea here suggested as a possibility for the case of Eyebright and the grasses connected with it is an ascertained fact in the case of some other plants. For plants are known which unite to form a single organism and thenceforward so co-operate in their functions that ultimately both derive advantage from the arrangement. The one takes food-stuffs from the substratum and from the air and transmits them to the other; whilst, in the green cells of the other, the raw material is worked up, under the influence of sunlight, into organic compounds. The organic compounds thus created are used by both for the further production of organs, and therefore a connection such as this must be looked upon as a true case of symbiosis, i.e. associated existence for purposes of nutrition.

The first place amongst social communities of the kind must be assigned to Lichens, a section of Cryptogams possessing an extraordinarily large number of species and differentiated into thousands of forms, representatives of which are

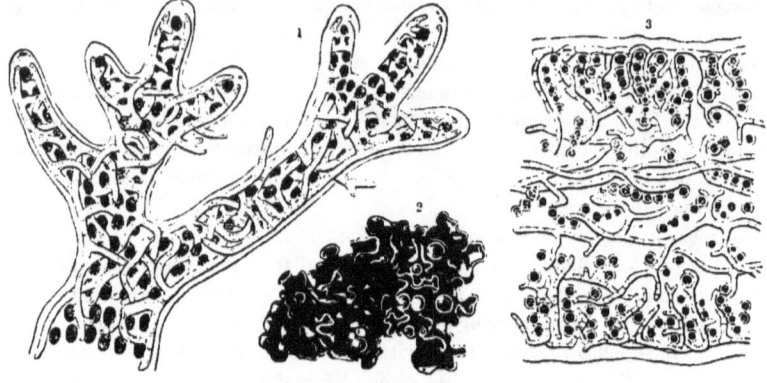

Fig. 57 Gelatinous Lichens.

¹ *Ephebe Kerneri;* ×450. ² *Collema pulposum;* natural size. ³ Section through *Collema pulposum;* ×450

everywhere distributed, from the sea-shore to the highest mountain peaks yet scaled by man, and from the tropics to the arctic and antarctic zones.

The partners in the Lichen communities appear to be, on the one hand, groups and filaments of round, ellipsoidal, or discoid green cells belonging to plant species included under the general name of Algæ; and, on the other hand, pale, tubular cells or hyphæ, which are destitute of chlorophyll, and pertain to species of plants comprised under the general name of Fungi (see fig. 58).

The form assumed by a large proportion of these lichens is that of incrustations on stones, earth, bark, or old wood-work; the entire structure of the lichen is either ensconced and imbedded in the depressions of weathered surfaces of stone, or else between the cell-walls of dead fragments of wood and bark, so that it often happens that attention is only drawn to its presence by the altered colour of the substratum, or by the fructifications which lift their heads above the substratum.

Lichens of the kind are termed Crustaceous Lichens, and the wide-spread Graphic Lichen (*Lecidea geographica*) may serve as an example. A second great group nearly allied to the first is that of Foliaceous Lichens. The form of the vegetative body in these is best compared to the foliage-leaves of the Curled Mint, with their corrugated or sinuate margins, or to those of *Malva rotundifolia*. It may also be described as a number of lobes radiating irregularly and bifurcating repeatedly, and only lightly joined to the substratum by root-like fringes, and therefore capable of being readily loosened and detached. The light-grey *Parmelia saxatilis*, which bear brown saucer-shaped fructifications, may be taken as a representative of these Foliaceous Lichens. The Fruticose Lichens are distinguished as a third group in which the thallus rises from the ground in the shape of a shrub, whilst the cylindrical, fistular, and ligulate stemlets, which ramify profusely, are only adherent to the substratum by a very small surface at the base. With these are associated the Beard Lichens, which hang down from the bark of old trees in the form of pale, copiously-branched filaments. Lastly, there is a fifth group, the

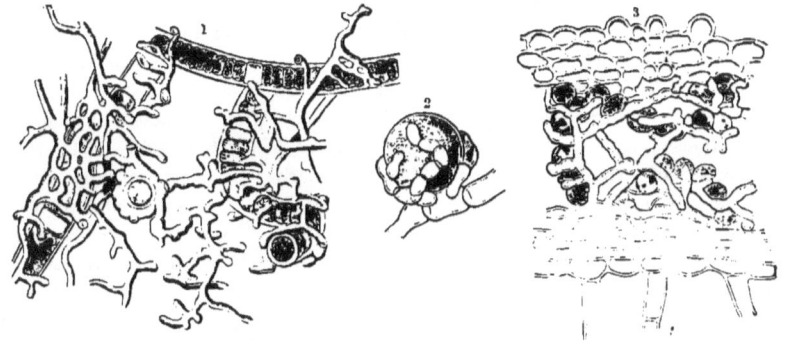

Fig. 58.—Fruticose and Foliaceous Lichens.

1 *Stereocaulon ramulosum* in conjunction with *Scytonema*; ×650.   2 *Cladonia furcata* with *Protococcus*; ×650
3 *Coccocarpia molybdæa*; section, ×650 (after Borzet).

Gelatinous Lichens, which when moistened look like dark, olive-green, or almost black lumps of wrinkled and wavy jelly or as if composed of variously-divided bands and strips packed together into little cushions.

In the gelatinous expansions last mentioned the algal cells are arranged in moniliform rows and are interwoven with the hyphal filaments of the fungus throughout the entire thickness of the thallus, as in *Collema pulposum* (see fig. 57 2 and 57 3), or else they form regular ribbon-shaped double rows, interwoven with few hyphæ, as in *Ephebe Kerneri* (see fig. 57 1). In crustaceous, foliaceous, and fruticose lichens, the algal cells constitute a disorderly heap and are crowded together in the middle stratum of the thallus, where they are imbedded between an upper and a lower layer of densely felted hyphal threads, as in *Coccocarpia molybdæa* (fig. 58 3).

Seeing the wide distribution of lichens it must be assumed that both partners occurring in the lichen-thallus are able to range about with extraordinary ease and latitude. When one observes how patches of the most various lichens are produced in a few years after a landslip on the freshly-broken surfaces of the stones which have fallen down into the valley beneath, one can only explain the phenomenon by supposing that the algal and fungal cells concerned have been blown together, and that the opportunity has been afforded them on the blocks of stone of contracting a union. Now, so far as regards one of the two partners, viz.: the one devoid of chlorophyll, and known as a fungus—the idea that everywhere in the air spores of fungi are swarming about is so familiar to us that the supposition of an occasional stranding of individual spores, which are being blown about by the wind, upon the moist broken surfaces of stones can encounter no opposition. Respecting those spores in particular which are ejected from the aërial fructifications of lichens, the discussion of their life-history and distribution must of course be reserved for a later section; but it is necessary to make here the one statement that provision exists for the most profuse and distant dissemination of these spores.

Thus, in the case of one of the partners, there is no difficulty in realizing its ubiquity. But when one comes to the Algæ, the name at first calls up to mind the green filaments which occupy our pools and ponds, or the brown wracks and red Florideæ of the sea-shore, and we ask ourselves how it can be possible for these plants to occur on fractured surfaces of stone, especially on the débris of mountain sides. Indeed, it is certainly not Algæ of these kinds that take part in the construction of Lichens. The name Algæ is properly only a general name for all Thallophytes containing chlorophyll, and it is applied to many small organisms besides those mentioned above, namely, to numbers of Nostocineæ, Scytonemeæ, Palmellaceæ, Chroolepideæ, and these are the kinds which fall in with the cells of fungi and form lichens in conjunction with them. Owing to their minute size, they are apt to escape observation, and, in general, only attract attention when myriads of them clothe the bark of trees, cliffs, stones, or earth. In these situations they need but little moisture, and it is not necessary for any of them to live under water like other algæ; they become desiccated without sustaining the slightest injury and make their appearance on the substratum occupied by them at the first stage of their development, as powdery coats, and, in this condition being extremely light, are liable to be blown away by a wind of moderate strength, and so distributed over mountain and valley.

That this dissemination is not merely hypothetical but an actual fact has been susceptible of easy proof by the following experiment, made in a mountain-valley in the Tyrol. A plane surface covered with white filter-paper, which was kept moist, was exposed to a south wind; in the course of a few hours numerous particles, like dust, adhered to the paper, and amongst them cell-groups of Nostocineæ and others of the above-mentioned algæ occurred regularly, in addition to organic fragments of the most various kinds, such as pollen-grains and spores of all sorts of mosses and fungi. All these bodies were deposited in the little depressions on the sheet of paper, and in the same way they rest in the grooves, cavities, and cracks in the surfaces of stone, bark, and old wood-work, where they succeed in reaching a further development as soon as the requisite quantity of water is provided. Now, if at these places the little algal cell-groups meet with hyphæ belonging to the other potential partner, the latter embrace and enmesh them, as is shown in the above figures, and thus is produced the confederacy called a Lichen. The member destitute of chlorophyll takes up nutriment from the external environment; it possesses, in particular, the property of condensing aqueous vapour, and has, besides, the power of bringing the solid substratum partially into solution by means of excreted substances: it effects adhesion to the substratum, and, in a majority of cases, determines the form and colour of the lichen-thallus as a whole. The second member, whose cells contain chlorophyll, undertakes the task of producing organic matter, under the influence of sunlight, from the materials conveyed to it; by this means it multiplies the number of its cells and increases in volume, whilst, at the same time, it yields to its mate so much as is necessary in order to enable the latter to keep pace with it in growth.

The number of algæ which enters into a partnership of this kind is, in any case, much less considerable than that of the fungi, and it must be assumed that one species of alga may unite with the hyphæ of different lichen-fungi. The extreme variety, moreover, in the combinations of the two sorts of confederate occurring on a very small area is obvious from the circumstance that it is not rare for half a dozen different species of lichen to spring up side by side on a patch of rock no bigger than one's hand. Whether they all achieve an equally hardy development, or whether some perchance are not crowded out and overgrown by others depends on various external conditions—on the chemical composition of the substratum, and particularly on the conditions of moisture and illumination of the site in question. Lichens are very sensitive in this respect, and the different sides of a single rock often exhibit quite different growths of lichens. A very instructive example of this is afforded by a marble column near the famous castle of Ambras in Tyrol. This column is octagonal, and has been standing in its place for more than two hundred years, with all its sides exposed to wind and weather. Lichens have settled on all the eight faces, and, indeed, are present in such abundance that the stone is quite covered by patches the size of a man's hand. Many of these growths are but poorly developed, and not susceptible of being identified with certainty; but altogether on this column there must be over a dozen different species, the germs of which can only have been brought by winds. These species are, however, by no means uniformly disposed; some prevail on one side, some on another, and a few are confined exclusively to one of the eight faces. Of three species of *Amphiloma*, the one named *A. elegans* is restricted to the warmest side, *i.e.* the face exposed to the south-west; a second, *Amphiloma murorum*, is to be seen on the upper part of the southern face; whilst *Amphiloma decipiens* occurs on the same face, but only near the ground. On the side with a northern aspect *Endocarpon miniatum* predominates, and on the north-west face *Calopisma citrinum* and *Lecidea* are the prevailing forms.

What thousands of spores and algal cells must have been blown on to this pillar to enable all these combinations to arise! What complex processes must have gone on before the selection of lichens best adapted to each different quarter of the compass was effected on this little marble column! It is necessary to add, however, that lichens growing on stone, bark, or any situation of the kind do not in all cases owe their original appearance on the substratum to a fresh union of Algæ and Fungi, but that there is a second mode of distribution of lichens. This method consists in the transportation by air-currents of already completed social colonies to places often situated at a great distance from the spots where the initial union between Alga and Fungus was contracted. The process is as follows: —in the interior of an old, large, and fully developed lichen-thallus certain groups of cells separate from the rest, each group consisting of one or more green algal cells enmeshed in a dense weft of hyphæ. When a sufficient number of these daughter-associations has been formed the thallus of the parent lichen is ruptured and the little miniature social-groups, which are termed "soredia", come to the surface. To the naked eye a single soredium is only visible as a bright dot, but all together they have the appearance of a mass of powder or meal lying loosely upon the old lichen-thallus. In dry weather this mealy efflorescence is easily blown away with other organic particles. If, then, a soredium thus removed comes to rest in the crack of a rock or on any suitable substratum, the alga and hyphæ composing it continue to develop, and the organism grows into a larger lichen-thallus, which is able to repeat the process just described. In regions where lichens abound, soredia of the kind are found regularly amongst the elements of the organic dust, and occur, indeed, mixed with fungal spores and algal cells, so that it certainly happens not infrequently that two spots close together in the same cranny of stone exhibit both sorts of lichen-growth, the one newly produced by the concurrence and union of algal and fungal cells, the other a daughter-association which has arisen from an old lichen, as a soredium, and is continuing its development.

Another case of symbiosis allied to that of lichens is manifested by certain Cryptogams which live socially together under water and have received the systematic names of *Mastichonema*, *Dasyactis*, *Enactis*, &c. In them also a plant containing chlorophyll, and belonging to the group of Nostocineæ, appears as one member of the partnership; whilst the second is some species of *Leptothrix* or *Hypheothrix*. The green moniliform rows of cells of Nostocineæ are enmeshed and wrapped round by the delicate, filamentous cells devoid of chlorophyll of the *Leptothrix* or *Hypheothrix*; and later, by repeated processes of division, whole colonies of green cell-filaments ensheathed in this manner are produced, which to the naked eye appear as small soft tufts, usually clinging to porous limestone in the spray of waterfalls. In many cases the filaments destitute of chlorophyll rest upon the moderately thickened cell-membranes of the green algæ, whilst in other cases they insinuate themselves into the thick cell-membranes, permeate them with their webs, and form in conjunction with them the sheathing envelope.

## SYMBIOSIS OF GREEN-LEAVED PHANEROGAMS WITH FUNGAL MYCELIA DESTITUTE OF CHLOROPHYLL—MONOTROPA.

Another instance of symbiosis is observed to exist between certain flowering plants and mycelia of fungi. The division of labour consists in the fungus-mycelium providing the green-leaved Phanerogam with water and food-stuffs from the ground, whilst receiving in return from its partner such organic compounds as have been produced in the green leaves.

The union of the two partners always takes place underground, the absorbent roots of the Phanerogams being woven over by the filaments of a mycelium. The first root that emerges from the germinating seed of the phanerogamic plant destined to take part in the association descends into the mould still free from hyphae; but the lateral roots and, to a still greater extent, the further ramifications, become entangled by the mycelial filaments already existing in the mould or proceeding from spore-germs buried there. Thenceforward the connection continues until death. As the root grows onward, the mycelium grows with it, accompanying it like a shadow whatever its course, whether the root descends vertically or obliquely, or runs horizontally, or re-ascends, as is sometimes necessary when it happens to be turned aside by a stone. The ultimate ramifications of roots of trees a hundred years old, and the suction-roots of year-old seedlings, are woven over by mycelial filaments in precisely the same manner. These mycelial filaments are always in sinuous curves and intertwined in various ways, so that they form a felt-like tissue, which looks, in transverse section, delusively like a parenchyma. As regards colour the cell-filaments are mostly brown, sometimes they are almost black, and it is rare for them to be colourless. The epidermis of many roots is covered as if by a spider's web, whilst the hyphae form a complex tangle of bundles and strands broken here and there by open meshes through which the root is visible. In other cases an evenly woven but very thin layer is wrapped round the root; and in others, again, the fungus-mantle forms a thick layer which envelops uniformly the entire root (see fig. 59). Here and there the hyphae insinuate themselves also inside the walls of the epidermal cells, and the latter are permeated by an extremely fine small-meshed mycelial net (see fig. 59[3]). Externally the mantle is either fairly smooth and clearly marked off from the environment, or else single hyphae and bundles of hyphae proceed from it and thread their way through the earth. When these branching hyphae are pretty equal in length they look very much like ordinary root-hairs. And they not only resemble them, but assume the function of root-hairs. The epidermal cells of the root, which would in an ordinary way act as absorption-cells, being inclosed in the mycelial mantle cannot exercise this function, and have relegated the business of sucking in liquid from the ground to the mycelium. The latter undoubtedly acts as an absorptive apparatus for the partner on whose roots it has established itself; and the water in the soil, together with all the mineral salts and other compounds dissolved in that water, are caused by the mycelial mantle to pass from the surrounding ground into the epidermal cells of the root in question, and thence onward, ascending into axis, branches, and foliage.

Thus the fungus-mycelium not only inflicts no injury on the green-leaved plant by entering into connection with its roots, but confers a positive benefit, and it is even questionable whether a number of green-leaved plants could flourish at all without the assistance of mycelia. The experience gained in the cultivation of those trees, shrubs, and herbs, which exhibit mycelial mantles on their roots, does not, at any rate, lead to that conclusion. Every gardener knows that attempts to rear the various species of winter-green, the bog-whortleberry, broom, heath, bilberries, cranberries, rhododendrons, the spurge-laurel, and even the silver-fir and

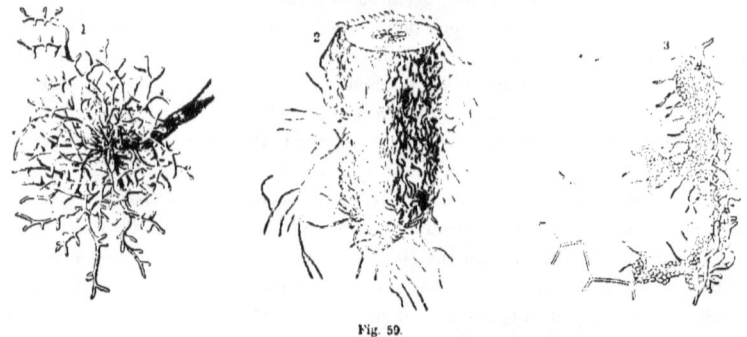

Fig. 59.

[1] Roots of the White Poplar with mycelial mantle. [2] Tip of a root of the Beech with closely adherent mycelial mantle; ×100 (after Frank). [3] Section through a piece of root of the White Poplar with the mycelium entering into the external cells; ×480.

the beech, in ordinary garden soil are not attended with uniform success. Therefore, as is well known, soil consisting of vegetable mould from the top layer of earth in woods or on heath is chosen for the cultivation of species of the genera *Erica*, *Daphne*, and *Rhododendron*. But it is not even every kind of forest- or heath-mould that can be made use of. When earth of that nature has been quite dry for a long time it is no longer fit for this purpose. On the other hand, it is known that the above-mentioned plants should be transplanted from their forest-home with the soil still clinging to the roots, and it is also laid down as an axiom that the roots of these plants should not be exposed and should be cut as little as possible. The following reasons account for all this. Firstly, fresh earth from a heath, or mould recently dug from the ground in a wood, contains the mycelia still alive, whereas in dry humus they are already dead; secondly, the mycelia woven round the roots are transferred together with the balls of earthy matter suspended to them into the garden; and, lastly, any considerable clipping of the roots would remove the ultimate ramifications which are furnished with the absorbent mycelial mantle.

The failure of all attempts to propagate the oak, the beech, heath, rhododendron, winter-green, broom, or spurge-laurel, by slips or cuttings, if the shoot which is cut off and used for the purpose is put into pure sand, is explicable in the same way. Limes, roses, ivy, and pinks, the roots of which possess no mycelial mantle, are notoriously propagated very easily by putting branches cut from them into damp sand. Rootlets are at once produced on those parts of the branches which are buried in the sand, and their absorption-cells carry on the task of taking up nutriment from the ground. But though cuttings of oak, rhododendron, winter-green, bog-whortleberry, and broom strike root, no progress in their development is to be observed, because the superficial cells of the rootlets, in these cases, have not the power of absorbing food when they are not associated with a mycelium. It is only when the slips from these plants are put into sand with a rich admixture of humus, the latter having just been taken from a wood or heath and containing the germs of mycelia, that some few are successfully brought to further development. The result is even then often not assured, and the cuttings of several of the plants enumerated die even in sand mixed with humus before they have produced rootlets.

Seeing also that the result of attempts to rear seedlings of the beech and the fir in so-called nutrient solutions, where there could be no question of any union with a mycelium, has been that the plantlets dragged on a miserable vegetative existence for a short time and ultimately died, we have good grounds for assuming that the envelope of mycelial filaments is indispensable for the Phanerogams in question, and that the prosperity of both is only assured when they are in social alliance.

The facts ascertained in cases of analogous relationship lead one to expect that the fungus-mycelia also derive some advantage from the flowering-plants, the roots of which they clothe, and to which they render the service of acting as absorption-cells. The benefit in question is undoubtedly the same as that derived by the hyphæ of a lichen-thallus from the enwoven green cells. The mycelial mantles withdraw from the roots of the Phanerogams the organic compounds which have been elaborated by the green leaves in the sunshine above-ground, and which are conducted thence to all growing parts, that is to say, downwards as well as in other directions, to the tips of the swelling and elongating roots. According to this, therefore, the division of labour between the members of the alliance for joint nutrition consists in the mycelium supplying the green-leaved plant with materials from the ground, and the green-leaved plant supplying the mycelium with substances which have been worked up above-ground in the sunlight.

The range of species which live in a social union such as is here described is certainly very large. All Pyrolaceæ, Vaccineæ, and Arbuteæ, most, if not all, Ericaceæ, Rhododendrons, Daphnoideæ, and species of *Empetrum*, *Epacris*, and *Genista*, a great number of Conifers, and apparently all the Cupuliferæ as well as several Willows and Poplars are dependent for nutrition on the assistance of mycelia. We find, too, that this condition recurs in every zone and in every region. The roots of the *Arbutus* on the shores of the Mediterranean are equipped with a mycelial mantle in precisely the same manner as those of the low-growing Whortleberry of the High Alps.

Special importance is given to the social life by the fact that the chief species of Phanerogams participating in it are of gregarious growth and cover whole tracts of country, forming boundless heaths and measureless forests, as, for instance, the various heaths, the oak, the beech, the fir, and the poplar. The conception of this subterranean life affecting every moorland and vast timbered tract is one full of wonder and interest.

We can now see why it is that the ground in woods is the abode of such a profusion of fungi. No doubt some of these fungi draw their nutriment exclusively from the store of dead plant-organs accumulated there; but others, as certainly, are in social connection with the living roots of green-leaved plants. It is true we cannot yet state precisely what are the species of fungi which contract this sort of union, or whether generally a definite elective affinity exists between certain fungi and certain green-leaved plants. There is much in favour of this supposition in a few cases; but, on the other hand, it is very unlikely that each of the various Phanerogams occupying a limited area of ground in a pine-forest, where a few square meters of earth contain so many tangled roots belonging to pines, spurge laurels, bilberries, cranberries, heath, and winter-green, that they can only be separated with difficulty, should select from the great host of fungi growing in the forest a different partner. In instances of this kind it seems just to suppose that the mycelium of one and the same species of fungus enters simultaneously into connection with all or several of the plants growing close together; it is similarly probable that the mycelia of different species of fungi render to one and the same flowering-plant the service of absorption according to the locality in which it occurs. This surmise is supported by the fact that when certain species, brought from distant parts and regularly exhibiting mycelial mantles on the ends of their roots, are reared in our gardens and greenhouses from seed, they unite in these abodes with fungus-mycelia, which certainly do not exist in the regions where the Phanerogams in question grow wild. Thus, for instance, the roots of the Japanese tree, *Sophora Japonica*, and those of the Epacrideæ of Australia, are found in European gardens in social union with fungi, which with us are native, but which certainly do not occur in Japan or Australia; and it is therefore scarcely open to doubt that the *Sophora Japonica*, to take one example, associates itself with different fungi in different regions.

Now that the symbiosis of fungi devoid of chlorophyll with green-leaved Phanerogams has been discussed, we are for the first time in a position to deal with that most remarkable of all cases of food-absorption wherein the subterranean roots of a flowering-plant are completely wrapped in a mycelial mantle, whilst the parts which shoot up above ground bear no green leaves, and, in general, possess no trace of chlorophyll. Such is the case of *Monotropa*, the various species of which are intimately allied in the structure of flowers and fruit with the Primrose and Winter-green, and are met with scattered everywhere in shady woods. Their stems, which are from 10 to 20 centimeters in height and emerge from the mould of the forest-ground in summer time, are thick, fleshy, succulent, and profusely beset with membranous and transparent scales, and the extremity of each is bent back like a hook. The cylindrical flowers are developed at the top of the stem with their open ends turned to the ground, and are half-covered by the scales. Everything about this plant (stem, leaf-scales, and flowers) is of a pale waxen-yellow colour, and the general impression it produces is much more that of a Toothwort, or one of the colourless forest orchids, than of a species of primula or winter-green. Towards autumn, when ripe fruits have been produced from the flowers, the hitherto drooping extremity of the stem lifts itself into an upright position, whilst the entire aërial portion of the plant turns brown and dries up. Every disturbance caused by the wind, however slight, shakes out of the spherical fruits many thousands of tiny seeds as fine as dust, which, like the winter-green seeds, consist of only a few cells, and do not admit of the recognition of any differentiated embryo within them. Moreover, underground, the rhizomes, from which the small group of pale stems have arisen in summer, continue to live through the winter, and a number of new buds are developed on them. On digging down to the hibernating plant and removing the mould which conceals it, one finds at a depth of from 10 to 40 centimeters bodies like coral-stems consisting of dense masses of roots crowded together and ramifying multifariously. All the root-branches are short, thick, fleshy, and brittle, and are matted together to form turf-like masses, which are not infrequently interwoven with the rootlets of pines, firs, and beeches, and have all their interstices filled with humus. Each rootlet is enveloped, right up to the growing apex, in a thick mycelial mantle. The hyphal filaments of this mycelium do not penetrate into the tissue of the root of *Monotropa*, nor do they send any haustoria into the superficial cells of these roots. The hyphæ and the epidermal cells of the root are, however, in such close and continuous contact that sections exhibit a complete continuity of the tissues.

*Monotropa* is therefore only able to withdraw nutriment from the hyphal weft of the mycelium so far as its subterranean parts are concerned, and, seeing that it is quite destitute of chlorophyll, and its aërial stem and leaves display no trace of stomata, the possibility of creating organic matter and of adding in general to its substance by means of its aërial parts is excluded. It therefore receives all the materials of which it is constructed from the mycelium of the fungus, whilst it is not in a position to render anything in return to this mycelium that it has not previously derived from the latter. If the mycelium subsequently withdraws any materials whatever from the still living or decaying *Monotropa*, the process is only one of restitution and not of exchange. Thus, in this case, there can be no talk of reciprocity in the processes of nutrition or division of labour such as occurs when there is symbiosis. The *Monotropa* grows in height and in circumference entirely at the expense of the mycelium in which it is imbedded, so that we have here the remarkable phenomenon of a Phanerogam parasitic in the mycelium of a Fungus. We so often come across the converse process in our experience that we cannot easily familiarize ourselves with the idea of a flowering-plant draining the mycelium of a fungus of nutriment: nevertheless there is scarcely any other interpretation possible in this case, for all the other hypotheses,—such as that *Monotropa* enters into connection with the roots of trees, or that it is parasitic in the first stages of development, but subsequently detaches itself from its host and becomes a saprophyte,—rest on inaccurate observations, and have long been disproved. As a parasite *Monotropa* ought to have been discussed at the same time as others in earlier pages, but it was not without intention that the description of this plant was reserved for this place, for it would have been difficult to state and explain the method of nutrition exhibited by it before some previous knowledge of the curious phenomena of union of the mycelia of fungi with the roots of green-leaved Phanerogams had been acquired.

## ANIMALS AND PLANTS CONSIDERED AS A GREAT SYMBIOTIC COMMUNITY.

If we look back at the cases of symbiosis already discussed and inquire what is their value, we find it consists in an integration of the functions of plants possessing chlorophyll and plants not possessing it. The reciprocity here implied is, however, at bottom, but a copy of the complementary interaction of plants and animals which takes place on a grand scale in the organic world. The associated plant, destitute of chlorophyll, in which capacity fungi are always the organisms concerned, really plays the same part in the social life as is taken by animals in the great economy of nature, and this is in harmony with the fact that in other respects as well fungi exhibit so many similarities to animals that in many instances one looks in vain for a line of division to separate them from animal organisms. Hence there is no need for surprise when cases come under observation wherein a quite unmistakably animal organism enters, instead of a fungus, as one of the partners in a symbiotic community. Certain Radiolariæ have small yellowish spots upon them, which were formerly held to be pigment-cells, but have proved to be little algæ, with cells furnished with true chlorophyll. Similar properties are exhibited by the fresh-water polyp, *Hydra*, and by the marine sea-anemones. Small algæ occur in social union with these also in the shape of cells with membranes made of cellulose and containing chlorophyll and starch-grains in their protoplasmic bodies. These algæ are in no wise injurious to the animals with which they are associated; on the contrary, their presence is beneficial, their partners reaping an advantage from the fact that the green constituents split up carbonic acid under the influence of the sun's rays, and in so doing liberate oxygen which may be again taken in by the animals direct, and serve a useful purpose in their respiration and all the processes connected therewith. Conversely, the alga, in association with the animal's body, will derive a further advantage from the latter, inasmuch as it receives at first hand the carbonic acid exhaled by the animal in breathing. The small algæ living socially with animals cannot be reckoned as parasites in any case, nor can the animals be looked upon as parasites of the algæ, but we have here the phenomenon of mutual assistance and of a bond serving for the benefit of both parties, precisely similar to that noticed in the case of lichens and in the others which have been described above.

Several of the liverworts which live as epiphytes on the bark of trees exhibit on the under surface of their leaflets (which are inserted on the stem in two rows, and are pressed flat against the bark) little auricular structures, and in species of the genus *Frullania*, these take the form of definite hoods or pitchers. The rain that trickles down the trunks of the trees, washing the bark and wetting the liverworts in its course, fills the hooded receptacles referred to with water, and is retained longer in these protected cavities than anywhere else, if a period of drought ensues and the liverwort becomes dry again. Now these cowls are the abode of tiny rotifers (*Callidina symbiotica* and *C. Leitgebii*), which live on the organic dust brought thither with the water. In return for the peaceful home thus afforded them in the hooded chambers of the leaves, the rotifers supply the liverworts in question with nitrogenous food. For as such must serve the matter excreted by the rotifers in the interior of the cowls. Without the intervention of the rotifers, the living organisms (Infusoria, Nostocineæ, and spores) contained in the water could not be converted into food by the liverworts, whereas the liquid manure arising from the Infusoria, Nostocineæ, and spores, digested in the bodies of the rotifers, contains highly nitrogenous compounds, which are of great value to the liverworts in question, as indeed they are to all epiphytes living on the bark of trees. It stands to reason that the symbiotic liverworts and rotifers derive also a mutual advantage from the fact that the oxygen set free by the former comes into the possession of the rotifers and the carbonic acid emitted by the rotifers into that of the liverworts by the most direct method.

Moreover, these cases of partnerships further remind us of other analogous relations existing between plants and animals, which it is necessary to refer to now, although they cannot be treated in detail till later on. A great number of flowering-plants excrete honey into their flowers, and so attract flying insects to them, which supply themselves plentifully, and in their turn render to the plants they visit the service of transferring the pollen from flower to flower, thus making possible the development of fruits and fertile seeds. Certain small moths which visit the flowers of *Yucca* bring the pollen to the stigmas, and force it into the stigmatic orifices in order that mature fruits and seeds may be produced from the rudimentary fruits, a result which is indeed a matter of vital importance to these moths. For the moths lay their eggs in the carpels of *Yucca*, and from the eggs larvæ are developed which live exclusively on the seeds of this plant. If the Yucca were not fertilized, and did not develop any fruit, the larvæ would die of hunger. A similar phenomenon occurs in many other cases of the kind, where both plant and animal reap some benefit. On the other hand, in the formation of galls, which are produced by animals laying their eggs in particular parts of plants, the advantage (with few exceptions) is all on the side of the animals, and these gall-structures might most justly be placed by the side of parasitic structures.

It is obvious from all this that such of the mutual relations of plants and of their relations to animals as are occasioned by the endeavour to acquire nutriment are extremely various and often linked together and complicated or deranged by one another in the most curious manner. Cases occur of a particular plant being socially connected with another, and at the same time also beset by vegetable and animal parasites. The absorption-roots of the Black Poplar are covered with a dense mycelial mantle, so that this tree is associated for purposes of nutrition with the fungus to which the mycelium belongs. Such parts of the roots of the Black Poplar as are left free from the mycelium are fastened upon by suckers sent forth by Toothwort plants, which withdraw from the roots the juices absorbed by the latter from the earth through the instrumentality of the mycelial mantles clothing them. Meantime, in the cavities in the leaves of the Toothwort various small animals are caught and made use of as nitrogenous food. Again, the poplar-tree bears Mistletoe on its boughs, and its presence there is due to the missel-thrush. The thrush takes the Mistletoe-berries for food, and, in return, renders the plant the service of dispersing the seeds and establishing them on other trees. The parasitic Mistletoe takes its liquid nutriment from the wood of the poplar-tree; but, on the other hand, its own stems are covered with lichens, and these lichens are themselves a symbiotic community of algæ and fungi. Within the wood of the poplar-stems spread the mycelia of certain Basidiomycetes (*Panus conchatus* and *Polyporus populinus*), whilst the foliage-leaves are covered with a little orange-coloured fungus, *Melampsora populina*. In addition, no less than three gall-creating species of *Pemphigus* live on the leaves and branches of the Poplar, and a number of beetles and butterflies are nourished by them. Certain lichens, mosses, and liverworts regularly settle on the bark of old trunks, and included amongst these may be the species of liverwort which is inhabited by rotifers. If all the plants and animals which live upon the poplar-tree, within it or in association with it, are counted, the number turns out to be not much fewer than fifty.

www.ingramcontent.com/pod-product-compliance
Lightning Source LLC
Chambersburg PA
CBHW060610030726
47498CB00005B/1627